Triumph of a Tsar

Tamar Anolic

CONTENTS

ACKNOWLEDGMENTS

Many people have helped make this book a reality. First, a thank you to my beta readers: Joyce Galun and Kerry O'Connor, your interest in Russian history and culture made you natural readers for my first drafts, and your insightful comments have improved the final version of this novel.

Once more, I would like to thank Bob Rubin for this book's fabulous cover artwork, and for the design of the outside of this book, front and back.

Part I

CHAPTER 1

March 1, 1881. St. Petersburg.

Tsar Alexander II walked along the Catherine Canal, visibly shaking. His boots crunched on the virgin snow, and his breath exited his mouth in hot clouds of vapor.

"Is Your Imperial Majesty harmed?" asked Colonel Dvorzhitsky.

For a moment, all Alexander heard was the ringing in his ears. "I am fine," he told his police chief, after reading the man's lips.

"I beg you to get to safety," Dvorzhitsky said. "There may be another assassin in the crowd."

"But I can't go anywhere- my carriage was damaged," Alexander said condescendingly. Was Dvorzhitsky stupid? Did he not see the obvious?

"My sleigh here will take you directly to the Winter Palace," Dvorzhitsky replied. "You must leave, Your Imperial Majesty."

"I must tend to the wounded." Alexander's vacant eyes moved to the body of a dead Cossack nearby, and then to the blood that glistened on the street's cobblestones. He moved forward. "Who else is hurt?"

Dvorzhitsky stopped him, even though it meant grabbing Alexander's arm, a serious breach of etiquette. Alexander glared at him. Dvorzhitsky quailed, then held firm. "That blood on the street could have been yours, Your Imperial Majesty, and it might still be if another bomb is thrown. I implore you to take my sleigh back to the safety of the Winter Palace."

"I am not a coward," Alexander replied. His eyes shot bullets at

Dvorzhitsky.

"I am not questioning Your Imperial Majesty's character. I am merely thinking of your family, and all you can still do for Russia."

Finally, Alexander took a breath, and his angry expression lessened. "You are right," he said. "I should not leave my children without their father." He headed towards the sleigh, and Dvorzhitsky sighed with relief. Then Alexander turned, and Dvorzhitsky readied himself for another round of arguments. "See to the wounded," Alexander said.

"Yes, Your Imperial Majesty," Dvorzhitsky said. He gave orders to two trusted deputies, and got into the sleigh with Alexander. He cracked his whip, and the four white horses in front of them leapt forward.

The sleigh raced towards the Winter Palace. The horses' manes tossed in the wind, and their leg muscles rippled as they galloped. Alexander felt the cold wind bite into his cheeks as the Palace came into view.

Dvorzhitsky only felt safe once the Palace gates were sealed behind them. As soon as the sleigh stopped, Alexander raced inside, barely seeing the guards that stood at attention all around him. It took him less than a minute to reach his children's nursery.

"Sasha, what on Earth-" his wife Catherine began as Alexander burst into the room.

"Oh, it's nothing," Alexander replied, trying not to worry her. Then he noticed their three young children looking up at him. He clenched his jaw, determined that they would not see his fear, but tears had already formed in his eyes.

Catherine stood and hurried to the door. "Wait here, children," she said.

Alexander followed her gratefully. As soon as they were in the hallway, Alexander threw his arms around his wife and buried his face in her neck.

"My God, Sasha, what happened?" Catherine asked.

"Another attempt on my life, Katya, a bomb thrown at my carriage. Will I never be safe?"

Catherine felt her giant husband trembling, felt his tears on her neck. "Thank God you escaped!"

"Only through the urgings of Dvorzhitsky, who bade me leave. I would have stayed, tended to the wounded…."

"It would have gotten you killed!" Catherine pulled herself away from her husband's tight embrace to look him directly in the eyes. "Thank God you listened!"

Alexander buried his face in his wife's neck again. Only slowly did he become aware of the commotion downstairs- Dvorzhitsky must have spread the news of the assassination attempt. Alexander raised his head slightly, mostly to send away any servants who came up the stairs. At that moment, he wanted nothing more than to hold Catherine in his arms, feel her heart beating. Then he realized that the door to the nursery was open, and that his children were staring up at him, tears coming down their faces. In a second, Alexander's own tears overflowed.

It was completely dark when Catherine awoke several hours later. Instinctively, she reached for her husband- surely he must need some comforting after what had happened that afternoon. But the other half of the huge bed was empty. Across the room, Catherine could barely make out the hands and numbers of the grandfather clock. They read just after midnight. Catherine bit her lip, praying that Alexander had not left the palace at this time of night.

Getting up and putting on a white dressing gown, Catherine slipped out of the room and went down the Palace's large staircase to Alexander's study. She was relieved to see light coming from beneath the door. She pushed the door open, and saw Alexander at the window, staring out at the night's interminable blackness. Catherine closed the door behind her and eyed the pile of papers on her husband's desk.

Alexander turned from the window and smiled. "I was wondering when you might come down."

"What is all that?" Catherine asked, nodding at the papers. "Surely you can't still be working after all that happened today."

"To the contrary, my dear Katya, you know my work is never done," Alexander chided softly, his words tempered by the love he felt for her.

Catherine sighed. "What is all that, then?"

"A constitution."

"A constitution, Sasha?" Catherine shrieked. "How can you even think of granting your people more rights when they nearly killed you today?"

Alexander shrugged. "I've been drafting it for weeks. It grants the people a responsible Duma. They can vote for their own representatives."

Catherine knew her husband had indeed been drafting this document for some time. "Even so," she sniffed. "Your people are hardly worthy of your kindness."

"Perhaps," Alexander said. "But I already signed it. I shall not let a few radical crazies get in the way of political progress."

CHAPTER 2

August 14, 1920.

Tsarevich Alexei Nikolaievich, thin and pale, stood at the window of the Winter Palace, squinting through his binoculars. The summer sun shone through the window, highlighting his auburn hair. Princess Ileana of Romania stood next to him, impatiently pushing her dark brown hair out of her face so that she could use her own set of binoculars. Princess Margarita of Greece and her sister, Princess Theodora, stood next to Ileana. They both wore matching white dresses, and their blond hair was braided into crowns around their heads. Each of these princesses, and more, had descended on St. Petersburg to join the festivities surrounding Alexei's sixteenth birthday. *It's too bad everyone can't stay longer,* Alexei thought. *I'm enjoying the company. And the attention.*

He scanned the long red façade of the Palace. Then he watched the sunlight dapple the sculptures on the roof. Even with the binoculars, the ends of the Palace disappeared slightly into the haze of an unusually warm day. Next to him, Ileana was examining the palace's famous black gate, with its gold Imperial coat-of-arms, when the gate swung open and two cars drove through it. Servants greeted the cars as a man stepped out of each.

"Who is that?" Ileana asked.

"Ministers Stolypin and Witte," Alexei replied. "They must be here to see my father."

"Which is the one who almost got killed a few years before the Great War?" Theodora asked.

"Stolypin," Alexei said. "Olga and Tatiana were in the theater with Papa when it happened. Luckily, one of Stolypin's servants thought quickly enough to step in front of the gunman."

Alexei lowered his binoculars and looked at the girls next to him, his blue eyes penetrating. They stared back at him.

"What happened to the servant?" Margarita asked.

"He didn't make it," Alexei said. "My sisters had nightmares for weeks." He watched the ministers' cars disappear into the garage. Then he looked at his companions, and his face lit up with a huge grin. "Want to take a ride?" he asked. "Papa has a lot of fast cars that I've been learning to drive."

"Mama's Rolls Royce is in the garage too," Ileana offered.

But Alexei shook his head. "Papa's got a purple Rolls Royce that I like better," he said. "Let's go."

They snuck downstairs. Alexei heard his boots clicking on the palace's polished parquet floors as he walked. He cringed, wishing that the thick rugs that covered the floors in other rooms of the palace were covering the hallways too.

"Are you sure we won't get caught?" Margarita whispered.

Alexei nodded, feigning more confidence than he felt. "Papa and his ministers are meeting in his study, Mama is in one of her receiving rooms with your and Ileana's parents," he said. "They won't be out for awhile."

"What about Marie and Anastasia?" Theodora whispered.

"Aunt Olga took them shopping," Alexei said. "They won't be back for awhile either."

They had reached a doorway. Alexei cautiously stuck his head out and scanned the long hallway to make sure there were no servants or footmen. The hallway was empty and silent. Alexei ducked into a small room on the first floor, and the girls followed him. Across the room, Alexei moved a portrait of Alexander II to reveal a secret passageway. He held the door open for the princesses. Then he ducked into the passageway and rearranged the portrait so that it would hang correctly once the door was closed behind them.

The four of them hurried down the dark passageway. At the end of it was a door that Alexei opened with a flourish, and they walked out into the garage of the Winter Palace. Nicholas' purple Rolls Royce Ghost, a 1914 model, was a short distance away. "Your father still has this old thing?" Margarita asked.

"It's the only one he'll let me drive," Alexei said. "Come on."

"Do you have the keys?" Ileana whispered as they ran.

Alexei pulled the keys out of his pocket with a grin.

"You've been planning this!" Theodora said.

"Indeed," Alexei said as they reached the car. "Get in."

A second later, Alexei was at the wheel with Ileana in the seat beside him. Theodora and Margarita were squeezed in the back. Alexei started the car and pointed it towards the door. Upon the car's approach, the mechanized door began to open, and Alexei pressed his foot to the accelerator. The car shot out of the Palace and into the street. As the car continued to accelerate, Alexei wound through the narrow streets of St. Petersburg. The car jumped and jostled over the cobblestones as Alexei steered it around horse-drawn carriages and other motorcars. Next to him, Ileana quietly held on to the door of the car to counteract the car's increasing speed. Behind them, Margarita and Theodora were more vocal about their fear. "Alexei, slow down," Margarita cried.

"No," Alexei replied. "I want to get across the city before anyone notices we're gone."

The golden dome of St. Isaac's Cathedral was just coming into view when a police car's siren sounded. Alexei ignored it as long as he could, weaving through the streets until it became obvious that the police were following him. Then he pulled over to the side of the road, somehow bringing the car to a screeching halt without actually hitting anything.

Behind them, the police car stopped. A policeman got out and walked up to the car, his uniform perfect, his stride confident. Alexei lowered the car window, an embarrassed grin on his face. The policeman took a deep breath, ready to go into his routine lecture, when he recognized Alexei. "Your Imperial Highness, I'm sorry," he said. Then he recovered slightly. "But you were going twice the speed limit."

"I know," Alexei replied. "I'm just out for a ride."

Knowing he could not ticket the heir to the throne, the policeman came up with a different solution. "Would it please Your Imperial Highness to return to the Palace with me?" he asked. "I'll drive."

"My father needs his car back," Alexei said.

"Not a problem, Your Imperial Highness," the policeman replied. "I will drive this car back, while my colleague drives Your Imperial Highness back to the palace in our car."

Alexei glanced behind him and saw a second policeman standing beside the police car. "What about my passengers?" he asked. "They are as important as I am."

"I will see that they get back as safely as you do," the policeman replied. "Would it please Your Imperial Highness to step away from the vehicle?"

Finally, Alexei complied, and the police officer took his seat at the wheel as Alexei joined his colleague in the police car. Within minutes, they were back at the Palace, and Alexei was disappointed. *Mama and Papa are going to be so mad.*

The policemen next to him stopped the car, walked around to the passenger's side and opened the door. Alexei got out as the Rolls Royce was driven up behind him. A number of servants greeted the car and their imperial master. Within seconds, Alexei, Ileana, Theodora and Margarita were herded into the Palace as the Rolls Royce was driven back into the garage.

Inside the Palace, impeccably uniformed Aide-De-Camps, their military decorations shining in the light of the Palace's lamps, opened the door to Nicholas' study, and the servants shoved Alexei and the three princesses inside. Tsar Nicholas II, seeing his son, rose from his desk and came towards the door. His dark brown hair and beard, now laced with gray, were impeccably trimmed against his pale face. His blue eyes were stern. Stolypin and Witte stood from their chairs at the study's small table, expressions of studied neutrality on their faces.

Next to the two ministers, Grand Duke Michael Alexandrovich, tall, thin, balding, and immaculate in his uniform, also rose. Alexei shot his favorite uncle a grin, and Michael sent him an amused look in return. Nicholas' stern expression remained unabated, however, and Margarita, Theodora and Ileana practically shook with fear as they were led into the presence of the Tsar of all the Russias.

Alexei stood eight inches taller than Nicholas' meager five foot seven, and suddenly he became aware of the difference. He looked Nicholas straight in the eye. "I'm sorry, Papa," he said, "but no one was hurt."

"Really?" Nicholas replied. "Your companions seem shaken up."

"They're afraid of you, Papa."

"Is that so?" Nicholas looked at the three princesses in front of him with a gentle smile. Then he looked back at Alexei, and his eyes narrowed. "Why would they be afraid of me, when it is you who just took them drag racing through the streets of St. Petersburg?"

Even in the short while they had been talking, news of Alexei's ride had made its way around the Palace. Alexei could hear his mother and Ileana's mother racing down the hall to see that they were unharmed. Queen Marie of Romania led the way. "Ileana!" she yelled. "I-le-an-a!!" In a second, Marie burst into the study and hugged Ileana to her chest. "Are you alright?" she asked.

"I'm fine," Ileana replied, her voice muffled.

Alexei's face nearly broke in half with an impish grin. Ileana managed to turn her head away from her mother just enough to see him. She smiled back.

Tsarina Alexandra appeared in the doorway behind Marie and Ileana, her cheeks red, her chest heaving. "Sunbeam, is everything alright?" she asked Alexei.

"We're fine," Alexei replied, embarrassed at his mother's use of his pet name. As he spoke, Prince Andrew and Princess Alice of Greece appeared behind Margarita and Theodora, quietly eyeing their daughters with nervous expressions.

Alexandra glared at her son, and Nicholas sought to reassure her. "They're unharmed, Alicky," he said.

"They could have been killed," Alexandra said shrilly.

"Yes, but they weren't," Nicholas said. "Relax, please."

Alexandra obeyed her husband enough to calm down slightly, but her nervous glance went back to Alexei.

The next morning, Alexei awoke to the sound of Alexandra screaming. From the vestiges of a dream, Alexei wondered if she was still mad at him for the car ride the day before. Hauling himself out of bed, Alexei stripped off his nightclothes and pulled on his favorite uniform. Then he headed over to his parents' apartments to see what his mother's fuss was about.

Even in the few minutes it had taken him to get dressed, Alexei's family and servants had gathered outside his parents' suite. Most of them eyed Alexei as they made room for him to pass. Alexei noticed Michael and thought, *I didn't realize he stayed overnight.*

Anastasia and Marie stood at the door to their parents' bedroom. Only as Alexei crossed the threshold to the bedroom did his sisters' tears and pained expressions sink in. He saw Alexandra standing next to her bed, still in her nightclothes. "Mama, what's wrong?" he asked.

Then he noticed that Nicholas still lay in bed. Eugene Botkin, the court physician, stood next to him. Alexei's confusion increased until it was a buzzing noise in his head that drowned out everything else. "Mama?" he said. "What's happening?"

"Your father is dead," Alexandra replied, tears pouring down her face.

Alexei froze, and a cold sweat covered his face. "Yevgeny Sergeievich, what happened?" he asked Dr. Botkin.

"Heart attack," Botkin replied, his face ashen, his voice tight.

Alexei could feel sweat dripping down his neck and back. Everything was silent. Everyone in the room was looking at him. He swallowed. When he finally spoke, it was in a firm voice, despite the lump in his throat and the tears in his eyes. "We need to make funeral arrangements," he said. "I'll call Olga and Tatiana and notify the rest of the family."

Anastasia and Marie crept into the room. Anastasia started talking. "I, Anastasia Nicolaievna Romanova, promise and swear to the all-powerful God…"

Then Marie started. "I, Marie Nicolaievna Romanova, promise and swear…"

What were they saying? It took Alexei a minute to realize that they were swearing the oath of allegiance- to him as Tsar. It was only when his sisters, now speaking in unison, put his own name after the word "Emperor," that the full gravity of the situation finally began to sink in. Then Alexei could hear Michael also pledging the oath of allegiance. Alexandra tried to get the words out, but she fell to her knees, sobbing. Alexei knelt beside her and embraced her. "I'm sorry," he whispered.

Then he stood up. He grabbed Dr. Botkin and steered him out of the room. "Help me make the arrangements," he said. "I need a death certificate, and my father needs to be moved and cared for."

"Olga and Tatiana!" Anastasia said as Alexei rushed past her.

"I know!" Alexei replied. He raced to the telephone. *I need to talk to Olga and Tanya,* he thought. *I need to hear their voices. But how do I deliver news like this?* His tears flowed and his hands ached as he dialed the telephone to call Belgrade, and he was relieved when his brother-in-law, Prince Alexander of Serbia, answered rather than Olga. "Sandro, it's Alyosha," he began.

"Is everything alright?" Alexander asked, hearing how rough Alexei's voice sounded.

"My father bids you live long."

"I'm so sorry."

"I was hoping to tell Olga."

"She's feeding the baby. Don't worry, I'll tell her."

"Can you come to Russia?" Alexei asked. "I know Peter's only six months old."

"We'll be there," Alexander said firmly.

As soon as Alexei hung up, he called Tatiana in Sofia.

"Oh, my God," Tatiana sobbed when she heard the news. "I'll tell Boris. We'll be there as soon as we can."

By the time Alexei had finished speaking to his sisters, the flags around St. Petersburg had been lowered, and the bells of all the city's churches were tolling the sad news. *Uncle Misha has been at work too,* Alexei realized. *Thank God he's here.*

Nicholas' body lay in state for a week. Alexei was relieved when his oldest sisters arrived at the Winter Palace. *I feel better already, just having them here,* he thought. "How are you feeling, Tanya?" he asked.

"Not too badly," Tatiana replied, rubbing her belly, which was only just beginning to protrude from her mannequin-thin body.

"Did it happen quickly, Alyosha?" Olga asked, tears in her eyes. "Was Papa in pain?"

"It happened in his sleep," Alexei reassured her. "It was peaceful."

Every day for the next week, Alexei attended at least one of the requiem services that were held in every church across the city. Bells wailed their mournful cacophony so often that Alexei stopped hearing them. One day, Alexei returned to the Winter Palace to find his uncle Pavel and aunt Elizabeth waiting to see him. "Is Mama still in her bedroom?" he asked, bewildered by Alexandra's absence.

"We haven't seen her," Pavel answered. "Alyosha, we're so sorry about Nicky." His eyes shone with tears.

"Thanks," Alexei replied as he embraced them both. "Why don't we go to one of the larger drawing rooms? We'll have tea." He tried his best to make small talk as they sat, but his heart was not in it.

Then Elizabeth and Pavel looked at each other, and Alexei realized this was not simply a condolence call. "Alyosha, Mitya has been in exile for over three years now," Pavel said of his oldest son, Dmitri.

"I know that," Alexei replied, hearing the clink of his teacup against its saucer as he put it down. "Papa exiled him after he and Felix Youssoupov killed Grishka."

The mention of Gregory Rasputin made both Pavel and Elizabeth grimace, but Pavel's voice remained calm as he continued speaking. "We don't condone what he did, but he and Felix were acting in good faith to protect your father- and Russia- from a revolution."

"And yet their actions put Papa in a very difficult position."

"Even so, they were close to your father before that happened," Pavel said. "They'd like to come back for the funeral."

"Absolutely not!" Alexandra said suddenly from the doorway, making them all jump. Wisps of gray hair had come loose from her auburn bun, and creases lined her face.

Pavel and Elizabeth stood up. "Alicky, I am so sorry about Nicky," Elizabeth began. "This can't be an easy time for you."

Alexandra's mouth twisted, and her eyes were red. Elizabeth approached her sister, but Alexandra stood stiffly as Elizabeth embraced and kissed her. "I've been better," Alexandra said. "And I'll not have Dmitry and Felix coming back for Nicky's funeral."

Alexei noticed that Olga, Tatiana, Marie and Anastasia all stood behind Alexandra, expressions of discomfort on their faces. *I'm sorry they have to see this,* he thought. "It's up to me in the end, Mama," he said calmly. He remained seated, teacup in his hand.

"They killed Our Friend!" Alexandra replied venomously. "You know how much Grishka meant to us."

"I do know," Alexei replied, his calmness purposely contrasting Alexandra's fury.

Alexandra looked back at Pavel and Elizabeth. "I suppose you'll also be asking for a full pardon for Dmitry and Felix?" she said.

"We were considering it," Pavel replied honestly, despite his niece's hostility.

"I'll not have it," Alexandra replied decisively. "They cannot be rehabilitated after what they did."

Finally, Alexei put his teacup down again and stood up. "Coming back for Papa's funeral and a full pardon are two separate things," he said.

"Dmitry and Felix are family, and Papa was their tsar. Besides, Irina and the girls have been in exile with Felix. They had nothing to do with Grishka's death, and Irina is Papa's only niece."

Alexandra frowned at her son. "I can't believe you're going to allow this."

"I think it's important they be here for the funeral," Alexei replied. He looked back at Elizabeth and Pavel. "I'll send the necessary telegrams."

The final funeral services were interminable. Alexei watched Nicholas' coffin being loaded into a carriage that was decorated with black bunting. The coffin was then drawn through the streets by horses covered in black, and Alexei cried until his eyes burned. The coffin moved slowly through the streets, surrounded by guards of the Preobrazhensky Regiment. The Regiment's green uniforms were familiar, but Alexei barely saw them.

Alexei was surrounded by his uncles, great-uncles, and cousins as they all walked behind the coffin. The women of the family followed in closed carriages. All around them, ordinary Russians stood in lines twelve or thirteen deep to pay their respects. Many of them sobbed and prayed loudly, their wails adding to the mournful noise of the church bells that filled the air. Their presence clogged the streets and slowed the progress of the funeral procession, and yet Alexei was grateful. *These are my people*, he thought. *I am not alone.*

Once inside the Fortress of Sts. Peter and Paul, Alexei's tears had stopped but his eyes still burned. He supported Alexandra, whose tears continued flowing throughout the service. Olga, Tatiana, Marie and Anastasia also surrounded Alexandra. Alexei looked at his sisters and could see that while Anastasia's eyes and cheeks were red, she too looked as though her tear ducts had finally dried up. Olga, Tatiana and Marie's tears continued to flow as copiously as Alexandra's.

It was just as painful for Alexei to see his grandmother, the petite, dark-haired Dowager Empress Marie Feodorovna. She was supported by her other children, Alexei's aunts Olga and Xenia, and his uncle Michael, but somehow the support did not seem enough. Marie had always carried herself regally, but now she was shrunken and stooped in her grief. Alexei could hear his family's murmurs as they, too, witnessed Marie's pain.

Alexei made his way over to Marie. Xenia and Olga parted to let him stand next to her. Marie clasped Alexei's arm gratefully, and Alexei was surprised by her strength. All around them, the priests chanted the familiar liturgy, their deep voices intermingling and filling the space of the sanctuary. The incense they lit filled the air with smoke and made Alexei's nose throb.

It was several hours later before the family finally returned to the Winter

Palace. Alexei felt completely drained of his strength, and yet he was in better shape than Alexandra. Alexei helped Alexandra into bed and left her ladies-in-waiting with her as he went to check on Tatiana.

Boris had already helped Tatiana lie down in their apartments. He was standing next to her, tall and majestic looking despite his increasing baldness, when Alexei arrived. Tatiana's porcelain skin matched the white sheets she lay on, and her black hair framed her head. Marie and Anastasia sat next to her, helping her eat some soup that a nervous servant had left. Olga and Alexander sat in chairs nearby. A bassinet sat next to them, and Alexei could see baby Peter inside it, sound asleep.

"How is Mama?" Tatiana asked.

"Sleeping," Alexei replied. "How are you?"

"Exhausted," Tatiana said. "But I'll recover."

Alexei nodded. "You should rest," he said.

"I am," Tatiana said, gesturing to show that she was lying down.

"How long can you stay?"

"We don't have to rush back quite yet. There's always state business to attend to, but this takes priority."

Boris did not disagree with his wife, but he looked nervous. "We'll have to get back at some point," he said. "The baby has to be born on Bulgarian soil."

Tatiana's eyes shot daggers at him. "We won't be here that long," she snapped. "I still have three months until my confinement."

Boris looked uncomfortable.

"I know my duty," Tatiana added. "I wouldn't keep the baby from being born in his homeland."

"I didn't mean-" Boris stuttered.

"Enough," Alexei interrupted. "This is a rough time for everyone."

Across the room, Alexander was comforting Olga. "I'm fine," Olga said when Alexei looked at her. Her red eyes conveyed a different message, and her blond hair had started to come loose from its formal styling.

"When do you get back to state business?" Alexander asked. His kind blue eyes conveyed his sympathy from behind his thick square glasses. "You're taking some time off, I hope?"

"I'll be taking a few days," Alexei said decisively, even if it was not something he had considered. "On some levels, because Papa laid in state, it feels like it's been awhile already."

"Still, it's not good to rush things," Alexander said.

"I know," Alexei said. "I won't."

That night, after Olga and Tatiana were asleep, Alexei joined Alexander and Boris in one of the Palace's drawing rooms. Alexander and Boris were smoking cigars, and the acrid smoke filled the room. Alexei, who had never gotten used to the taste or the smell, took a cigar from Alexander but did not light it. Still, he found the presence of his brothers-in-law comforting, and he eagerly listened to Boris' tales of ascending the throne after his father's abdication. Alexander had been acting as Regent because of the Serbian king's ill health, and he had plenty to add.

"It doesn't get easier, does it?" Alexei asked wearily.

"It takes time to gain confidence in your ability to rule," Boris admitted. "Though it might be easier to come to the throne after your father's death rather than through an abdication- it's a more natural way to transfer power."

"The ruling does get easier," Alexander added, running a hand through his black hair. "Surround yourself with people you trust, and be sure you have wise, competent ministers. Otherwise, governing will be impossible."

Boris nodded in agreement. "I don't envy your youth in this regard, Alyosha," he said.

"No, I wouldn't have wanted to take the throne at sixteen either," Alexander said. "You have a difficult task in front of you."

A few days later, Alexei said goodbye to his oldest sisters with a heavy heart. *My happiest memories are of the times when the family was together. Besides, I need their support now more than ever*, he thought. *But both Alexander and Boris have countries of their own to rule.*

Tatiana and Boris gave Alexei one last hug before they departed. "You know how to use the telephone," Tatiana reminded her brother. "Call us anytime."

Alexander gave Alexei a serious, sympathetic look as Olga prepared to board their train, carrying Peter. "If there's anything I can do to help, don't hesitate to call on me," he said.

"I won't," Alexei promised.

When the family had left and the Palace was quiet, Alexei crept into Nicholas' study to attend to the state business his father had left behind. *It's my study now*, Alexei told himself, but the thought belied the reality of the place. Nicholas' scent still hung in the air, and all of his belongings, so neatly arranged, remained untouched from the last time he had been there.

Alexei went around the office's heavy mahogany desk and sat in the chair. A small portrait of his mother sat on the desk in front of him, and photographs of Alexei and his sisters sat in various places nearby. Both the pictures and the papers surrounding them were arranged with an extraordinary neatness. Opening one of the desk drawers, Alexei saw a line of pens, all arranged exactly the same way, and a line of pencils, all sharpened to exactly the same length. They reminded Alexei of his father- so meticulous, so insistent upon doing everything himself that he did not have a secretary. *He was the same way about preparing me to rule*, Alexei thought as he realized he felt comfortable in the study.

He took a deep breath. *A few more years of education would have helped, though*, he thought. *Despite Papa's own lack of preparation when he ascended the throne, he was a full ten years older than I am now.*

Alexei swallowed. Then he stood up, looking at the portrait of Nicholas that hung across the room. Tears sprang into his eyes. Had it really been only two weeks ago that Nicholas had reprimanded him for joyriding in his Rolls Royce? The memory made Alexei smile through his tears.

After a minute, he looked down at the papers that sat on the desk. Some were marked as being urgent, and many already had Nicholas' comments and edits in the margins. Alexei pulled a pen from one of the desk drawers, and sat down again to review the papers more fully. Then he worked well into the night, reading until he had finished the last piece of paper in front of him.

CHAPTER 3

When Alexei awoke in his bedroom the next morning, warm sunlight was streaming through the window, making the icons in the room gleam. Alexei's eyes were drawn to the icons, and he rose, crossed himself, kissed the icons, and said a few prayers. When he stuck his head outside his room, he saw several servants in full court dress arranging a tray of black bread and hot tea. They all stood at attention when they saw him. "Thank you," Alexei said, grateful for the food and his servants' presence of mind.

When he was done eating, Alexei made his way to his study. To his surprise, he found Michael sitting outside, as if he were expecting a formal audience. "Uncle Misha," he said. Then he saw one of his mother's ladies-in-waiting, and he stood up straight. "I'm sorry," he said. "Is my mother waiting to see me too?"

"She is, Your Imperial Majesty," the lady replied, and it took Alexei a minute to acclimate himself to the weight of the new title. Luckily, Alexandra appeared from around the corner, and with a nod, Alexei waved her and Michael into the study.

"How late were you working last night?" Michael asked. Already, he had taken a seat across from the mahogany desk that his brother had so recently occupied.

"I couldn't tell you," Alexei replied. "It was until whatever time I finished reading and approving the legislation Papa had been working on."

Early morning sunlight flowed through the Palace's windows, and the parquet floor glowed. Without thinking, Alexei sat in the comfortable chair at the desk. When he looked up, his mother had tears in her eyes, and Michael was eying him gravely.

"I'm sorry," Alexei said. "This can't be easy for either of you." He paused slightly. "But the government must be run somehow, and I am Tsar."

"Actually, that was what we wanted to talk about," Michael said carefully. "You are only sixteen, so your mother and I were discussing the possibility of a Regency."

"What for?" Alexei asked, his face smiling, his tone serious. "Last time I checked our Fundamental Laws and constitution, they said that a tsar can take power on his own at sixteen."

"Even so," Michael said, "Nicky had been preparing for the transition in power, and he had a regency set up in case he passed on before you turned twenty one."

"He wanted me to have a Regent for another five years?"

Michael nodded. "Nicky made me and your mother regents. It's why I've become so much more involved with running the government recently."

"I didn't know that," Alexei said. "In fact, the way I heard it, Uncle Misha, you were quite relieved when I was born, because it meant that you were no longer Tsarevich."

"That's true," Michael replied, smiling at the memory. "But as I've gotten older, I've realized the importance of the family's leadership."

"No, you've just grown up and become a mature adult," Alexandra sniped.

Michael's face tightened, but he kept his eyes on Alexei.

"Don't worry, Misha, I know you've been involved," Alexei said. "In fact, people have been impressed by your low-key presence. As such, I would like you to remain in your current position. However, I intend to rule as tsar on my own, without a regent."

Michael and Alexandra looked at each other. "You are hardly ready to rule, Sunbeam," Alexandra said.

Alexei felt his face grow warm. *I'll never be ready to rule if she keeps calling me that,* he thought. "The tsar I am named for took the throne at sixteen, as did his father before him," he said. "Both Mikhail Feodorovich and Alexei Mikhailovich had just come of age, and they were the first two Romanov tsars. I have had many generations since then to learn from."

"When did you start paying attention to your history tutors?" Michael teased.

"Oh, come on, Misha," Alexei said, becoming slightly annoyed. "Papa has been preparing me to rule since I was born. Putting me under the power of a Regent when I am already of age would undermine the power of the throne!"

Michael and Alexandra looked at each other again.

"That is not to say I couldn't use the help," Alexei said, his tone becoming more conciliatory. "Misha, are you interested in remaining in the government? It would be most welcome."

"What about me?" Alexandra sputtered.

Alexei looked her, fearing an outburst.

"I should like to remain as involved with your government as I was in Nicky's," Alexandra said.

"Absolutely not," Alexei answered. "You are not a politician, Mama, and your choices for ministers were often disastrous."

"How dare you talk to me like that!" Alexandra exploded. She leapt to her feet.

Michael stood up too, a worried look on his face.

Alexei remained seated, trying to look calm even as his heart raced. He splayed his hands out on his desk and felt the cool wood beneath his palms. "I'm only speaking the truth, Mama," he said. "Most of the ministers you picked, especially during the Great War, were so old or so incompetent that it was scary."

"Russia won the war," Alexandra reminded him.

"Only because we are a constitutional monarchy, and the Duma had the sense to carry out the good policies that Papa and his competent ministers promulgated."

"Your father never had enough backbone," Alexandra said. "I was constantly encouraging him."

This conversation is giving me a headache, Alexei thought. For a moment, he stared out the room's tall windows. Then he looked back at his mother and uncle. "I am tsar now, and I intend to rule on my own. I am of age, and I will not accept a regent. I do want your expertise, though, Misha, and that of Papa's ministers, until I find my own way."

"What do you want of me?" Alexandra asked, sounding defeated.

"You are the Dowager Empress," Alexei said.

"Behind your grandmother."

"This is a first in the history of the dynasty, but you still have the charities you support, the churches you visit…"

"Your grandmother has tried to have preference over me since I married Nicky," Alexandra sniffed. "There's no way she'll consent to allowing me to go ahead of her now!"

Alexei sighed. "I thought you developed different charities to support for that very reason," he said. "And Amama doesn't support nearly the number of churches and monasteries that you do. Being Dowager Empress is a ceremonial role, Mama. You could do a lot with it."

But Alexandra shook her head. "My focus has always been the family," she said.

"Perhaps a greater involvement in the capital's social events would add prestige to the dynasty," Michael suggested, and Alexei was glad for his input. "In fact, your isolation from the extended family and the rest of society is something that should be rectified."

Alexandra's face tightened, and Alexei could tell she was unhappy. But instead of saying anything else, she simply turned and fled out of the study. Looking uncomfortable, Michael followed her. *Good,* Alexei thought as they left. *Maybe Misha will calm Mama down.*

Once they were gone, Alexei wanted nothing more than to put his head down on his desk and sob. Instead, he went outside to the Palace's gardens, where the cool September air greeted him, perfumed by copious flowers. Beyond the palace gates, he could hear the clop-clop of horses and the sound of the occasional motor car. Suddenly, he became aware of the palace's guards around him, separating him from the rest of the world.

Alexei shivered. Then, hearing footsteps behind him, he turned to see Alexander Spiridovich, the Chief of his personal police, approaching. "Alexander Ivanovich, can you read minds?" Alexei asked. "I was just thinking of security issues."

Spiridovich smiled. "That is why I am here, Your Imperial Majesty," he said.

"Let's walk," Alexei said. As they marched across the open lawn, Alexei breathed in the smell of fresh cut grass. "So what brings you here, Alexander Ivanovich?"

"For some time now, my agents have been following Vladimir Ilyich Lenin," Spiridovich replied.

"Who is that?" Alexei asked.

"A Communist. He was in exile in Switzerland until after Rasputin was killed. Then- even before the Great War ended- he slipped back into Russia, thinking he could instigate a revolution."

"The Communists always think a revolution is at hand," Alexei said. "Nevertheless, letting a man like Lenin back into the country is poor police work."

"We're not sure how he got in," Spiridovich admitted.

"He's been back in the country for two years now and you're not even sure how he got here?" Alexei asked pointedly. Spiridovich swallowed uncomfortably. "Why are you bringing him to my attention now? Is he going to throw a bomb at me?"

"It's always a possibility, Your Imperial Majesty," Spiridovich said. "He definitely wants some contact with you, and incredibly, it seems his first attempt is through legal channels."

"What do you mean?" Alexei asked, his eyebrows coming together in a frown.

"He put in a petition to meet with you here at the Palace."

They had reached a small grove of trees with a marble bench under it. Alexei paused from his high speed walking and rested his foot on the bench. "There's an entire stack of petitions on my desk," he said. "I'll have to take a look at them."

"Please be careful, Your Imperial Majesty," Spiridovich warned. "This may be nothing more than an assassination attempt."

"Perhaps," Alexei conceded. "But bringing him to the Palace puts him here on our terms."

"Even so, it's not a course I recommend."

"Of course not," Alexei said with a smile. He thought for a minute. "Let me find that petition. I'll let you know what I decide."

The next day, Alexei located Lenin's petition from among the stack on his desk. The carefully worded document requested a meeting to discuss the living and working conditions of the working class and veterans from the Great War. Alexei doubted that was all Lenin had in mind, but he granted the petition and set a meeting date for the following Monday. *I would be amenable to having him disappear into Siberia, but he made it back into the country during the War,* Alexei thought. *Simple banishment is probably not the answer.*

In locating Lenin's petition, Alexei came across a second petition that he deemed equally important- Prince Igor Konstantinovich's petition to retain his Aide-de-Camp position in Alexei's reign. *Igor served Papa loyally,* Alexei thought as he pictured his tall, pale cousin who had retained his round cheeks even into adulthood. *Besides, having a trusted ADC is not an opportunity I intend to pass up.* He picked up the telephone and called Pavlovsk.

"Hello?" a deep voice answered on the other end.

"Hello Gavril," Alexei replied, grinning at the prospect of talking to one of Igor's older brothers. "It's Alexei."

"Alyosha, are you back at work already?" Gavril asked.

"I am," Alexei confirmed. "I have so many petitions on my desk that I could cover the walls of the Winter Palace. I have to start somewhere."

"Just put in the same number of hours your father did, and it'll all work out," Gavril advised.

"I don't know," Alexei said doubtfully. "I never did have my father's work ethic." They both laughed. Then Alexei said, "Listen, Gavril, I have Igor's application to be my ADC. Is he still interested?"

"I'm sure he is," Gavril said. "Let me put him on."

A minute later, Igor was on the line. "I'm still interested," he said. "I would be humbled if you would consider it."

"I've already considered it," Alexei replied. "If you want it, it's yours."

"I want it."

"When can you start?"

"As soon as I tie up some loose ends with my regiment."

"I was counting on that, Igor, but I do have one assignment for you while you're doing that."

"Of course. Anything."

"Do you think you could procure me a pistol?"

"What are you going to do with a pistol, Alyosha?" Igor asked. "Are you unhappy with me already?"

"It's not you," Alexei reassured him, and they both laughed. "I have a meeting with Vladimir Ilyich Lenin next week."

"The revolutionary?" Igor asked. "I've heard he's crazy."

"I don't think this will be a simple meeting," Alexei agreed.

"I'll see what I can do," Igor promised.

It was the first Monday of September. Alexei leaned on the desk in his study as Michael stood at the window, staring out at the trees in the Palace's park, which were beginning to show signs of autumn. "I'm not happy about this, Alyosha," Michael said. "I don't trust Lenin one bit."

"Me neither," Alexei replied. "But I'm hoping that a meeting with him will forestall-"

"Forestall what?" Michael interrupted. "You will never change that man's revolutionary intentions, and having him here in the Palace could get us all killed."

Just then, a servant knocked on the door. "Come in," Alexei ordered.

"Your Imperial Majesty, a Vladimir Ilyich Lenin has arrived at the Palace to see you," the servant said.

"Bring him in," Alexei ordered.

The servant bowed and left. He returned a minute later with Lenin on his heels, and Alexei was given his first glimpse of the famed revolutionary. Lenin was short and balding, and the top of his head looked like it had been polished. He also had slanted eyes that reminded Alexei of the Orientals that lived on the fringes of his empire. Alexei eyed Lenin, and Lenin glared back at him with a cold stare. At the window, Michael watched nervously, biting his lip.

There was a silence, which Alexei broke by saying, "have a seat, please."

Lenin obeyed, sitting in the chair across from Alexei's desk, never taking his eyes off Alexei as he moved. Alexei sat too, facing Lenin. Michael remained standing by the window, eyeing them both uncomfortably. Alexei folded his hands on his desk and looked at Lenin for another minute before saying, "so what can I do for you, Vladimir Ilyich? Surely you did not request this meeting simply to stare at me without speaking."

"Of course not," Lenin replied. "I am only here to advocate the case of my people- the working class. We have been trying to achieve better representation in the Duma, and all of our attempts have failed."

"People are allowed to refrain from voting for your party as they see fit," Alexei replied. "I'm not sure what you would like me to do."

"With the death of your father, we were hoping that the government would make a transition to one that is completely Duma-run."

"Are you asking me to abdicate?" Alexei asked.

"That would certainly be an acceptable course of action."

Out of the corner of his eye, Alexei could see Michael's jaw drop. Inwardly, he agreed, but outwardly, he just smiled. "You think I should give up my right to rule? On what grounds?"

"You and your entire class are nothing but parasites! You are only a boy who is completely unqualified for the position you now hold."

Alexei shrugged. "What would you do if I abdicated?"

"Put you on trial for your crimes against humanity and redistribute your wealth. It is only fair. Your money was obtained on the backs of your people."

"Nothing you say will persuade me to give up my throne. I'm sorry you wasted your time in coming here." Alexei put his hands on his desk and pushed his chair back. Then he lowered his hands enough to open the desk's top drawer.

"Don't dismiss me so quickly," Lenin warned.

"Why not? You've done nothing but insult me. I'll have a servant escort you out." Immediately, a servant appeared at the door.

Lenin shook his head. "I'm not moving until you hear me out!"

"Is that so?" Alexei glared at his visitor.

Lenin glared back without blinking. "For too long the tsars of Russia have repressed their citizens," he said. "This ends now."

Although both of them were seated, Alexei sensed that Lenin's hands were moving in his lap. Alexei grabbed the loaded pistol in his desk drawer. Lenin began to stand up. Suddenly, Michael pulled a knife from his belt and hurled it at Lenin. The knife crashed into Lenin's chest, nearly tipping him backwards.

At the same time, Alexei raised his pistol and fired. The gun let out a bang that reverberated through the study as Lenin's revolver clattered to the floor. Alexei's bullet tore through Lenin's head and kept going, finally coming to rest in a portrait of Alexander II. Lenin slithered to the floor as his blood sprayed across the room. Alexei leapt to his feet and raced around his desk. He stood over Lenin, aiming his pistol again. But Lenin did not move, and Alexei slowly lowered the gun.

Michael knelt beside Lenin and felt for a pulse. "He's dead."

Michael had barely finished speaking when Alexei threw down his gun and ran for the door. He dashed into the hallway- and straight into the horde of servants that were sprinting towards the study. Among the servants were Marie and Anastasia, both of whose eyes were round with fear.

I need to get out of here, Alexei thought. He pushed through the mass of people and raced down the hallway, not sure where he was going, only caring about getting away from the dead body in his study. Eventually, he ended up in one of the Palace's formal ballrooms, whose wide open space appealed to him. He took a deep breath and slowly walked to one of the windows.

When Michael and Anastasia found him a few minutes later, tears were running down his face. "I saw such suffering during the Great War," he said. "After that, I never thought I'd be able to do something so brutal."

"Would you have preferred he killed you?" Michael asked calmly.

"No."

"Then you did the right thing."

Alexei sniffed. "I was hoping to be a kind and compassionate tsar," he said. "Instead, one of my first acts was to blow out the brains of one of my subjects."

"He didn't have much of a brain to lose," Anastasia reassured him. Alexei almost smiled.

"If it had been up to Lenin, you never would have had the chance to be tsar," Michael said seriously.

"You're right," Alexei said. "And I've wanted to be tsar my whole life." He turned and looked around, taking in the expanse of the ballroom. "Also, that was an impressive knife-throw, Uncle Misha."

"Thanks," Michael replied, a smile twitching at his lips. "It was a lesson well-learned from my Savage Division during the Great War."

Across the ballroom, Alexandra and Marie hesitantly entered, but Alexei's mind was no longer on the vast space in front of him. "I can't work in that study anymore," he said.

Anastasia nodded. "The servants are already cleaning up in there," she said. "I also told them to move your desk to a different room of the palace, so you can work somewhere else."

Alexei looked at his sister and smiled through his tears.

CHAPTER 4

By the time Colonel Spiridovich reported to the Winter Palace the next day, the news of Lenin's demise had been reported across the country and abroad, and Alexei's summons did little to calm him. As he was led to Alexei's makeshift study, Spiridovich noticed the servants packing trunks full of the imperial family's belongings. When he arrived in Alexei's presence, he still had a questioning look on his face.

"We're moving back to the Alexander Palace," Alexei said.

"Are the Empress and Grand Duchesses going with you?" Spiridovich asked.

"Yes," Alexei replied. "We all feel safer there." His eyes hardened. "Speaking of safety-"

"I am sorry, Your Imperial Majesty," Spiridovich interrupted. "But it was your decision to see Lenin here at the Palace."

"That's not what worries me," Alexei said, his voice rising. "How is it that anyone- let alone a man like Lenin- could make it all the way through the Palace and into my presence with a loaded revolver?"

"I can't imagine how that happened."

"You are my Chief of Police!" Alexei shouted. "How do you train your men?"

"We use the most up-to-date technology and training," Spiridovich replied indignantly.

"Like hell you do! I want your resignation now."

"You're firing me? Your Imperial Majesty-"

"Yes, I'm firing you. Your poor police work resulted in Stolypin's near-assassination back in 1911, and my father was too weak to fire you then-"

"Your Imperial Majesty-"

"That shooter was a policeman who was also double agent," Alexei continued. "How many more near assassinations are we going to have before someone important ends up dead?"

Spiridovich did not have a good answer, and his silence showed that.

"You have until the end of today to vacate your office and hand me a list of recommendations for your successor."

"That's completely unfair!"

"I was almost murdered right here in my own Palace because you failed to do your job properly, and all I'm doing is firing you," Alexei yelled. "Don't tell me what's unfair! Would you prefer a permanent vacation in Siberia?"

Spiridovich swallowed. He met Alexei's gaze without flinching, but he managed to hold his tongue.

"Very well," Alexei replied. "You're dismissed."

Glowering, Spiridovich stormed out of the Palace.

It was nearly midnight when Marie and Anastasia found Alexei sitting at a table in the Palace's expansive library, surrounded by books. His right leg rested on the chair next to him, and a warm compress was pressed against his knee.

"Ah, there you are," Marie said.

"Looking for me?" Alexei asked.

Anastasia nodded. "It's nearly midnight. We thought you'd be asleep already, but your apartments were empty."

Alexei checked his watch. "There aren't enough hours in the day," he complained.

Then Marie noticed the warm compress. "What happened?"

Alexei grimaced. "I must have strained my knee running out of my study yesterday. Hopefully the bleeding won't be too bad." He shook his head. "I'm finally tsar and I would almost give my kingdom to be free of my hemophilia."

Marie and Anastasia eyed their brother uncomfortably. "Why are you in the library?" Anastasia finally asked. "I've never seen you surrounded by this many books, even during your lessons."

Alexei sighed. *I didn't enjoy my studies when they were happening, but now I wish I had more time for them.* "I'm preparing my speech for the opening of the Duma," he said. "There's a lot of history I wish I knew more of."

"Your education was interrupted whenever your hemophilia struck," Marie reminded him.

"I know," Alexei said. He sighed and put his head down on the table. Despair emanated from him. "I've always wanted to be tsar," he said. "Now I also wish I were an adult as well."

"You're of age, and you didn't want a Regent," Anastasia reminded him.

"I hope that wasn't a mistake," Alexei said as he sat up.

"It wasn't," Marie said emphatically. She sat down across the table from her brother, and the room's light shined off her golden hair. "How are you planning on delivering your speech?"

"I told the Duma that I will come to the Tauride Palace for the opening session next week."

Anastasia frowned as she thought about it. "Papa always made them come here when he wanted to open a session."

"From the interpretations I've been reading, that might have been a mistake."

Marie and Anastasia exchanged a look. "I can't imagine that Mama will be happy about the change either," Marie said.

"Let me handle Mama," Alexei said. He checked his watch again and stood up, curling the warm compress in his hands as he stood. "It is now officially midnight. I'm going to bed." His sisters followed him out of the library.

"One more thing," Marie said. "Spiridovich disappeared from his office today, cleaning out all of his belongings in the process. As police chief, that's-"

"It's because I fired him," Alexei said abruptly. "He let an armed assassin into the Palace."

Marie and Anastasia looked at each other again.

"Don't worry, I'll soon find a replacement," Alexei reassured them. "Now, how about we get some sleep?"

The next morning, Alexei sat in his makeshift study with Michael and Ministers Stolypin and Witte. Once more, Alexei had applied a warm compress onto his aching knee, but now he kept his legs under his desk so that the ministers would not see it. *Most of the country doesn't know about my hemophilia*, he thought. *Mama and Papa always kept it a secret.*

"I'm glad you're doing this, Your Imperial Majesty," Stolypin said, and Alexei had to remind himself that Stolypin was talking about his speech to the Duma. Stolypin's thinning, graying hair was cut short, and his curling black moustache moved when he spoke. "Despite the constitution, your father regarded the Duma as something to be contravened so that he could do his job correctly."

"Many of us are hoping for a change with the new reign," Witte added. He had retained his full head of dark hair and full, dark, mustache and beard, but Alexei thought his skin had never lost the sallow complexion it had gained following a brain tumor that had been removed in 1915.

"Russia has been a constitutional monarchy since before I was born,"

Alexei replied. "And I intend to work within its confines." He squirmed slightly, feeling both his knee and the cramped surroundings. "You met with my father the day before he died. What were you working on? What are the delegates in the Duma most worried about?"

"The state of the economy," Witte said immediately. "Frankly, Your Imperial Majesty, the country is still recovering from the Great War, as is most of Europe. Our infrastructure and economy may not have been damaged as badly as Germany's, for example, but our economy was not as advanced as theirs, either."

Alexei nodded. "I remember the constant shortages of guns, ammunition and food, as well as the problems we had transporting everything to the front."

"Our economy is still primarily agrarian, and we're not even using the best farming techniques," Witte said with a nod. "We're very far behind the industrialization of the rest of Europe."

"What does that mean?" Alexei asked.

"We have fewer factories to produce materials, fewer mining operations to extract minerals, ores, and so forth from the ground, fewer miles of railroad track and trains to transport these materials to the factories."

"We also have a huge empire, and huge distances over which to transport the materials," Alexei said.

"It certainly aggravates the problem," Witte agreed.

There was a silence as Alexei contemplated the situation. "Okay," he said finally. "We need to improve our agriculture and our mining so as to produce more from the Earth, we need to improve our railroads to get food to the cities and other materials to the factories, and we need our factories to produce more from those goods." He took a deep breath. "All of that takes a lot of work and money. Where do we start?"

A week later, Alexei was adjusting his uniform's epaulets when Jim Hercules, one of the two tall Abyssinian Guards that stood watch over his private chambers, opened the door to allow Alexandra to enter the room. She was fully dressed, and looked magnificent in her long skirts, pearls, and tiara. Her eyes, however, remained sad. "I can't believe you're doing this, and that you wanted the whole family there," she said.

"The Duma and its representatives want to get to know me, and to know what kind of ruler I will be," Alexei said.

"The Duma is nothing but a bunch of rogues and revolutionaries."

"And yet our constitution says that we have to work with them."

"Your father did all he could to prorogue the Duma."

"To the detriment of the country, I think," Alexei said. Alexandra looked horrified. "I believe in the monarchy," Alexei reassured her. "But our constitution is going on its fourth generation now."

As they left the Palace, Anastasia and Marie surrounded their brother. "Don't worry, you're doing the right thing," Anastasia said as Marie rested her hand on Alexei's arm.

"Thanks," Alexei said with a grin. *Thank God somebody supports me.*

When they exited the Palace, however, Alexei regretted the rush to leave- the procession of cars awaiting them seemed like too many. Then he realized that quite a number of those cars were for policemen, and indeed, he found himself nearly alone in the car but for the policemen that surrounded him. Even the car's tinted windows separated Alexei from the outside world. As they drove, Alexei saw people on the streets, driving and walking at their own paces. He shook his head. *I'm now one of the most powerful people in the world, and my freedom has been reduced for my own safety,* he thought.

Prince Igor Konstantinovich, Alexei's newly appointed Aide-De-Camp, was the only other non-policeman in the car. Alexei smiled at his cousin, glad for Igor's stoic presence. Igor smiled back. "My family and I are looking forward to this," he said.

The thought of Igor's four brothers, two sisters and mother assembling at the Tauride Palace to hear him speak calmed Alexei slightly. *And at least my knee is better, so I'll be able to stand up straight when I speak,* he thought. Even so, when the Winter Palace disappeared behind them and the Tauride Palace came into view, Alexei's only thought was, *from one gilded cage to another.*

Inside the Tauride Palace, the Imperial family took its place at the front of the hall, and the delegates took their seats. Immediately, Alexei was struck by the difference in the Imperial family's court dress and military uniforms and the way some of the delegates were dressed. The conservative delegates, who were mostly pro-monarchy, were all dressed in immaculate military uniforms. By contrast, the Communists wore street clothes. *I never would have guessed that they were delegates,* Alexei thought.

Alexei spent an extra minute eyeing the Communists as the delegates continued to assemble. *Lenin's party,* he thought. *I wonder how they'll adapt to the change in leadership.* He could see a couple of delegates who looked like they were in charge. One was a man with wiry glasses whose eyes shone with a penetrating intelligence. A mop of curly black hair covered his head. Next to him stood a more imposing man, also with black hair but whose eyes were so cold they shot daggers of ice in Alexei's direction. Alexei shivered and looked away.

Looking back at his family, he could see Alexandra staring at the delegates in front of her with a haughty expression, the same expression he had seen in old photographs of his parents in prior sessions of the Duma. By contrast, Anastasia and Marie were smiling and watching the proceedings with interest. Their expressions were mirrored on the faces of the younger members of the Imperial family.

Then the delegates quieted and took their seats. A respectful silence descended as Alexei went to the podium to speak. Seeing hundreds of eyes upon him, Alexei suddenly became nervous. By the time he stood at the podium, fully facing the delegates, his heart was pounding and his hands were shaking. He swallowed and forced himself to speak.

"Thank you all for coming," he began. "The beginning of a new reign is a chance to start on a different path. Like a few of my forefathers, I come to the throne at a very young age, and I come to power at a fragile time for Russia.

"Our country and our lives are very different than when my father began his reign. We have just been through a terrible war that shattered many of our illusions. It is peacetime now, but a delicate peace. Threats continue, both internally and abroad. At home, our population has been depleted by war and famine at a time when our economy needs additional human capital, and investment capital, to grow and prosper. Our soil is fertile, but our farms remain untilled. We need additional factories and additional workers to fill them. Outside our borders, foreign aggressors such as Germany have been pacified, but unless we take intelligent measures to ensure peace, they will become our aggressors again.

"As tsar, I pledge to tackle these issues straight away, but I ask for your support in doing so. Gone are the days when tsar and Duma could work against each other and still hope to accomplish these difficult tasks. The fact that our country was nearly ripped apart by an internal civil war while still fighting an external enemy is not acceptable. I am a firm believer in our country's constitutional monarchy. As such, I welcome the existence of the Duma and value your opinions, but I will not tolerate unrest for the sake of unrest. This Duma is a forum for your opinions and intelligent debate that benefits Russia- violence is not the right path.

"Thus, I ask again that we work together to achieve our common goals. Together, we can make this country greater than any of our neighbors and allies."

Thunderous applause filled the chamber as Alexei finished speaking. Alexei, relieved to be finished, stepped back from the podium and acknowledged the applause. When it was quiet again, several of the delegates approached to introduce themselves. Alexei spoke to each of them in turn before making his way over to where the Communists stood, talking amongst themselves. They became quiet when they saw him, but at least they had the courtesy to introduce themselves. The man with wiry glasses and intelligent eyes was Leon Trotsky, and the man who had given Alexei the chills was Joseph Stalin.

I might almost be able to work with Trotsky, but Stalin makes my stomach turn,

Alexei thought. *Maybe I should deal with him the same way I dealt with Lenin.*

Throughout it all, Alexei was aware that Michael and a bodyguard hovered protectively- and nervously. Alexei could also see his sisters and grandmother all engaged in conversations with various delegates. Anastasia spoke to several delegates at once, her humor and impertinence coming through- all of the delegates were laughing. Marie was speaking to several of the Obolensky princes- Nikolai, in particular, it seemed, though quite a few of his family members surrounded them.

The other members of the Imperial family were also making conversation with the people around them. Alexandra, however, remained standing by herself near the podium, watching Alexei. *No wonder so many people think she's unapproachable,* Alexei thought, feeling a stab of sadness penetrate his stomach.

CHAPTER 5

Five days after Alexei's speech to the Duma, the family moved from the Winter Palace to Tsarskoe Selo. Alexei and Michael sat together in one train car as Marie, Anastasia and Alexandra made noise in the next car. Igor Konstantinovich stood discreetly at one end of Alexei's car, keeping an eye on Alexei and Michael and an ear on the women next door.

"Have you made any progress in selecting a new police chief?" Michael asked.

"Yes," Alexei said, pulling a piece of paper from his pocket. "When I fired Spiridovich, I asked him to provide me with a list of possible replacements."

"How do you know that list will be good?" Michael asked. "He may have given you a list of the most incompetent bureaucrats, just out of spite."

Alexei shrugged. "I fired him because Lenin got all the way through the Palace with a loaded gun. I couldn't continue to employ him because of the message it would send. That doesn't mean I thought he was totally incompetent."

"So you trust his judgment, despite that incident?"

"I think he knows his own staff. I thought this list would be a good start, not an exhaustive list."

"Let me see it," Michael said. Alexei handed him the paper. "You've already crossed off a few people."

Alexei nodded. "A few of them have been around awhile. I think they're more interested in retirement than promotion."

"I'm not familiar with all the names on this list," Michael admitted.

"Me neither, but I've started checking. There a few that I think are solid. I'm meeting them tomorrow, one after the other. I want you to be there."

Michael nodded. "The family's safety has always been the highest priority."

"It's not just that," Alexei said. "Our police staff has always been understaffed an underpaid. I'm thinking of expanding the police service and paying them better."

"That's a very autocratic thing to do," Michael joked.

"No, the autocratic thing to do would be to leave their pay as it is." Alexei shook his head. "Our public servants have always been underpaid- it's why so many of them take bribes, just to survive. We rely on our police force pretty heavily- I want to make sure they're reliable."

"If you raise the salaries of one sector, the rest will be clamoring for it too."

"And if they do, I'll consider it."

Michael eyed his nephew. "How will we get the money to do that?"

Alexei stared out the window of the moving train as he thought about it. "Higher taxes, I guess," he said finally.

"The peasants can't withstand higher taxes," Michael said. "It's why we almost had a revolution at the end of the Great War. We were having trouble paying for the War, too."

"Witte and Stolypin have been advocating a change to the tax structure for years," Alexei said. "Taxing the clergy, the monasteries, and the wealthy would certainly go a long way."

"Then we'll really have a revolution, except that it'll be the nobility leading the way."

Alexei laughed. "The United States is just now instituting an income tax because its customs duties no longer bring in enough money," he said. "I'm not a fan of taxation, but we need to do something."

When Michael left, Alexei found Igor smiling at him from the other end of the car. "What?" Alexei asked. Igor had been so quiet that Alexei had forgotten he was there.

"Look at you, Alyosha," Igor said. "Restructuring our whole government and society. Following in the footsteps of Alexander II and Peter the Great."

"I'm not doing anything that radical."

"I don't know," Igor said. "You're certainly getting some resistance, even from within the family. That's usually a sign that you're doing something radical."

Alexei frowned. "Alexander II got more than resistance from within the family," he said. "He almost split the family apart. I was hoping to avoid that."

Igor came over and sat across from his cousin. "Alexander made the family angry because he kept a mistress while his wife was alive, and he flaunted it to everyone- he even had a second family with her! And when the Empress passed, he married his mistress even before the official mourning period was over."

"I know," Alexei said. "I'm not planning on doing anything like that. Even so, if I did rewrite the tax code, I'd probably have to start taxing our family. Politically, I don't think I could avoid it."

"It would be a difficult change," Igor admitted. "But if it's good for Russia, I can't see too much resistance from my branch of the family."

Alexei smiled. "Your branch of the family has always been the most patriotic. I still remember when you and your brothers went to fight in the Great War."

Igor nodded. "Losing Oleg to his wounds was one of the worst periods of my life, but people finally realized that the imperial family was willing to risk its own."

Alexei was in the gardens of Tsarskoe Selo, supervising the removal of a few dead trees, when Drs. Botkin and Derevenko were led out. Alexei smiled at them as he wrapped his coat around himself in the chill of the autumn air. "Walk with me," he said, and started moving along a path that would take them further into the woods. "The foreman can handle the rest of the tree cutting."

Botkin and Derevenko struggled to keep up as Alexei strode forward with long, confident strides. "Please be careful, Your Imperial Majesty," Botkin said.

"Or what?" Alexei asked, turning to look at him. "You're worried I might hurt myself, aren't you?"

"I have spent my whole life worried about that," Botkin admitted.

"Keeping watch over you has always been a major part of our job," Derevenko added.

Alexei eyed the doctors in front of him. He wasn't glaring at them, but his eyes really burrowed into them. Botkin and Derevenko looked away uncomfortably.

"My parents protected me because they were afraid," Alexei said finally.

"Of course they were," Botkin said. "Any cut or bruise could kill you. You're quite familiar with the effects of your hemophilia by now."

"Do you think me disease makes me unfit to reign?" Alexei asked.

"You are already reigning," Derevenko replied.

"That was not the question," Alexei said pointedly.

Botkin swallowed and looked away. Alexei felt a cool breeze wash over him as the silence lengthened.

"What is it, Yevgeny Sergeievich?" Alexei asked as they continued walking.

"Your father asked me that same question."

"When?"

"About the time the Great War was ending."

"What did you tell him?"

Botkin swallowed and looked at the ground.

"You told him that you didn't think I could reign," Alexei surmised incredulously.

"I'm sorry," Botkin said. His face showed his misery.

Alexei stopped walking and sat down on a tree stump. Light filtered through the trees around him, and dappled light fell on his shoulders. "Look, Yevgeny Sergeievich and Vladimir Nikolaevich, I don't blame you," he said. "My parents were probably looking to you to provide confirmation of what they already thought. But I've spent my whole life learning how to manage this disease, and preventing its attacks are something I wish I knew more of. Can you help me with that?"

The doctors looked at Alexei, uncertainty on their faces.

"Can you do research, confer with experts?" Alexei pressed. "I need to stay alive at least long enough to marry and produce an heir, and I'd like live long enough for my heir to reach maturity."

"Yes," Botkin replied finally. "There is research we can do, medical conferences we can attend."

"Good," Alexei said. "I'd rather have that knowledge, and protect myself, than live in fear."

The next morning, Alexei awoke early in his bedroom at the Alexander Palace. Its familiarity made him smile, even as he realized that he was in his childhood bedroom. *I'm tsar now,* he realized. *I should have different apartments.* Over breakfast with Alexandra, Alexei discussed his plans to interview for a new police chief that day.

"It sounds like another long day, Sunbeam," Alexandra said.

"Mama, please stop calling me that," Alexei said. "You make me sound like I'm four years old."

"You are still my child," Alexandra reminded him.

"And I am still tsar," Alexei reminded her.

Alexandra swallowed. "Fine," she said.

It was more than eight hours later when Alexei and Michael conferred before interviewing the last candidate on their list. Around them, the parquet floors of one of the Alexander Palace's staterooms glowed in the late afternoon light as the sun neared the horizon. The curtains of the nearly floor-to-ceiling windows had been pulled back to let in as much light as possible. Beyond the windows, the famous flowers of the Palace's park still shown brightly, even though Alexei knew that their beauty was fading in the crisp autumn air.

Alexei had decided to use the staterooms for the interviews, and now he was glad. A few of the candidates had been intimidated by the Palace's opulence, and Alexei made a mental note to strike them from consideration. Then he looked despairingly at Michael. "I'm not overwhelmed so far," he said. "Some of these men might be competent policemen or detectives, but I'm not getting a sense from any of them that they could handle my security."

"Unfortunately, I can't disagree," Michael replied. "But let's interview this last man on our list and go from there. He's someone that I've actually heard of, so that gives me a little more confidence."

"Who is he?" Alexei asked.

"Ivan Maximovich Gorvenko. He had a hand in defusing a conspiracy against your father."

"I never heard about that."

"It was long before you were born- right around the time of Nicky's coronation. There was a plot to kill him while he was taking the oath, and Gorvenko found out about it."

"That's the most impressive thing I've heard about anyone we've met all day," Alexei said. He looked at a servant. "Bring Gorvenko in."

The servant immediately disappeared, and Gorvenko was soon led in. His boots clicked on the wooden floor as he strode across it. Alexei studied him, and Gorvenko looked back at him steadily, but not rudely. He was a tall man, but still shorter than Alexei. His brown hair was tied back into a neat ponytail and his cold blue eyes shone from his pale face. He remained composed as Alexei examined him, showing little emotion. Only a small rivulet of sweat running down his face betrayed his nervousness at meeting Alexei for the first time.

"Please, sit down," Alexei said finally.

"Thank you, Your Imperial Majesty," Gorvenko replied. His voice was a rich baritone.

"So you work for Spiridovich?" Alexei asked.

"Yes, Your Imperial Majesty, I do. Or, well, I did, until-"

"Yes, until I fired him," Alexei said. "How long have you been in police work?"

"More than twenty years, Your Imperial Majesty. I started as a beat cop, walking the streets of St. Petersburg during the nighttime shift."

"And then what?" Alexei said. "You seem to have moved up through the ranks pretty quickly."

"I started surveillance work even while walking the beat."

"What kind of technology have you been using for this surveillance?"

"Wiretaps, bugs, tracking devices. We also get a lot of technology from the military- telescopes, weapons, that sort of thing."

"Where do you stand politically?" Alexei asked.

"I have been a staunch monarchist as long as I can remember," Gorvenko replied.

"What do you think of the Bolsheviks?"

"I think they're agitators who would do away with the very foundations of society if they could."

"And yet they have representation in the Duma," Alexei said. "Aren't people allowed to vote for whomever they want, including the Bolsheviks?"

"I don't think many people realize the depth of hatred or propensity for violence that the Bolsheviks possess," Gorvenko replied. "They talk about equality, but they want to achieve it by violence."

The interview lasted for over three hours. By the time Gorvenko left the palace, it was dark outside and Alexei was exhausted and more than ready for dinner. "I'm starving," he told Michael. "I could really use some borscht and sour cream right now. And some baklava."

"You're not allowed to skip the main courses and only eat desert," Michael reminded him.

"Then what's the point of being tsar?" Alexei asked. "It's not worth it if I can't even change the food service around here."

Michael and Alexei looked at each other and burst into laughter as the servants around them bowed and opened the Palace's doors for them.

Across the city, Gorvenko paced the streets of St. Petersburg. Throughout the interview, he had been struck by Alexei's sense of purpose, but also by his youth and inexperience. *People thought Nicholas Alexandrovich was too young when he came to the throne,* Gorvenko thought, *but Alexei Nikolaievich is younger still.*

Gorvenko walked along the Neva River until he came to the Alexander Nevsky Bridge. In the middle of the bridge, Gorvenko finally stopped and stared out over the city. He breathed deeply, smelling the water below him and feeling the chill in the air as the breeze swept over him.

I really want this job, he realized. *Becoming tsar has been Alexei Nikolaievich's destiny since he was born, but he is still so young.* Gorvenko swallowed as he stared down into the swirling waters of the Neva. *I would give my life to protect the Tsar,* he realized. *If only I were given that chance.*

Three days later, Gorvenko was working in his office when his assistant, Vladimir Alexeievich Kormenov, came running in, startling him. "His Imperial Majesty is on the telephone," Kormenov blurted out, before

Gorvenko could upbraid him for the intrusion.

Gorvenko rushed to the telephone. "Good afternoon," he said into the receiver. His voice was calm, but his heart was pounding.

"Good afternoon Ivan Maximovich," Alexei said on the other end of the phone. "How are you?"

"Fine," Gorvenko replied. "What can I do for you, Your Imperial Majesty?"

"Are you still interested in being the head of my security?"

"Absolutely," Gorvenko replied. "More than interested."

"Good," Alexei said. "Given that the position is currently vacant, I need you to start as soon as possible."

"I can start whenever you need me to."

"How is tomorrow?"

"Fine."

"Great. Come to the Alexander Palace tomorrow."

"Thank you."

When the conversation was over, Gorvenko raced to St. Isaac's Cathedral, where he knew the mass schedule well enough to know that one would be starting in a few minutes. Inside the church, Gorvenko threw himself to his knees, thanking God for the opportunity that had just befallen him. He remained prostrate throughout the mass, barely hearing the priest's intonations through his own fervent prayers.

It was only after the mass had ended that Gorvenko looked up and saw a familiar figure a few pews in front of him- a heavyset man with thick black hair and a mustache. *Joseph Stalin,* Gorvenko thought. *I wouldn't have expected him in church, except that his wife is religious.* He looked away, hoping his hatred for the man was not obvious. *My work is just beginning.*

CHAPTER 6

Three days later, Gorvenko made his first report to Alexei. When a servant led him into Alexei's study, Alexei was scribbling notes on official documents, and Gorvenko could hear the scratching of his quill pen. The servant cleared his throat.

Alexei looked up from the legislation he was drafting. "Thank you, Oleg Vasilievich," he said, and Oleg bowed and disappeared. "Have a seat, Ivan Maximovich," Alexei added, gesturing at one of the ornate mahogany chairs that faced his desk. Gorvenko complied, and Alexei eyed the stack of papers he was holding. "What is that?"

"These are reports on some of the subjects that Your Imperial Majesty asked me to look into," Gorvenko replied. He handed Alexei two sets of bound papers one at a time. "This one is an initial report on the state of the police force, and this one is an intelligence report on how Lenin made it back into Russia."

Alexei nodded as he took the second report. "I am most interested in this one," he said. "Thank you."

Despite his interest, Alexei had so much other work consuming his attention that it was late that night when he finally sat down with the reports. *The one on the police force can wait a few days,* he thought. *I need to see the one on Lenin now.*

Over an hour later, the clock in his study struck midnight, but Alexei barely heard the twelve chimes as he read. The report detailed Lenin's exile in Switzerland, and his negotiations with German agents and diplomats to get back into Russia. When Alexei finished reading, sweat was running down his face. He got up and went to the window.

The Germans were behind Lenin's attempts at revolution even before the Great War ended, he thought. *A German train got him from Switzerland to Russia- through a war zone! He was guarded by German soldiers and funded with German money that has only increased since the end of the War.*

Alexei clenched his hand into a fist and swung at the window in front of him, remembering just in time not to strike the glass. For a second, he looked back at the paper on his desk. *If the Germans wanted reconciliation after the War, or even more lenient terms of recovery,* he thought, *they're out of luck!*

As he entered his study for a meeting with Witte and Stolypin, Alexei looked at his calendar. *I can't believe it's nearly October already,* he thought. *Where does the time go?* But the trees in the park at Tsarskoe Selo were already colorful, and Alexei knew their leaves would soon litter the grounds of the park.

"I need to appoint someone new to be Governor-General of Moscow," he said to Stolypin and Witte a few minutes later. Michael sat at the table with them, and behind them, Igor quietly listened and took the minutes of their meeting.

"Prince Shuvalov is incompetent and exhausted by the demands of the office," Witte agreed.

"What should I be looking for in a candidate?" Alexei asked.

"Someone strong," Stolypin said. "You don't want the revolutionaries to take over."

"But you don't want someone who's so headstrong that they won't take direction from you," Michael said. "My uncle Sergei was Governor-General during Nicky's coronation- the first tragedy of Nicky's reign happened during the coronation, and Sergei wouldn't listen to anything that said that it could have been his fault."

Alexei nodded. "I need someone who will listen to me and to history."

"But you also need someone who's relatively liberal," Witte said. "Sergei was a reactionary who instituted pogroms and may have blocked the kind of economic progress that the country needs."

Alexei frowned. "I'm trying to decide between putting a family member in there and putting an industrialist in, like one of the Voronstovs or Obolenskys," he said. "Normally I'd put one of the Grand Dukes in, but the number of Grand Dukes are dwindling since Alexander III limited the title. The family now has more Princes than Grand Dukes, and most of the Princes are my age or only a little older. I'd like them to get more experience before I start appointing them to these positions." He looked at Igor. "Unless your older brothers are interested?"

"I'm not sure they would be," Igor replied. "Gavril is still in love with his regiment. Konstantin will be in the army for life."

"Ioann could be finished with his regiment if he wanted to take this position," Alexei replied.

Igor shook his head. "Ioann's too gentle for a position like this," he said. "And he's too religious. When he leaves his regiment, he'll do it to establish a religious school or monastery."

Alexei looked back at Michael, Witte and Stolypin. "Who does that leave us with? My aunt Xenia's sons are too young. Some of the older Grand Dukes? Dimitri Konstantinovich, perhaps?"

"No way," Michael said. "He's too… eccentric."

Witte nodded. "Let him enjoy his retirement and his horse farm," he said.

"Grand Duke Kirill Vladimirovich was also on my list," Alexei said. "I think he's been handling himself with dignity recently, especially after the death of Aunt Miechen."

"I don't disagree, despite his history of going against your father's wishes," Michael said.

"He's served in the Navy admirably, especially in the Great War," Alexei said. "Besides, he's got three kids now. Maybe he's finally settling down."

"Maybe," Michael said doubtfully.

"You're not in a position to judge, Misha," Alexei said. "If you hadn't married morganatically, there would be more Grand Dukes around."

"I wouldn't have married morganatically if your father had let me marry the princess I wanted to," Michael replied.

Alexei sighed. "Enough," he said. "Kirill Vladimirovich, can we make a decision on his appointment for Governor-General?"

"Fine," Michael said.

Alexei looked back at Witte and Stolypin, who looked uncomfortable. "Sorry, gentlemen," he said. "But at least that matter is decided. So, where are we with that taxation bill the Duma was working on?"

Not wanting to waste any time, Alexei summoned Grand Duke Kirill on October 1. At the appointed hour, he found Kirill pacing nervously. "Relax, Krill, I'm not going to bite you," Alexei told him as they went into his study.

"Even so, a summons from the tsar, and one wonders what it's about," Krill said. For the first time, Alexei was struck by how much he looked like a typical Romanov- tall, thin, handsome and with a thick, dark moustache.

He looks like the typical Romanov of Papa's generation and earlier, Alexei thought. *I don't intend to grow a moustache or a beard, and Igor and most of his brothers have also remained clean-shaven.* "Prince Shuvalov is ready to leave his position as Governor-General of Moscow," Alexei said. "I need someone to replace him. Are you interested?"

For a minute, Kirill sat in stunned silence. When he collected himself, he said, "Moscow has always made a real impression on me. I would be honored."

"Think about it, though. I don't want you to make a decision like this so soon after your mother's passing. Both are huge changes."

"It's okay, Alyosha. I want this position. I really do."

"It's a lot of work, Kirill. Are you sure you're willing to take on everything the position entails? It means a lot of social engagements in addition to the work."

"I know. I have no problem with that."

"I also need you to be in line with my policies. Right now, that means rebuilding Russia's economy through industrialization and improving our agricultural techniques."

Kirill smiled. "You made your agenda pretty clear in your speech to the Duma," he said. "I agree with it."

"Good," Alexei replied. "Moscow is our country's ancient capital, and you'll have a lot of power in that position. I can't have you straying from the official line. I need family unity as well as political unity."

"Family unity was pretty strong in past generations," Kirill said. His voice trailed away, and he looked away from Alexei for the first time.

"I know it frayed while my father was Tsar," Alexei said, and Kirill swallowed uncomfortably before looking back at him. "I want to change that. Papa was a good father and husband, and I want that example to be held up for the rest of the family, but I intend to reign more firmly. Can you follow me in that regard as Governor-General?"

"Absolutely," Kirill replied.

"You'll also be responsible for the preparations for my coronation," Alexei pressed.

Kirill nodded. "I can handle that," he said. "When are you thinking of having the coronation?"

"I haven't set a firm date yet. This spring is too soon. It may be the following spring."

"That'll give us plenty of time to plan it." Kirill smiled. "I'll tell Ducky to pack her bags for Moscow. My children will be happy as well."

"Good," Alexei replied. "I'm glad we've settled this. It's definitely a weight off my shoulders."

Two weeks later, it was the middle of October and the weather in St. Petersburg was already cold. Inside the Alexander Palace, there was a lot of rushing around as Alexei and his family got ready to vacation in the Crimea.

As Alexei placed some belongings in his suitcase with one hand and held reports from his ministers in the other, Alexandra appeared in the doorway. "Are you sure this vacation is the right thing to do, so soon after Nicky's passing?" she asked.

Seeing the tears in his mother's eyes, Alexei put down everything he was holding and went to comfort her. "I realize that hasn't been that long," he said. "But the forty day anniversary has past, there have been multiple memorial services…"

"The traditional mourning period is a year," Alexandra reminded him.

"I can't go that long without a break. Maybe the change in climate and scenery will do you some good as well."

"My heart's not in it. It's too soon."

"We have been through a lot as a family. But we've always enjoyed these times aboard the Standart."

"That's true," Alexandra said.

"You should come," Alexei coaxed. "I'd hate to see you stay at the Palace alone."

A little over a week later, the family disembarked the Imperial train in Sevastopol on the Black Sea. The weather was fine, and the town was more than happy to welcome them. A light breeze made the water ripple, and the Standart hulked in the background, docked and waiting.

"I'm really looking forward to this vacation," Anastasia said. "I'm so glad Olga and Sandro are coming."

"Me too," Alexei said. "It's just too bad Tanya can't come."

"She is about to give birth."

"I know, but still. Even Uncle Misha decided to go to his country estate rather than come with us."

"He needs a vacation too," Anastasia said.

All around them, crowds lined around the streets, cheering, and flags were flying everywhere. Alexei grinned, and found himself getting caught up in the crowds' enthusiasm and excitement. A red carpet led the way between the imperial train and the quay where the Standard was docked. Alexei stopped to shake hands with the people in crowd. When he caught up to his sisters and mother, he saw his Romanian cousins. King Ferdinand and Queen Marie stood waiting. Princess Ileana and two of her siblings, Nicholas and Mignon, stood next to them, waving as the Russians approached.

"I know you invited them, but I didn't expect them to come," Alexandra said sourly.

"I would have been disappointed if they hadn't," Alexei replied.

Alexandra's expression did not change.

"Oh, come on, Mama," Anastasia put in. "Marie is always a lot of fun, and Ileana is cute."

Alexei grinned at his sister. "I like them too," he said.

The officers aboard the Standart stood at attention as the two families boarded the yacht. The 420-foot long ship was also 50 feet wide and displaced over 5500 tons. Even on deck, the mahogany paneling gleamed in the sunlight. Olga and Alexander were already on board, arranging their cabin and keeping Peter from fussing. After greeting them, Alexei stood on deck, leaning against the railing, waiting for the anchor to be lifted. In the gathering twilight, he watched the shoreline for any signs of the ship's movement. Then he caught sight of Gorvenko on shore and gave him a nod. Gorvenko nodded back.

Suddenly, Anastasia pulled a chair next to her younger brother and stood on it so that they could be closer in height. Alexei eyed her with amusement. "He's staying ashore?" Anastasia asked of Gorvenko.

"No, he'll be coming aboard, but he'll be following us on a smaller ship for awhile first."

Anastasia looked back at Gorvenko. "He's looking at us," she said.

"He's supposed to be watching us," Alexei reminded her. "He's my Chief of Police, remember?"

Anastasia stuck out her tongue at Gorvenko, who looked away. Anastasia burst out laughing. When Gorvenko looked back at her, she made more faces at him.

"Stop it!" Alexei said.

"No!" Anastasia replied.

Without warning, Alexei grabbed his sister around her waist and flung her over his shoulder. Anastasia let out a shriek as Alexei took off down the deck of the Standart. Anastasia's skirts flew around her brother, and she wriggled wildly. "Let me go!" Anastasia yelped. "I would pound you if you didn't bruise so easily!"

"When are you ever going to stop your antics?" Alexei demanded, even though he was laughing. "How am I ever going to marry you off, with how you behave?"

"Who said I have to marry?" Anastasia demanded. "Let me go!"

Finally, Alexei dumped his sister back onto the deck. Anastasia lost her balance and ended up on her rear. "What are you going to do if you don't marry?" Alexei said. "You can't live in the Palace for the rest of your life!"

"I'll get my own palace, and I'll throw parties every day!"

"Of course," Alexei replied. He and Anastasia burst out laughing.

From the shore, Gorvenko watched them with amusement, even if he could not hear their conversation. Slowly, the Standart pulled away from the shore and began heading towards Yalta.

Alexei went to bed late that night, and still he could not sleep. After tossing and turning for the better part of an hour, he got up and made his way to the deck of the Standart. As he passed his parents' cabin, he instinctively hesitated so that he could hear his parents' voices.

Mama and Papa always stay up late, Alexei thought, wondering whether his father would be working or reading aloud from a book he enjoyed. But the cabin remained silent, and Alexei wondered if his parents had already fallen asleep.

A minute later, in the darkness of the hallway, Alexei remembered why he would not hear Nicholas' voice. His eyes filling with tears, Alexei continued to the deck. As the familiar salty smell of the sea air wafted to his nostrils, Alexei's tears made their way down his face. Up above, the sky was clear and the stars were bright.

Alexei struggled to take a few deep breaths through his constricted chest. Slowly, it felt as though air was reaching his lungs. Then he became aware of voices nearby. Following the sound, Alexei saw Olga and Alexander several feet away. Alexei tried to be as silent as possible, and still Alexander turned.

"I'm sorry," Alexei said, feeling that he was intruding. "I didn't mean-"

"No, not at all," Alexander said. "We couldn't sleep."

"Me neither," Alexei admitted. "I thought the sea air would help."

Olga leaned over to look at her brother. "Me too," she said. "I always loved being aboard the Standart as kids."

Alexei nodded. "It was always so much fun," he said. "And the Crimea was always a tropical paradise."

Olga smiled. "I'm looking forward to getting there," she said. "I've been dreaming about it for weeks now. Still, it's going to be hard without Papa." Her smile disappeared.

Quiet footsteps announced Anastasia and Marie's arrival. "Figured you all would be out here," Anastasia said.

"It does seem weird, to be doing this trip without Papa," Marie added, having heard Olga's comment.

"I think it's the right thing to do," Alexei said.

"Oh, none of us is complaining," Anastasia said.

Alexei leaned on the ship's railing again, breathing in the night air. "I'm glad you all are here," he said. A second later, he could see another, smaller, figure coming over to join them. "Ileana," he said with a grin. "I hope your parents are asleep, at least."

"They are," Ileana said.

The group continued talking until late in the night. Then, one by one, they drifted off to their respective cabins. Soon only Alexei and Ileana stood on deck, staring at the night sky as the stars continued to twinkle.

"I really didn't mean to interrupt anything," Ileana apologized. "I'm sure you all miss your father."

"Even when I first got up, I expected him to be in his cabin with Mama," Alexei admitted. "I'm sure my sisters felt the same way."

"I wish there was something I could do to ease your pain."

"Thanks," Alexei said with a smile. "Your being here is doing just that."

Ileana smiled back at him as the Standart continued to sail forward into the night.

CHAPTER 7

The next morning, Alexei awoke to the smell of flowers. The ship's lack of movement told him that they had arrived in Yalta. After the obligatory receptions, Alexei gratefully returned to his cabin and changed into more casual clothing. Then he and his family decamped to Livadia. Inside the Palace, Alexei only took the time necessary to get his belongings into his apartments. *I can't wait to get outside and walk,* he thought. At the gates of the Palace, he caught sight of Igor, and they walked out together.

"Thanks for sitting through those meetings," Alexei said. "Everything's more casual aboard the Standart, but those receptions are still tedious when it's nice out."

"I actually don't mind them so much," Igor said.

"Then I'll send you in my place."

"I don't like them that much," Igor protested. They both laughed.

A warm breeze washed over them, and Alexei could hear his sisters' laughter on the beach. *I think I'm relaxing already,* he thought. "Which way do you want to go?" he asked. "It sounds like the rest of the family is on the beach."

"Don't let me stop you if you want to go that way," Igor said, "but I told my brothers I'd meet them at Oreanda."

"Oooh," Alexei said, and they started walking in that direction. "I've always enjoyed walking through there. Is it true the Palace burnt down because the Grand Duke Konstantin Nikolaievich was plotting against the throne?"

"Anything was possible with Konstantin," Igor said. "But that might also just be family lore. The way my father told it, there was just some accident after a party, and everyone was too drunk to do anything but run outside and watch the place burn."

"That sounds like a possibility too," Alexei had to admit, and they laughed again.

Soon, they arrived at the dilapidated estate. The ruins, while always fun, also gave Alexei the chills. Soon, he heard the voices of the other Konstantinovichi princes- first Gavril, then Ioann. To Alexei's surprise, he could hear Marie's voice, followed by a voice he did not immediately recognize. "Hello," Igor called. "Ioannchick? Gavril?"

A second later, Gavril appeared, tall and pale. "Iiiigooorr," he said.

"Gaaaaavrilll," Igor replied, just as dramatically, and both brothers burst out laughing. Alexei rolled his eyes at them.

"So good of you to show up, even if you are a bit late," Gavril teased.

"It's my fault," Alexei said. "I made him attend a few receptions this morning."

"Oh, good, you made him work," Gavril said. His grin broadened. "Alyosha, how are you?"

"I'm better, now that we're here."

"I know. I love this place."

Behind Gavril, Ioann appeared, followed by their brothers Konstantin and George. "Ioannchik, Kostya, Georgy," Alexei greeted them. "Ioannchik, where are Elena and the kids?" He looked at Konstantin. "What about Pilar and Sergei? Where is everybody?"

"Back at our Palace for now," Ioann said.

"Though Sergei is just itching for the beach and the water," Konstantin said. "I think Pilar might try to bring him down later, after he takes a nap."

"I hear you're expecting another child," Alexei said to Ioann.

"Where'd you hear that?" Ioann asked.

Alexei looked at Igor, who put his hands behind his back and looked up at the sky. When he looked back at Ioann to apologize, he realized that Ioann was joking. They both laughed.

"I'm expecting our new arrival early next year," Ioann confirmed. "Right around the time Kostya and Pilar are expecting their next one."

"Very good," Alexei replied. "I'm looking forward to meeting him or her."

"I'm hoping for a him," Ioann admitted.

Just then, Marie and Prince Nikolai Obolensky appeared behind Konstantin, and Alexei realized that it had been Nikolai's voice he had heard but not recognized. "I didn't realize your family was here, Nica," he said.

"Oh yes, we got here yesterday," Nikolai replied.

"Masha, I thought you were down at the beach," Alexei said to his sister.

"Olga and Nastia are there with Mama," Marie replied. "I decided to come here instead."

Igor looked at his brothers, and Alexei, seeing the look, said to Marie and Nikolai, "why don't we walk to the beach?"

Alexei could smell the water before he saw it. All around them, roses and other flowers were in bloom. "It's so beautiful here," Alexei sighed. *Now I understand why we used to come here,* he thought. *Papa must have relished getting away from ruling for a little while- it's really a heavy burden.* He stared at the water in front of him. *It's time to get whatever secretaries and other personnel will alleviate that burden.*

The family's two weeks in the Crimea flew by. The day before their scheduled departure, Alexei stood by himself on the beach, his feet in the water, wishing he did not have to return to St. Petersburg. Then Anastasia appeared next to him, and Alexandra came over and stood at Alexei's other side. "Thinking of staying here?" Alexandra said, smiling.

"I am," Alexei replied, not altogether joking.

"I'm definitely staying here," Anastasia said seriously.

"No, you're not," Alexei replied, just as seriously.

"Are you going to stop me?" Anastasia asked with a grin. In a split second, she turned and dashed down the beach.

Without giving it a second thought, Alexei dashed after her.

"Sunbeam, don't-" Alexandra began. She watched nervously as her two youngest children raced down the beach. Behind her, Olga, Alexander and Marie looked amused.

Several feet away from them, Ileana, grinning, watched her cousins race. "I'm going after them, Mama," she said, and took off down the beach.

Up ahead of her, however, the race ended suddenly. Alexei, who had nearly caught up to Anastasia, slipped on a wet portion of the sand. Seeing a rock in his path as he fell, Alexei tried to avoid it, to no avail. As he fell to the sand, his left knee came into contact with the rock- hard. "Ouch!" he yelped.

Anastasia immediately stopped running and turned to look at him. "Oh my God," she said when saw him sitting on the beach next to the rock, clutching his knee.

By then, Ileana had caught up to them and saw the fearful look on Anastasia's face. She frowned. "Are you alright?" she asked Alexei.

"I will be," he said, but it was through clenched teeth. After a minute, though, his face relaxed, and he started to get up.

Anastasia helped her brother to his feet. By now, the rest of the family had reached them, and Ileana saw the worried looks that Olga, Marie and Alexandra were giving Alexei. "I'm fine," Alexei reassured them.

"I hope so," Alexandra replied, not looking convinced.

By the time the family arrived back at Livadia, Alexei's knee had become swollen and painful. Still, with a package of ice on it, he spent the rest of the day packing his trunks. It was only when he tried to stand up after a long period of sitting on the floor next to one of his trunks that he realized how much more immobile and painful his knee had become. A feeling of dread washed over him. He rolled up his trouser leg, and sure enough, his knee was discolored and swollen.

Alexei tried to get up, but the pain was too great. He tried again, and failed. "Mama!" he called.

Olga appeared in the doorway. "She's outside with Masha and Mimi," she said. Then she caught sight of her brother's knee. "Oh, no!" she exclaimed, and rushed forward to help him. "I knew this was going to happen." She helped Alexei up and into his bed.

Alexei nodded. "As soon as I fell, I knew it too. Can you get me some more ice?"

Olga rushed around, making sure her brother was comfortable. "Hopefully this won't be a bad one," she said.

I'm more worried about this than I want to admit, Alexei thought. Alexander and Ileana appeared in the doorway, looking concerned. Alexander's expression told Alexei that Olga had told her husband about his hemophilia.

"Ileana, can you find my mother?" Olga asked.

Ileana nodded and dashed outside.

"The Romanians know nothing of my hemophilia, and I didn't want Ileana finding out this way," Alexei said through clenched teeth. *God, my knee really hurts*, he thought, *and the ice is no longer helping*.

"She'll have to find out somehow," Alexander said. He moved aside as Alexandra rushed into the room, her faced creased with worry. Behind her, Ileana had joined Alexander at the doorway, and Marie stood in the hallway behind her daughter.

"It's okay, Mama," Alexei said. "I can still move."

"Keep your leg as straight as possible, so that it doesn't get bent," Alexandra replied.

Alexander put a hand on Ileana's shoulder and led her from the doorway to another part of the palace. Marie followed. "He's going to be fine," Alexei heard Alexander say as they walked down the hall.

Olga shot a grateful look at her husband's back as she and Alexandra continued to help Alexei. Soon, Alexei began to drift off to sleep, only vaguely aware that Anastasia had come in to help.

Alexei awoke again after night had fallen, sweating. His fever had risen, and his blood continued to flow into his knee. He could hardly move his leg now, and his knee was swollen and painful. As his eyes acclimated to the darkness, Alexei realized that he was alone in his room, though he doubted that Alexandra was far away.

In a split second, Alexei thought of all the times his mother had cared for him during his hemophiliac attacks, barely leaving his bedside. The thought of that remaining unchanged even now that he was tsar was almost too much for him to bear. As the pain in his knee increased, Alexei's tears rolled down his face.

Why? he wanted to shout. *Why me? Why now? Can't this disease ever go away?* Alexei buried his face in his pillow to muffle the sound of his sobs.

The next morning, Alexei slowly came awake, aware that someone was changing the ice pack and bandages on his knee. He opened his eyes, expecting it to be Alexandra. Instead, it was Ileana.

"I didn't mean for you to take care of me," Alexei said, starting to move away from her.

Ileana shook her head immediately. "You should stay still," she said.

Alexei lay back down. "How long have you been in here?" he asked.

"A little while," Ileana replied. "Your mother was here most of the night, but she needed to sleep too."

Soon, Marie appeared in the doorway. "Sweetie, we have to go soon," she told her daughter.

Alexei suddenly remembered that the vacation was supposed to end today. "I'm sorry," he said. "I didn't mean for it to end this way."

"What can you do about it, honey?" Marie responded.

"I'd better get changed," Ileana said. "Our train leaves in an hour."

Alexei wanted to apologize again, but he bit his lip as Ileana left the room and Alexandra and Anastasia came in. "What about us?" he asked. "We were supposed to go home today too."

"We're not going anywhere until you're better," Alexandra said firmly.

As the Romanians departed, Alexei's fever rose again, and his blood continued to flow into his knee. Soon, shooting pains made him cry out incessantly, and he was unaware of his doctors' arrival, or that they leaned over him to treat him. For three days, the Imperial family remained in the Crimea as Alexei's fever remained unabated. Each day, he moaned in pain, and Alexandra never left his side.

"Mama," Alexei said at the end of the second day, "why can't I just die and have the pain go away?"

"Oh, Alyosha," Alexandra said, tears running down her face. "You know I can't bear to hear you speak like that."

The next day, when Alexei's condition remained unchanged, Alexandra looked at Dr. Federov. "We should prepare the medical bulletins. The country should know how sick their tsar is." Her voice shook as she said it.

"What should the bulletins say?" Federov replied in a whisper.

"Tell the truth!" Alexei cried.

Both Alexandra and Federov eyed Alexei. Then they left the room. From the furtive look on his mother's face, Alexei knew that she would not listen to him.

She's been keeping it a secret my whole life, Alexei thought. *Most of the family doesn't even know. That's not going to change now.* Much as he wanted to object, Alexei felt his fever getting the best of him again, and he fell sleep.

On the morning of the fourth day, Alexei awoke around noon to find that the attack had largely abated. His fever was gone, and the pain in his knee was minimal. He heaved a sigh of relief. Then he looked around. Alexandra was asleep in the chair next to his bed. Dr. Federov stood at the window, looking out. In a second, the surgeon turned and looked at Alexei.

"Did those medical bulletins ever go out?' Alexei whispered, trying not to wake his mother.

"No, they didn't," Federov replied. He moved forward to examine Alexei.

"Careful," Alexei said. "I'd hate to have the hematoma get dislodged again."

"I can't believe how much better you are, or how quickly," Federov said.

"That seems to be the nature of it," Alexei replied. "At death's door one minute, alive and well the next."

"Indeed," Federov said. "I just wish there were better ways of controlling it."

Upon finding Alexei so much better, the joy of Alexandra, Olga, Marie and Anastasia knew no bounds. Olga finally felt comfortable departing for Belgrade. Still, it was nearly a week later when Alexei and the rest of his family departed for St. Petersburg. By then, Alexei was able to walk, but only with the aid of a brace on his leg and crutches. When Alexei stared at his reflection in the mirror, he could see how pale he was, and how large the dark gray bags under his eyes were. As they arrived in St. Petersburg, Gorvenko helped Alexei off the train, an expression of relief and alarm on his face.

"I feel better, Ivan Maximovich," Alexei reassured Gorvenko as they drove back to the Alexander Palace through several feet of snow.

"I certainly hope so, Your Imperial Majesty," Gorvenko replied.

Alexei could tell he had further questions, but he said nothing more, and they passed the rest of the ride in silence.

The next morning, Alexei was awake early, reading the reports that had piled up on his desk during his illness. One in particular drew his attention, so much so that when Gorvenko entered the room, he found Alexei sitting at his desk, his hands folded, studying the report intently. "Tell me, Ivan Maximovich, did you know about this?" Alexei asked.

"About what, Your Imperial Majesty?"

"This report says that Joseph Stalin has died, probably by poisoning."

"I heard about that, yes."

"Did you have anything to do with it?"

"What do you mean?"

"We share a hatred of the Communists," Alexei said. "All I'm asking is if you had a hand in Stalin's death?"

"Absolutely not," Gorvenko replied, a little too quickly.

Alexei eyed his police chief.

Gorvenko looked away and swallowed. There was a pause. Then Gorvenko looked back at Alexei. Alexei was still watching him, his gaze penetrating. The silence lengthened. Then, Alexei, seeing a question on Gorvenko's features, said, "what is it, Ivan Maximovich?"

"May I ask you something, Your Imperial Majesty?"

"Ask away."

"For years now, there has been talk of your ill health, and clearly something plagues you. What is the problem?"

"You don't know?" Alexei asked.

"Not at all. Your health has been a state secret since you were born."

"How much does the general population know?"

"Nothing. Speculation has always run rampant, but there have been no hard facts."

Alexei swallowed. He reached for his crutches, then hauled himself up and hobbled to the window. Gorvenko moved to help him, but Alexei shook his head. Immediately, Gorvenko fell back, and Alexei made it over to the window by himself.

For a full minute Alexei stared outside. *If you answer him honestly now, it will be a huge change in the family's policy,* he thought. *You were thinking of telling the whole country, though,* he reminded himself. *You have to start somewhere.* He looked back at Gorvenko. "I have hemophilia," he said.

Gorvenko sucked in a breath. "The hereditary blood disease," he said. "I heard it affects many of the royal houses of Europe. I didn't know you had it too."

"What were you expecting?" Alexei asked.

"I don't know," Gorvenko admitted. "The rumors have been rife with every possibility."

"Any fall or cut could kill me, and a few nearly have," Alexei said, wanting to make sure Gorvenko understood the implications of the disease. "This is but another reason why my security is paramount."

"I understand, Your Imperial Majesty."

Alexei stared at him for a moment. Gorvenko returned his gaze without blinking. "Listen, Ivan Maximovich, I realize that this is new information for you- information you didn't have when you took this job. If you feel like my disease adds too much, let me know."

"To the contrary, Your Imperial Majesty, I will only redouble my efforts to protect you."

Alexei smiled at that. "Thank you."

As Gorvenko left, however, Alexei contemplated the situation. *The country is almost entirely ignorant about my health,* he realized. *I don't even think my whole family knows- certainly Ileana doesn't. That has to change. But how? Another speech to the Duma?* Alexei frowned. *I don't want to talk to the Duma. I want to talk to the people.*

At breakfast the next morning, Marie and Anastasia chattered excitedly. Next to them, Alexandra looked tired as she sipped her tea. Alexei eyed his sisters as he leaned his crutches against the wall behind them. His knee still felt stiff, and he winced. "What's put you two in such a good mood?" he asked his sisters. Igor, seated at the table, also watched his cousins with amusement.

"We're going shopping with Aunt Olga!" Marie said happily.

The family was just finished eating when Olga arrived. Alexei and Alexandra stood to greet her as Marie and Anastasia scampered off to their apartments to get ready. "It's always good to see you," Alexei said, giving his aunt a hug. "Where are you taking my sisters?"

"To some of the dress shops downtown," Olga replied. "They want to see the latest fashions in anticipation of the winter social season."

Alexandra harrumphed. "Balls and social events," she said dismissively. "They have better things to do."

"Like what?" Olga asked.

"Like going to church and visiting hospitals and helping the poor," Alexandra replied. "It is only befitting their station in life."

"That may be so," Alexei cut in, "but even I know how much fun Masha and Nastia have had at the balls we've had since the War. Tanya and Olga had enormous fun at their first balls too."

Alexandra was about to reply when the phone rang.

"Why don't you get that, Mama?" Alexei suggested.

Dropping her napkin onto the table, Alexandra hurried out of the room.

Alexei looked at Olga. "Don't worry," he said. "I know how isolated my parents kept us was when I was growing up. Mama in particular hated the capital's social scene, but I don't plan on following that path."

"That's certainly a relief," Michael said as he entered the room. He greeted his sister with a kiss. "Taking the girls into the city?" he asked.

Olga nodded. "We're leaving as soon as they're ready." She and Michael exchanged a look.

"What?" Alexei asked.

"Nothing," Olga and Michael said at the same time.

"I doubt that," Alexei said. "What was that look for?"

"I'll meet you in your study whenever you're ready, Alyosha," Michael replied. He left the room.

Alexei eyed his aunt. "What was that about?" he asked.

"There are a lot of reasons your sisters enjoy going out with me," Olga said. "You're right that it gets them away from the isolation of the palace to spend time with people their own age. Increasingly, that's meant romantic prospects as well."

"Like who?" Alexei demanded.

Olga swallowed. "Masha has been meeting with Nica Obolensky for some time now," she said.

Instantly, Alexei thought of the times he had seen them together. "You let them see each other without a chaperone?" he asked incredulously.

"No, of course not," Olga replied indignantly. "Someone is always watching them, whether it's one of my ladies-in-waiting or me."

Alexei looked over at Igor, who was studying his fingernails as if he had never seen them before. "Igor," he said. "You knew about this."

Igor's head jerked in Alexei's direction.

"Masha kept it quiet because she was afraid Nicky would find out," Olga said.

"I've never known Masha to be afraid of Papa," Alexei replied with a smile. "What was she worried about?"

"That your father wouldn't think Nica was good enough for her."

"Why would he think that? The Obolenskys are princes, one of the oldest families in Russia. They've been serving Russia, and our family, forever."

"Your sisters are some of the most eligible brides in Russia," Olga replied pointedly. "Every time your parents talked about their marriages, it was about a political match- one that they wouldn't let happen if your sisters weren't in love, but political matches nonetheless."

Alexei sighed. At that moment, Marie and Anastasia came bouncing back into the room with their boots and heavy winter coats. Immediately, Alexei acted as though he and Olga hadn't been talking about anything serious. "Have fun," he told his sisters.

"We will," they called over their shoulders as they dashed for the door.

"Bye," Alexei said to Olga as she followed Marie and Anastasia. Then he looked at Igor. "Come with me," he said, grabbing his crutches. "There's a report on my desk that's been bothering me." In his study, Alexei handed Michael and Igor copies of Stalin's death notice, and held out the police report he had received from Gorvenko. "Did you hear about this?" he asked.

"I heard about Stalin's death, of course," Michael said as he took the police report. "It did seem a little… sudden."

"The Duma has been in turmoil over it," Igor added. "Between Lenin and now Stalin, the Bolsheviks' leadership is practically gone."

"Trotsky has pledged to continue the party," Michael said. "He's a smart man, but Lenin and Stalin were in charge. The party might not hold up without them." He frowned as he read the police report.

Igor read the report over Michael's shoulder. "Wow, maybe it wasn't an accident," he said. "I didn't hear that."

"Me neither," Michael admitted.

"I wonder if the police were involved," Alexei said, before recounting his conversation with Gorvenko.

"It sounds like you're uncomfortable with that," Michael said.

"I guess I am," Alexei said. "If Gorvenko did this, he certainly wasn't acting on my orders."

"Still, it may be something to reconcile yourself with, Alyosha," Michael advised. "Protecting a tsar has never been an easy task. The police have always kept an eye on groups that pose a threat, and that includes the Communists."

"I'm well aware," Alexei said. "I haven't forgotten my meeting with Mr. Lenin, much as I'd like to."

"And yet killing your opponents bothers you," Michael said.

"He's keeping his moral compass," Igor said. "I think that's a good idea."

"It's not a bad idea," Michael said. "But politics is politics. The Communists would kill all of us without hesitating."

Two days later, Alexei got a phone call he had been expecting: Tatiana had given birth to a daughter. "Congratulations!" Alexei said happily. "What did you name her?"

"Marie Louise, after Boris' mother," Tatiana replied.

"That's nice. How are you feeling?"

"Tired. It's been tough."

"How so?" Alexei asked, concerned.

"It was a long labor," Tatiana replied. "Everything still hurts. Besides, people are upset that it was a girl."

"Everyone was hoping for a boy," Alexei said understandingly. "Some things don't change."

But the conversation upset Alexei enough that he made sure to check in with Tatiana frequently over the next few weeks, and was frustrated that she did not always come to the phone. "Are your servants keeping you from the phone or something?" he demanded when he finally got a hold of his sister. "Are they not telling you that I call?"

Tatiana sighed. "It's not that, Sunbeam."

"What then?" Alexei asked as he watched snowflakes dance just outside his window. A sudden gust of wind rattled the window, making Alexei jump.

"I'm having a tough time of it," Tatiana said. "I don't always feel like coming to the phone when you call."

"What's that supposed to mean?"

"I've been have a lot of trouble since Marie Louise was born. I'm not as attached to her as I thought I would be, and I'm sad all the time."

"Has the feeling that she should have been a boy affecting all of this?" Alexei asked. "Mama and Papa always loved you anyway, even when the rest of the country was clamoring for them to produce an heir."

"And Mama became totally neurotic after awhile, trying to have a boy," Tatiana replied. "I don't want to turn into that."

"Don't worry," Alexei reassured her. "You've got awhile before that happens." There was a silence, but Tatiana's shuddered breathing told Alexei that she was crying. "Tanya, what's wrong?" he asked.

"I feel so sad and awful all the time," she said.

"Have you spoken to the doctors about it?"

"No."

"Why not?"

"I don't want them to take the baby from me."

"Why would they do that?"

"They'll only think I'm an unfit mother, and nothing else."

"No, they won't," Alexei said. "How could they think that?"

"The doctors are all men, Alyosha," Tatiana said. "They don't understand." She was still crying.

"You've got to do something," Alexei said. "Do you want me to visit? I'm happy to talk to them."

"No, no, no," Tatiana said. "You've got enough to do, running the country."

"You're as important as everything else I do," Alexei replied.

"Thanks," Tatiana said.

"Would it help if I sent Masha and Nastia?" Alexei asked. "They certainly want to see you and the baby." *And I'm completely out of other ideas. My knee is still bent from the hemophiliac attack in the Crimea, and I can't afford the time to travel again.*

"That's not a bad idea," Tatiana said finally. "Being so far away from the family has always been hard."

When Alexei got off the phone, he stood very still, and very silently, for a long time.

CHAPTER 8

Marie and Anastasia were more than willing to go to Sofia, and Alexei's conversation with Tatiana bothered him enough that he made the arrangements quickly. Not wanting his sisters to travel with just their ladies-in-waiting, Alexei arranged for his aunt Olga and uncle Pavel to go with them. "I don't want Tanya to be overwhelmed by so many people coming, though," Alexei warned.

"Don't worry," Pavel replied. "We'll be discreet."

"We'll send Masha and Nastia in as the advance guard," Olga added with a grin. "If Tanya is interested in the rest of the army, we'll be there."

Finally, Alexei smiled. "Please make sure she's taken care of," he said.

In his sisters' absence, Alexei found that the Palace was much quieter, and it gave him more time to work. Because it was already the first week of December, that work included getting ready for Christmas and the New Year. After a single conversation, Alexandra made arrangements for the Christmas tree, and started ordering gifts for the family. Alexei, too, began making lists of gifts to order.

One of the first tasks on Alexei's list of state business was to visit schools, especially the universities, to recruit secretaries and other public servants. His first visit was local, to the Imperial Alexander Lyceum. "I didn't intend for this visit to be such a production," Alexei said as his car sloshed through the mixture of white and melted snow on the street, surrounded by police cars.

"Get used to it," Igor advised. "Now that you're tsar, you won't be able to do things quietly anymore."

At the Lyceum, guards in uniform stood at attention, and bands played military marches. Alexei returned the salutes of everyone around him. When he glanced behind him, Igor was doing the same, and Igor's military background was obvious. *He's lucky he had the chance to serve,* Alexei thought.

It's customary for the heir to the throne to serve in a regiment too- when that heir doesn't become tsar at 16.

Inside, the whole student body had turned out to see their new tsar. Even the older students, who were close to Alexei's age, stood watching him in awe. Not wanting to miss an opportunity, Alexei walked up and down the line of students, shaking hands, asking their names and about their families.

After the obligatory speeches, Alexei and Igor joined Alexander Obolensky, the director of the Lyceum, and the rest of the school's high-ranking officials for a formal luncheon. As the informal conversation died down, Alexei turned to Alexander. "How has the Lyceum's enrollment been, Alexander Nikolaievich?" he asked.

"It has continued rising, Your Imperial Majesty," Alexander replied. "Some of the instructors and I were just discussing expanding the school and its classes if enrollment continues at this rate."

"The Lyceum has always had a first-rate reputation," Alexei replied. "I can hardly fault anyone for wanting to attend."

"Your Imperial Majesty is too kind," Alexander replied modestly.

Alexei smiled. "The school's academic reputation is what brought me here today."

"How do you mean?" Alexander asked. His attention, and that of everyone around him, was focused intently on Alexei as their plates were cleared and new dishes were brought.

"My father managed his workload without even a secretary," Alexei replied. "Unfortunately, it's not a model I can continue. I'm looking for people to work for me- starting with secretaries, but also ministers and diplomats. Do you have any of your graduates in mind, or pupils who will soon be graduating, that you can recommend?"

Alexander looked thoughtful, and his expression was mirrored on the faces of the instructors around him. "I know of a several recent graduates who were star pupils," he said. "And I'm sure my colleagues have promising students that they can recommend as well."

The instructors around the table nodded.

"We'll get a list together straightaway," Alexander said.

"That would be perfect," Alexei said.

A week later, Alexander Obolensky sat across from Alexei in his study at the Winter Palace. His son Nicholas sat next to him. *I'll bet anything that Alexander brought Nica because he wants to discuss the possibility of his marriage to Marie,* Alexei thought.

Alexander looked around at the small study as he settled into his chair, making Alexei wonder whether he should have been using a larger room. "This room was only intended as a temporary replacement," he said apologetically. "Someday I'll upgrade to a better space."

"Nonetheless, I'm glad you escaped from your last study unharmed," Alexander replied.

"God smiled upon me," Alexei agreed. "So, tell me about the people on this list."

For nearly three hours, Alexei and Alexander discussed the names Alexander had compiled- their lineage, their education at the Lyceum, their experience after graduation. When they were done, Alexei was ready to move the discussion to a different venue. "Would you care to join me for lunch?" he asked. "Marie and Anastasia are in Sofia visiting Tatiana, and it's been quiet without them."

"We would be delighted, Your Imperial Majesty," Alexander said.

Nicholas suddenly looked nervous.

"Relax, Nica," Alexei said. "We're not going to eat *you*." As they walked to the Palace's dining room, they made their way past strings of Christmas lights and sprigs of holly and pine trees, whose fresh scent reached Alexei's nose. As they sat down to eat, Alexei asked, "so, Alexander Nikolaievich, does your cousin Dimitri still have a glass factory on his estate in Penza?"

"Yes, he does. He used it to produce military items during the war, and business has only gotten better since the war ended."

Alexei smiled. "I remember the Faberge items he used to make before the war. Papa always looked forward to his gifts."

Both Alexander and Nicholas smiled in return. "Mitya has always loved that estate," Nicholas said.

"I'm glad it's productive," Alexei said. "The country's manufacturing sector badly needs improvement. I don't suppose Dimitri could share some of his secrets with me?"

"I'll speak to him," Alexander said. "I'm sure he would be happy to show you the facilities."

It was not until the soup had been cleared that Alexander started the next round of the conversation. "Your Imperial Majesty," he said, "my son has asked me to broach the subject of his marriage to your sister Marie."

Alexei nodded. "I was expecting that," he said. He looked at Nicholas. "Are you interested in marrying Marie?"

Nicholas nodded, and sweat broke out on his forehead. "More than interested."

"Have you spoken to Marie about it at all? Does she share your interest?"

"Yes, she does," Nicholas said. "We spoke about it as recently as when we were in the Crimea."

"Their interest has been mutual for a long time," Alexander added. "I would not be here if it weren't, or if I thought my son were a bad match for your sister."

Alexei smiled. "Is there a father in this country who thinks his son would be a bad match for a Grand Duchess?"

"I'm sure plenty are interested, but few have the lineage, education and service to Russia that Nicholas has," Alexander answered. "And Marie's interest speaks for itself."

Nicholas shot his father a grateful look.

"Well, when Marie returns from Sofia, I'll discuss it with her," Alexei said.

There was a brief pause. "Where do you stand on the subject, Your Imperial Majesty?" Alexander asked.

"I'm not opposed to it by any means," Alexei replied. "But Marie will have the final say. It is her life, after all."

When Anastasia and Marie returned from Sofia a week later, the Winter Palace was completely decked out for Christmas. A large tree was decorated with ornaments, and lights filled the Palace. Even in the few seconds Alexei spent at the window watching his sisters arrive, he could see extra trunks being unpacked, and he knew his sisters had been Christmas shopping while abroad.

When Marie and Anastasia got inside, the Palace was bustling with activity. Alexei had taken over a few rooms adjacent to his study and had filled them with desks and cabinets. Several men now sat at those desks, working. They all jumped to their feet and stood at attention when the two Grand Duchesses came in.

"What is all this?" Anastasia asked.

"I hired secretaries," Alexei replied.

His sisters' eyes lit up at the prospect of meeting new people, so Alexei introduced them. "This is Sergei Petrovich Kamensky," he began.

"I remember you," Marie interrupted. "You served as a kamer-page for my Aunt Olga a few years ago, right?"

Sergei nodded. "As did my brother Vladimir before me. I'm impressed that you remember me, Your Imperial Highness."

"The rest of these men are graduates from the Lyceum," Alexei said. "This is Peter Pavlovich Alexeiev, Ilya Dmitrievitch Tolstoy, and Andrei Feodorovich Suvarov."

Each man seemed taken aback by meeting Marie and Anastasia in person, but soon the sisters' warmth put them at ease as they continued questioning each one about his background and family. From the edge of the room, Alexei and Igor watched with amusement.

"It's always the same," Igor said. "People are intimidated by the family, but whenever they meet us, a lot of misconceptions fall away. Your sisters are good at that. Your grandmother is too."

Alexei nodded. "I wish my mother could be like that too," he said sadly. "It's a shame she's as shy as she is."

After awhile, however, Alexei ushered his sisters to the door. "Alright, enough already," he teased, his customary grin lighting up his face. "I need to hear all about Tanya, but I need to finish a mountain of work first. Shall we meet for dinner?"

"Yes, yes, yes," Anastasia said, pouting as she was ejected from the room. "But we'll only talk to you if you're on time."

"I'll be there," Alexei promised. Igor was already laughing, but Alexei could tell his new employees didn't know what to make of the scene in front of them. "Relax, gentlemen," he said. "Don't you have families that you joke around with?"

Later that night, after dinner was finished, the family adjourned to one of the drawing rooms. Once more Igor stayed to dinner and joined the family afterwards as well. "If you keep doing this, you might need apartments in the Palace," Alexei teased him.

"I'll start scoping out empty ones," Igor replied, just as humorously.

"So, how was the trip?" Alexei asked his sisters as soon as they were seated. "How's Tanya?"

"The trip was fine," Anastasia replied. "We would have stayed longer, but we wanted to be home for Christmas."

"How is Tatiana?" Alexandra pressed.

"She's doing much better," Marie said. "It's been tough on her with the baby, but she was better by the time we left."

"What was the problem, exactly?" Alexei asked.

"Everything," Anastasia said.

"Her birth was hard, her recovery was hard, she was having trouble connecting with the baby," Marie clarified.

"Why would she have trouble dealing with the baby?" Alexei asked, bewildered.

"It happens every once in awhile," Alexandra replied. "Ella said she's heard a lot more about it in the hospitals she runs than we do in our circles, but it does happen to women that after the birth of a child, they become incredibly sad and detached."

Alexei frowned. "Do they recover from it?"

"Oh, yes," Alexandra said. "It takes time and effort, but they recover."

"Tanya was definitely on the mend when we left," Anastasia assured her brother.

When the conversation died down, Alexei looked at Marie. "While you were gone, I met with Alexander and Nicholas Obolensky."

Marie looked down at the floor and swallowed. Then she looked back at Alexei.

"I thought they were here with personnel recommendations," Alexandra said.

"They were," Alexei replied. "But they were also here because Nica is interested in marrying Marie."

"No," Alexandra said immediately.

Marie looked like she was about to cry.

"I'm not asking you," Alexei said to his mother. "I'm asking what Marie thinks. Masha, are you interested in marrying Nica?"

Marie nodded wordlessly, her tears threatening to overflow.

Alexei looked back at Alexandra to see his mother opening a book she had brought into the drawing room. "What is that?" he asked.

"The Almanac de Gotha," Alexandra replied. "I was hoping for a slightly different match for Marie, perhaps one in England." She looked at her daughter. "Would you be willing to marry one of the British princes?"

"I thought you were going to arrange a British marriage for me," Anastasia said.

"I wanted to," Alexandra said honestly, "but I don't know who would take you." A rare smile lit up her face.

"We'll answer that question when we come to it," Alexei said, amused but seeing the uncomfortable look on Igor's face and wanting to finish the conversation he had started. "Frankly, Mama, I'm amazed you'd be against Nica. He has a lineage that can be traced back to the 1300s, and he is a prince."

Alexandra sniffed. "He's still not high-ranking enough for Marie," she said. "If she wants to stay in Russia, she'll have to marry one of the Grand Dukes or a Prince of the Imperial Blood. Otherwise, it would have to be to a high-ranking foreign prince, preferably one who was in line for a throne."

"Come on, Mama," Alexei said. "The Obolenskys could have come to power after the Time of Troubles just as easily as our family did, and I doubt they would have shunned us for it."

"I really want to marry Nica!" Marie burst out suddenly. "You and Papa had a love match," she said to her mother. "I thought that's what you wanted for all of us!"

"I do," Alexandra said. "But I have to consider rank as well."

"Papa let Irina marry Felix, even though Felix is 'just a Prince'," Marie said. "Nica's family is just as old as Felix's, and just as titled."

"Irina is a princess, not a grand duchess," Alexandra reminded her. "And it was still considered a morganatic marriage."

"And maybe you're just a snob who doesn't want me to be happy!" Marie cried. Her tears started flowing down her face.

"That's not true," Alexandra said. "I love you very much."

"Enough!" Alexei said. Anastasia and Igor looked ready to sneak out of the room, and Alexei felt like joining them. "Much as I want this marriage for you, Masha, Mama does make one point- the Obolenskys are aristocracy but not royalty. This would be a morganatic marriage. You'd have to renounce your right to the throne, and that of your children."

"I don't care about that," Marie said. "I'm far down in the succession anyway."

"Still, I don't have an heir yet," Alexei said. "I'd like to keep as many options open as possible."

"Then perhaps you should work on your own marriage and children rather than denying mine."

"Masha!" Alexandra burst out. "Where are your manners?"

"She's not wrong," Alexei said mildly. He looked at Marie. "I'm not looking to block the marriage." He looked back at Alexandra. "I think Nica would make a good match, Mama. Why don't you think about it for awhile?"

With the conversation over, Anastasia and Igor finally scrambled out of the room. Marie followed in short order.

Alexei followed them to the door. Then he turned back to Alexandra. "Please think about this some more," he said. "The Obolenskys are waiting for our answer, and they deserve a response sooner rather than later."

Alexandra pressed her lips together and looked away from him.

"Fine," Alexei said. Then he left the room, leaving Alexandra alone.

CHAPTER 9

Breakfast the next morning was a quiet affair. Marie decided to remain in her apartments, and Alexandra did the same. The table suddenly felt too large for just Alexei, Igor and Anastasia, especially as there were more servants in the room than people eating. "I'm sorry about last night," Alexei said, feeling like he was speaking more to Igor than Anastasia. *Anastasia has dealt with Mama's moods, and Marie's responses to them, our whole lives, but it's not something I want the rest of the family to see.*

"I understand how families are," Igor reassured him.

"Even so," Alexei said. He had not missed how uncomfortable Igor had looked, but Igor genuinely seemed reassuring, so Alexei looked at Anastasia. "Have you spoken to Marie at all?"

Anastasia nodded. "She's a little calmer now. She really does want this marriage, though."

"She always wanted to get married and have twenty kids," Alexei said. "I'll have to talk to Mama again. Otherwise this whole thing will be decided by silence, which will end in a negative answer rather than a positive one."

"I'll talk to Mama," Anastasia said. "I'm sure I can convince her."

"If it were up to me, the marriage would go forward, but I don't want to ignore Mama altogether."

Anastasia nodded. "Let me see what I can do," she said.

Later that day, Alexei took a break from his work to go to Marie's apartments. His sister was still there, and it was clear that she had not left all day. "You can't stay in your room forever," he told her. "It's not healthy."

"Go away," Marie said.

"Don't get angry at me," Alexei replied. "I'm in favor of this marriage, remember?"

"So?" Marie said. "It won't happen unless Mama approves."

"I wouldn't be so sure."

Marie frowned. "What do you mean?"

"I am Tsar, remember? Not Mama."

"Mama made plenty of decisions when Papa was tsar."

"That doesn't mean it will continue that way. It hasn't been that way since I became Tsar."

There was a silence.

"Do you still want to marry Nica?" Alexei asked.

"Yes," Marie said.

"Then I'll convince Mama. Anastasia's talking to her already."

It took several days before Alexandra agreed, and even then, it was reluctantly. "I still think she could do better," she said.

"I disagree," Alexei said shortly. *I'm tired of this argument,* Alexei thought. *And that's just within the family. How am I going to handle international negotiations, or the negotiations with businessmen that I have coming up?*

On Christmas Day, Alexei awoke to a Palace that was uncharacteristically quiet. It took him a minute to realize that he had given his secretaries and ministers the day off. *I also made sure Igor went home. I want him to celebrate Christmas with his mother and siblings.* At breakfast, Alexei sat across from Anastasia at an otherwise empty table.

"Mama isn't feeling well enough to come down," Anastasia said, "and Masha is trying on dresses again, though I've lost track of whether it's for church tonight or that ball that we're having next week."

Alexei groaned. Then he and Anastasia burst out laughing.

"We shouldn't complain," Anastasia said. "We spent the war years darning our own socks and repairing every hole in every piece of clothing. It's nice to be able to get new clothes for a change."

"There were shortages of everything," Alexei agreed. "So many people were badly off."

"Even before that, though, Mama had us living frugally."

"It's her English upbringing. Papa was always pretty Spartan too, though."

"It's nice to live a little," Anastasia said. "I'm so glad you decided to have that ball so soon after Christmas. We never used to do anything like that growing up."

"I'm hoping it's well-attended," Alexei replied. "It'll be boring if we're the only ones there."

"It won't just be us," Anastasia said, laughing. "Didn't you get a lot of replies to your invitations?"

"After a fashion. I didn't get any replies at all for a while. It made me worry that the invitations got lost."

"I think it was just a stunned silence," Anastasia said with an impish grin. "Mama and Papa really isolated themselves. People have become unaccustomed to invitations from the Palace."

When breakfast was over, Alexei was restless. For a moment, he stared out the window to the mounds of snow outside. Then, suddenly making up his mind, he got a hold of Gorvenko. "Get a couple of Cossack guards on horseback," he said. "I want to take a sleigh ride down the Nevsky Prospect."

"Now, Your Imperial Majesty?" Gorvenko asked.

"Yes, Ivan Maximovich, now," Alexei replied.

A few minutes later, with the Cossack guard on horseback thundering alongside him, Alexei was flying through the streets of St. Petersburg in an open sleigh with Gorvenko beside him. The cold air tingled through his hair and stung his skin. All around him, he could hear the bells attached to the horses he passed. The bells of the surrounding churches added to the cacophony. Soon, they were along the Nevsky Prospect. As they flew past the frozen river, Alexei breathed the cold air deep into his lungs as he watched other horse-drawn sleighs cross the river. All around him, he could hear vendors hawking warm beverages and lit candles.

Further up, Alexei stopped the sleigh as they arrived at the Alexander Nevsky Bridge. Then he got out and walked to the center of the bridge. Behind him, Gorvenko had also dismounted and was keeping an eye both on Alexei and on everyone around them. His hand remained on the pistol at his side. Alexei's Cossack guard remained mounted and moving as Alexei moved.

For a minute, Alexei enjoyed a rare moment of anonymity. Then he looked towards the other end of the bridge, where a few of the city's citizens stood agape. Alexei smiled at them, and in a second, they came over to him.

"Your Imperial Majesty, we were not expecting you to be out in the city," one of them said.

"Of course not," Alexei said. "But I couldn't resist the opportunity to see the city in all of its holiday splendor."

In a second, a crowd gathered. Just as quickly, both Gorvenko and Alexei's Cossack escort pressed in on Alexei, but with a gesture, Alexei told them to step back. For nearly two hours, Alexei shook hands with the crowd around him, talking to each person individually. It was only when he checked his watch that he realized how much time had passed.

"Christmas services start in an hour," he said. "If I'm not back at the Palace soon, my mother's going to panic."

The crowd laughed and parted just enough to let him get on his sleigh.

"Was that so bad, Ivan Maximovich?" Alexei asked as the doors of the Palace closed behind them a few minutes later.

"You could have been killed," Gorvenko replied.

"There will always be assassins looking over my shoulder. But the crowd that gathered today was quite the opposite."

"God smiled upon you, Your Imperial Majesty."

In church that night, Alexei smiled to see how much of his family was there- Anastasia, Marie and Alexandra, of course, as well as Michael and Natasha and their son George. Two rows back, Pavel and his family were there as well.

Alexei looked across the aisle at the Konstantinovichi brothers, their sisters Tatiana and Vera and their mother, Elizaveta. His grin broadened. "I never thought I'd get you out of Pavlovsk," he whispered to Gavril.

"We wouldn't pass up an invitation to celebrate Christmas Mass with the Tsar of all the Russias," Gavril replied with a grin.

"You can call me Alyosha," Alexei reminded him. They both laughed. Alexandra sent her son a disapproving look, and it took all of Alexei's self-control not to laugh harder. *It's so nice to have so much of the family here*, he thought.

Just over a week later, the Winter Palace was lit up, and its doors were thrown open. As the hour approached ten, Alexei stood in one of the drawing rooms near the Grand Ballroom. As he listened to the sound of his guests enjoying themselves in the ballroom, Alexei stood in front of the drawing room's large mirror, absentmindedly adjusting the epaulets on his uniform. His fingers then moved to medals that hung beneath them.

Without even looking up, Alexei could sense Gorvenko's presence behind him without ever having heard him approach. He turned, and sure enough, Gorvenko stood behind him. "Your Imperial Majesty," Gorvenko said with a nod.

"Good evening, Ivan Maximovich," Alexei replied.

There was a moment of silence as Gorvenko eyed Alexei. "You're angry with me, aren't you?" Gorvenko finally asked.

"I'm not *angry*," Alexei said. "I just need to know the truth. Did you have a hand in Stalin's death?"

Gorvenko looked away. He took a deep breath, smelling the flowers that were in the ballroom as he did so. Then he looked back at Alexei. "Yes," he said finally. "That man was as much of a threat as Lenin."

"I don't disagree with you," Alexei said. "But if you're going to do something like that in the future, I need you to tell me- *before* it actually happens."

"Yes, Your Imperial Majesty, I will."

"We're going to have some tough decisions ahead of us, Ivan

Maximovich, and I need to see all sides of everything if I'm going to be fair. I need you to protect my person, but shielding me from the truth is not in either of our interests."

"I understand that, Your Imperial Majesty." There was another pause. Gorvenko's brows came together in a frown, and he turned to the door of the drawing room.

A second later, Anastasia came into the room. "How is it that you saw me coming even before I came into view?" she asked Gorvenko.

"Just one of my skills, Your Imperial Highness," Gorvenko replied. Then he slipped out of the room.

"You look great," Alexei told his sister. He was so accustomed to Anastasia's minimal way of dressing that he had had to look at her twice to recognize her in her formal ball gown, pearls, and makeup. A small diadem stood on her head, and its diamonds sparkled in the light from the chandelier.

"Thank you," Anastasia replied. "Aunt Olga made me buy all these cosmetics when we went shopping the last time." She made a face. "Masha's more into that stuff than I am."

"Maybe you should get used to it a bit more," Alexei advised. "It looks good."

"If you keep having entertainments like this one, maybe I will."

Alexei looked at the clock. "It's almost time for us to go in," he said. "Are Mama and Masha waiting for us?"

Anastasia nodded. "They're just outside. Igor and his family are there too."

"Well, then, let's go," Alexei said.

Together, the family walked into the Nicholas Hall. Alexei smiled as he looked around. The spacious room had been turned into a grove of palm trees for the occasion, and small tables had been placed around the room. *Those tables won't hold more than six or eight people each,* Alexei thought. *I'm glad this won't be a huge gathering.* But he was happier for the smell of the food wafting through the air. *I'm hungry.*

As the Imperial family entered the room, their guests stood. Men in uniform bowed, their decorations flashing in the light. The women curtseyed, their long and colorful gowns swaying around them. Alexei continued smiling. As his sisters, mother and cousins sat at various tables, Alexei made his way around the room, talking to his guests. Finally, however, Alexei made his way to his own seat.

"Thank you for coming," Alexei said to the guests at his table as servants brought their soup.

"It was our pleasure," said Victor Tolstoy, who sat two seats away from Alexei. His daughter Elizaveta sat next to Alexei. Her blond hair had been curled for the occasion, and her blue eyes shown from her pale face.

She's my age, Alexei remembered. "How is your mother doing, Elizaveta?" he asked.

"She's on the mend, Your Imperial Majesty," Elizaveta replied. "Luckily, she only had a bad cold. We feared something worse, and we're happy it wasn't."

Once everyone at the table had been served their soup, Alexei lifted his spoon to start eating, and noticed that everyone else waited for him before doing the same.

After dinner, the dancing started. Alexei's first partner was Elizaveta. After the first dance ended, Alexei could see his mother taking leave of the guests and went to say goodnight. "I'm glad you came, Mama," he said.

"I am too," Alexandra replied, "but I am tired now."

"I know," Alexei said. "I'll see you tomorrow."

The dancing continued long after Alexandra left. In the wee hours of the morning, in between the spinning of the dancers, Alexei caught a glimpse of snow falling outside, illuminated by the light the ballroom cast outward. *Being tsar hasn't been easy,* he thought. *But at least this part is nice.*

The time flew by, and it was the middle of February before Alexei finally sat down to write a letter. It was late at night, and most of the Palace was dark. Piles of papers surrounded Alexei as he wrote. Many dealt with plans for his coronation. *That's still over a year away,* he thought, *but the more I get into the planning of it, the more I'm glad I started early. I will be one of the only Romanov tsars who will be crowned without having been married first,* he realized. The thought made the letter he was writing all the more important.

"Dear Ileana," he began. "I hope this letter finds you well. I am writing for a few reasons. Plans are underway for my coronation, which will happen in Moscow next spring. Furthermore, my sister Marie will soon be married. I hope you and your family can come to Russia for both events."

Alexei took a deep breath and continued writing. "I apologize for the way we parted last time. I feel much better now, but you deserve to know what happened. I have hemophilia, which makes it impossible for my blood to clot properly. It is almost unimaginable to think that hitting my knee on a rock in the Crimea could endanger my life, but it is a reality I've been living with since I was born."

Alexei frowned, wondering how to continue. "My parents kept my health a secret, and I think it aged them beyond their years," he wrote. "I have therefore decided to pursue a different course. Soon, I will be telling the country about my disease, but I wanted to share it with you first. I hope it doesn't come as a shock to you, and I hope you remain interested in seeing me again."

"Give my greetings to your family," Alexei finished his letter by saying. Breathing a sigh of relief, Alexei placed the letter in the pile of outgoing mail and went to bed.

In Cotroceni Palace in Bucharest, Ileana finished her lessons one morning to find a letter waiting for her. Seeing the Russian Imperial double eagle on it, Ileana eagerly ripped it open. Over an hour later, she was still rereading the letter when Ferdinand appeared at the door of her bedroom. "What is that?" he asked, seeing the paper she held.

Ileana jumped. Her sister Mignon appeared behind their father, also looking concerned. "I've never known you to be late for tea," Mignon said. "Are you alright?"

"I'm fine," Ileana said. "I just got a letter from Alexei, that's all."

"How's he feeling?" Ferdinand asked. "The last time we left him, he was in a pickle."

Ileana did not need to be reminded of Alexei's moans of pain. "He's fine," she said. "His health has improved, and he's planning a speech about it."

"Another speech to the Duma?" Ferdinand asked.

"No, this one is going to be to the people directly. Alexei says he's going to speak on the balcony of the Winter Palace, the same way his father appeared there when the Great War began."

In St. Petersburg, Alexei found that his letter to Ileana helped him frame how he wanted to announce his illness. After weeks of writing and editing, Alexei sent his speech out for publication in newspapers and to be read in churches on the same day that Alexei would deliver it from the Winter Palace the first week in April.

"I really wish you wouldn't do this, Sunbeam," Alexandra said as the plans were finalized.

"I think it's brave," Igor said.

"People are going to question his ability to rule," Alexandra replied.

"People questioned it during the Romanov Tercentenary, when Alyosha had to be carried around by a Cossack because the hemophilia had crippled him," Igor replied.

Behind Igor, his brothers all nodded in agreement. "There have been rumors about your health forever, Alyosha," Ioann said. "I think addressing them head-on is the only way to dispel people's fears."

When the day arrived, however, Alexei was nervous. He had

deliberately chosen a Sunday so that people would not be working. He went to church very early, and as he knelt in the family's private chapel, he prayed for guidance.

Am I making the right decision here? he wondered. *Mama is against it, and the cult of secrecy that has surrounded me my whole life also speaks volumes against it.* When Alexei opened his eyes again, mass had ended and his family was getting ready to leave.

"You alright over there, Alyosha?" Gavril asked from the doorway. "Any last minute changes to the plan?"

"I don't think so," Alexei replied.

In his study a few minutes later, however, Alexei tried to read his speech over one more time, but the noise of the people who had gathered in the square outside distracted him. Then Michael and Gorvenko appeared at the door of the study. "Everything is in place, Your Imperial Majesty," Gorvenko said.

"Then it is time to begin," Alexei said. Michael and Gorvenko followed him down the Palace's long hallway.

At the end of the hallway, pages opened the doors to the balcony that overlooked Palace Square. Without hesitation, Alexei walked out into the bright sunlight. He squinted but felt the warmth of the sun on his face. The square in front of him was packed with thousands of people, who all burst into cheers. Alexei, smiling, waved to crowd in front of him. When it was quiet, he took a deep breath and started speaking.

"For nearly seventeen years, a cloud has hung over my head," he began. "When I was just six weeks old, I started bleeding from my navel and couldn't stop. It wasn't long before my doctors diagnosed me with hemophilia, a disease that prevents my blood from clotting properly. A single fall could kill me, and a few nearly have."

A murmur ran through the previously silent crowd.

Alexei continued speaking. "As I grew up, my parents took great pains to protect me, and my physicians sought every cure possible. It is with great difficulty that we have come to realize that while there is no cure, this disease can be managed. As a child, I was prone to the wild games of any boy, and to the bumps and bruises that came with them. As an adult, and as tsar, I have pledged to manage my health more effectively, so that I may continue to serve my country and my people. Today I declare that my condition shall not stand in the way of that service. I am as fit to rule as each tsar was before me.

"My illness has remained a secret for far too long. While I understand the choice to keep it hidden, I have decided on a different path- one of openness, one of honesty. I will not shrink from my hemophilia, nor will I be defined by it. To the contrary, I will be defined in the same way as my forefathers: by my heritage, by my dedication to Russia, and by my faith in

God. I firmly pledge to serve Russia as long as I live.

"I am honored that so many of you have come to hear me speak today. May God bless each and every one of you."

When Alexei was finished speaking, the square went from profound silence to thunderous applause. Suddenly, spontaneously, the crowd burst into song, and the sounds of the national anthem reverberated throughout the square. Alexei smiled as tears ran down his face. It was hours later before the square was completely empty and Alexei was back inside the Palace.

In Bucharest, Ileana listened to Alexei's speech with her family. Marie looked at Ileana as the speech ended and she turned down the volume on the radio. "You don't seem surprised by what Alexei had to say," Marie said.

Ileana shook her head. "He wrote me a letter a couple of weeks ago, telling me what he was planning."

Marie and Ferdinand exchanged a look.

"What?" Ileana asked. "You two don't seem surprised either."

Marie sighed. "I had an uncle with hemophilia. Alexei's symptoms always sounded a lot like that."

"Uncle Leopold?" Ileana asked, putting her mother's stories together for the first time. "What happened to him?"

"He died young, of a hemorrhage."

"How old was he?"

"In his thirties. He had enough time to get married and have children."

"What was he like?" Ileana asked.

Marie smiled. "Alexei reminds me of him in a lot of ways," she said. "Leopold was high-spirited, always playing pranks. His attitude often belied his illness."

"Hmmm," Ileana said thoughtfully. "Alexei made it sound like was managing the hemophilia. Maybe he'll live longer than Leopold."

CHAPTER 10

In early May, the Palace was bustling again as Alexei prepared for another trip. "Do you ever stop moving?" Marie asked.

"Nope," Alexei replied. "There are places out east I can barely identify on a map. I'm starting in Moscow and then heading to Siberia. My people deserve to see me, and I would have done this as heir if I'd hadn't become tsar so early."

"The ancient cities around Moscow have some wonderful cathedrals," Alexandra said nostalgically. "I haven't seen them since the tercentenary."

"You're welcome to come with me, Mama," Alexei said.

"I can't," Alexandra said. "My sciatica, my neuralagia- I haven't been able to travel for a long while now."

"I know," Alexei said. "That's why Anastasia, Aunt Olga, Michael and Igor are coming with me."

Marie broke into a grin. "Mama and I are going to plan and execute my wedding while you're gone," she said. "When you get back, I'll be a married woman."

"Don't you dare!" Alexei exclaimed, but he and Marie were laughing.

Two days later, the Imperial train steamed out of St. Petersburg. "This is going to be great," Alexei said to Anastasia as they stood at the window of the train, waving at the crowds that had gathered to see them off.

As the train approached Moscow, Alexei stood at the window again. He could see the red walls of Kremlin, and the domes of the churches within it. In a different direction, he could see the towering, multi-colored façade of St. Basil's Cathedral. Surrounding it all, he could see the sparkling waters of the Moskva River. Just then, Michael came into the train car. Alexei was about to say something when he heard noise as the train continued to pull into the station. "What is that?"

"It's people cheering," Michael said.

"Oh, my God," Alexei said. He pressed his face to the window, and sure enough, he could see a huge crowd of people surrounding the station. Many were peasants, identifiable by their colorful blouses and headscarves, but many of the city's officials were visible in front of them.

"These people are waiting to see you," Michael said, as Igor, Anastasia, and Olga joined them in the car.

Alexei looked at his family and then back at the crowd in front of them, feeling a little dumbfounded. Anastasia joined him at the window of the train, and began waving at the crowd in front of them. Alexei smiled and began waving also. The crowd roared. Finally, the train came to a stop, and the family disembarked. Alexei smiled to see Grand Duke Kirill at the head of the official deputation. Kirill stepped forward. "Your Imperial Majesty, welcome to Moscow," he said.

"Thank you," Alexei said, and Kirill greeted the rest of Alexei's party individually.

"Are you ready to go to St. Basil's?" Kirill asked a few minutes later.

Alexei nodded. "I've been looking forward to hearing a Te Deum there for weeks," he said.

Before he actually got into the car in front of him, however, Alexei took a few minutes to shake hands with the peasants who had gathered in front of him. Most looked at him in wonder, their eyes round. Despite their goodwill, Alexei could feel the crush of people around him, and struggled against the claustrophobia that suddenly arose within him. A few minutes later, he was relieved to be in the car with Michael and Kirill as they rode into the heart of the city.

Kirill smiled as they rode. "Some of those people have been waiting at the station for hours to see you, Alyosha," he said. "Many of them were gathered here even before dawn."

Alexei shook his head. "That's insane."

"Your people hold you in high regard," Kirill replied. "They want to see you succeed."

Alexei looked out the window again, where people were still lined up along the streets. He waved. Seeing him, the people cheered loudly. When he looked back at Michael and Kirill, they were both smiling at him. "What?" he asked.

"I spent much of Nicky's reign wishing that he and your mother would show themselves more to the people, spend more time in society," Kirill said. "The fact that you seem inclined to fulfill that wish makes me happy."

When they arrived at St. Basil, ropes blocked off the entrance by a wide berth, giving the cars plenty of room to pull up to the cathedral. Nonetheless, a row of policemen stood just outside the ropes, keeping the crowd back. Inside, Alexei relaxed in the warm atmosphere of the cathedral. He looked up in awe at the view all the way up to the top of the towers.

Sun flowing in from the windows in the towers enhanced the inherent brightness of the iconostasis, and Alexei felt as though the eyes of the saints on the icons were watching him. A few minutes later, Alexei closed his eyes briefly as he knelt in one of the chapels. When the choir began the Te Deum, Alexei sung along.

When the service was over, Alexei, Michael, Igor, Olga and Anastasia piled back into the cars outside. "I'm very happy to have you here, Alyosha," Kirill said as they drove to his mansion for a formal reception and lunch. "When you offered me the Governor-General's position, I realized that I'd be the first member of the family to hold the position since Sergei left it more than fifteen years ago."

"I didn't mean to make you nervous," Alexei said.

"I wasn't worried for my safety," Kirill replied. "I mean, who can forget that Sergei was murdered carrying out his duties? But the revolutionaries haven't been as active recently."

"Only because Alyosha's been removing their leadership," Igor said with a grin.

Alexei glared at him.

"Relax, Alyosha," Kirill said as they arrived at the maroon Governor-General's palace. "I think you've handed yourself quite well when dealing with the Bolsheviks. I doubt Lenin expected you to be as prepared as you were."

"It was still pretty gruesome," Alexei replied.

"I don't doubt that," Kirill answered. "But it would have been much worse for Russia if he'd succeeded in killing you." He took a breath. "I hear Trotsky's in charge of the party now. On some levels, maybe it makes sense to pacify him rather than simply killing him."

Alexei nodded in agreement. "He's joining us at some of the factories in the Urals."

"Be careful it doesn't turn into a riot, though," Kirill warned.

"I'm worried about that," Alexei admitted. "But given that we've been opening so many more factories, the working class has only grown. Right now I think it's wise to listen to him. Given Lenin and Stalin's deaths, he's already seen what we can do. Perhaps he'll tread a moderate line."

"We should only be so lucky," Kirill said.

Then an elaborately dressed footman opened the door to the car. Kirill gestured for Alexei to exit before him, and Alexei stepped outside once more into the bright sunshine.

The next morning, Alexei grinned at Michael as he waited to review a military parade. "I've been looking forward to this since we organized it," he said. "I really do wish I could have served before I became tsar."

Michael smiled back. "I wouldn't trade my military service for anything," he agreed. Then he became more serious. "Don't forget that Nicky lowered the conscription age to 18, and lowered the age at which men could volunteer to 16. He also put out a conscription decree in early 1919. Even though the war was over, he wanted to maintain a larger standing army that could mobilize faster than we did in 1914."

Alexei nodded. "I remember," he said. "A lot of soldiers have remained in the army."

"It could mean they wanted to become professional soldiers," Michael replied. "Maybe many of them have had better opportunities in the military than anywhere else."

Alexei bit his lip as he thought about that, unconsciously lifting his teeth away from his flesh at the last minute so as not to actually cut himself. When the parade began, he intently watched the regiments marching in front of him. He saluted as they passed, even as the sun poured down, heating his body and threatening to obscure his vision.

When the parade ended, Alexei sought out several soldiers and officers to speak to. His eye had already fallen on the stocky squadron commander of the Fourth Regiment of the First Moscow Cavalry Division. *It's too bad my hemophilia keeps me from riding a horse regularly*, Alexei thought. *I'd love to ride the way these men were.*

Alexei tried not to notice the awe with which the soldiers were watching him. *I should be looking at them like that,* he thought. He focused on the squadron commander. "Your soldiers performed nicely in this parade," he said.

"Thank you, Your Imperial Majesty," the commander replied.

"What is your name?"

"Georgy Konstantinovich Zhukov."

"Pleased to make your acquaintance."

"The pleasure is mine."

Alexei bombarded the man with questions about his upbringing and military training. *He fought in the Great War and was awarded quite a few medals,* Alexei realized. *He's definitely someone to remember.* After a few more minutes of talking, Alexei moved on to another regiment.

Both Michael and Kirill eyed Alexei as they returned to the Kremlin, waiting for him to speak. Finally, as the red brick walls came into view, Alexei looked back at them. "Papa met Major Kulik during the Great War, and he was impressed with him," Alexei said, naming an officer he had just met.

Kirill and Michael glanced at each other, and then out the windows of the car.

"What?" Alexei asked.

"Many soldiers complain of his incompetence," Kirill said.

Alexei frowned as he thought. "Perhaps he's good at giving a good impression, then," he said. "I liked him, though I guess I'll have to keep an eye on him. I thought more highly of some of the other commanders we met today, though- Zhukov, Rokossovsky, a few others."

Now, Michael and Kirill both nodded in agreement, and Alexei was relieved. "Both those men's squadrons think highly of them," Michael said.

Alexei eyed his uncle and cousin. "So you've been asking around as to their reputations," he said. "Why didn't you tell me that?"

"We're discussing it now, aren't we?" Kirill teased. Alexei glared at him.

"We wanted you to get your own impressions, Alyosha," Michael said seriously. "You need to be able to make your own decisions."

That night, Alexei, Michael and Igor spent the night on the imperial train, en route to Penza to visit Dimitri Obolensky's estate and glass factory. Anastasia and Olga remained in Moscow to attend festivities in their honor and visit hospitals the next day. "We're going to a lot of the nobility's estates on this trip," Igor observed.

"Many of them are very wealthy and have huge factories like this one," Alexei replied. "I'm hoping for either their monetary investment in the country's manufacturing sector, or their willingness to build more factories." He looked out the window of the train and watched as the city of Moscow disappeared behind them. Suddenly, he yawned as his fatigue hit him intensely. "I am *so* tired."

"Get used to that," Michael advised. "Your work as tsar never ends."

Next to Alexei, Igor was struggling to keep his eyes open. Alexei poked him in the shoulder. "Why didn't you say you were tired?" he asked. "You don't have to sit up with us."

Igor groaned. "If you're awake, I should be too," he said.

"Well, I'm going to bed," Alexei said, standing up.

"Me too," Igor said, getting up in a hurry and heading to his sleeping car.

When their train arrived the next morning, the Obolenskys' carriages were waiting for them at the station, and Prince Dmitri exited from the first one as the train came to a stop. Behind him, Alexander and Nicholas exited from the second carriage. All around them, hundreds of peasants were also waiting, hoping to get a glimpse of Alexei. Many of them cheered when Alexei disembarked.

Alexei grinned. "Dmitri Alexandrovich, thank you for hosting us," he said.

"The honor is mine, Your Imperial Majesty," Dmitri replied as

Alexander and Nicholas struck up a conversation with Michael and Igor. "In fact, I am the indebted to you for allowing Nica's marriage to Marie."

"I think both our families gain from it," Alexei said. He looked at the peasants that were gathered, the men in their bright shirts and the women wearing colorful headscarves. Many cheered when he looked over at them, and Alexei couldn't resist going over to them to shake hands and greet them. After awhile, he pulled himself away, and Dmitri's carriages began their journey to Gorodishche.

Alexei looked out the window of the carriage as he rode with Igor sitting next to him and Dmitri sitting across from them. Outside, vast acres of green land met his eye, and peasants worked the land as far as he could see. *Agriculture*, Alexei thought, remembering what Stolypin and Witte had told him. *The farmers need better machinery, and they need motivation to use it. Stolypin and Witte's stories of farmers not wanting to use the better machinery are hard to believe. There's got to be a way of changing it.*

Alexei looked back into the interior of the carriage to find Igor looking out the window on the other side of the carriage, and Dmitri watching them both. "Is all this land yours, Dmitri Alexandrovich?" Alexei said.

"Yes, it is. My home is up that way-" Dimitri gestured in one direction- "and the factory is up this way." He gestured in the direction in which they were headed, and a minute later, Alexei could see a huge building with smoke coming out of various smokestacks. As they went inside, he could hear the tremendous noise of all the glass being produced.

Dmitri led his imperial guests to the floor of the factory, where all of the workers were moving at great speeds in front of bustling machines. Many of the workers, noticing their master, stood at attention. With a small wave, Dmitri bade them continue working. They all did, but most, recognizing Alexei, kept their eyes on him.

Dmitri, Alexander and Nicholas stopped walking and watched Alexei, waiting for him to get his bearings and ask questions. Michael stayed with them, wanting his nephew to take the lead. Alexei, awed at the sight, stared around at the huge factory, the long rows of machinery and thousands of workers. Slowly, he began walking forward, examining both the machines and the workers hands as they moved. Igor, too, looked around in wonder. He stayed behind Alexei, but he moved at the same pace, and he looked at everything that that Alexei did.

The furnace in the middle caught Alexei's eye, and he moved towards it as if hypnotized. He stopped when got within a few feet of the worker who was standing in front of the furnace. The man wore huge gloves on his hands and a mask on his face. Immediately, Alexei understood why- the heat from the furnace was intense. Nonetheless, he watched, fascinated, as the man repeatedly turned the object he was holding. Slowly, the glass, nearly liquid, changed shape.

Quickly, the worker pulled his oblong object from the furnace and rushed it to a nearby worktable. Alexei hurried to keep up. Already, he could tell that the man was making an egg. The worker placed the brightly colored glass onto the table and pulled his mask from his face. It was only then that he noticed Alexei, and began stuttering an apology.

"Please, don't let me stop you," Alexei said, a grin lighting up his face. "I just want to see you work."

Grabbing his tools, the man attacked the glass in front of him. "This is how we finishing shaping the hot glass," he explained.

"What is your name?" Alexei asked him.

"Vladimir Petrovich Sergov."

"How long have you worked here, Vladimir Petrovich?"

"About four years, Your Imperial Majesty."

"Do you enjoy the work?"

"Oh yes. Very much. It sure beats working on the farm."

"You used to work on a farm?"

"Most of my family still does," Sergov replied. "I'm the only one that works here, though a couple of my brothers are thinking of joining me."

"Why do you prefer this?"

"The wages are better, the hours are better."

A few minutes later, in a different part of the factory, Alexei watched as a group of female workers pressed hot glass into icons. "Those are really beautiful," he said. Instantly, one of the workers pressed her completed icon into Alexei's hand. "Thank you," he said sincerely.

The woman's face broke into a wide smile. "I have a daughter who's your age," she said.

"What is her name?" Alexei asked.

"Ekaterina Pavlovna. Her eyes are big and blue, like yours."

Alexei grinned. "Maybe I'll meet her someday," he said.

Alexei, Igor and Michael left long after dark, when the factory was closing and the workers were heading home. As they drove back to the Obolensky palace, Alexei was quiet, contemplating everything that he had seen.

Two days later, Alexei sat at the window of the Imperial train as it traveled eastward. A stack of papers sat in front of him, but he was not looking at them. Instead, he stared out the window as the train approached the Ural Mountains. The sun was setting behind him, and yet it glinted off the tops of the snow-covered mountains ahead of him. Far below the mountaintops, the verdant valleys were dotted with farmers and livestock.

Alexei checked his watch and sighed. Much as he hated to pull himself away from the window, his foreign minister, Anatoly Andreievich Demetrikov, had been asking for an appointment with him for several days now. Alexei stood as Demetrikov was led into the train car. "Good afternoon, Anatoly Andreievich," he said. "Have a seat."

Demetrikov obeyed, settling himself in a plush armchair before one of many tables that were covered in reports and other papers. The chair, the table, and the papers all shook slightly as the train lurched forward.

Alexei steadied himself by leaning on a chair. "Now I know why it took our troops and supplies so long to reach the front during the Great War," he said. "If I do nothing else on this trip but secure financing to rebuild and expand the railways, it will be a success."

"Your Imperial Majesty, I know your attention is focused on Russia," Demetrikov replied. "But there have been developments abroad that require your attention as well."

Alexei's expression was serious as he sat opposite Demetrikov. "What should I be aware of?"

"There are changes happening Germany that could prove problematic."

"Germany was crushed at the end of the war, and the reparations the rest of the world placed on her were intended to keep it that way."

"Therein lies the problem. There has been talk that the reparations are preventing Germany from recovering from the war, and that the German people are unhappy as a result."

"It hasn't even been three years since the war ended. This type of change doesn't happen instantaneously."

"I agree that it takes time, but in that time, discontent has been growing." Demetrikov handed Alexei a report. "The German monarchy fell after the war, allowing political parties to fill the void. This one seems to be on the rise."

"Die Nationalsozialistische Deutsche Arbeiterpartei," Alexei read aloud.

"They call themselves the Nazis," Demetrikov said. "In particular, their new leader has risen through their ranks quite quickly."

"Adolph Hitler," Alexei said, picking up a picture of the man from the file as the train car continued to shake around him.

"He's a decorated veteran of the Great War, and a gifted orator," Demetrikov said. "I saw him speak when I was in Germany a couple of weeks ago, and I was impressed. He's good at playing to people's fears and frustrations. I don't think we can dismiss him easily."

Alexei eyed Demetrikov unhappily. "Germany has been a thorn in my side for awhile now."

"And I don't expect that to change, unfortunately."

"Well, the German people may have lost their Kaiser, but it looks like they're about to replace him with another strong leader." Alexei shook his head as he flipped through the file. "Do you think this Hitler would start another war, though?"

"Right now, no," Demetrikov replied. "Germany is too weak, both economically and politically."

"But you think it might be possible a few years from now?"

"Hard to say. It'll depend largely on how quickly Germany recovers."

Alexei sighed as he closed the file. "Having just been through a war on the scale of the Great War, I can't imagine anyone starting hostilities again."

"Let's hope the rest of the world shares your common sense, Your Imperial Majesty."

Two weeks later, as the Imperial train finally inched its way back to Moscow, Alexei felt his eyes burning with fatigue as he hunched over his teacup. Igor sat next to him, and Anastasia, Olga and Michael sat across from him in the Imperial train's dining car as they finished breakfast. "I'm really looking forward to sleeping in my own bed again," Alexei said.

Igor, Anastasia and Olga smiled at him sympathetically, but Michael eyed his nephew seriously. "This trip was a good one, Alyosha. People that far east haven't seen much of our family since Nicky took a tour of the empire as Tsarevich. If you'd accomplished nothing more than making yourself more visible and popular, that alone would have been worth the trip."

Alexei was about to respond when the train shook even more than usual. "What was that?" he asked, feeling the same alarm that he saw on Anastasia and Olga's faces.

Michael and Igor stood up, looking around worriedly. Alexei was about to follow suit when a loud bang sounded from the front of the train. In a second, the train flew off the tracks and hurtled into the surrounding woods. The train sunk into the muddy permafrost, rammed into a tree, and turned on its side. Alexei howled as he was thrown from his seat and into a nearby armchair. Anastasia and Olga both screamed as they were tossed onto their sides, and Michael and Igor were groaning from having been thrown from a standing position.

With the train now stationary, the dining car was besieged by Alexei's policemen. As Alexei pulled himself to his feet, he could see Gorvenko struggling with the door to the car. "That door must be jammed!" Igor said as he got to his feet, wincing. Then he pulled his gun from its holster.

"What are you doing?" Alexei yelled.

Igor did not respond before he took aim at the window closest to the door and fired. The sound of the shot reverberated around the car, and Alexei felt as though the sound was echoing through his head as well. But the window's glass shattered with the force of the bullet, and the family had a way out of the car.

Michael helped Olga to her feet and Igor helped Anastasia to her feet as Alexei went to the broken window. Gorvenko was already clearing away the glass from the window. "Be very careful, Your Imperial Majesty," he warned as Alexei folded his body to climb through the window. He held out his hand as Alexei tried to avoid the broken glass that surrounded him.

Alexei grabbed Gorvenko's arm, and Gorvenko pulled him from the train car. Behind him, the rest of the family pulled themselves from the car. No sooner were they all out than Alexei heard a smaller explosion, this one coming from the back of the train. "We need to get out of here!" he yelled.

He and Michael grabbed Olga's arms and pulled her forward as they ran. Behind them, Igor grabbed Anastasia's arm as they ran away from the train. Alexei's boots sunk into the same permafrost that had slowed the train. His legs began to hurt almost immediately, and his breathing came in gasps. *That looks like a road just up there,* he thought. *If only I could make it.* Just as he was thinking that his whole body would give out, Alexei saw his Cossack guard struggling up onto the road on horseback. *Horses,* he thought. *That would help.*

A strong arm grabbed his shoulder and pulled him up onto the road. Looking up, Alexei saw Gorvenko pulling him to safety, his eyes full of concern. Two of the Cossacks that had just made it to the road dismounted, and Gorvenko helped Alexei mount one horse before he mounted the other and began leading Alexei up the road.

"Where are we going?" Alexei asked, feeling as though he was in a haze.

"You don't look well at all," Gorvenko replied. "We're not far from Moscow. We should be able to find a hospital."

Alexei managed to kick his horse forward, but as he rode, he realized that Gorvenko was right- his whole upper body hurt. *I must be bleeding somewhere,* he thought as the rest of the Cossacks surrounded him protectively. It was not long before Alexei thought he recognized his surroundings, but he also felt himself growing weaker. Unable to hold onto his horse any longer, Alexei slipped off and fell to the ground. He was barely aware of the uproar that followed- shouting voices, a cry for a stretcher. Everything was far away as he slipped into an abyss of darkness.

CHAPTER 11

Alexei slipped in and out of consciousness for what seemed like an eternity. In some moments, he was aware of the sharp pains in his torso. Sometimes, he could also hear voices surrounding him, and he was aware of Alexandra's presence by his bedside. At some point, he saw Michael hovering in the doorway. Grand Duke Kirill stood just behind him, and Alexei thought he heard their conversation.

"You gave up your right to the throne when you married morganatically," Kirill said. "If Alyosha doesn't make it, the throne goes to me next."

Michael's reply was sharp and tense. "He'll survive."

"I don't know, Misha. It's not looking good."

In some of his more conscious moments, Alexei was aware of someone feeding him soup, and the hot liquid felt good. When he finally blinked awake into full consciousness, he did not recognize his surroundings. Then he saw both Alexandra and Anastasia sitting by his bedside, praying fervently. Icons surrounded his bed. "Where am I?" he croaked.

Anastasia jumped, then put her prayer book aside. "You're awake!" she said.

Alexandra put her bible down more slowly. "How do you feel?" she asked.

Alexei had to shift in his bed slightly to be able to answer that question. "Better, I guess. What happened?"

"The train's derailment caused you to hemorrhage internally," Alexandra said.

"This hemophilia is going to be the death of me," Alexei said. "Where are we?"

"Back at the Obolensky's estate in Gorodishe," Anastasia said. "This is the hospital on the estate."

"How long have I been here?"

"Almost three weeks," Alexandra said. "Misha has been running the government since the train wreck."

"Oh my God," Alexei said.

Even as his health returned, Alexei felt the toll that the attack had taken on him. One morning, he tried to read reports in bed, and only managed an hour of work before his strength left him. When Father Vasiliev came to Alexei's bedroom carrying an icon, he found Alexei lying in bed, tears running down his face. "Your Imperial Majesty, is everything alright?" the priest asked. "I thought your health was returning."

"It is," Alexei said. "That's not what bothers me."

"What, then?"

For a moment, Alexei stared out the window, and tears continued to roll down his face. Then he looked back at Vasiliev. "Is it really worth living like this?" he asked.

The priest was visibly taken aback at the question. "Of course it is," he said. "You have your whole life in front of you."

"What kind of life? I'll be in pain all the time, and always in fear of dying. It's no way to live."

Vasiliev swallowed, and Alexei watched his Adam's apple move up and down. "Think of your family, and your people," Vasiliev said finally. "All of them care about you enormously. Think of your country. You've wanted to be tsar your whole life, and now you finally hold that position. You're also a young tsar who could do so much good. Think of your future, and all it could hold. Think of your faith, and of God, which will sustain you."

Finally, Alexei took a deep breath and looked at the icon that Vasiliev was holding. "You're right," he said. "God ensured that I lived through this latest attack, as he ensured that I lived through the rest of them. He is truly watching over me."

Alexei remained in Moscow for another three weeks as he slowly healed. He spent the time at the Petrovsky Palace in the Kremlin, working as much as he was able. "What made the train derail?" he asked Gorvenko about a week after he was working again.

"A whole series of bombs right on the tracks. We have already arrested the culprits."

"How many were there and who are they?"

"We have arrested five main conspirators and twelve others who were indirectly involved. Unfortunately, Your Imperial Majesty, they were Communists who had hoped that your death would spark a revolution."

"Dammit!" Alexei burst out. "You may be right about this after all, Ivan Maximovich. Killing the entire party may be the only option I have. Was there any evidence that Trotsky was involved?"

"No, Your Imperial Majesty, none whatsoever."

"I still find it suspicious. Trotsky met us at various factories along the trip, and he knew when I was leaving for Moscow."

"It is suspicious," Gorvenko agreed. "But so far, we haven't found a shred of evidence linking him to the bombings."

"That's too bad," Alexei said. "But we still have to deal with the perpetrators you arrested." He frowned as he thought. "For reasons of my health, I need to remain here in Moscow for at least another two weeks. Can we put them on trial here in Moscow in such a short time?"

Gorvenko nodded. "Charges can be brought as early as tomorrow."

"See that it happens," Alexei ordered.

Huge crowds gathered outside the main courtroom of Moscow when the charges were announced, and crowds packed the courtroom to watch the trial. When the trial ended in a guilty verdict a week later, many spectators cheered. The cheers grew louder as the death penalty was announced.

Michael, who had come in from St. Petersburg as the trial was ending, looked at Alexei as they received the news of the verdict and sentence. "It's your right as Tsar to commute that sentence," he said.

"There is no way in hell I'm commuting it," Alexei replied. "Those people tried to kill all of us."

"I'm well aware," Michael said. "How will you carry out the sentence?"

"A public hanging in the streets of Moscow."

"Alyosha," Michael said uncomfortably. "That sounds like something out of the Middle Ages."

"Perhaps," Alexei said. "But first it was Lenin, now it's this." He shook his head. "I will not show mercy."

On the day of the hanging, Alexei stood in the window of the Petrovsky Palace with his binoculars and watched. Once the punishment had been administered, Alexei finally felt comfortable, and well enough, to return to St. Petersburg.

"I'm not happy about that hanging," Michael said as they traveled.

"Get over it Misha," Alexei said. "Even if I regretted it, I couldn't take it back."

When Alexei returned to St. Petersburg, it was early July, and preparations for Marie's wedding were in full swing. "I'm glad to see you used my time away wisely," Alexei teased Marie and Alexandra one evening as they sat in one of the drawing rooms, discussing the latest plans.

"It was at your orders, Your Imperial Majesty," Marie said. She stood up and went into a deep curtsey.

Alexei burst out laughing. "You are ridiculous," he said.

Over a month later, it was a week before the wedding, and Alexei took advantage of the fact that guests had not begun arriving yet to start work early. Despite the hour, however, the study was not empty- Sergei Kamensky was just putting a stack of documents on his desk as he arrived. "What is that, Gega?" Alexei asked.

Sergei jumped. "I didn't even hear you come in, Your Imperial Majesty," he apologized. "These are the documents you requested from your father's coronation. The coronation proclamation is on top, followed by your father's amnesty manifesto and many others."

"Thanks," Alexei replied, and Sergei returned to his desk.

Alexei sat down and began his reading the coronation proclamation. "Our Most August, Most High and Puissant Sovereign, Nicholas Alexandrovich, having ascended the hereditary throne of the Empire of Russia..." Almost immediately, Alexei's eyes had trouble focusing. *Who writes this stuff?* he wondered.

But it was the language at the end of that paragraph that stuck in his throat. "Furthermore," he read, "His Majesty has commanded that his august spouse, the Empress Alexandra Feodorovna, should participate in this holy function."

Alexei put down the document and sighed. *I'm going to be the first Emperor since Peter the Great who wasn't married before his coronation*, he thought. *I feel quite deficient.*

In the antechamber just outside his study, Alexei could hear his secretaries standing up from their desks in unison, and the sound distracted him. A second later, Marie and Anastasia were standing in the doorway. "Are you still working, Alyosha?" Marie asked, pouting slightly.

"Were you expecting anything else?" Alexei said with a smile. "The wedding preparations are completed and the guests haven't arrived yet."

"I'm still getting my dress fitted," Marie said. "The preparations aren't totally complete."

"Alyosha doesn't need to be there for your dress fittings," Anastasia said, pushing past her sister into Alexei's study. "What are working on, Alyosha?"

"My coronation proclamation."

"The coronation is eight months away and you're working on that rather than on my wedding?" Marie said, but she was smiling as she followed Anastasia into the study.

"The coronation is as important to him as your wedding is to you," Anastasia said. "In fact, we should let him work." She turned and started pushing Marie back towards the door.

Alexei laughed. "Was there an actual reason you two came in here?"

"Oh yes," Anastasia said, speaking over her shoulder. "We just got telegrams from Olga and Tatiana. They're on their way to St. Petersburg."

"Great!" Alexei said. "I'll meet them at the station."

As Marie and Anastasia disappeared, Alexei continued to smile. *I'll miss them both when they're married and living somewhere else.*

One week later, on the morning of the big ceremony, Alexei awoke very early, and, after a quick breakfast, he put on his dress uniform. Outside, the August sun beat down, and Alexei could see the heat rising in shimmering waves. *I can't believe it's been just over a year since Papa's death,* he thought. *Time really flies. It's the only reason we were able to hold Marie's wedding now, though- the traditional mourning period just ended.*

Alexei made sure that the Obolenskys were comfortably situated in the Winter Palace's Great Cathedral Church. When they were inside and Alexander was checking on the last details of his son's uniform, Alexei slipped away and went to the Malachite Drawing Room to see Marie. When he got there, the door was firmly shut, but Alexei, holding his ear close to the door could hear plenty of noise inside. He knocked.

"Who is it?" Alexandra asked from inside.

"It's me."

The door opened a crack- just enough for Alexei to see past his mother to where Marie was sitting in front of the room's large silver-gilt mirror. She was wearing her wedding dress, made of heavily embroidered silver cloth. Behind her was their grandmother Marie, who was supervising the hairdresser. "What do you want?" Alexandra asked.

"I'm just checking on her," Alexei said.

"We're getting her ready," Alexandra said. "Don't you have to be downstairs to greet the guests?"

"I'm going, I'm going," Alexei said, holding up his hands in self-defense. Alexandra closed the door, but not before Alexei caught his sister smiling at him. Downstairs, the guests were arriving, making their way to the staterooms by way of the palace's white and gold Jordan Staircase. For a moment, Alexei paused on the staircase, watching Olga and Tatiana make their way up, their children in their arms.

Alexei grinned. The light that poured in from the tall arched windows sparkled over his oldest sisters' jewels, and their satin, brocade and velvet dresses were colorful. Next to them, Alexander and Boris looked dashing in their military uniforms and decorations. Then Alexei caught sight of Anastasia on the other side of the staircase, greeting the guests that were coming up on that side. *Good for her,* he thought. He looked back at his oldest sisters and their families, who had joined him at the top of the staircase.

Olga smiled. "It is so good to be home again, and this time for a happy occasion," she said. Tatiana nodded in agreement. After a few words with Boris and Alexander, Alexei let them walk into the church. "Tanya," he said. "How are you feeling?"

"Much better," Tatiana replied. "We're discussing having another baby."

"Are you ready for that?"

Tatiana shrugged. "I'm not sure," she admitted. "But Boris does want a son, which I understand."

As Tatiana followed Boris, Olga and Alexander, Alexei turned to see the Romanian royal family arriving, and he smiled. Ileana grinned and waved, and Alexei lifted a hand in return. Ileana started up the Jordan Staircase, and Marie followed her. Behind them, Ferdinand followed his wife and daughter, and the rest of his children followed.

Marie hugged Alexei as she and Ileana made it to the top of the staircase. "Congratulations, honey," she said.

"Thanks," Alexei said, and gave Ileana a hug too.

"So, where is your sister?" Marie asked.

"Upstairs. My mother and grandmother are helping her get ready."

"Is your mother happy?" Marie asked.

"I think she's nervous. Amama's pretty excited, though."

Marie sighed. "That's the way it's always been, I'm afraid."

Alexei wanted to ask her what she meant, but the rest of her family had just joined them. As the rest of the family congratulated him, Alexei stole a glance at Ileana. She was staring around the huge palace in wonder. When the rest of her family headed into the church, Alexei gave her a poke. "What are you looking at?" he asked. "You've been here before."

"I know," Ileana said. "It's still an incredible place."

Nearly an hour later, Alexei finished greeting the last of the guests. By then, the priests and the deacons were ready to begin the ceremony. Inside the church, Nicholas waited near the iconostasis, resplendent in his uniform. *He looks great, but he's nervous,* Alexei thought, watching Nicholas trying to breathe deeply.

Alexei looked around the church, his eyes resting on the gilded angels and the images of the four evangelists that were painted on each of the pendentives. All around, the church was decorated with roses and other flowers.

The Metropolitan of St. Petersburg made his way to the door of the church. His gold cape shimmered in the sunlight that streamed down from the top of the church. The rest of the clergy, in their richly embroidered vestments, surrounded him. The Metropolitan opened the door, and Marie stood on the other side of it. Slowly, she entered the church, and the light caught every jewel on her silvery white gown. Alexei grinned. *She really does look beautiful,* he thought.

Nicholas stood riveted at the front of the church, watching his bride walk through the chapel to join him. When Marie got to where Nicholas stood, they both lit candles and held them, and the rich sounds of the choir filled the church with the Te Deum that began the extensive service. It was a couple of hours later when the service ended, and by then Alexei was tired and hungry. *I'm so glad that lunch is next,* he thought. *I'm happy for Marie, and I'm happy to have paved the way for her marriage, but my God… there is so much other work to do.*

The day after the ceremony, Alexei made a point of putting down his work for a couple of hours, and he spent the time walking through the gardens behind the Palace with Ileana. As they walked, Alexei took a deep breath, smelling the greenery and the flowers around them.

"It really is beautiful here," Ileana said.

Alexei nodded. "I'm so glad the weather cooperated. I was worried that it would rain."

"Nah," Ileana said. "Everything was perfect. Besides, your sister seems really happy."

"She is," Alexei said.

"Was her dress and train very heavy?" Ileana asked, her blue eyes wide. "They looked like a lot of fabric."

"They are heavy," Alexei said. "Before the ceremony, I heard Mama and Aunt Ella reminiscing about their wedding days. The ceremony is so long, and the dresses are so heavy, that they were both exhausted by the end of it."

Ileana nodded, listening intently.

"Ella remembered that before her own wedding, my father slipped a coin into one of her shoes for good luck," Alexei added.

"That was nice of him."

"Except that she was stepping on it for the whole ceremony."

"Ow," Ileana said, scrunching up her face. Then she looked back at the Palace.

"What is it?" Alexei asked, looking back as well.

"I think my mother is watching us," Ileana said.

"She's probably worried we'll steal her Rolls Royce," Alexei joked.

Ileana laughed at the memory of their fast ride through St. Petersburg. "We should try that again," she said, rubbing her hands together as her eyes gleamed. "What do you say we sneak out in the middle of the night? I doubt the police would stop us if we go late enough."

Alexei joined her laughter. "I don't think they'd have to," he said. "I think my police chief would be on to us even before we snuck out."

"Who, Gorvenko?" Ileana asked, more seriously. Alexei nodded. "He really watches you closely."

"Is it that obvious?"

"Yes. But as much as he watches you, he watches everything else too. I really think he sees everything."

"That's good," Alexei said. "That's why I hired him."

Ileana nodded. "I also noticed all of your secretaries and extra ministers," she said.

"You're observant," Alexei said with a smile.

"I guess I'm interested also," Ileana said.

"Why?" Alexei asked seriously.

"I just am. You're only a few years older than I am. I've spent my whole life knowing you'd become tsar, but it happened sooner than I thought it would."

"Yes, I think that's true for everyone, including me," Alexei said, somewhat sadly, as he eyed the flowers and garden around them.

"Do you regret your position at all?"

"No, no, not at all. It's just hard work, and a lot of work."

"Is there anything I can do to ease the burden at all?"

Alexei looked back at her and smiled. "You can keep writing to me," he said. "I always enjoy getting your letters."

Ileana shook her head. "I can't believe you have the time to read my letters."

"It's state business, like the rest of it," Alexei teased, and they started walking back to the palace.

It was late at night, so late that most of the Palace's lights were out and most of its inhabitants were slumbering. The silence seemed even deeper when compared to the hustle and bustle that Marie's wedding had brought. Despite the hour, Alexei remained awake, standing in his study, staring out into the night. Not one fiber in his body felt like sleeping. A half empty bottle of vodka sat next to him in a bowl of ice. On his other side sat a number of chilled shot glasses. Having already warmed up one shot glass from holding it for so long, Alexei reached for a different glass, hoping that it was still cold.

"Nice night, isn't it?" Michael asked from behind Alexei.

Alexei jumped. "You shouldn't scare me like that, Misha," he said when he saw who it was. Then he saw Pavel behind Michael. "Uncle Pavel, I thought you'd gone home."

"And miss out on some of the best vodka in the empire?" Pavel said. "No way."

It was only then that Alexei noticed that both of his uncles had full bottles and shot glasses of their own. "Here to drink with me?" he asked.

"That's certainly one reason we're here," Pavel said.

"What more could you possibly want?" Alexei teased.

"We were hoping to find out what you wanted," Michael responded seriously. "Tsar of all the Russias, drinking alone in his study late at night…"

Alexei rolled his eyes at him. The silence lengthened as they all drank.

"So…" Pavel said finally. "Are you going to talk to us?"

Finally, Alexei turned and looked at him. Even as he did, though, his mind felt somewhat distant from his body. *It must be from the vodka*, he thought. "What do you think my chances are with Ileana?" he said finally.

"The Romanian princess?" Pavel said.

Alexei nodded.

"She's still pretty young for marriage."

"I know, but she acts older."

"She saw a lot of harsh stuff during the war. Romania was completely destroyed. The family had to evacuate the capital, and the conditions where they stayed got pretty desperate."

"I know," Alexei said. "Papa and I took supplies there after the war ended. It was a mess."

"That kind of experience can change people," Michael said. "But still, given her age, I don't think her parents will say yes to anything right now."

"I'm not talking about marrying her tomorrow," Alexei replied. "I'm talking about speaking to Mimi and Nando about it having it happen a few years from now."

Pavel eyed Alexei for a minute. "The Greek princesses are closer to your age," he said. "If you're looking to get married soon, I'd start there first."

"Margarita and Theodora don't have the same personality that Ileana has," Alexei said. "Ileana is spunky and caring."

"Even so," Pavel said, "you could get married sooner if you chose one of them. Perhaps that's a good idea, given your hemophilia."

Alexei poured himself another shot of vodka and stared out into the night. Pavel and Michael eyed their nephew, but allowed him his silence. Finally, Alexei looked back at his uncles. "If I'm going to marry, and it's imperative that I do, I want it to be to Ileana."

"Fine," Michael said. "I can talk to Mimi and Nando if you want."

"I can do it myself," Alexei replied. "I'm not afraid of them, and I am tsar. That ought to make some difference."

"Alright," Pavel said. "But she still is barely thirteen. I would give it another two years before saying anything."

Alexei frowned. "Is it possible Mimi and Nando would promise her to someone else by then?"

"I'll think they'll keep her options open," Michael replied. "Marie married quite young, and had to move to Romania to do it. It was a difficult transition for her. Given how important Ileana is to her, I think Marie will shelter her more than anything else."

"At the same time, I think you'll get more suitors in the next couple of years, not fewer," Pavel said.

Alexei shrugged. Pavel frowned at him. "Don't worry, Pavel," Alexei said hastily, not wanting his uncle to think that he was simply dismissing him. "It'll always be worth it to consider whatever other options there are. But if I know I want Ileana, why not move forward?"

CHAPTER 12

A month after Marie's wedding, Alexei decided that his coronation would take place the following May, and set a date of May 21. *Papa's coronation was May 14, Alexei thought. I don't want mine to be the exact same date, but I do want to do it while the weather is nice.*

In advance of other preparations, Alexei wrote his personal manifesto, to be published the day of the coronation. *Papa used his to reduce sentences of people in exile, reduce peasants' taxation arrears and similar things. It's a well-trod path. I plan to do all of that, but there's also something else I need to attend to.* He swallowed. *I still haven't forgotten that Ella and Pavel asked for a full pardon for Dmitri, or that the Youssoupovs asked for the same for Felix. I've been thinking about this for awhile now, and the coronation is a good time to do it.*

Alexei looked at the portrait of his father that sat on the wall across from his desk. *Papa wouldn't be happy about me doing this, and Mama will be furious when she finds out, but I think it's necessary. I don't think Felix and Dmitri did the right thing in killing Grishka, but perhaps I could get something out of them in return for their repatriation.*

As the coronation approached, Felix Youssoupov returned to Russia with Irina and their two daughters in tow. One of his first acts upon arriving home in St. Petersburg was to meet with Alexei to express his gratitude. Alexei could hear the couple's two little girls playing before he even reached the Palace's drawing room. Felix and Irina stood when Alexei came into the room. Alexei greeted them and then looked at the two little girls wondrously.

"You remember Bebe, don't you?" Felix said of his older daughter.

"You've gotten so big!" Alexei said as he knelt next to her. She giggled. "How old are you now?" he asked.

"Six," she said.

"Six?" Alexei asked. "When did you get so old?"

Irina picked up the smaller girl. "This is our younger daughter, Alexandra," she said.

Alexei stroked the little girl's hand. "It's good to meet you," he said.

"I can't tell you how happy we are to be back, Alyosha," Felix said seriously.

Alexei stood up. "I'm glad to hear that," he said.

"I've spent the last several years wanting to raise my daughters in Russia," Irina said. "I'm so grateful you're gracious enough to let us do that."

"My pleasure," Alexei replied. *I think it's gracious that they've come to see me. I haven't heard a peep out of Dmitri. I only know he's home because Pavel told me.*

A while later, as the girls were starting to get sleepy, Irina looked Alexei and Felix. "We should take them home," she said.

Alexei nodded. "Do you have a few extra minutes, though, Felix?" he asked. "There was some business I'd wanted to discuss with you."

"Of course," Felix replied. He looked at Irina. "Why don't you take the girls home?" he said. "I'll meet you back there later."

By the second week of October, preparations for Alexei's coronation were in full swing. Thousands of invitations were sent to royalty, foreign delegations, Duma members, local zemestvos, peasant delegations and members of the press, both domestic and foreign. Copies of the Coronation Proclamation and Alexei's coronation manifesto were printed by the thousands. Pages were appointed to each member of the Imperial family, and a running list of all the participants in the coronation was drawn up. By the time April, 1922, arrived, an entire administrative section in Moscow was staffed to oversee the cuisine and lodgings of the Imperial family when they arrived in the city. 1300 full-time servants and 1200 part-time servants were hired to assist in the preparations.

Inside the Kremlin, the Uspensky Sobor was renovated. The electrical station that had been built in the Kremlin for Nicholas' coronation was given an overhaul. Outside the Kremlin, the Petrovsky Palace was also renovated. The buildings along the route that Alexei and his family would travel to the ceremony were cleaned, painted and decorated with flags, portraits of Alexei, coats-of-arms and emblems of the Imperial family.

Huge arches with banners embroidered in gold and silver were built at large intersections. The silver and gold strands of each banner ended in a long, fancy tassels. Columns thirty feet high were placed at each railroad crossing and decorated with patriotic slogans. Large decorative shields with the city and country's coats-of-arms were placed at the beginning of Tverskaia Street, where the Governor's Mansion stood.

Homes all around the city, from Strastnaia Square to the Iverskaia Bell Tower, were also colorfully decorated. The huge building of trade was specially decorated with the Imperial double-headed eagle, and the building's sidewalls were covered with coats-of-arms, flags, and flowers. Not one square inch of the building's façade could be seen. Flowers and other decorations also covered the Kuznetsky Bridge.

In the middle of the frenetic preparations, as Alexei was arranging for his regalia to be transported from St. Petersburg to Moscow, Grand Duke Kirill called, and his voice conveyed an exhaustion that Alexei felt. "Don't worry about me," Kirill said when Alexei voiced his concern. "I'm happy to do this, and I want it to be perfect."

"Still, it's been a lot of work for both of us."

"Truly. At least Andrei and Boris have been in Moscow for the last several weeks, helping wherever they can," Kirill said of his younger brothers.

"I'm relieved to hear that," Alexei said. "You can't do it alone. Listen, Kirill, I'm planning on distributing a lot of gifts to the ordinary Russians that come, like mugs, food, and the other items we were discussing."

"Of course. All of those items have been ordered, and I'm expecting them to arrive a couple of days before the coronation itself."

"I'm more concerned about the location of the distribution," Alexei said. "I'd like to avoid doing it at Khodyinka Field."

"Don't worry, Alyosha," Kirill reassured him. "No one who was in Moscow for your father's coronation has forgotten the significance of that place. I'm still deciding on an alternate location, but I've already surveyed three different places that I think will be suitable."

"Good," Alexei said. "The other thing I need from you is to make sure that the Duma members have sufficient participation in the festivities. Make sure there's a place for them in the procession into the Kremlin, and make sure there's at least one other event for them- a banquet, a luncheon, whatever it is. Set it up and I'll make sure I attend."

There was a brief silence on the other end as Kirill absorbed Alexei's orders.

"My father never got comfortable working with the Duma, and his failure to include them in his coronation celebrations didn't go unnoticed," Alexei said, uncomfortable with Kirill's silence.

Kirill sighed. "I'm afraid the older members of the family haven't gotten used to the idea of working with the Duma. Just the fact that the Duma exists is seen as an infringement on the Tsar's power."

"We've been a constitutional monarchy for more than three generations now," Alexei said. "Much as the family may dislike it, the Romanovs haven't been absolute monarchs since 1881."

"I know that," Kirill said. "I'll make sure they're represented."

On May 13, Alexei moved from the Winter Palace to the Petrovsky Palace in Moscow. Anastasia, Alexandra, Marie Feodorovna, Michael, Natasha and George moved with him. An honor guard of an Uhlan regiment met them at the train station, wearing plumes on their helmets. With the sun shining brightly in an intense azure sky, Alexei and his family climbed into open carriages. They were surrounded by a cavalry escort, made up of officers led by Grand Duke Nicholas Nikolaievich. Even at sixty-five years old, Nicholas stood tall on his horse, his shoulders unbent.

The escort galloped ahead of the carriages, and the sight made Alexei smile. The horses were tall and powerful, and their muscular legs flexed as they galloped. The officers riding them were all in parade uniform. As they galloped, the Circassians' helmets reflected the light of the sun, and the Hussars all wore capes around their shoulders that swayed in the wind.

At the front of the escort, Nicholas Nikolaievich was clearly visible to Alexei, his six-foot-six inch frame making him tower above the officers around him. His closely cropped gray hair remained unmoved by the wind, and the authority he projected was unmistakable. Alexei felt his pride swell within him.

At nine o'clock the following night, there was a concert at the Petrovsky Palace. The choirs of the Moscow Imperial Opera, the Russian Choir Society, the Moscow Concert Society and the Moscow Philharmonic Society had all come to perform, and the singers numbered more than a thousand. Each singer held a staff with a torch on top of it, and the flashes of fire lit up the Palace. As the music soared, from the deepest basses to the highest sopranos, Alexei finally felt himself relaxing.

When the concert ended, Alexei consulted with Kirill one last time. "Are all of our guests accounted for?" he asked.

Kirill nodded as Boris and Andrei appeared behind him. "I've met the majority of them at the station myself," he said. "And the few times I've gotten tied up in other business, Andrei and Boris have met them for me."

"Thank you," Alexei replied, nodding at Boris and Andrei.

Nicholas Nikolaievich appeared behind the Vladimirovichi brothers, and they parted to let him through. "Alyosha, I'm so glad I could be here," he said.

"I'm grateful you're here too," Alexei replied. "That escort was magnificent."

"Thank you," Nicholas replied sincerely. For a moment, Alexei thought he saw the shine of unshed tears flash in Nicholas' eyes as he looked around the room. When Nicholas looked back at Alexei, however, his eyes were focused. "I never thought I'd live to see you crowned."

"Well, you have," Alexei replied. "I'm glad you came all the way from your Crimean estate for the ceremony."

"I wouldn't have missed it for anything."

Alexei spent the last three days before the coronation fasting, in a ritual prescribed by the Orthodox church. *Every tsar before me has done this*, he thought. *But I wonder how. I'd give anything for a decent meal right now.* The lack of food and the unfamiliar surroundings had also been taking a toll on his sleep, and Alexei hardly remembered a time when he had slept so poorly, except when he had been afflicted by his hemophilia.

For a moment, he looked into the full-length mirror in his apartments. His pale face stared back at him. His eyes looked unnaturally large and were highlighted by the dark rings underneath them. *Can I do this?* he wondered.

The day of the coronation dawned without a cloud in the sky. By noon, the bright sun illuminated each copula of every church in the city. The highest dignitaries began arriving at the Petrovsky Palace, and the court's Kamer-pages escorted the trains of the Grand Duchesses and Princesses as the women, in full court dress, made their way into the inner rooms of the Palace.

With a half hour to go before the procession, Alexei was relieved to see his sisters, mother and grandmother all congregating around him. Olga, Tatiana, Marie, and Anastasia all hugged their younger brother as Alexandra watched, tears coming down her face. Nearby, Alexander held nearly-three-year old Peter, who grinned at his uncle. "Where are the babies?" Alexei asked Olga and Tatiana.

"In the nursery at Kirill's palace," Olga said. "Only Peter was old enough for this, and even so, I'm worried about him."

"He'll be fine," Alexei said with a grin.

"Easy for you to say," Olga said, swatting her brother. "You don't have to take care of him if he starts fussing."

In the last few minutes before the procession started, Alexei gathered with Michael, Kirill, Nicholas, Igor, and the rest of the family's Grand Dukes and Princes for any last conferring and planning. Then he took a deep breath and looked at his watch. "It's almost one," he said. "Should we get into place?"

At one o'clock exactly, the procession into Moscow began. A long column of cavalry units marched out, signaling the start of the procession.

Behind them, hundreds of Astrakhan Kubans rode in red coats with long waists. Cossacks followed them, hot in pursuit, wearing blue jackets and carrying long spears. Then came representatives from the eastern end of the empire, colorful and Oriental looking: Khirghiz, Kalmyks, Bokharans, all wearing native red costumes and riding horses decorated to the hilt. They were followed by a deputation of Cossack officers and sixty members of the Russian nobility, all vying for the honor of the most splendid horse.

The columns of horsemen that poured down the street soon gave way to a procession of court officials, all dressed in gold. They were intermingled with escorts plumed with ostrich feathers in complicated headdresses, and court lackeys in triangular hats. The officials, the lackeys and the escorts all wore camisoles decorated in gold, giving the entire procession a golden sheen. Court musicians followed them, and the Master of Ceremonies followed the walkers in a carriage.

Back at the Petrovsky Palace, Alexei appeared on the porch of the Palace, and a cannon blast was fired. Alexei was brought a white horse wearing silver horseshoes. Taking a deep breath and trying not to hurt himself, Alexei swung himself up into the saddle. A second blast of the cannon sounded out. When Alexei rode out of the gates of the palace grounds, the cannon fired again. On cue, the thousands of church bells all across the city began ringing in unison. The crowd, hearing the cannon and the bells, began cheering, and a deafening "hurrah!" could be heard across the city.

At the gate, Alexei waited long enough to receive a report of Grand Duke Nicholas Nikolaievich, who was commanding the troops participating in the procession. "Everything is in place, Alyosha," Nicholas said.

"Good, let's get moving," Alexei replied.

Nicholas nodded and joined the Imperial Suite. He was now behind the ministers of the court and the military personnel who were following directly behind Alexei. Behind the Grand Dukes was a large number of adjutant generals and wing-generals, impressive in their white lambskin hats and dress coats with gold decorations. Boris, Alexander, and other foreign royalty rode with this group, each dressed in native uniforms. *That's a pretty colorful group there*, Alexei thought.

Alexei could hear the sounds of the bells and the cheers, and he felt the sun on his neck. For a second, he looked up into the deep blue of the sky and saw several doves soaring upward. As the cheers around him grew louder, Alexei began his march forward, his tears burning his eyes. *This is incredible*, he thought. *My coronation. It's happening. I've spent my whole life wondering if my hemophilia would prevent me from living this long.* His heart beat faster as he rode.

Behind Alexei, Alexandra and Marie Feodorovna rode in identical carriages. Alexandra's came first, and Marie's rode some distance behind her. Both golden carriages sparkled in the sun, and four pairs of decorated white horses pulled each one, their manes flowing in the wind. Two pages in court dress sat on the seats between the coachmen's benches and the body of the carriages. Two officers rode alongside each carriage, and six Kamer-pages on white horses rode behind them.

Behind Alexandra and Marie, several carriages followed. One carried Olga, Tatiana, Marie, and Anastasia, who waved to the crowd from the windows. The carriages behind them carried the family's other Grand Duchesses and Princesses. Alexandra and Marie's ladies-in-waiting also had their own decorated carriages. A squadron of Ulan guards rode behind them. Loud cheers went up as each carriage passed.

As Alexei glanced around at the thousands of people lining the route, they all seemed to be looking back at him and cheering wildly. The sound was deafening. Alexei stared around him as he rode, his eyes wide. All around him were masses of people, all packed in to watch the procession. Every window of every building was open, and people were standing at each window. Every balcony was crammed with people of all nationalities, wearing every type of uniform and dresses of every color. Magnificent hats also caught Alexei's eye from every angle.

As he continued to ride, Alexei finally became aware of just how long the procession really was. *I'm beginning to feel my saddle*, he thought. *Though I'm probably the only one- this wouldn't be an issue if I'd been able to ride more growing up.* Finally, however, Alexei could hear the beginning of the seventy-one gun salute that signaled his approach to the Kremlin. As the shots ended, a large deputation of merchants and workers' unions greeted Alexei. Behind them, a large group of Duma members greeted him, and Alexei saw Trotsky among them. Behind the Duma members was a group of aristocrats and court officials, also waiting to welcome their Tsar into the capital. Their colorful clothing and decorations were all set off against the red walls of the Kremlin.

Just inside the Kremlin walls, the Preobrazhensky guards that had begun the procession from the Petrovsky Palace waited, standing in rows that filled the square. Seeing this proud regiment made Alexei sit up taller in his saddle. All around them, the cathedral bells continued to ring, and the tension was palpable as everyone in the square waited to see Alexei. As he appeared at the gate, the Preobrazhensky Guards stood at attention, and a row of drummers pounded out a beat. Loud hurrahs continued to fill the air.

Alexei dismounted from his white horse and smiled at the guards in front of him. Their faces remained stern, but their eyes twinkled back. When Alexandra's carriage arrived, Alexei helped her out. Behind her, pages ran up and adjusted her train. When Marie's carriage entered the Kremlin and stopped, Alexei also supported her.

Marie leaned on her grandson. "My third coronation," she said. "I never thought I'd see this."

When Alexei looked over at Alexandra, he saw that she had tears coming down her face. Behind his grandmother, Alexei could see the rest of the carriages arriving, and he was glad that the rest of his family was there. The procession had been thrilling, but he was beginning to feel lightheaded and weak. Then he, Alexandra and Marie began their ascent into Uspensky Sobor for the coronation ceremony itself. The crowd around them roared, and Alexei wondered if he would go deaf. As he was about to enter the cathedral, the cannons fired another salute.

Inside the cathedral, Alexei, Alexandra and Marie began climbing the Red Staircase. Four pages held the trains of Alexandra and Marie's dresses. Cavalier Guards stood at attention along the steps, their faces unmoving and white as marble, their decorations glittering on their chests. At the top of the staircase, the master of ceremonies stood waiting to receive them, a baton in his hand. When Alexei, Alexandra and Marie reached the top of the staircase, they bowed again to the people that had gathered, and the crowds again roared again. Somewhere, despite all the noise, Alexei could hear the Court orchestra playing "God Save the Tsar."

Then, in an instant, everything fell silent. Gone were the bells, the cheers, the music. The silence was nearly a reverent one. The Metropolitan of Moscow stepped forward to greet Alexei, Alexandra and Marie. They entered the cathedral, following metropolitans, bishops and other clergy, who were singing a psalm as they entered. Court officials walked in front of them, carrying the Imperial insignia- the banner of the Empire, the orb, scepter and imperial mantles. The Metropolitans all carried crosses and icons, and Alexei could smell incense. Everything around him blazed in color, from the clergy's gold vestments to the court marshal's gilt staff, covered in jewels.

Once Alexei was inside the cathedral, the service began. The Metropolitan of St. Petersburg led the service, assisted by the Metropolitans of Moscow and Kiev. They were surrounded by bishops and choirs. The choirs began the ceremony's opening Te Deum, and the hymn's familiarity finally slowed Alexei's racing heart. The clergy led Alexei, Alexandra and Marie to the icons, which they kissed and knelt to. Then they sat on the three thrones next to the icons.

The Metropolitan of St. Petersburg approached Alexei. "What is Thy belief?" he intoned.

Alexei responded with the Nicene creed. "I believe in one God, the Father almighty, maker of heaven and earth, of all things visible and invisible," he began. He finished the creed in a loud, clear voice, but it sounded as if the words were coming from somewhere other than his body. *Where am I getting the strength to do this?* he wondered.

When he finished his statement of faith, the Metropolitan, accompanied by all of the bishops, said softly, "the blessing of the Holy Ghost be with thee."

The choirs began singing, and their majestic voices soared throughout the cathedral. When they finished, the Archdeacon of St. Petersburg read from the gospel. The Bishops of St. Petersburg and Kiev then approached Alexei with the Imperial insignia. They fastened the ermine cape and jeweled collar of St. Andrew around Alexei's neck a little tighter than was comfortable. Then Alexei knelt, and the Bishop of St. Petersburg placed his hands on Alexei's head in the form of a cross and blessed him.

The Bishop presented Alexei with his crown, round and with a cross on top whose jewels sparkled in the light of the cathedral. Alexei took the crown and placed it on his head, but he was unprepared for how heavy it felt. *What were you expecting?* he asked himself. *This thing has more than 2500 diamonds and two full rows of pearls. That ruby under the cross the largest in the world.*

Once the crown was securely on Alexei's head, the Bishop proclaimed him Tsar, and Alexei's heart raced again. When he took his orb and scepter from the Bishop, it was with slightly shaking hands. *That scepter is heavy too,* Alexei thought, *but no wonder- it's got that Orlov diamond in it, which is as large as an egg.*

For a second, the Bishop glanced back towards the empty chair on which the crown, orb and scepter had just sat. Alexei's eyes automatically followed his gaze, and he understood the bishop's hesitation. *If I were married, I would now be crowning my Empress,* Alexei thought. Once more he felt an absence. His concentration broken, Alexei's gaze traveled from the clergy to his family and the royal guests that were crowded into the cathedral. In a second, his eyes had located Ileana, looking small next to her parents. She gazed back at him, her eyes round with wonder. When she saw him looking at her, she smiled.

Then Alexei sat down on the throne, and the coronation was complete. Outside the cathedral, 101 guns fired in salute, and bells rang again across the city. In front of Alexei, the Bishop of St. Petersburg had regained his composure, and the service resumed. For the next two hours, icons were brought to Alexei to be kissed, and the bishops administered Communion. Then, for the only time in his life, Alexei was allowed to enter the Holy of Holies- the church's inner sanctum- which he did alone.

Grateful to be alone in silence after all the noise and hoopla, Alexei fell to his knees and prayed. *I need a wisdom that belies my age,* he begged. *I need the fortitude to make sound decisions that will benefit my country and my family. I also cannot do this alone- I need a wife that will support me. I need strong sons that will continue my legacy and come of age before my hemophilia separates me from them.* He took a deep breath and sent a supplicating look upwards. Then, calmed by the silence around him, Alexei stood.

Outside the lonely chamber, the service resumed when Alexei rejoined the clergy and his waiting family and guests. The Bishop of St. Petersburg anointed Alexei with holy oil. "Impressio doni Spiritus Sancti," he said. The Bishop then proceeded with the rest of the mass, finishing with a Benediction.

With the service over, Alexei's family lined up to congratulate him. Alexandra was first. Alexei hugged her, and she nearly sobbed. Marie was not much more composed than Alexandra had been, and after having to comfort them, Alexei was almost in tears himself.

Olga, Tatiana, Marie and Anastasia were next, and Alexei was relieved-his sisters were all genuinely smiling. Each kissed his hand and offered their congratulations, and Alexei found himself unprepared for their show of deference. Their husbands came next. "Congratulations," Alexander said, and as usual, Alexei found himself riveted by his brother-in-law's penetrating blue eyes.

"Thank you," Alexei said. He grasped little Peter's hand, and the boy squealed with delight.

The Grand Dukes were next. Nicholas Nikolaievich remained grave, his eyes focused on his young cousin. "Congratulations, Alyosha," he said.

"Thank you," Alexei replied. "I hope you're staying in Moscow for a few days, at least?"

"Yes, of course," Nicholas replied. "I wouldn't miss the festivities."

"Good," Alexei replied. Kirill, Boris and Andrei were next in line. "Thank you for all of your hard work," Alexei said. "Everything has gone by without a hitch."

"Thanks be to God," Kirill replied. "I am honored to be in such an important position at such an august time."

"Thank you for your kindness, Alyosha," Andrei added. "We're quite pleased to be here."

Behind them, Igor grinned at Alexei before kissing his hand. His brothers gathered around and did the same. "We're so happy to be here, sharing this with you," Gavril said sincerely.

"I'm glad I've gotten to be your ADC all this time," Igor said.

"This whole ceremony has been incredible- so moving," Ioann added.

"Ioann has had tears coming down his face the entire time," Konstantin teased his brother.

"So true," Ioann said. "And I have nothing to apologize for."

Ioann's oldest children, eight-year-old Vsevolod and nearly seven-year-old Ekaterina, stood next to him. Ekaterina curtsied deeply to Alexei, but Vsevolod, following his father's example, took Alexei's hand and kissed it. Alexei laughed and hugged both children. Behind them, Igor's mother and sisters- Grand Duchess Elizabeth Mavrakilevna and her daughters, Princesses Tatiana and Vera- kissed Alexei's hand and congratulated him.

Behind them, Ileana was on tiptoes, trying to see around the tall Konstantinovichi brothers. Alexei had to hold his laughter in at the sight. "I'm so glad to see you," he said as he hugged her.

Glad as he was to see his family and speak with them individually, Alexei was even happier for the next part of the ceremony- removing the regalia, including the heavy crown, and having dinner. *I haven't eaten in nearly four days,* he thought as his hunger burned a hole in his stomach. *If there's food, I'm there.*

He moved to the Palace's banquet hall, the Granovitaja Palata. The room was huge, so large that Alexei wondered if he was really seeing the wall on the other end. The room's low ceiling cast shadows everywhere. Oil lamps had been lit to alleviate the darkness, and their glowing light shone in circles around them. On one end of the room was a dais with three thrones, surrounded by a canopy. Alexei, Alexandra and Marie made their way there. As they walked, everyone around them bowed.

Members of the court stood opposite the thrones, and Alexei found himself increasingly aware of his legs as he approached his seat. For a second, the walls seemed to spin, and Alexei put a hand out towards a nearby chair. In an instant, a strong hand was grasping his arm and holding him upright. When Alexei blinked back into reality, Nicholas Nikolaievich was holding his arm.

"I'm alright," Alexei said when he caught his breath. "Thanks, Nikolasha."

Even so, Nicholas guided Alexei to one of the thrones before releasing him. "Your father had a similar incident at his coronation," he said. "Several days of fasting may be good for the spirit, but the body says otherwise."

"That's certainly true," Alexei said, enjoying the safety of his seat. As Nicholas made his way back to his place, Alexei looked around the room. The walls and ceiling were decorated with frescoes, and the floor was made of inlaid wood with floral designs on it.

Then Alexei saw his food being brought towards him, and his eyes focused on the plates as they were handed from one officer to another, all throughout the room, until they finally made their way to him, and the last officer holding the plate knelt as he placed it on the table. Alexei's mouth watered as he smelled the food in front of him. Finally, Alexei called for some wine, which was the signal for the members of the court to leave, which they did, bowing as they disappeared. The banquet's guests took their seats, and their food was soon served.

Alexei, relieved, took a sip of wine and felt it immediately. Putting his wine glass down, he reached for a glass of water and drained it. It was immediately refilled by a servant, and Alexei drank a second glass. "Be careful," Marie warned her grandson. "The day Sasha was crowned, I found out the hard way that it's better not to eat too quickly."

Alexei laughed, even as he tried- and failed- to picture his huge grandfather sitting in the seat he currently occupied.

Then a toast was offered by the Chamberlain of the Court. "To a long life and a long reign," he said, holding his glass high. As was customary, the toast was drunk in silence, but Alexei could see the smiles and warmth of his sisters and their husbands all directed towards him, and he grinned in reply.

That night, all of Moscow was illuminated by strings of light. Strings covered the Kremlin, illuminating its architecture with green, red and white lights. *I've never seen anything so beautiful,* Alexei thought as he stepped onto a balcony of the Petrovsky Palace to take in the sight. Crowds of people still clogged the streets, and upon seeing Alexei, they all cheered. Alexei acknowledged the ovation with a wave.

A minute later, fireworks exploded across the sky. Huge balls of light in every color stretched from horizon to horizon. Alexei's face split with a grin, even as he was sure he was about to go deaf from the sound. In a second, Anastasia appeared next to Alexei, her eyes round with wonder. "This is incredible!" she said.

Alexei nodded, his eyes on the sky above them, where the tails of the last burst of fireworks still hung in the sky, trailing fire of every color. The rest of their siblings joined them- Marie and Nicholas first, followed by Olga, Alexander, Tatiana and Boris. Alexander held a lit cigar in one hand, but it was Boris who held something closer to Alexei's heart: a huge bottle of chilled vodka and several chilled shot glasses. "Congratulations, Alyosha," Boris said, handing him a full glass.

"Hear, hear," Alexander said as Boris passed around the shot glasses and poured from the huge bottle. "These past few days have been incredible, especially today."

"Indeed," Olga said, raising her glass. Tatiana, Marie and Anastasia did the same. "To the newest Russian tsar," Olga said. Alexei grinned. They all drank.

"I'm so happy you're all here," he said, looking from their familiar faces to the next round of fireworks that were exploding in the sky. When he looked back at his family again, the light from the fireworks had lit up everyone's faces. Boris refilled Alexei's glass, and as Alexei drank again, he could feel both the vodka and his exhaustion coursing through his veins.

When the round of fireworks had died down, Anastasia looked Alexei. "So, where's your shadow?" she asked.

Genuinely bewildered by the question, Alexei looked behind him, expecting some shadow from the fireworks.

Anastasia made a face at him. "I meant Ileana," she said.

"She's with her family, at some of the royal apartments in the city," Alexei said. "What did you expect?"

Anastasia looked back at the sky. "I don't know," she said. "But she's always keeping an eye on you, you're always keeping an eye on her."

"I thought you liked her," Alexei said.

"I do," Anastasia replied. "And I sort of expected her to be here."

"She's with her family, I'm with mine," Alexei replied, glad that the next round of fireworks was starting.

Alexei spent the next three days receiving congratulatory deputations from every corner of Russia and abroad. In particular, he eyed American President Warren Harding and First Lady Florence Harding with interest. After greeting them cordially, his eyes fixed on Vice President Calvin Coolidge and his wife, Grace. "Thank you all for coming," he said. "It is my honor to host you."

"We are the ones honored to be here," President Harding replied. "We hope you will return the honor by visiting America sometime soon."

"I'm planning on it," Alexei replied.

The next day was the luncheon with the Duma representatives that Alexei had asked Kirill to arrange. Leon Trotsky was among the first delegates to arrive, and for the first time since the coronation proceedings had begun, Alexei felt the presence of Gorvenko and the other palace guards.

For all his smiling of the past couple of days, Alexei's mirth now felt forced. *Maybe Kirill was right about this,* he thought, remembering his cousin's trepidation. *Trotsky makes me nervous.* The sight of Gorvenko eyeing Trotsky hatefully made Alexei feel a little better, but even so, he sought to reassure his police chief. "Relax," he said. "I don't want Trotsky thinking you're going to kill him."

"No, *you* relax," Gorvenko advised. "It's your coronation. It's my job to make sure you get through it safely."

Under the watchful eyes of the police, Alexei made his rounds, going from one table to the next, speaking with all of the delegates, making sure not to spend too long at any one table. When the food started coming out, Alexei poured himself a glass of wine from a bottle on his table. Looking around, he noticed that the delegates were pouring themselves drinks that varied by political leanings- the monarchists and conservatives all poured themselves wine, but the Communists poured themselves vodka.

Then Trotsky stood, a shot of vodka in his hand. The room got quiet.

Alexei tried to remain calm. Trotsky raised his glass. "A toast," he said. "To Your Imperial Majesty's health. May these coronation festivities be but the beginning of a long and fruitful reign. May we see the continuation of the wise policies you have already begun."

The room burst into applause, and the delegates rose to their feet, holding their drinks. Alexei gave Trotsky a nod and raised his own glass. Everyone in the room drank. When the meal began after several more rounds of toasts, Alexei kept an eye on Trotsky and the other communists. They all downed shot after shot of fine Russian vodka, barely touching anything else. *They can really drink,* Alexei thought.

The next day brought visits and congratulations from more delegations, including a Polish delegation whose importance Alexei realized as soon as they were introduced. Their leader was Stanislaw Czartoryski, and Alexei nodded immediately upon hearing the name. "Your ancestors served Alexander I," he said, sizing up the man in front of him. *He doesn't look more than ten years older than me.*

Stanislaw nodded as his sharp black eyes focused on Alexei. He had thick black hair that he wore slightly long. "Adam Jerzy Czartoryski was my great-great-grandfather," he confirmed. "We hope that Your Imperial Majesty might visit Warsaw in the near future."

"I'm planning on it," Alexei said. "The Polish question has always loomed large for us Romanovs."

Stanislaw introduced Alexei to his younger brother, Teodor. Teodor shared Stanislaw's thick black hair, but had cut it short. His blue eyes danced in his face, and his face radiated excitement at everything that was going on around him. *He is definitely younger than I am,* Alexei thought. As the conversation went on, Alexei found himself liking Stanislaw. *He would make a good ally,* he thought.

When the day was over, the coronation celebrations were officially over as well. Despite the magnificence, Alexei was relieved. That night, many revelers were still out in the streets, but it was also obvious that many visitors were on their way home. For awhile, Alexei watched Olga and Tatiana pack their trunks before Ileana and her family arrived for one last goodbye.

Alexei, Anastasia and Ileana went to one of the Palace's balconies to watch the crowds below them. It was a mild night, and Alexei felt the warm breeze swish through his hair. Slowly, he inhaled the smell of the coming summer, and felt relief, and a certain sadness, that the coronation ceremonies were over. "I'm glad your family came over," Alexei told Ileana. "I was wondering if I'd see you again before you went home."

"These last few days have really been spectacular," Ileana said. "It definitely matches the stories my mother tells of your father's coronation."

"That's too bad," Alexei said. "I was hoping to exceed those stories."

They both laughed, and Anastasia rolled her eyes and stuck her tongue out at her brother.

A large, gilt carriage pulled up across the street from them, and Stanislaw and Teodor Czartoryski exited the building in front of it. "Hey, it's the Poles," Ileana said.

"You met them?" Alexei asked.

Ileana nodded. "A couple of times now- first at one of the balls, then at one of the operas, then at a luncheon."

"Sounds like you really got around the city," Anastasia said.

"There was a lot going on," Ileana replied. "I wanted to do everything. Luckily, Mama has a lot of energy, so we did a *lot*."

Alexei watched as the Czartoryskis got into their carriage. The driver cracked his whip, and the stately horses in front of the carriage jumped forward. "What did you think of Stanislaw and Teodor?" he asked Ileana.

"Stanislaw is a politician, through and through," Ileana said. "He definitely made a beeline for Mama and Papa. Teodor is training for politics but preferred the opera and dancing."

"He sounds a lot like me," Anastasia said.

Alexei grinned at her. "Maybe I should arrange your marriage to him," he said teasingly.

"Don't even try it," Anastasia warned him seriously.

Alexei looked back to the scene in front of him, with the buildings of Moscow all decked out in festive gear, and the many people below him in the streets, dancing and celebrating. *I am tsar now,* he thought, *and the whole world is celebrating with me.*

CHAPTER 13

Alexei spent the five days after his coronation in Moscow, attending to some last matters. Those matters included a flurry of telegrams with the Polish delegation as he made arrangements to meet with Stanislaw Czartoryski and other members of the Polish aristocracy.

"The conversation will be about Polish independence," Michael said.

"It won't be an easy meeting," Alexei agreed. "That's why I was hoping you'd be there. Stolypin and Witte have agreed to meet me in Warsaw too."

Michael nodded. "That's a good idea. Don't worry, I'll be there." He eyed his nephew for another minute before asking, "so what's your strategy going to be? The Poles have wanted independence forever."

"Yes, they have," Alexei replied. "And if Russia had been on the losing side of the Great War, the Versailles Treaty may have given it to them."

"That's only speculation, Alyosha. It's still our land."

Alexei sighed. "My point is that it may be time to grant their independence," he said. "Maybe it doesn't make as much sense to have an empire that spans one-sixth of the globe as it did two hundred years ago."

Michael looked at him, aghast. "You'd willingly give away all of our territory?"

"It's not all of our territory, it's just Poland, and it's not completely willingly. We may have been able to use force to keep the empire together when Catherine the Great sat on the throne, but having just been through a huge war across Europe, I'd hate to have that kind of war inside our borders."

"You think they'd fight for their independence?"

"They might. I'd rather give it to them in exchange for their allegiance and strong diplomatic ties."

"You're putting a lot of faith in the Poles," Michael said. "They could just as easily be hostile because they've been under our yoke for so long."

"That's why I'm having this meeting," Alexei said. "Maybe we'll get a sense of how they'd act."

It took Grand Duke Dmitri Pavlovich the entirety of the five days that Alexei spent in Moscow to set an appointment with him. By then, Alexei was wondering, half-jokingly, whether Dmitri had made it back for the coronation at all. By the time Alexei made it to the appointed drawing-room, Dmitri was already seated and examining the biscuits in front of him. A steaming cup of tea sat next to his elbow. He jumped up as Alexei arrived. "Sorry the tea's already on the table," he said. "I couldn't stop the servants from putting it out."

"They're enthusiastic," Alexei said with a smile as he waved Dmitri back into his chair. "Besides, I'm a little late."

"I'm sure the job is keeping you busy," Dmitri replied sympathetically. A servant came forward to pour Alexei's tea, and Dmitri shifted his attention back to the basket of biscuits in front of him long enough to take one and offer Alexei one as well.

"It is a lot of work, but sometimes I almost think it's worth it." Alexei laughed as he held up his plate to accept the biscuit that Dmitri was holding out. Then he inhaled the scent of the freshly baked bread.

Dmitri smiled in return, but his vacant stare chilled Alexei. "I don't envy you, Alyosha," he said. "Being tsar is not a job I'd ever want, especially at such a young age."

"What job would you want?" Alexei asked.

Dmitri looked confused.

"You're young, wealthy and good-looking," Alexei clarified. "What do you want to do with your life?"

Dmitri shrugged. "Who says I have to do anything?"

Alexei smiled. "Honesty. I like that."

"I am serious, though," Dmitri said as he sipped his tea and chewed his biscuit.

"Are you glad to be back in Russia, at least?" Alexei asked, trying to draw his cousin out. *Olga was once very interested in marrying him,* Alexei thought. *I wonder what she saw in him besides his looks.*

Dmitri paused. "It's certainly nice to see my family," he said finally. "I missed my father and sister."

"But?"

"The climate in Persia was good for my health."

Alexei nodded at that. "You do look better than I've seen you look in years," he admitted.

"I could say the same of you," Dmitri replied. "And announcing your hemophilia to the whole country- that was brave."

Alexei shrugged. "I thought it was the right thing to do." For a moment, he stared out the window, watching huge white clouds scuttle across a blue sky. Then he looked back at Dmitri. "Are you still so interested in horses? I haven't forgotten that you represented Russia in equestrian at the Olympics."

"That was nearly ten years ago!"

"I'm still impressed by it. Your father said you continued training while in exile."

Dmitri nodded.

"Would you be interested in continuing that, now that you're back in Russia?" Alexei asked. "Uncle Sergei ran a horse farm on Ilinskoe before he left you the property. It could be your base of operations."

Dmitri looked uncertain. "What do you want of me, Alyosha?" he asked.

"I want you to be happy," Alexei said, as he continued to feel the warmth of his teacup against his hands. "But ruling Russia is difficult work, and I'm trying to get the family to help as much as possible."

"I can help you rule Russia by running a horse farm outside of Moscow?"

"Having Russian athletes compete in the Olympics would make us look good, and you'd be involved with society. You're obviously talented, and I'd hate to see your wealth and good looks put you on a path to complacency."

"My father thinks I'm already on that path."

"I didn't talk to him about this, I promise." They both laughed. Then Alexei said, "I'm serious about this, Mitya. Please consider it."

Two days later, Dmitri left Pavel's palace to have dinner with Felix Youssoupov. "It is so good to see you, Mitya," Felix said as Dmitri was led into his library at the Volkov Palace.

Dmitri kissed him and then his wife Irina. "Thank you for having me," he said.

"Our pleasure," Irina said. "Both Felix and I are so glad to be back in Russia, and to able to entertain in our own home again."

It's partially because of me that you weren't able to, Dmitri thought, but he left the words unsaid as Felix and Irina's daughters raced into the room. "Your girls have gotten so big."

"I know," Irina replied. "It scares me sometimes. Have you even met Sasha?"

"No, I haven't," Dmitri replied.

"How would he have?" Felix asked. "She was born in Rakitnoye."

"Born in exile," Irina said, shaking her head. "It's nothing I would have wanted."

"At least you were exiled to one of your estates," Dmitri said mildly. "There are worse punishments."

Hours later, after they had eaten dinner, Felix and Dmitri sought refuge in the palace's newest addition, a porch whose open windows afforded a comfortable breeze. It was a pleasant evening, and the weather was mild. Felix lit a cigarette and took a deep breath. "It is so nice to be home," he said. "Our years in exile felt very long." They were silent for awhile. Felix continued to smoke, enjoying the way the evening breeze played with his hair. "It's nights like that I'd rather be in the Palace on the Moika. At least we could take advantage of the weather by walking along the Canal."

Dmitri played with his cigarette but did not light it. "How can you live there, after what we did?"

"You regret killing Rasputin?"

"I'm not sorry he's dead, but I am sorry for my role in it."

Felix shook his head and looked out the window. "I would do it again, and again- as many times as it took to rid Russia of that scourge." He looked back at Dmitri. "I believe in Russia and I believe in the monarchy, and I would do anything to preserve both."

"My loyalties are the same, but I can't believe I killed over it."

Felix shook his head again, his disbelief evident. Then he changed the subject. "I heard you had a meeting with Alexei," he said. "What did he ask of you?"

"What makes you think he asked anything of me?"

"Well, he asked about my family's mines and factories, as well as our mills and oil fields."

"What about them?" Dmitri asked, and Felix could tell that he was genuinely interested.

"He wanted to know how the family runs them, how many people we employ, that sort of thing. He's looking to industrialize the country."

"And he wants your help in doing that?"

"Well, I have the money to invest in new factories, to develop the oil fields, that kind thing. The country certainly needs the investment, and if it leads to more jobs and better lives for the peasants, I'm happy to support it."

"Hmmm," Dmitri said.

"So he didn't ask anything of you?" Felix pressed.

"Of course he did," Dmitri said. "He was impressed by my equestrian turnout at the Olympics and wants me to train athletes."

"Guess our little Alyosha is turning out to be smarter than we thought."

Dmitri shrugged, his disinclination obvious.

"I think it's a good idea," Felix said. "Do you have any other plans?"

"No, and that was Alexei's argument too."

Felix smiled. "Think of it as a condition of our exile being revoked," he said. "We're investing in Russia's future at the behest of the Tsar!"

Dmitri shrugged. "I can't say I'm as enthusiastic as you are."

"You don't have to run out and start tomorrow. Take some time and think about it."

That same night, Alexei, Anastasia and Alexandra boarded the imperial train for Skerenvizi. "I'm surprised Igor isn't here," Alexandra said.

"He'll be joining us in Warsaw," Alexei replied. "But for now, he and the rest of his family are going back to Pavlovsk. He needs the rest as much as we do."

Alexei wanted to spend more time with his mother and sister, but as soon as he was in his own compartment, his bed looked too inviting to pass up, and soon he was asleep. When he awoke the next morning, he expected to see the greenery of the countryside, and plenty of the grass remained green. The forests lacked the density that Alexei remembered, however, and no large game moved within the trees.

When they arrived at their estate, Alexei was glad to be off the train and into the palace. Later that afternoon, he arranged a carriage ride for the three of them. "At least we'll get to see the property," he said. "Even if I do wish I were able to go hunting, like the family used to do in prior generations. Those hunts were really legendary."

Alexandra nodded as the carriage pulled away from the Palace, but she remained silent.

"What's wrong, Mama?" Alexei asked.

Alexandra sighed. "At the end of the war, there were reports that the Germans had really destroyed these woods and the game in them," she said. "I was almost too afraid to return here for fear that it was true."

"The woods seemed mysteriously still as our train arrived," Alexei agreed.

"I noticed that too," Anastasia said. "I remember seeing huge elk and other animals when we used to come here, and I didn't see any this time."

As he looked around, Alexei realized that the woods were indeed empty. Many trees were burned, and their blackened forms looked like huge monsters, even in the daylight. Smaller saplings and grass had begun to fill in the emptiness, but the new growth could not hide the destruction- to the contrary, it was so new that no flowers bloomed. Just as obviously, no animals filled the woods, and as the imperial carriage creaked through the burnt trees, it seemed to be the only thing moving. Alexei opened the window of the carriage and heard little but the sound of the wind rustling through the tops of the burnt trees. Few birds sang.

Alexei felt his heart sink. Looking at his mother and sister, he saw that their eyes were filled with tears. "We made so many happy memories here," Alexandra said. "So much has changed."

Back at the estate, Alexei could see just how much the building itself had fallen into disrepair. *It's really going to take a lot of work and money just to get the Palace back to its original condition,* he thought. *I'm not sure it's worth it without the hunting possibilities.* By the end of their planned week there, Alexei's spirits were subdued, and he thought the same was true of his usually high-spirited sister. He was glad to leave for Spala, but his relief changed to further disappointment as the family settled into the Spala estate.

I never realized what a dark and gloomy Palace this is, Alexei thought. *My memories of the last time we were here are completely taken up by my hemophiliac attack.* He looked around, first standing outside the Palace, and then inside. *It's more of a large wooden villa than a Palace, and it's really dark inside. If the weather's bad at all, it's really going to be gloomy in here.*

The dining room on the ground floor was large enough to accommodate the family, but Alexei had to turn on the electric lights even in the daytime. The bedrooms and the dressing rooms also seemed dark, and Alexei found himself in his mother's rooms most of the time because they were among the few light rooms in the building. When Alexei finally plucked up the courage to go into his father's study two days after his arrival, he was pleased to find that the room was as bright as his mother's. *I guess this is my study now,* Alexei thought.

Alexei was glad for the hours of quiet time, which he spent reading reports and legislation. He did most of the work either reclining or lying in bed, so that he could apply a warm compress to his groin, which remained sore after the long procession into Moscow. *I will never be a normal tsar,* Alexei thought, and a feeling of sadness washed over him.

On June 1, Gorvenko reported to Alexei. "Your Imperial Majesty, we've been following Trotsky's movements since he became head of the Communist party," he said.

"Anything interesting?" Alexei asked.

Gorvenko nodded. "He's been leaving Russia a lot, and traveling all over eastern Europe, inspecting factories, meeting with workers and union leaders. He's been in Hungary most recently. We think he's trying to incite a revolution."

"Interesting that he's doing it everywhere but Russia," Alexei replied. "Though his absence from the Duma hasn't gone unnoticed. His Communist colleagues have had to lead the discussion of their legislation without him."

"With Lenin and Stalin gone, he may think he has less of a chance in Russia right now, or he may think that once the smaller countries around us fall, we will too."

"Or he's trying to start a revolution all over, all at once."

"If so, he's been most successful in Hungary. There have been large numbers of strikes there, and a lot of unrest. But the country has been a mess since the War, so that may be Trotsky's advantage."

Alexei sighed. "That seems to be a theme these days," he said.

When the family made the hour-long trip into Warsaw the next day, they were driven in two cars. Alexei, Michael and Igor were in the first one, and Alexandra and Anastasia were in the second with Natasha and George. *I'm really glad the Poles arranged social time for the family,* Alexei thought as they drove. *Mama really doesn't get out much anymore.*

In Warsaw, they were treated to an elaborate luncheon in the Czartoryski family's Potocki Palace. As they were led inside, Alexei eyed the unfamiliar palace, with its grey exterior and red mansard roof. After the luncheon, Alexei, Michael, Igor, Witte and Stolypin joined Stanislaw and a host of Polish diplomats at a long table in a rectangular-shaped room on the first floor. Several pitchers of water sat in the center of the tables, and glasses sat at each chair. Upstairs, the rest of Alexei's family joined Teodor Czartoryski and several women of the Polish aristocracy for a tour of the Palace and other entertainments.

"Thank you all for coming," Stanislaw said. Igor and Sergei Kamensky sat behind the table, along the wall of the room, taking minutes of the meeting. "I'm glad you've traveled all the way to Warsaw, and with such an esteemed group. It speaks well of how seriously you take this discussion. It's a gravity we Poles share."

"No doubt," Alexei replied. "The Polish question has been one we Russians have contemplated since Catherine the Great."

"Rumor has it she was contemplating Polish independence," Stanislaw replied, seeing no reason not to get right to the point. "And, as you noted at your coronation, Your Imperial Majesty, my forefathers were active under Alexander I, trying to get the same mission accomplished."

"I'm well aware that you seek your country's independence," Alexei replied. "But I would like to see stability in the region. We have many enemies in common, internal and external. I can't imagine that any of them would be easy for a new state to navigate."

"Poland would hardly be a new state. We have a long history of independence and our own institutions of government and justice."

"Institutions which have been subjugated to Russia for centuries now."

Stanislaw took a deep breath and looked away, but he did not dispute Alexei's point.

Alexei glanced around him, and saw Michael leaning forward tensely. His attitude was mirrored in their Polish counterparts across the table. "I don't doubt that you could get your state back up and running, but it would take time and strong leadership, not to mention practicalities such as taxation and voting," Alexei said.

"If we received our independence, Russia would not have to concern herself with how we run our government," Stanislaw said. "Our leaders are strong and patriotic."

"If Poland received its independence, both it and Russia would face common threats," Alexei replied. "That is my concern."

"What are your biggest fears?"

"A stronger Germany that harbors the same aggressions it did in 1914, for one. Could Poland mount an army and fight for its borders?"

"What internal issues worry you?"

"We, too, are still rebuilding from the war, much like Poland is."

"Yes, that is one challenge our nation faces, I cannot deny that."

"The Communist threat is also large. Lenin and Stalin are out of the picture, but Trotsky still has plans of some sort."

Stanislaw looked away and swallowed hard. Suddenly, tension seemed to roll off him in waves.

Alexei leaned forward. "What is it?" he asked. Stanislaw did not answer. "Stanislaw?" Alexei prompted. "Is there something about Trotsky that I should know?"

Stanislaw took a deep breath. He poured himself a glass of water from the pitcher in front of him. Other than the sound of the moving water, the room was so silent that Alexei could hear footsteps on the floor above them. Finally, Stanislaw spoke again. "Mr. Trotsky was here to see me last week," he said. "He wants a Communist revolution, and he's been working all across Europe to get it started."

"And he wants it to start in Poland?"

"Either Poland or Russia."

"Damn him!" Alexei burst out. He shook his head. "While I don't deny that Polish independence makes a certain amount of sense, having

Poland as a strong ally against the likes of both Trotsky and Germany would be one condition of my granting that independence."

The discussion lasted for four hours, and when it was over, the diplomats and aristocrats dispersed back to their own homes. Then Stanislaw took Alexei outside to the Palace's courtyard, and Alexei was glad for the fresh air and the trees.

"I'm not opposed to close ties with Russia," Stanislaw said as they finished walking and stood with their backs to the Palace, looking out over the towering trees and dense leaf canopies. "But my priority is independence."

"I understand that," Alexei replied. "And while I support an independent Polish state, I would rather see Poland remain a part of Russia than see an independent Poland become our enemy."

Stanislaw shook his head. "I would spend every ounce of my being ensuring that Poland didn't fall to either Germany or Communism."

"And yet you're unwilling to fully commit to Russian ties unless you first get full independence, no strings attached."

"Only because I have seen Russian policy against Poland too many times, Your Imperial Majesty."

"Is there anything I can do to sweeten the deal?" Alexei asked. He broke into a grin as he remembered his conversation with Anastasia at his coronation. "Perhaps I can offer my sister as a wife?"

Suddenly, Stanislaw simultaneously jumped and gasped. Alexei, not knowing what was happening, jumped back and threw his arms over his head. Nothing else happened, though, except that Stanislaw continued to gasp. Slowly, Alexei lowered his hands and stood up straight, looking at his Polish counterpart with concern.

Stanislaw stood still, covered from head to toe in water. Water dripped from every part of his body and formed a puddle at his feet. One ice cube sat on his shoulder, another on each of his shoes. His hair, so perfectly curled a moment ago, now hung limply to his shoulders. His uniform, previously so perfectly starched, was now plastered to his skin.

Alexei spun around to look at the Palace. Directly above them, one of the Palace's second floor windows was open. Anastasia stood just inside the window, an empty bucket in her hand. "What did you do?" Alexei yelped. He looked back at Stanislaw, who was slowly regaining his composure.

A few servants rushed out to help Stanislaw, who managed to get his tongue working again. "I'm alright," he croaked.

Alexei dashed into the Palace. When he got upstairs, Anastasia was racing down the hall, the bucket still in her hands. Alexei raced after her and grabbed her arm. "What is wrong with you?" he yelled.

"Nothing!" Anastasia said.

"You dumped an entire bucket of water on him!" Alexei shook his sister. "How could you do such a thing?"

"Alexei," Alexandra said uncomfortably from behind them.

Alexei ignored his mother and continued to shake Anastasia. "Answer me!" he demanded.

"I don't want to marry Stanislaw," Anastasia finally managed to stutter, shocked by the force of her brother's anger.

"I wasn't even being serious!" Alexei shouted. "You shouldn't have been listening to our conversation!" He let her go with a shove.

Anastasia stumbled backwards until she hit the wall behind her, which she leaned on for support until she had regained her balance. Then she stared at Alexei defiantly.

"I can't believe you're still playing pranks, especially on an aristocratic diplomat!" Alexei yelled. "It was fine when we were kids, but we're not kids anymore." He shook his head. "How am I ever going to marry you off? No one will put up with you!"

"I don't want to get married," Anastasia replied.

"That's not an option, Nastia, you know that," Alexei said, finally calming down slightly. "Besides, I don't want you to be moping around as an old maid, ten years from now, complaining about being unmarried." He turned around, and saw the rest of his family standing in the hallway, looking uncomfortable. Sergei in particular looked like he was about to flee. Alexei took a deep breath. "Come," he said. "We should be going, and I need to check on Stanislaw before we depart."

Outside, Alexei watched as George, Natasha, Anastasia and Alexandra piled into the first motorcar that was waiting to take them back to Spala. Michael, Igor and Sergei got into the second car, and Alexei looked at Stanislaw. "I'm sorry," he said genuinely.

"You can't always control the actions of others," Stanislaw replied.

Alexei could tell his pride was wounded. *I'm ashamed by Anastasia's behavior too,* he thought. "The worst of it is that I was joking about the marriage."

"I know you were," Stanislaw replied. "I'm promised elsewhere as it is, and I think that even Teodor's eyes have been drawn elsewhere too."

"Really?" Alexei asked, amused.

"To one of the princesses he met at your coronation, actually."

"Really?" Alexei said again, seriously this time. "Who?"

"One of the Romanians. There's one that's close to his age."

Alexei bit his lip. "Ileana?" he asked, his chest constricting.

Stanislaw nodded. "Yes, Ileana," he said. "I have no idea whether her parents would allow that, but..." He shrugged.

Alexei looked back at the nearby cars. The closest one still had its door open, and a Cossack guard was standing at attention next to it. Inside the car, Michael was watching, and Alexei could tell he was listening to the conversation. He looked back at Stanislaw. "I'm amenable to continuing our conversation about Poland's future," he said. "I'll leave my sister home next time."

Finally, Stanislaw smiled. "Don't worry," he said. "This was the beginning of the conversation, not the end."

The drive back to Spala was a silent one. Despite how much of a dialogue he had had with the Poles, Alexei's thoughts focused on Anastasia's behavior and Teodor's interest in Ileana. *I have more to do than just political diplomacy*, he realized. *I need to get back to St. Petersburg.*

CHAPTER 14

Four days after his return to St. Petersburg, Alexei was working at his desk when a servant announced Marie's arrival. Alexei stood up and grinned. "I'd forgotten you were coming, Masha," he admitted sheepishly.

"You have a lot on your mind," Marie replied. "Mama told me what happened in Warsaw." She looked amused.

"And yet, from a state perspective, Nastia's behavior was probably the least of it."

"Still, I doubt her shenanigans make your job easier."

"Have you told Nastia that? I think she could use the perspective."

"I'll tell her, don't worry," Marie replied. "We're spending the afternoon together, having lunch and then shopping downtown. There'll be plenty of time to win her over, even to something as weighty as marriage."

"You'd talk to Nastia about getting married? She hasn't listened to me once."

"I know," Marie said. "But she acted as an intercessor between me and Mama when I wanted to get married. Repaying the favor is the least I could do."

Alexei smiled. "I appreciate your efforts," he said. He looked at his watch. "It's early. What are you doing between now and lunch?"

"Paying a visit to the factory and hospital of which I am patroness."

"I'd forgotten that you'd funded a factory," Alexei said. "The women of our family have always been involved in nursing and hospitals, but a factory? That's new territory."

"It's a modern world, Alyosha," Marie replied, a grin lighting up her face. "Besides, this factory makes medical supplies, so it's connected to the hospital."

"That's very smart," Alexei said. "Well, don't let me keep you. I'm really glad you're involved with Russian society."

"I'm a Grand Duchess," Marie said. "And I don't want anyone to forget it." They both laughed, and Marie left.

A week later, Alexei was rushing again, packing his bags, getting the Imperial train ready, and making certain that extra trains full of hospital supplies, food and other supplies were also being readied for the trip into Bucharest. Alexei used one hand to shield his eyes from the summer sun pouring through the window as he used his other hand to continue packing.

"What do you expect to accomplish?" Michael asked, watching his nephew's frenzied actions.

"A betrothal would be nice."

"It's not going to happen, Alyosha," Michael said reasonably. "Ileana's only thirteen. Even if she has other suitors, Mimi and Nando won't give you a firm answer."

"It's still worth the journey," Alexei replied. "I've never even told them I'm interested."

"I think it's obvious that you are, and that the interest is mutual on Ileana's part."

Alexei stopped packing for a moment and looked at his uncle. "You think I shouldn't go?"

Michael sighed as Alexandra appeared in the doorway next to him. "I guess it couldn't hurt," he said. "I just wouldn't expect the outcome that you want for another few years." He looked at Alexandra. "You're going with him, right?"

Alexandra nodded. "And if Nicky were alive, he'd be coming too."

"That's why I invited Misha to come with us," Alexei said. He looked at Michael. "Are you coming?"

"Yes," Michael said.

Two days later, Alexei sat in Cotroceni Palace in Bucharest, having tea with Ileana, Nicholas and Mignon. Ileana shifted in her seat, and then cringed as a loud whack, and then another, sounded near her feet. "Sorry," she said. She jumped up and started rearranging things on the floor.

"What happened?" Alexei asked, standing briefly so that he could see what Ileana was doing.

"I knocked over all of my schoolbooks," Ileana said sheepishly.

"If you didn't stack them like the Tower of Pisa right next to your feet, you wouldn't knock them over so easily," Nicholas reprimanded his sister.

"You could also read fewer books," Mignon advised. Neither she nor Nicholas had moved at all.

Alexei eyed them, then realized they were teasing. "Does this happen often?"

"All the time," Ileana said. She finished straightening her books and sat back at the table. A warm breeze blew through an open window nearby, and a couple of birds sang a happy tune. Both Ileana and Alexei turned towards the window. "I'm so glad he weather has improved," Ileana said as she looked back at Alexei. "Everything has started to bloom again. We should go for a ride later."

When tea was over, Alexei snuck upstairs to where Michael and Alexandra were meeting with Marie and Ferdinand. For a minute, Alexei leaned towards the closed door, trying to hear the conversation inside.

"She's too young, Misha, and a lot can happen in a few years," Ferdinand was saying. "I'm not going to promise anything."

There was a silence, and Alexei could hear Michael and Alexandra standing up. Not wanting the conversation to end like that, Alexei knocked on the door, then pushed it open. Michael looked at Alexei, then back at Marie and Ferdinand. The Romanian monarchs had slightly guilty looks on their faces.

"She's had other suitors," Alexei said, ignoring Michael's subtle gesture telling him to keep quiet.

"And we told them the same thing," Ferdinand replied. "We're not going to promise a thirteen-year-old into marriage."

"I know it's unusual," Alexei said. "I wouldn't even be asking, except for my hemophilia, and the fact that my father's sudden death left me on the throne at such a young age."

"We're sympathetic, Alyosha," Marie said. "And Ileana likes you so we're open to an engagement several years from now. But I was a few years older than she is now when I married Nando, and I still felt too young. I'm trying to save my daughter from a similar fate."

The next day, Alexei was on the train back to St. Petersburg. He sat near the window in the dining car, not wanting to be in his own compartment, not wanting to be in the train at all, really, but not wanting to be back at home yet either. *Home is in another palace in another city*, he thought. *It's all the same.*

Michael sat down next to Alexei as the train continued to move forward, and Alexei did not even have to look at his uncle to know who it was. "That trip was a bust," he said as he continued to stare at the sunlight-dappled trees.

"I told you not to get your hopes up," Michael replied. "But, on the positive side, Mimi and Nando are aware of Ileana's interest in you."

"So? She'll be thirty before they let her marry." Alexei folded his arms across his chest and stared glumly at Michael.

Michael looked amused. "They won't wait *that* long."

"But it'll definitely be several years. I may not have that long. My hemophilia could kill me at any time."

Michael looked away and swallowed. "You can't think like that," he said. "You have to act as if you have a long future- both for your family and for your country." He heaved a breath. "Now, what about those telegrams you were sending the British before we left? Did anything come of that?"

"Oh, yeah," Alexei said, unfolding his arms and sitting up straight. "I'm still trying to negotiate for political alliances and financial investment so that we can continue rebuilding Russian's infrastructure. We've been discussing it by phone and telegram, but the time has come to be in the same room together."

Michael nodded. "Are they coming to St. Petersburg?"

"Yes, next week."

"Good," Michael said. He stood up. "Stop moping. Everything will work out, I promise."

When the British arrived in St. Petersburg a week later, Alexei met the delegation at the train station and was glad to see that George was traveling, not only with his official party, but also with his son Henry. Back at the Winter Palace, Alexei made sure that his cousins were comfortable and served the best tea possible. Many of the Palace's windows had been cleaned and opened to take full advantage of some of the few fine days of the St. Petersburg summer.

The conversation then moved into Alexei's study and a more formal atmosphere. After more than five hours discussing the state of Europe after the war and how to improve it, Alexei was ready to locate his bed and stay there for a few days. George, however, had one more topic he wanted to discuss. "Alexei, let me be frank," he said. "I want to make sure that my sons make the right decisions in the marriage market. In particular, I feel that Henry could use some help in that area."

Alexei shot Henry a look of amusement and found that his cousin was groaning. "Come on, Father," Henry whispered.

George's eyes never left Alexei's face. "Your sister Anastasia, where does she stand?"

"I'm sure she's amenable to a proposal," Alexei replied.

"That was not the warmest endorsement I've ever heard," George said, his pale blue eyes searching Alexei's.

"My sister is warm and loving, and she has cared for me her whole life," Alexei said. "But she also has a strong personality. I want to make sure she's happy, and I don't want to force her on anybody."

George smiled, and Alexei was relieved to see that Henry was smiling also. "Anastasia's willfulness is well known in the family," George said. "As is her penchant for playing pranks on the people she loves."

"Including tossing water on a Polish diplomat," Henry said with a laugh.

Alexei buried his face in his hands. "I haven't overcome my embarrassment from that one," he admitted.

"Try not to be too embarrassed, Alyosha," George advised. "Henry and I consider her an attractive bride despite that."

"I can't tell you how relieved I am," Alexei said. He took a deep breath and looked at Henry. "Still, I want my sister to be happy, and the ultimate decision is hers. If she consents to your proposal, then I have no objections."

Two days later, Alexei was finishing lunch with Alexandra, George, Michael and Igor when Anastasia burst into the room. "Henry asked me to marry him," she announced.

The room became so quiet that Alexei could hear his heart thumping. "Did you accept?" he asked.

"Yes, I did," Anastasia replied. She threw a balled-up handkerchief at Alexei. "And all this after you thought I wasn't marriage material!"

Alexei plucked his sister's handkerchief from the floor and stood up. "Did you accept because you're interested in marrying Henry or to prove me wrong?"

"Both!" Anastasia said, her expression a combination of a smile and a snarl.

"I want nothing more than for you to be happy," Alexei replied as Henry appeared in the doorway behind Anastasia. "Congratulations to you both."

George stood as his son came into the room. "Congratulations," he said as he embraced Henry. "You've made a good choice."

At the beginning of August, in the middle of the wedding preparations, Alexandra came to talk to Alexei. "What is it, Mama?" Alexei asked, standing at his desk and shuffling through his papers as he looked for one in particular.

Alexandra took a seat opposite her son. "I've been thinking about this for awhile, and I've made my decision," she said. "After Anastasia's wedding, I will be retiring from society, like Ella did."

Alexei stopped looking through the papers in front of him and sat down as he contemplated what his mother was saying. "Are you going to start your own convent, like Ella did?"

"No, I will retire to an existing convent, where I will pray and continue to explore the Orthodox faith."

"Do you have a specific place in mind?" Alexei asked.

Alexandra nodded. "The Ipatiev Monastery in Kastroma. I have been corresponding with them, and they're happy to have me."

"I didn't know that," Alexei said.

"I didn't want it made public until I made a decision," Alexandra replied.

Alexei folded his hands on his desk and stared at them for a few moments. When he looked back at his mother, he said, "it would be nearly unprecedented for a Dowager Empress to retire like this."

"I'm aware of that," Alexandra said. "But your grandmother would still be involved with public life, and the fact remains that I could never compete with her. I'm a very shy person, and public appearances have always been difficult for me. The family has been my life's work ever since I married your father, and now that Anastasia is marrying and leaving the country, there seems little left for me."

"I'm still here, Mama, and I haven't married yet."

"I know," Alexandra replied. "But I have no doubt that Mimi and Nando will come around. Your marriage will take place sooner than you think."

The night before they left for England, Alexei and Anastasia stood at the window of the Alexander Palace, staring out into the night. It was already too dark to see the brown leaves that were being swept from the trees in the cold October wind, but Anastasia sighed anyway. "I will miss this place," she said.

Alexei studied his sister. "Did you accept Henry's proposal just because I said you'd never marry?"

"That was part of it," Anastasia admitted. "But I do care for Henry, and I've spent most of my life thinking I would marry one of the British princes."

Alexei swallowed, then went back to staring out the window.

"You feel guilty about it, don't you?"

Alexei nodded. "A little."

"Don't feel bad. The whole family has always told me what an imp I am."

Alexei smiled. Behind them, the phone rang, making Alexei jump. "It's late," he said as the phone rang a second time. "Why don't you get some sleep?" Anastasia left the room as Alexei answered the phone.

"Alyosha, it's Gavril Konstantinovich," Gavril said on the other end.

"Hello, Gavril," Alexei said. "Is everything alright?"

"I'm not sure. Is Igor still with you? I was expecting him home awhile ago."

Alexei frowned. "I let him go some time ago already. Are you sure he's not at Pavlovsk?"

"I'm sure," Gavril said, his concern deepening his voice.

Alexei bit his lip, trying to quell the uneasy feeling in his chest. "Why would he disappear now, on the eve of Anastasia's wedding?"

"I don't know," Gavril replied. "We're all supposed to leave for England together in the morning."

"Let me look around," Alexei said. "I don't know why he'd still be here, but…"

"Would you let me know if you find him?" Gavril asked.

"Of course," Alexei replied. He dropped the telephone into the receiver in a hurry, and headed upstairs to Igor's apartments. The rooms were dark, however, and Alexei was about to go look somewhere else when he caught sight of Igor's form at the window, visible in the darkness only because of his light khaki uniform.

For a minute, Alexei stood next to Igor and stared out the window into the dark night. Only the occasional movement of a patrolling sentry broke the blackness. Finally, Alexei looked back at Igor. "Gavril called," he said. "Your family was expecting you home hours ago. Why are you still here?" Igor sighed, and for the first time, Alexei could see tears in his eyes. "What's the matter?"

"I never wanted this wedding to happen."

"What?"

"I've always been interested in Anastasia," Igor said, and his words shocked Alexei. "Your family was always so busy getting bees in your bonnets about her pranks and her impertinence, but I always thought it was funny. My brothers did too. I would have been happy to marry her."

Alexei looked at his cousin, simply listening as the torrents of words escaped the normally reserved Igor. When Igor stopped speaking, his tears were flowing down his face. "Why didn't you say something?" Alexei asked.

"I didn't need to," Igor replied. "Your mother realized I was interested, and she told me she wouldn't entertain the thought of Anastasia marrying me."

"She said that?" Alexei asked, incredulous. Igor nodded. "Why didn't you come to me?"

Igor shrugged and looked back out the window. "Your mother said she couldn't believe that I would even be interested in a daughter of hers. I couldn't imagine standing a chance after that conversation."

Alexei took a deep breath, inhaling through his nose to compensate for his clenched teeth. *Maybe Mama's retirement isn't the worst thing that ever happened,* he thought. "I wish you had come to me. I would have taken you seriously." He looked out the window again, just in time to see another guard checking the perimeter of the palace. "I'm sure there's another princess who would be happy to accept your proposal," he added.

Igor shook his head. "The marriage boat has passed me by," he said. "I'm twenty-six years old. I don't have a chance. Most of my family married as soon as they were able."

"That's not true at all. Look at your brothers. Ioann didn't marry until he was twenty-five. Konstantin didn't get the first marriage he wanted either, and he found someone else."

Igor just shrugged. "I don't know," he said. "Even Vera has started getting proposals, and she's the baby of the family."

"Gavril married that dancer mistress of his without Papa's permission," Alexei said, trying to say something that would make Igor feel better.

But Igor shook his head again. "They separated awhile ago. The divorce is nearly final."

"Really?" Alexei asked incredulously. "I didn't know that."

"Gavril's purposely been quiet about it."

"What happened?"

"He wanted children, and she wasn't conceiving. He's looking at eligible princess now too. Things are different, Alyosha. Your reign has changed things." Igor turned from the window to look at Alexei. "Your father's morals and family values were impeccable, but he wasn't strong enough to make sure the rest of the family stayed in line."

"I'm too young to be a strong leader," Alexei said.

"Your youth has inspired the family's sympathy," Igor replied. "And you've made wise decisions while staying firm. The family is falling in line behind you."

For a moment, Alexei stared out the window, unsure how to respond. "Please don't despair, Igor," he said finally. "You have a lot to offer a prospective bride." He looked away from the window and back at Igor. "Why don't we discuss this again when we get home from England? In the meantime, it's late, and you should go home." Alexei grabbed Igor's elbow, led him to the door of the palace and made sure he was in a carriage home.

When the carriage was out of sight, Alexei went to bed, and his tears wet his pillow for a long while before he finally fell asleep.

In England, the wedding meant a gathering of Europe's royals, and Alexei was only too happy to see Olga and Tatiana and their families again. His oldest sisters were far enough along in their pregnancies that they were showing, and both seemed happy. "I think it'll be okay this time," Tatiana whispered to Alexei as they waited in the church for the wedding to begin.

"Would you give me a call if you're having problems again?"

"Absolutely," Tatiana promised.

Having just been through his coronation, Alexei was happy not to be at the center of attention. *Nastia really looks beautiful,* he thought as he watched Anastasia and Henry recite their vows. *Mama was expecting differently because Nastia's so short. And she does look happy, contrary to what I was expecting.*

Despite his sister's happiness, Igor's tears still ate at Alexei, and when he looked for his cousin in the church, Igor was hidden behind his taller older brothers, so Alexei could not tell what he was thinking. *I don't want to spend my entire reign acting as the family's matchmaker,* he thought. *I'd never have time for anything else. But I do owe Igor that much. He's been a trusty aide-de-camp, and having him around has been very good for me.*

Alexei spent a good amount of time with Anastasia after the ceremony. "The palace is going to be empty without you," he said.

"You should have thought of that before you rushed off to marry me," Anastasia teased.

"I wasn't in a rush," Alexei said. "I just wanted to see that you were well taken care of."

Alexei slept most of the way back to St. Petersburg. As his train neared the Russian border, however, Alexei finally dragged himself out of bed for some breakfast. On his way to the dining car, he banged on Igor's sleeping compartment. "I'm awake," Igor said, even if he did not sound happy about it.

A few minutes later, Alexei and Igor were sitting across from each other. Steam emanated from their teacups as they buttered black bread. "How are you feeling?" Alexei asked.

"Fine," Igor mumbled.

They had barely finished eating when Sergei rushed in with a telegram for Alexei. "Your Imperial Majesty, this just came for you," he said.

Startled by his secretary's speed, Alexei read the telegram. "Oh, my God," he said.

"What happened?" Igor asked, suddenly looking more alert.

"There's been an explosion at a factory in St. Petersburg," Alexei replied, his heart beginning to race.

"Which one?" Igor asked.

Gorvenko appeared in the doorway. "It's the factory that your sister Marie supported, Your Imperial Majesty," he said.

Alexei and Igor jumped up at the same time, practically knocking over their chairs in the process. "Is Marie hurt?" Alexei shrieked, before realizing that his sister could not have made it back to St. Petersburg yet.

"She's still in London," Igor said. "She wasn't supposed to leave for another day or two." His words were reassuring, but his stricken face gave a different impression.

"Damn," Alexei spat. He looked at Gorvenko. "Is there any other news?"

Gorvenko nodded, and his face remained calm. "My informants have been telling me that Trotsky has been using your absence as an excuse to start riots in the capital. He's been planning a workers' strike at this particular factory for while."

"Why?" Alexei asked. "He could have hurt Marie!"

"Her patronage of this factory was probably the point," Gorvenko replied.

"Was Trotsky there when the explosion happened?" Alexei asked.

"I don't know yet," Gorvenko replied.

Alexei looked at him, his eyes narrowing.

"I had nothing to do with it, Your Imperial Majesty, I swear."

Alexei thought he was telling the truth, but his feelings of horror were reflected on Igor and Sergei's faces. "Is there any word on how many have been killed?" he asked.

Sergei shook his head. "That telegram is the only one that came through," he said.

"I haven't heard anything yet either," Gorvenko said.

As soon as the imperial train arrived in St. Petersburg, Alexei hurried into a waiting car. Igor and Sergei followed.

Many of the roads leading to the factory had been sealed off by the police and fire brigade, but the policemen guarding the blockades opened them for Alexei. When he arrived at the factory, he saw that only one small section of the block-long building still stood. The rest of it was smoldering black ash with wisps of smoke rising from it. The heat that emanated from the scene felt even hotter in the damp November air. The fire brigade's hoses were putting out the last of the burning ashes, but Alexei could still smell the smoke that rose from every corner of the burnt factory. Smoke covered the sun and gave the scene a gray aura. Soot covered the faces of every member of the fire brigade, and many of the policemen's faces as well.

Alexei covered his nose with his hand. Next to him, Sergei was doing the same, and Igor's face was twisted. "My God," Alexei said. He walked over to Gorvenko. "What about the victims?" he asked.

"The ones who survived were brought to all of the hospitals in the area," Gorvenko said. "The ones who didn't are at the morgue."

Alexei looked at Sergei, and thought of his other secretaries. "Please send my sister a telegram, letting her know what happened. Send Peter Pavlovich to the morgue to get a list of the victims who were killed."

"I don't know how many have been identified yet, Your Imperial Majesty," Gorvenko put in. "It is very soon."

"They may have a partial list, though," Alexei said. He looked back at Sergei. "Petya will have to keep up with the list so that we can notify the families. Have Ilya Dimitrievich and Andrei Feodorovich meet me at the hospitals. I'm going to visit the victims." Sergei nodded and dashed off. Alexei looked at Igor. "You're coming with me."

At the hospitals, the worst burn victims were in separate wards and could not be visited, but Alexei went to the bedside of each victim that could be. When Sergei found him, Alexei was talking quietly to one victim whose face was completely covered in bandages. Alexei was quiet and composed, but Sergei could not help but grimace.

When he was done, Alexei went to the doorway, where Sergei was waiting. "Any news?" he asked quietly as they stepped into the hallway.

"The two Empresses have gone to the other hospitals where the victims are being treated," Sergei replied of Alexandra and Marie Feodorovna. "Your sister Marie got my telegram and is on her way back to Russia."

"Any news on identifying the ones that didn't make it?"

"Yes," Sergei said. "Trotsky was among the victims, as were a number of other members of the Communist party."

Alexei grabbed Sergei's arm. "Are you sure about this?" he asked forcefully.

"It's true," Gorvenko replied from behind them.

Alexei jumped, startled, then turned to face his police chief. "Are you absolutely certain?" he asked.

Gorvenko nodded. "I know the medical examiner personally. He identified Trotsky himself, and had one of the hospital's top surgeons confirm it."

Alexei took a deep breath, trying to process the information. There was a silence as his mind worked. "Has his family been informed?" he asked.

"Yes," Gorvenko replied. "His wife is already at the morgue."

"Make sure she positively identifies the body as well," Alexei said. "Same for the other Communists that were killed. I want this done correctly. When it's certain, I want a full report on my desk. I'm sure the Communists are trying to figure out their future, but I need a plan as well."

"Yes, Your Imperial Majesty," Gorvenko replied. He disappeared.

When he was gone, Alexei heaved a sigh and walked down the hallway. Sergei followed slowly, giving him his space. In the middle of the hall, Alexei stopped walking. First his arm, and then his forehead hit the wall in front of him. When he looked up, Igor was coming out of one of the rooms nearby, his face screwed up in pain.

"Someone else didn't make it?" Alexei asked.

Igor shook his head. At the other end of the hall, the door to the hospital opened and Gavril entered. Ioann, Konstantin and George were on his heels. Alexei straightened up, but Gavril had already seen him, and he and his brothers came over.

Gavril put his arm around Alexei. "Tough day," he said. Alexei nodded.

Ioann put his arm around Igor. "These things never get any easier," he said.

Two weeks later, Alexei sat at his desk, reading reports on the explosion. A combination of the eyewitness accounts and Gorvenko's police reports gave Alexei a sense of what had happened. *Trotsky was planning this revolt for months,* he realized. *Strikes at this factory were supposed to lead to other workers' strikes across the capital and the nation.*

Alexei shivered. *Could a Communist revolution have been that easy?* he wondered. *It was only a fight in the factory that ended it. A monarchist worker shoved one of the Communists' plants right as one of the machines was starting up.* Alexei remembered the burns on the victims he had visited at the hospital and shuddered.

When he picked up the last document in front of him, he realized that it was a petition from the remaining members of the Communist party. "Owing to the death of our leaders and many of our members in the explosion at the Marievna Factory," it read, "the Communist Party has come to the difficult realization that it can no longer remain a viable political party at the present time. We request that new elections in the Duma be held, so that the people may obtain delegates that can better serve them and their nation."

"Hallelujah!" Alexei cried, standing up and punching the air with his fist. "That's exactly what I wanted!"

Sitting back down, Alexei picked up his pen and granted the petition. Then he began drafting the order for new elections in the Duma. *With God's grace, the Communists' seats will go to more worthy political parties,* he thought.

Part II

CHAPTER 1

April 26, 1925.

"Are you comfortable?" Alexei asked his uncle Pavel.

Pavel lay in bed, unmoving. He looked pale and sickly. *Did he hear me?* Alexei wondered. Then Pavel slowly looked over and nodded. Alexei felt relieved. A minute later, however, Pavel's eyes closed. His chest fell and did not rise again.

Alexei felt his heart sink. Behind him, he could hear Marie Pavlovna begin to sob. Dmitri put a hand on his sister's back to comfort her, even as he held his own emotions inside. Their younger half-siblings, Vladimir, Irina and Natalia, sobbed. Princess Olga Paley, Pavel's wife, had not stopped crying since the night before, and her tears continued to flow.

"I'll send out the telegrams," Dmitri said.

"I'll help you," Alexei replied, standing up.

"I'll call the priests and have them tend to the body," Vladimir said.

Dmitri barely gave Vladimir a nod before dashing out of the room. "You never fully accepted him, or Pavel's second family," Alexei realized as they raced towards the telegraph machine.

"What's it matter now?" Dmitri said. "My father is dead."

His response was a harsh one, and Alexei cringed. "You're not the only one who's lost something."

Dmitri shrugged. "Do you want to telegraph the Romanians?" he asked. "Papa was Marie's last surviving uncle."

Alexei thought about it. "No, you do it," he said.

"Maybe it wouldn't sound like a solicitation if you hadn't been so forthcoming about your interest in Ileana," Dmitri said.

Alexei glared at him. "What is wrong with you?" he demanded. Dmitri did not respond, and the silence lengthened. "I'll telegraph my sisters, mother and grandmother," Alexei said finally. "You contact the rest of the family. You can *start* with the Romanians if you'd like."

It was not until the funeral that Alexei fully began to feel the effects of the loss, and his tears came down his face. Much of the family stayed for several days, and Alexei was grateful to see that Dmitri had pulled himself together to accept visitors graciously.

The Romanian royal family stayed for nearly a week after the funeral so that Marie could visit the grave of her mother and other Russian relatives. When the family returned to the Palace, Alexei stood at a window and watched them exit their car. Ileana had grown to a lofty five foot ten, and was starting to look older than her age for the first time since Alexei had known her.

"She's really grown up, hasn't she?" Michael said from behind Alexei.

Alexei jumped. "I didn't see you, Misha," he said.

"Because you were too busy looking out the window," Michael teased. Then he became serious. "I think it would be a good time to ask Mimi and Nando."

"I was hoping it would be," Alexei said.

One afternoon, Alexei paid Marie and Ferdinand a visit when he knew they would be in their apartments. "I know what you want," Marie said as soon as Alexei was led in.

"Relax, Mimi," Ferdinand said. "Ileana is sixteen now. It's much more of an appropriate conversation now than last time we had it."

"She's still too young," Marie replied. "And it's up to her in the end. If she says no, that's the end of it."

Alexei was not surprised by Marie's conditions. "The wedding wouldn't happen tomorrow even if Ileana wanted it to. *If* she's interested, would late this year or early next year be acceptable?"

Ferdinand and Marie looked at each other. "It would be," Marie said finally, and Alexei's heart jumped.

The next day, Alexei took advantage of the fine weather to take Ileana for a walk around the Palace's gardens. All around them, birds sang and the leaves looked ready to burst forth from their buds. "How is your mother?" he asked. "This can't be easy for her."

Ileana shook her head. "It's been tough. Maybe not as bad as Grandmama's death, but my mother has been watching her ties to Russia slowly dwindle."

"She'll always have me," Alexei said.

"I know," Ileana replied. "But she loved coming here as a kid, because she always had these wonderful uncles that would spoil her. Between Pavel and Sergei and the rest of them, it was always a wonderful experience for her. And of course, the Russian court was always dazzling while the Romanian court was always austere."

Alexei nodded. "Would those differences be a problem for you, do you think, if you came to live here?"

Ileana looked at him quizzically.

Alexei took a deep breath, and his heart started pounding. His mouth was suddenly dry and metallic tasting. "Ileana, your parents have given me permission to ask for your hand in marriage. It could be a long engagement, though. The wedding wouldn't have to happen for awhile- I mean…" Alexei tried to swallow and looked at Ileana. He was unsure what to say and he did not want his torrent of words to keep flowing unabated.

For a moment, Ileana stared back at Alexei. Then her face split into a grin. "Absolutely," she said. "I'm interested."

Alexei grinned back. Ileana opened her arms and Alexei hugged her to his chest. A feeling of relief overwhelmed him. As they walked back to the Palace, he reached out and took Ileana's hand. "You don't seem surprised by the proposal."

Ileana paused as she thought about it. "I'm not," she said finally. "For whatever reason, this is something I've assumed would happen."

"Was I that obvious in my interest?" Alexei asked.

"Don't worry," Ileana reassured him with a smile. "I think it was a combination of things- our families have become closer since your became tsar, for one thing."

The wedding date was set for September 15, and as the preparations moved forward, Alexei visited Bucharest with jewelry and other gifts. The day after his arrival, he watched as Ileana sat in front of a mirror, trying on various items. Then his eye fell on a stack of cards on a nearby table. Even from across the room, Alexei recognized Anastasia's handwriting on the first card. "What are these?" he asked.

"Congratulatory cards from your sisters and cousins."

"Aaawww," Alexei said, smiling as he looked through them. *Igor and all of his siblings each wrote one*, he thought as his eyes stung with tears.

"It's helped me keep straight who's married to whom," Ileana joked.

Alexei laughed as he looked at the missives from Igor and Sophie, Gavril and Maud, Konstantin and Pilar, and Ioann and Elena.

"Elena is Sandro's sister, right?" Ileana asked.

Alexei nodded. "When Olga and Sandro got engaged, Olga went to Elena for advice on Serbian customs."

"Did Gavril meet Maud at Anastasia's wedding?" Ileana asked.

"Yes. Her father is the Duke of Devonshire. Igor met Sophie at the wedding, too. It was the most talkative I'd seen him in awhile. And Konstantin's wife Pilar is a princess of Bavaria."

"Sophie is a Princess of Hohenberg, right?"

"Yes." Alexei smiled at the memory of Igor and Sophie's wedding. *I don't think Igor stopped smiling the whole night. It was one of the first times I thought he stopped feeling like he was second best because Mama wouldn't let him marry Anastasia.*

Ileana broke into a grin. "I met Igor and Sophie's boys when our engagement was announced- they're adorable."

Alexei grinned as well. "Yeah, Nicky and Petya are great, and Igor, at least, wants more." He nodded at Ileana's reflection in the mirror. "That necklace looks nice on you."

"Yes, I'm rather fond of it already," Ileana admitted. She turned to look at Alexei himself, rather than looking at his reflection in the mirror. "Thank you for giving it to me," she said sincerely.

"You're welcome."

"I mean it, Alyosha."

"I know that."

Ileana looked away for a moment, and when she looked back, her eyes shone with tears. "I don't think you understand what all of this means to me," she said, her voice quavering. "It's not just the necklace, it's all the jewelry and all the clothing- the wedding dress! It's just incredible to me." She shook her head. "I never felt poor growing up because Mama was good at making us feel like we had a lot, but..." She heaved a breath and looked back at the mirror.

Alexei put his hands on her shoulders, and Ileana looked back at him. "All the jewelry, the dress and everything are just material possessions," he said. "You mean more to me than all of it."

The day of the wedding dawned clear and bright, with a breeze that smelt of the rain that had passed through the night before. Alexei awoke with anticipation and dread fluttering in his stomach like butterflies. *I've really asked a lot of Ileana,* he thought. *I hope she doesn't regret this.*

Inside the church, Alexei stood up straight and unmoving, and the light in the church made the decorations on his uniform gleam. The church was packed with his large extended family, but he barely saw them. Instead, he closed his eyes and pictured Ileana in the Malachite Room, being dressed in the same way he had seen Marie getting dressed before her wedding.

When he opened his eyes again, the Metropolitan of St. Petersburg was opening the door of the church and escorting Ileana through.

Ileana's dress was a silvery white that somehow also managed to match the blue of her large eyes. Her hair had been done up in the curls of a Romanov bride, and pearls cascaded through her hair. She also wore the pearl necklace that Alexei had given her for their engagement. She caught sight of Alexei watching her and smiled. After Ileana had joined Alexei in the narthex of the church, they were given lit candles that had been decorated with flowers and ribbons. The service began when the deacon intoned, "bless, Master."

Father Vasiliev spoke: "Blessed is our God, always, now and ever and unto ages of ages." As the choir began singing, their voices rose throughout the church, and Alexei could smell the lit incense.

When the choir's voices died down, Father Vasiliev lifted Alexei and Ileana's wedding rings. Using Ileana's ring, he made the sign of the cross over Alexei, and with Alexei's ring, he made the sign of the cross over Ileana. "The servant of God, Alexei Nikolaievich, is betrothed to the handmaiden of God, Ileana, in the name of the Father, and of the Son, and of the Holy Spirit. Amen. The handmaiden of God, Ileana, is betrothed to the servant of God, Alexei Nikolaievich…" When he had repeated this three times, Alexei and Ileana exchanged their rings, and Father Vasiliev continued praying.

Alexei and Ileana followed the priest to the center of the church. Their lit candles flickered as they moved. All around them, the choir continued singing. Alexei glanced at Ileana long enough to see her jeweled dress glittering from the light of the candles and the light coming in through the windows of the church. He grinned.

Father Vasiliev lifted the golden nuptial crowns. "The servant of God, Alexei Nikolaievich, is crowned unto the handmaiden of God, Ileana, in the name of the Father, the Son, and the Holy Spirit. Amen. The handmaiden of God, Ileana, is crowned unto the servant of God, Alexei Nikolaievich…" The priest then blessed Alexei and Ileana three times each, saying, "O Lord our God, crown them with glory and honor."

It was several hours later before the service was finally finished, and Alexei felt an exhaustion that was mirrored in Ileana's eyes. His stomach was also growling, and he hoped no one could hear it. As they made their way to the celebratory dinner, Alexei could smell the food. He remembered all the time and effort they had spent putting the menu together and hiring chefs and cooks, and now he was glad.

As he and Ileana walked side by side towards their dinner, he felt Ileana's hand touch his. He looked at her and smiled. "Is your dress as heavy as you were worried it would be?" he asked softly.

"Yes," she said.

"It's almost over, I promise."

"I know." Ileana took a breath. "The food smells good. I'm hungry."

"Me too."

The long tables sat over a thousand guests. Once everyone was seated, Alexandra surprised Alexei by rising to make the first toast. "If I remember anything about my own wedding day, it's that you both must be hungry and tired, so I'll be brief," she said, to the laughter of the guests around her. "However, I am very happy to be here today. There were times when you were little, Sunbeam, that I wondered whether I'd ever see you live long enough to get married, and my heart is bursting with happiness and pride to witness this occasion. I know, too, that Nicky would have loved to be here as well. We spent a lifetime together looking forward to it." She sniffed, but managed to continue. "Now, you've found a wonderful bride who shares so many of your best characteristics. I wish you both a long life of happiness."

The room burst into applause as she sat, tears coming down her face. Grand Duchess Elizabeth, seated next to Alexandra, gave her sister's hand a squeeze. Alexei rose to give his mother a hug. When he returned to his chair, Marie and Ferdinand had also risen to give a toast.

"I'll leave most of the talking to my wife, as she's better with words," Ferdinand began. "But I have always wanted the best for you, Ileana. You are a special young woman, and I watched your decision to enter into this marriage with great difficulty. You may spend most of your time in Russia now, but you'll always be welcome in your homeland, and I hope to see you often." He sat.

"It is always difficult to see a child leave your home, especially one as special as you are," Marie continued. "But I have known Alyosha since he was a wee baby, and I have been impressed by the man he has grown into, and by the leader he has become. I echo the sentiments of those before me, and wish you a long life of joy and happiness."

Once the festivities had ended, Alexei and Ileana boarded the Polar Star, the smaller of the Romanovs' yachts, and began cruising towards the fjords of Finland. The stiff breeze smelt of the fresh sea, and Alexei could feel himself relaxing immediately. He and Ileana had discussed many destinations for their honeymoon, but now that they were on the water, he was glad. As Ileana joined him on deck, wearing an extra jacket to guard against the breeze, Alexei was aware of Gorvenko and other policemen surrounding them, but he did not care. He looked at Ileana and grinned.

Ileana grinned back. Then she looked over the deep blue waters of the Gulf of Finland. "This is so beautiful," she said.

"My family used to go cruising here all the time," Alexei said. "It's hardly happened at all, though, since my sisters got married and my mother retired."

"We could always invite everybody to go once a year or something," Ileana suggested.

"I like that idea," Alexei replied. He looked up. The sun had already set. The sky was a deep navy blue in the east and a lighter aquamarine in the west.

"I see a star," Ileana said.

For two weeks, Alexei and Ileana cruised the Finnish fjords, taking in the deep blue waters and the beauty of the towering glaciers. On one of their few land excursions, they met Marie Feodorovna for a luncheon. "It is so good to see you again, Alyosha," Marie said as they ate.

"Because it's been a whole ten days since you saw me at the wedding," Alexei teased.

Marie waved her hand at him. "It's nice to see how happy you are."

After the luncheon was a military parade. Alexei reviewed the troops that marched in front of him in colorful local costumes. At the end of the parade, a large group of schoolchildren presented Ileana with bouquets of flowers. Ileana, smiling, spoke to many of them before she and Alexei departed for the Polar Star. "Does your grandmother spend a lot of time in Finland?" Ileana asked when they were back on board.

Alexei nodded. "She loves it, and she's very popular there."

"Do you think Finland will ask for its independence the same way Poland did?"

Alexei sighed. "They already did," he said. "I got the petition right before the wedding."

"What are you going to do?" Ileana asked as they walked back to their cabin to change into more informal clothing.

"In the end, the Duma will vote on it, the same way they voted on the Polish independence, but my attitude is the same as it was for the Poles. I'd rather have a number of independent allies at our borders than a simmering discontent within the country."

"And you don't have any estates in Finland, so at least you wouldn't have to relinquish them like you did with your Polish estates."

"I didn't *have* to sell Spala and Skernevizi back to the Polish government," Alexei corrected. "I did it because I felt like the properties weren't worth owning anymore."

"Do you regret it?"

"No, I think it was a good deal. The Poles got their land back, and I got to invest the money in Russia's industrialization."

"And Stanislaw Czartoryski is President now. I remember what a politician I thought he was at your coronation."

Alexei nodded. "I'm proud of him," he said. "He wanted this so much, and he's worked so hard for it."

Once their honeymoon was over, Alexei and Ileana spent only a few days back in Russia before going to Germany to meet with President Paul von Hindenburg. In Berlin, Alexei met with Hindenburg as Ileana toured nearby hospitals with Hindenburg's daughters. *It's getting cold again*, Alexei thought as he was led into Hindenburg's office. *But it is almost November already. Almost another year gone.*

Once he and Hindenburg had exchanged pleasantries, Alexei wasted no time in getting down to business. "President Hindenburg, I have been concerned about Adolph Hitler's rise for a few years now. Is he as popular as he seems?"

Hindenburg sighed. "I'm afraid he is," he said. "I dislike him and would have remained retired but for my need to make sure he doesn't get elected to office."

Alexei shook his head in frustration. "Wasn't he imprisoned last year because he tried to gain power?"

"Yes, but it hasn't deterred him at all," Hindenburg said. "To the contrary, he used the time in prison to write his autobiography and consolidate his supporters. If anything, he's more popular now."

"I'm glad, at least, that we agree to oppose him," Alexei said.

"I share your concerns," Hindenburg replied. "I will do everything I can to ensure that he does not gain power."

CHAPTER 2

A week after they returned from Germany, Alexei was eating breakfast and reading the newspaper when he realized how late it had gotten. *Where's Ileana?* he wondered. *She's usually down by now.* Concerned, he went to their apartments. He saw no sign of his wife at first, but then he heard the unmistakable sound of her retching in the washroom. Alexei rushed over pushed the door to the washroom open. "Ileana?" he said. "What's the matter?"

"Go away," Ileana moaned, clutching her stomach.

Alexei knelt next to her and put a hand at her back. "What's happening?"

"I don't know," Ileana said. "I felt fine last night, but I got up feeling like this." Within seconds, she was vomiting into the toilet again.

Alexei held her hair back as she got sick, and handed her a glass of water when she was done. "I don't like this at all," he said.

Less than an hour later, Dr. Botkin was examining Ileana. He asked a slew of questions, but after the tumble of words stopped, the examination proceeded in silence. Alexei stood near the door of their bedroom as Ileana sat on the bed while the doctor examined her.

"What's the diagnosis?" Alexei asked, unable to handle the doctor's silence any longer.

Dr. Botkin remained silent as he put his stethoscope away and packed up the rest of his instruments. Alexei was about to repeat his question when Botkin finally looked at Ileana and spoke. "You're pregnant," he said.

Alexei's eyebrows shot up, and the beginning of a smile curled at his lips. Ileana's eyes widened. "Are you sure?" she asked.

"Absolutely," Botkin replied.

Alexei and Ileana looked at each other, and Alexei's face broke into a grin. "Any chance of a son?" he asked the doctor.

"It's too soon to tell," Botkin replied. "And of course the risks remain through the first few months of the pregnancy."

"How far along is she?" Alexei asked.

"About a month."

Ileana got up and went to the window. "I don't believe this," she said.

"Are you unhappy?" Alexei asked, going over to her.

"No, just in shock. It happened sooner than I was expecting."

Alexei saw that Dr. Botkin was edging towards the door. "Yevgeny Sergeievich, you're not to tell anybody about this yet," he said.

"I understand," Botkin replied.

When the doctor was gone, Alexei rubbed Ileana's back. "I'm happy about this," he said.

Ileana nodded slowly. "I am too," she said finally. They were quiet for awhile before Ileana asked, "what are you thinking?"

"I'm thinking of the conversation I was having with the American ambassador yesterday. I've been promising him a trip to America since the president and vice president came to my coronation, and I was thinking of going in March."

"You should go."

Alexei looked worried. "I was hoping you would come with me," he said.

"We'll see how I'm feeling as it gets closer. I'd love to go, but if it has to happen some other time, that's fine too."

There was a knock on the door. Alexei and Ileana turned to see Dr. Botkin in the doorway, holding ginger and crackers. "These should help with the sickness," he said as he came into the room.

Ileana moved toward him with a relieved look. "Thanks," she said.

"Remember, secrecy, Yevgeni Sergeievich," Alexei said. "We'll make the announcement when we're ready."

Botkin nodded. "I know," he said. Still, a hint of a smile glinted in his eyes as he left the room.

For the next five months, Alexei watched as Ileana's morning sickness subsided and her belly grew. Finally, when it could no longer be concealed, the announcement about the pregnancy went out, first to the family, and then by bulletin to the rest of the country. "An heir, I hope!" Anastasia said boisterously when she heard the news. "Hopefully you won't have to wait as long as Mama and Papa did."

"I'm concerned about that," Alexei admitted. "It's one reason I married so young."

Ileana stood nearby as Alexei hung up the phone. She was about to say something when she and Alexei heard noise out in the street. They listened for a few seconds, and the noise turned into people cheering and singing the national anthem.

Alexei rushed to the window of the Palace and pulled back the curtain. "There's a whole crowd of people marching towards the Palace with large portraits of us!"

Ileana joined him at the window. "Oh, my God," she said when she saw the long lines of people, many dressed in their best clothing, filling the large boulevard in front of the Palace.

Alexei's secretaries rose from their desks and joined them at the window. They looked astounded, but also somewhat protective. "Please be careful," Sergei implored.

Gorvenko rushed into the room. "Your Imperial Majesty-" he began.

"I see them, Ivan Maximovich," Alexei interrupted.

"Please step away from the window," Gorvenko said. "Any one of them could have a gun or other weapon."

Alexei took Ileana's hand, and they both walked into the middle of the room. Alexei, however, eyed Gorvenko. "Those people out there are celebrating!" he said. He looked at Ileana. "Let's go out on to the balcony and greet them!" His face lit up with excitement.

"No!" Gorvenko said immediately.

"Relax, Ivan Maximovich. I really want to show myself to my people. I don't want to repeat my father's mistakes." Gorvenko looked unhappy. "Remember Bloody Sunday?"

"That was a completely different situation," Gorvenko said.

"Let's make sure it stays different," Alexei said. He looked at Ileana. "Come on," he said. He put a hand at her back at they went to the nearest balcony that overlooked the mass of people outside. Gorvenko made sure that they were surrounded by policemen who watched from every window and balcony.

Outside, the crowd cheered loudly when they saw Alexei and Ileana. Many fell to their knees, and the singing of "God Save the Tsar" rang out even louder. Ileana waved, and Alexei, keeping one hand protectively at her back, waved with his other hand.

It was more than an hour later when Alexei and Ileana returned inside. Outside, the crowd dispersed slowly and peacefully. "See, Ivan Maximovich?" Alexei teased his police chief. "Every once in awhile, you have to relax. Otherwise, you're going to have a heart attack!"

Gorvenko just shook his head.

When it came time for Alexei to leave for America, Marie, Alexandra and Elizabeth came to the Winter Palace to care for Ileana. Outside, snow remained on the ground, and their entrance into the Palace let in a gust of cold air. Immediately, Marie handed her daughter an extra shawl. "I'm not a child," Ileana complained. "I can handle this. I'm not even getting sick in the mornings anymore."

"I know that," Alexei replied. "But knowing that we have family here makes me feel better." He swallowed. "Promise you'll call me if anything happens? And I mean anything at all."

"I'm not a china doll," Ileana told him. "I won't break while you're gone."

"Relax, Alyosha," Marie said. "You need to take this trip to America, and Ileana will be fine." She shooed her son-in-law to the door, where Michael, Igor and Gorvenko were waiting for him.

"Ready?" Michael asked.

Alexei looked over his shoulder and smiled at Ileana. She smiled back. Alexei turned back to his uncle, cousin, and police chief. "Ready," he said.

Outside, a Cossack guard galloped in front of Alexei's carriage, escorting him to the Imperial train. After a train ride to England, where they stayed overnight at Windsor Palace as guests of George VI, Alexei and his entourage boarded the frigate *Tsarevich* for its first voyage across the Atlantic. As the frigate steamed out of the harbor, Michael and Alexei stood on deck, the wind blowing through their hair. Alexei held his cap to make sure it did not blow away.

"You know this ship was named after you?" Michael said. "The title was never updated."

"We started building it while I was still heir," Alexei said. He smiled. "Besides, if Ileana's pregnancy goes well, we won't have to rename it."

Michael smiled also. "An heir would be a welcome event."

That night, the ship was tossed around on the high seas. Huge gusts of wind howled. In his cabin, Alexei struggled to stand upright as he went to one of his trunks to find a book. All of a sudden, an intense nausea overwhelmed him. He dashed for the nearest toilet and heaved up the contents of his dinner. *This must have been what Ileana felt like for the first couple of months of her pregnancy,* he thought. *I can't wait until we're on dry land again.*

Five days later, Alexei could finally see American shores coming into view as he stood on deck, binoculars to his eyes. As the Russian vessels neared the Port of Baltimore, he could see American ships waiting in the harbor.

The *Tsarevich* dropped anchor about 500 yards from the *Congress*, the

American flagship. At Alexei's orders, the Russian flag was hoisted up from the *Tsarevich*. A few minutes later, the American flag was hoisted up from the *Congress*, followed by the Russian flag. Alexei laughed and gave the order for the American flag to be hoisted up the *Tsarevich*. When the American flag was flying from the Russian vessel, a 15-gun salute sounded from the *Congress*. Much to Alexei's glee, the *Tsarevich* responded in turn.

Then a barge left the *Congress*, bound for the *Tsarevich* and carrying Admiral William Sims. Without any ado, Admiral Sims boarded the *Tsarevich* and shook Alexei's hand. He was introduced to Michael and Igor. "Pleasure to meet you," he said.

"The pleasure is ours," Alexei said. "I have been looking forward to this visit for a long while."

"So have we, Your Imperial Majesty."

Onshore, Alexei got into one car with Igor, Michael, and Admiral Sims, and Alexei's entourage filled the cars behind them. As they made their way towards Washington, Alexei's Cossack guard led the way on horseback. Their colorful costumes made them stand out from the scenery around them, and their whips and cries kept the gathered crowds at a respectful distance.

Inside the first car behind the Cossack guard, Admiral Sims cringed at the guttural cries all around them. Alexei smiled at him. "Relax, Admiral," he said. "They are only here to protect me." He waved at the crowds that lined the roads. Many of the people along the road saw him waving and cheered in return. All along the route to Washington, people stood in line, often three or four deep, to see Alexei pass by.

As they neared the capital, Admiral Sims finally smiled. "Your Cossacks are legendary," he said. "Being escorted by so many of them is nothing I thought I'd ever see in my lifetime."

When they arrived in Washington, Alexei checked into his hotel, where he was happy to take a hot bath. Soon, he was ready for his formal dinner with the president. As his motorcar and Cossack guard took him to the White House, Alexei reviewed his notes on President Calvin Coolidge and Vice President Charles Gates Dawes and discussed his agenda with Michael and Igor. "I need allies, both politically and militarily," he said.

Michael and Igor nodded in agreement. "The Americans would make fine allies," Michael said. "And between their economic power and military might, we can't afford to have them as our enemies."

Once more, people thronged the sidewalks as Alexei, Igor and Michael were driven up Pennsylvania Avenue to the White House. Alexei looked out the car's windows to see a wide avenue surrounded by cherry trees that were starting to bloom. Up ahead, the White House stood, tall and imposing, its façade nearly glowing in the afternoon light.

Alexei eyed the President's home. "It's not a palace, but it is stately," he said. As he got out of the car, his ears were bombarded with cheers. All around, photographers snapped pictures at a rapid pace. Alexei, feeling as though his space was invaded, shot the photographers a bewildered look. "What was that about?" he whispered to Michael as they were ushered inside.

"I imagine they were from the newspapers," Michael said.

"And they're allowed to just take pictures like that?"

"America has a free press."

"That's dangerous," Alexei joked. He looked around eagerly as he was lead through multiple reception rooms on the first floor of the White House, and to the second floor, where the President, Vice President and their wives were waiting to meet him. When he saw his American hosts, Alexei's face lit up with his customary grin. "President Coolidge," he began. "Thank you for having me. It is an honor to be here. Mrs. Coolidge, it is nice to see you again."

President Coolidge smiled. "Being at your coronation was a once in a lifetime event," he said. "I'm glad we could return the favor and host you."

Grace Coolidge smiled also. "I have been telling anyone who will listen about our trip to Russia."

The President then introduced Alexei to Vice President Dawes and his wife, Caro. Alexei exchanged pleasantries with them and was immediately taken by Caro Dawes' wide smile and pleasant manners. He introduced Michael and Igor.

Many of society's ladies and gentlemen had been invited to the White House for the reception, and Alexei, Michael and Igor made their rounds. When everyone was seated for dinner, Caro looked over at Alexei. "How is the Tsarina doing?" she asked. "The news of her pregnancy even made the newspapers here in Washington."

"She's feeling quite well," Alexei said. "Our mothers are taking care of her while I'm here."

"I was looking forward to meeting her," Grace said.

"She was looking forward to coming," Alexei said. "But the doctors thought it best if she not take such a long journey."

"She'll have to come on your next visit," President Coolidge said with a smile.

"She's planning that visit already," Alexei said, and the group laughed.

Alexei, Michael and Igor made it back to their hotel in the early hours of the morning. In his room, Alexei had already changed into his nightclothes when he heard a knock at the door. He frowned, wondering who it was. *The Cossacks are standing guard outside the door, and we have the whole floor of the hotel for security reasons. It wouldn't be anyone the guards didn't trust.* He opened the door to find Igor in the hallway, holding a newspaper.

"Alyosha, you're big news," Igor said, waving the newspaper.

"What is that?" Alexei asked, bewildered, as he stepped aside to let his cousin into his room.

"They were selling early editions of today's paper in the hotel's lobby," Igor said as opened the newspaper and put it on Alexei's bed. "I got to buy one without anyone knowing who I was."

"That's exciting," Alexei said sarcastically.

"Oh, come on, Alyosha," Igor said. "In Russia, we can't go anywhere without being mobbed. I've never bought a newspaper in my life."

Finally, Alexei conceded his point. "What's so special about this newspaper?"

Igor pointed at the headline. "Boy king visits America!" it read.

"I'm not a king, I'm a tsar," Alexei said irritably. "And I'm not a boy anymore, either."

"The smaller headline gets it right," Igor said, pointing, and Alexei saw that it read, "Russian Tsar Alexei II in Washington for first American visit."

"Interesting," Alexei said, picking up the paper and reading the article.

At the formal meetings the next day, the Americans got right down to business. "What do you want from these conversations, Your Majesty?" Coolidge opened the meeting by saying.

"I'm hoping to accomplish several goals, Mr. President," Alexei replied. "Russia would like an ally that shares its desire to prevent another war."

"How likely is another war, though?" Coolidge asked. "Europe has been pretty quiet since the peace talks."

"It's quiet now," Alexei answered. "But I don't trust the Germans. I think they are unhappy with the terms of the peace, and I'm concerned about what that might lead to."

"The peace disarmed the Germans for a reason," Dawes put in. "The whole world wanted to prevent them from starting another war."

"I'm aware of the disarmament," Alexei said. "But I also know German patriotism. There's been a void in leadership since the fall of the monarchy, and the Germans have always been militaristic. My fear is that a new, powerful, leader may take advantage of his people's unhappiness and turn their society back into a military force to be reckoned with."

"How would such a leader do that while the country is not allowed to rearm itself?" Dawes asked.

"I don't know," Alexei admitted. "But my lack of imagination would not preclude them from finding a way."

"The United States has long followed a policy of isolationism, Your Majesty," Coolidge said. "And it is a policy that we're looking to continue at present. I don't see us getting militarily involved in Europe's affairs again without some real provocation."

Alexei swallowed unhappily. It was the answer he had been expecting, and still he was disappointed. "I understand your position against military involvement," he said, deciding to switch gears. "But are you willing to invest in Russia, both monetarily and in terms of the goods you produce? It's no secret that my country has yet to reach America's level of industrialization, and that's something I'd like to change."

Both Coolidge and Dawes nodded at the suggestion. "Any overseas investment that raises our exports is going to be good for America," Coolidge said. "What are you thinking of investing in?"

"Better agricultural techniques and machinery, more railroads and factories, better mining techniques, to name a few things," Alexei said, shifting in his seat slightly as he became aware of how hard his chair was.

"I'm sure we can arrange some type of exchange program, where farmers and agricultural students go to Russia," Dawes said. "The same could be said across other economic sectors."

"And we have many businessmen, bankers, and philanthropists that would be willing to invest the necessary monetary capital in your country," Coolidge said. "Many have expressed interest in meeting you while you're here. I can arrange those meetings with just a few phone calls."

"I would really appreciate that," Alexei said.

Alexei was silent on the way from the White House to a luncheon at the Russian Embassy. "What are you thinking?" Michael asked as they turned onto Wisconsin Avenue, where cars swarmed around them in the spring sunlight. "I warned you that we probably wouldn't be able to shake them from their isolationist policies."

Alexei sighed. "It's much easier to be isolationist when you have two oceans separating you from everyone else," he said. "But they made it sound like they'd have to be attacked before they responded with military action."

"I don't think that's likely at all," Michael said.

Alexei nodded in agreement. "Anyone that considers attacking the United States should be committed to an asylum."

Alexei spent the next couple of days in meetings with the Russian ambassador, wealthy Americans, and the Russian émigré community, raising capital to build Russia's railroads, factories and mines. While he attended those, his servants scoured the finest shops in Washington for gifts for Ileana, Marie, Alexandra and Elizabeth. By the time Alexei returned late one night, boxes had been piled in his hotel room, and Alexei, looking through their contents, was pleased to see fine hats, watches and other items. His servants had also bought ornate crosses for Alexandra and Elizabeth, as well as a diamond necklace for Marie.

Nice, Alexei thought. *This is exactly what I wanted.*

Alexei spent his last day in America attending meetings with venture capitalists and representatives of the Russian Orthodox Church. But finally, his business for the day was finished, and he found himself back in his hotel room at four in the afternoon. Wanting nothing more than to be left alone, Alexei dismissed Michael and Igor to do whatever they wanted before taking a hot bath.

Once his bath was over, Alexei felt much more relaxed, but he also realized just how little of his surroundings he had seen. He thought of the open space in front of the famous American monuments. *The National Mall,* he thought. In an instant, he decided to go there.

He called Gorvenko and his Cossack guards together, but also decided that he would go as quietly as possible. He pulled on civilian clothes rather than his customary military uniform, and ordered Gorvenko and the Cossacks to follow him on foot rather than on horseback.

"How are the Cossacks supposed to protect you that way?" Gorvenko objected.

"They have weapons, don't they?" Alexei replied. Soon, he was walking down a concrete path. In front of him was the National Monument, whose white tiles shone in the gathering dusk. Behind him was the Capital Building, but Alexei barely looked behind him in the glowing purple light of sunset. All around him, the National Mall was bathed in the mildness of early evening, and Alexei breathed in the smell of fresh-cut grass.

He could see a group of boys playing baseball off to his right. As he watched, one boy threw the ball he was holding. It flew towards another boy holding a bat, nearly getting lost in the darkness. But the boy with the bat swung, and the ball came bouncing towards Alexei.

Alexei ducked involuntarily, fearing the bruise that would follow being hit by the ball. *Damn hemophilia,* he thought. It was only when the ball was rolling slowly on the ground that Alexei felt comfortable picking it up and lightly tossing it to the boy closest to him. A few minutes later, he realized that the boys playing were all around his age- and that they had had no idea who he was. *I rule over a country that's larger than theirs, I'm married and I have a child on the way,* he thought as he watched them. *But they don't have a care in the world.*

Still, Alexei smiled as he kept walking. All around him, the sky was purple, the temperature was comfortable, and he could feel the breeze playing with his hair. He was aware that both the Cossacks and Gorvenko were nearby, keeping an eye on him, and yet still he felt free.

CHAPTER 3

Back in Russia, Alexei waited impatiently for the birth of his first child. As Ileana's June due date approached, Marie and Alexandra made the trip to St. Petersburg again. "How do you feel?" Alexei asked Ileana two days after their mothers' arrival.

"If I promise to tell you when I think the baby is on the way, will you stop asking?" Ileana replied, her large eyes focusing on her husband.

"Have I been asking a lot?"

"Yes."

"I'm sorry. I just wish that there was something I could do."

"You could relax."

At breakfast the next day, Alexei, Ileana, Alexandra and Marie were eating quietly. They were just finishing their eggs when Ileana put down her fork decisively. "Call Dr. Botkin," she said, and rushed upstairs. Marie and Alexandra hurried after her as Alexei picked up the telephone.

For ten hours, Alexei tried to concentrate on the papers on his desk. He gave up late in the afternoon. Upstairs, he paced in the hallway outside Ileana's birthing room, struggling not to listen to her howls of pain. Instead, he focused on the palace's ornate wooden floors, which gleamed under the Palace's newly installed electric lights. "I'm sorry," he whispered. "I didn't mean for it to be like this."

Then everything went silent in the room in front of him. Alexei tensed. Suddenly, he heard the unmistakable sound of a baby wailing. He dashed into the room, not caring about protocol. For a moment, all he saw were white sheets stained with bright red blood. He recoiled. "Oh my God," he stuttered.

At the edge of the room, in front of the windows, Dr. Botkin was weighing and measuring the new arrival. Alexei stood as if nailed to the floor. "It's a boy," Botkin said as the baby wailed again. He began wrapping the baby in swaddling clothes, and Alexei's stricken eyes sought Ileana.

"We need to clean her up," Alexandra said, pushing her son out of the room.

"Wait, I'm taking the baby with me," Alexei said, finally forcing his tongue to function. When the child was placed in his arms, Alexei looked at Dr. Botkin. "Please take care of Ileana," he pleaded. "That's a lot of blood."

The doctor nodded, and Alexei backed into the hallway, looking down at his new son for the first time. Immediately, the child began to wail, and Alexei, not completely sure what to do, pressed him against his neck. *He's so little*, Alexei thought. *He does seem to have a healthy set of lungs, though.*

Alexei kept an eye on the door in front of him as he paced the hallway. Finally, Alexandra opened the door and gave him a nod. Alexei moved past her into the room, where Ileana was lying down, looking exhausted. Marie sat next to her, looking nervous. The floor had already been cleaned and the bloody sheets removed, and Alexei was relieved by how much better everything looked.

He went to Ileana's bedside and sat next to her. Then he handed her the baby. Ileana smiled as she took the infant, who started wailing again. Ileana comforted him and he quieted down. "How do you feel?" Alexei asked.

"Tired," Ileana said. "I'm glad it's over."

"Are you still in pain?"

"No, Dr. Botkin gave me medication for it."

"Don't be afraid to use it," Alexei said. "I don't want to see you suffer."

Finally, Alexandra and Marie left the room.

"Were you really worried about giving birth?" Alexei asked.

Ileana nodded. "I was scared of how much it would hurt, and how long it would take. I've definitely heard horror stories about how bad it could be."

"Why didn't you tell me any of this?"

"You were already worried enough."

Alexei clasped Ileana's forearm. "I would have preferred you tell me." They were quiet for awhile, looking at the baby, before Alexei asked, "so, what should we name this little guy?"

Ileana smiled. "Actually, he's not that little." She nodded at the piece of paper next to the bed.

Alexei picked it up and found his son's measurements scribbled in Dr. Botkin's handwriting. "4309 grams," it read. "57 centimeters length."

"Wow," Alexei said. "I'll bet he turns into a tall adult, too."

Ileana shifted slightly in bed, managing to do it without waking their son. "Are you still feeling obligated to consider naming him Nicholas?"

"A little," Alexei admitted. "But much as I'd like to remember my father, I'm hesitating to do it this way. Igor named his son Nicholas after my father. So did Gavril. Besides, he'd reign as Nicholas III." He shook his head. "I want him to have a different name."

"Are you still thinking of Konstantin?" Ileana asked. "I like that name."

"I do too," Alexei said. "So many men in the family have been named that, but none of them was in line for the throne."

"Then let's do that."

"Let's." They smiled at each other again, and Alexei stood up. "I need to inform the family, and the country." His smile widened into a grin. "You may need to hold your ears in a few minutes. The 301-gun salute to a new heir is a loud one."

"Hold my ears?" Ileana said, shaking her head. "No way. I'm going to be *listening* for that salute."

Alexei laughed as he left the room. Within the hour, the saluting cannon at the Winter Palace began to boom. The batteries at the Fortress of Peter and Paul also started thundering in salute. Soon, the cannons of other fortresses and palaces roared with them- at Kronstadt and at Peterhof, at the Alexander Palace and at Gatchina, cannons exploded their joyful news.

Soon, church bells were clanging as well. From St. Petersburg to Siberia and all the way to Vladivostok, bells pealed, filling the air. In Moscow, the sound of church bells drowned out everything else. The churches in the Kremlin began the cacophony, and soon the multitude of churches across the city were following suit.

Back in St. Petersburg, as the Imperial family rushed to the Winter Palace's church for a Te Deum, the streets had filled with people and waving flags. Everywhere Alexei looked, he could see his citizens celebrating with him.

A week after Konstantin's birth, Alexei snuck into the nursery when Ileana and the governesses were not there. That usually meant that Konstantin was asleep, but Alexei found his tiny son awake in his bassinet, staring up at him with huge blue eyes. He lifted Konstantin from the white sheets that surrounded him and hugged him close. Konstantin's thin film of blond hair looked more like a sheen than a head of hair.

"I hope you're healthier than I ever was," Alexei whispered as he rocked Konstantin back and forth. "I don't want you to have the childhood I did."

He walked over to the mirror and turned Konstantin around so that they both were looking into the glass. Then he looked at their reflections and smiled. *The future of the dynasty seems real for the first time*, he thought. *This is the next Tsar of Russia.*

Alexei took a deep breath and felt tears spring into his eyes. *I have to live until he's an adult*, he vowed. *Konstantin will take the throne when he's old enough. There will be no regency.*

Alexei clenched his teeth and stared at his own reflection in the mirror. *No more accidents, no more hemophiliac attacks*, he resolved. *I'm really going to be more careful from now on.*

When Konstantin was christened two months later, Alexei and Ileana waited outside nervously, feeling the August heat and regretting the Orthodox custom that prevented parents from being present. When the service was over, they rushed into the church to find their baby, only to be surrounded by Igor and all of his brothers.

"You named the heir after Papa!" Igor exclaimed. He kept his arm carefully around Sophie, who was far enough along in her third pregnancy to be showing. Next to them, Gavril, Konstantin, Ioann and George stood grinning. Behind them, their sisters Vera and Tatiana smiled, and their mother Elizabeth was glowing.

"We're very honored that you have chosen this," Ioann said. "Our family will finally have a Tsar Konstantin."

Elena appeared next to Ioann, holding their youngest child, two-year-old Gleb. The rest of their children gathered around them. Their oldest son, Vsevolod, now twelve, stood closest to his father, and Ioann put his arm around him.

Alexandra appeared behind them, holding little Konstantin. Ioann and his family parted to let Ileana through to take the baby, and Alexei enclosed his hand around his son's fist.

Vsevolod took a step closer to get a better look at Konstantin. When he saw that Konstantin's eyes were open, he started making faces, trying to get him to smile. Konstantin continued staring at his older cousin, but remained stoic. Behind Vsevolod, his four-year-old brother Vyacheslav laughed. Their nearly eleven-year-old sister Ekaterina rolled her eyes at her brother's antics as she looked at Alexei. "Sevka was acting like that before that ceremony began, too," she said.

"He is capable of behaving, however," Ioann said pointedly, putting his arm around his son's neck in an iron grip. Vsevolod, looking worried, stood up as straight as his father's grip would allow. Only then did Ioann release him.

Two months later, Igor called Alexei with the news that Sophie had given birth to another son. Even over the phone, Alexei could hear Igor beaming. "Congratulations!" he said.

Two days after the baby's birth, Alexei went to Pavlovsk to see his newest cousin. When he arrived, Ioann and Vsevolod led him towards Igor's apartments. Peter and Nicholas were playing in the room outside where their new brother lay, and Alexei could hear their laughter as he approached.

Ioann smiled as he listened to his nephews. "They've been as happy as Igor to have another child in the house," he said.

As soon as Alexei, Ioann and Vsevolod appeared, Peter and Nicholas ran to them, and Alexei swept them up in a large hug. "How's the baby?" he asked.

"Great!" Nicholas said enthusiastically.

"How's little Kostya?" Peter asked, holding up his two index fingers an inch apart.

"He's not *that* little," Alexei replied, as Ioann and Vsevolod guffawed behind him.

"What are you laughing at?" Peter asked indignantly.

Vsevolod dashed around Alexei. "What if we called you 'little Petya'?" he asked, bending down and pinching Peter's round cheeks. Peter pushed his hands away and made a face at him. Vsevolod made a face back.

Just then, Igor opened the door from one of the apartments' inner rooms. Peter instantly stood up straight, even as Nicholas giggled behind him. Igor looked at his oldest son suspiciously. "I'm behaving, Papa," Peter said. "And I want to see the baby."

"No," Igor said. He closed the door behind him and dove toward Peter. Peter tried to duck away, but Igor grabbed him and picked him up. Nicholas, seeing an opportunity, raced behind his father and ducked into the room where his new brother was in his crib.

Peter objected strenuously, struggling in Igor's arms and yelping. "Papa!" he shrieked. "Nicky just ran into the baby's room!"

Igor, Ioann and Vsevolod burst into laughter. Alexei joined them. Then Igor put Peter down, and they all went in to see Igor's newest addition. Igor lifted his tiny son from the crib.

"Aww, what a sweetie," Ioann cooed.

Igor rolled his eyes at his older brother. "You've had six kids of your own," he said. "I can't believe you're still such a softie."

Ioann shrugged and smiled. "I'm not apologizing for anything," he said.

Vsevolod grimaced at his father. "Were you that way with me?" he asked.

"No, I was worse," Ioann teased.

Alexei reached out with one finger and stroked the baby's tiny hand, feeling how soft his skin was. "What are you going to name him?" he asked.

"I'm thinking Oleg, after my brother," Igor said.

Ioann raised his eyebrows. "I like it," he said. "But I worry about the fate that Oleg met."

"I'm trying not to be superstitious about it," Igor replied. He looked at Alexei. "Perhaps he and Kostya can have their lessons together when they're old enough."

Alexei smiled. "I'm planning on it already," he said.

Two years later, Konstantin was toddling around the palace. His blond hair grew like a mop on his head, and his clear blue eyes stared at everything around him. By then, he had already taken several tumbles down the palace staircase and smacked himself on the table at which his parents took tea. Each of these incidents had caused his parents' hearts to race, but as each incident had only produced a regular bruise that had quickly healed, Alexei and Ileana had found themselves relaxing.

One day, Ileana and Alexei were at tea together when the phone jangled, making both of them jump. Konstantin laughed at his parents' reactions as Ileana got up to answer the phone. "Hello?"

For a moment, there was nothing but silence on the other end, and Ileana frowned, wondering if the caller had either hung up or forgotten how to use the phone. But then she heard a shuddering breath being taken and released, and somehow, in that second, Ileana knew who was on the other end. "Mama?" she asked. "What's wrong?"

Behind her, the governess had already lifted Konstantin from his chair and was heading back towards the nursery. Alexei was about to return to his study when he heard Ileana's question. He waited, frowning, to see what the phone call was about.

Finally, Marie spoke on the other end of the phone. "Nando passed away this morning," she said.

"Oh my God," Ileana said. "What happened?"

"The doctors are still examining his body," Marie said, her voice thick.

"We'll make travel arrangements," Ileana said. She replaced the phone in its cradle and stood with her hand still on the phone.

"I'm sorry," Alexei said from behind her.

For a minute Ileana was silent. Then she burst into tears. Alexei put his arms around her and held her until the tears had stopped. The next day, they were on the Imperial train with Konstantin, heading towards Bucharest, where they remained for several days. Only once Marie could bear to be parted from her daughter did they return home. Ileana spent much of the journey back staring out the window contemplatively, watching the arc of the sun, high in the azure June sky. "What are you thinking?" Alexei asked.

Ileana sighed. "I think Romania is going to be very different under Carol than it was under my father," she said.

"You don't seem happy with your brother's ascension at all," Alexei said. "I thought you two were close."

"We were growing up," Ileana said. "But he's changed a lot, and made some bad decisions. He fell in love with a woman he couldn't marry and even abdicated over her. The government had to reinstate his position as heir. He's married to Helen, but you wouldn't know it, given how badly he treats her." Ileana shook her head. "I'm afraid for what the country will look like under his rule."

"It's a tough thing, to be born into this station in life," Alexei agreed. "Maybe he'll grow into his new role."

Once they returned to Russia, it became obvious that Ileana was pregnant again. As her pregnancy progressed and her stomach grew rounder, Alexei came to one of her checkups with Dr. Botkin. He watched as the doctor examined Ileana, prodding her and putting one end of his stethoscope up to her stomach to listen for the baby's heartbeat. He took one listen, frowned, and moved the stethoscope to a different location.

"What's the matter?" Alexei asked forcefully.

Botkin spent another minute listening before he responded. "I hear two heartbeats," he said.

"Ileana's and the baby's?" Alexei asked, wondering if that was obvious.

"No, two babies," Botkin replied.

"Twins?" Ileana said.

"That's my guess," Botkin said.

Ileana's eyes had gone as wide as they could, and Alexei's eyebrows shot up. "When will you know for sure?" Alexei asked.

"When they're born," Botkin said.

"Seriously, Yevgeny Sergeievich," Alexei said. "Please tell me the truth."

"It will be impossible to know for certain until they're born," Botkin said, speaking more seriously now. "But it may become clearer as the pregnancy progresses."

But the doctor's intuition proved correct. In the middle of January, 1929, as large snowflakes added to the seven feet of felt snow outside the Winter Palace, Ileana gave birth to identical twin boys. Alexei could not contain his joy. He ordered two sets of cannon to be lined up, and for each to give the three-hundred gun salute. A few minutes later, his face lit up with glee as the force of the cannons seemed to shake the walls of the Palace.

As soon as it was safe for him to do so, Konstantin crept into the nursery to see his new brothers. For a few minutes, he stood looking at the two tiny humans that were sleeping in their bassinets. Alexei and Ileana watched him from the doorway. Then, as one of the little boys started wiggling in his crib, his eyes still closed, Konstantin turned to his parents. His eyebrows screwed up and he pointed a little finger at his brothers, as if trying to direct his parents' attention.

Both Alexei and Ileana laughed, and Alexei went and knelt down next to his oldest son. "These are your brothers, Kostya," he said. He pointed to the boy on the left. "This is Dmitri, and that one is Rostislav."

Konstantin looked back to the twins, and, waving his hands in the air, let out a laugh.

In February, Igor surprised Alexei with happy news of his own. "Sophie's pregnant again," he said one day as he arrived at the Winter Palace and pulled off his huge winter overcoat.

"That's great!" Ileana said with a grin. Igor grinned as well.

"How is she feeling?" Alexei asked.

"She's fine," Igor said.

Two weeks later, however, just when Alexei was expecting Igor at the Winter Palace, the phone rang instead. "I can't come today," Igor said. "Sophie is sick."

Alexei frowned. "What's going on?"

"I'm not sure," Igor replied, and Alexei heard the concern in his voice. "But the doctors are already here, so I'll know more later."

That evening, Ileana looked worried when Alexei repeated the conversation to her. "That doesn't sound good," she said. "I hope it's not about the baby."

"I'm concerned about that too," Alexei admitted. He and Ileana looked at each other for a moment. Then Alexei picked up the phone and dialed Igor's number. When Igor's brother Konstantin answered instead, Alexei knew something was wrong. "Kostya, what's happening?" he asked. "Is Sophie alright?"

Konstantin sighed. "No, she lost the baby," he said.

"Oh my God," Alexei said, his chest constricting. "Is there anything I can do? Should I come over?"

"One second," Konstantin replied, and Alexei could hear him handing the phone to someone else and saying, "it's Alyosha."

A moment later, Igor was on the phone. "All of my brothers are here," he said, despite how strangely silent it was in the background.

"Igor, I'm really sorry," Alexei said. He could tell his cousin was crying. "I know you wanted this child."

"Yes, I did," Igor replied. "But the doctors warned us it would be a risk. We should have listened."

"How is Sophie feeling?"

"Uuummmm," Igor said, making Alexei contemplate going to Igor's mansion. "She was in pain before, but I think she's feeling a little better now. She's lying down, anyway." He sniffed.

Alexei was at a loss for words. "Well, let me know if there's anything I can do," he said finally, before hanging up. The phone was barely back in his cradle before Alexei's tears began to fall from his face. Ileana, who had been standing close enough to hear the conversation, put her arms around her husband, and Alexei buried his face in her neck as he sobbed.

When Igor also did not make it to work the next day, Alexei decided to go see his cousin in the evening. He and Ileana made their way to Igor's mansion on the Nevsky Prospect, leaving their children in the care of their governesses. As they were being driven over, Alexei stared out the window of the car, noticing that the clouds had been blown away by the fierce wind. Up above, he could see the sky, black as ink and dotted with stars. He felt his stomach writhe as they arrived at Igor's.

Inside, Alexei was not surprised to find Igor surrounded by his brothers. He sat in one of the mansion's drawing rooms with Igor, Ioann, Konstantin, Gavril and George as Ileana slipped upstairs to see Sophie. "Are your mother and sisters here?" Alexei asked Igor.

Igor nodded. "They're upstairs with Sophie." Tears glistened in his eyes, and he worked hard not to let them fall. "I've made such a mess of things," he said.

"This isn't your fault," Alexei said, putting his hand over Igor's.

"I was the one that wanted that child," Igor said. "Sophie doesn't even want to see me now. Maybe if I hadn't pushed so hard…"

Ioann shook his head at his younger brother. "You can't blame yourself," he said.

Igor just shrugged. "How come this never happened with any of your kids?" he asked, looking around at each of his brothers. "Why is this only happening to me? What have I done wrong in my life?" His tears finally fell from his eyes, and his brothers stood up and surrounded him.

Gavril put his hands on Igor's shoulders. "Your life has been exemplary," he said. "What's happening now is not a reflection of that."

Nicholas and Peter snuck into the room, looking tiny next to the tall men around them. Igor was the only one still seated, and both boys crawled onto their father's lap. Igor hugged them. "I should check on Oleg too," he said.

"He's asleep," Nicholas said, his voice muffled as his face remained pressed against Igor's chest.

"Is he?" Igor asked, lightening his grip on Peter and Nicholas just enough for them to look up at him and nod.

"We looked in on him before we came downstairs," Peter said.

Alexei gripped Ileana's hand as they were driven home that night. "Sophie blames it on herself too," Ileana said.

Alexei shook his head in despair. "I hope they talk to each other," he said. "Otherwise this is just the beginning of the pain."

When Igor began showing up for work again and becoming more engaged, Alexei relaxed, but all it took was another early morning phone call from Igor to rattle his nerves. "Sophie's gone, Alyosha," Igor said as soon as Alexei answered.

"What?" Alexei asked. "Gone where?"

"Back to Vienna."

"When?"

"Late last night or early this morning. She left a note saying she was leaving, and not to come after her."

Alexei took a deep breath. *I really have no idea what to tell him,* he thought, his stomach sinking. "Do you think it would help her- or you- to leave her be for a few days?" he asked.

Igor shook his head. "I may have been willing to do that, except that she took Oleg."

"Oh my God."

"She wasn't the only one to lose that child- I did too," Igor said firmly. "Taking Oleg only makes it worse."

"I agree," Alexei said. "Why don't you sit tight for a minute? I'll be right over."

Once more, Alexei and Ileana made a high speed drive over to Igor's mansion, where they again found Igor surrounded by his brothers. "You should go after her, Igor," Gavril was saying as Alexei and Ileana entered Igor's apartments. "You're not going to see her or Oleg again if you don't."

"You really need to talk to her," Konstantin agreed. "She's not the only one suffering, and she needs to see that."

Igor looked over at Alexei. "I think you should go after her," Alexei concurred. "Especially now that Oleg is involved."

"Leave Petya and Nicky with me," Ioann said. "I'll take care of them while you're gone."

"You have six kids of your own," Igor reminded him. "Can you handle two more? They can be pretty rambunctious."

"There were eight of us growing up," Ioann replied. "It's not a problem."

"Or any of the rest of us can take them," Konstantin offered.

Igor sighed. "I didn't mean for them to be a burden too," he said.

Ioann put his arm around his brother. "They aren't," he said emphatically.

Igor looked back at Alexei. It was clear that he could not make up his mind. "Leave Nicky and Petya with Ioann," Alexei ordered. "Go find Sophie and work something out."

It took Igor several days to drive to Vienna. When he arrived, he checked into an upscale hotel. *Still feels like a step down from the last time I was here, when I was about to propose to Sophie.* He took a deep breath and stared at the sky, which was turning from red to purple as the sun set. *I just hope Sophie will see me tomorrow. I really want her back, and I want Oleg too.*

The next day, Igor felt his heart race as he was led to Sophie's apartments in Artstetten Castle. In front of him, Prince Jaroslav knocked on Sophie's door. Nothing but silence greeted the knock. "Are you sure she's in there?" Igor whispered.

Jaroslav nodded. "Sophie," he said, speaking in a normal voice. "Igor's here. I think you should talk to him."

"Go away," Sophie said.

Jaroslav looked at Igor and held up his hands in resignation. Then he left. Igor had no intention of going so quietly. He waited until Jaroslav had disappeared before knocking on the door himself. "Sophie, let me in," he said.

"No," Sophie said.

"You can't stay here forever."

"Yes, I can."

"I want you to come back to St. Petersburg, and I want Oleg too."

There was a silence. "I don't think I can make it back there," Sophie said finally.

Now Igor felt like throwing up his hands. "Would you at least give me another chance?" he asked.

Another silence ensued, and Igor, at a loss for words, put his hand on the doorknob. It turned, and he realized the door had been unlocked the whole time. Still, something stopped him. *I can't just walk in,* he thought. *That's not fair.* In the continuing silence, however, Oleg suddenly started crying, and that was too much for Igor. He pushed the door open and went inside.

Oleg sat in a crib in the center of the room. Tears ran down his face and mucus ran out of his nose. He saw his father and let out another wail. Sophie stood at the window, her back to Igor. Igor hesitated, not sure where to go first. Then he went to Sophie, and saw that tears were running down her face too.

Igor put a hand around his wife's shoulders. "I'm really sorry about all of this," he said. "But I love you and I want you to come home with me."

Finally, Sophie rested her head against Igor's shoulder. She still faced the window. Igor put his hand on her shoulder and pulled her around so that she was facing him and clutched her to his chest. They stood like that for a minute before Sophie finally put her arms around her husband.

Then Oleg wailed again, and tears continued to flow down his face. Unable to take it anymore, Igor went over and picked him up. He used his handkerchief to wipe the tears from his face and the snot from his nose. When Oleg's face was dry, Igor clutched him to his chest and felt Oleg rubbing his face back and forth against his uniform.

When they returned to St. Petersburg, Alexei and Ileana were waiting for them at Pavlovsk with all of Igor's siblings and their families. Ioann and Elena stood in front of the family, holding Peter and Nicholas by the hands.

Igor was the first to get out of the car, and Peter and Nicholas ran to him. "Papa!" they cried. Igor swept them up into a big hug and carried them to the other side of the car, where he put them down and opened the door for Sophie.

"Mama!" Peter and Nicholas cried, throwing their arms around their mother's legs and waist, which was only as high as they could reach. Sophie smiled and bent down to hug them.

Igor lifted Oleg from the back seat, and Nicholas and Peter grinned at him. "Oleg," they said. Nicholas rubbed his little brother's hand, and Peter grabbed one of his feet. From the vantage point of their father's arms, Oleg put a tiny hand on Peter's nose and pressed on it. The three brothers laughed as the family went inside.

CHAPTER 4

It was October 29, 1929. Alexei felt jittery as soon as he got out of bed. The day before, the American stock market had begun to plunge. Given the time difference between St. Petersburg and New York City, Alexei spent most of the day working, concentrating as best he could. In the evening, he turned on the radio. For nearly an hour, he stood riveted as newscasters described the market's continued plunge, and the intense frenzy of shares being sold.

As Alexei shuddered, Igor appeared in the doorway, a grim expression on his face. The two cousins shared a horrified look. "We've spent all these years worried that Germany would rearm and wipe us off the planet," Igor said, "and the biggest aggressor may turn out to be the financial markets."

"It's nothing I could have ever anticipated," Alexei agreed.

"The Americans have been investing in our economy ever since we visited Washington," Igor added. "If their economy collapses, will ours too?"

"I don't know," Alexei admitted. "We have plenty of financing aside from that, and plenty of railroads, roads, and other infrastructure still left to build, so maybe that will protect us from total collapse."

"Maybe," Igor said. His expression of doubt mirrored Alexei's.

They both turned back to the radio, where stories of investors being ruined by millions of dollars in losses continued. Alexei rubbed his temples. "I have to call a meeting of the Duma," he said. "We need a plan."

Alexei spent the next couple of months feeling like he was going downhill in slow motion. He watched in horror as the American economy spiraled out of control. The stock market crash had obliterated many people's savings. People that had been spectacularly wealthy a year ago now lacked the money to buy food. Many made a run on the banks, thinking that what little money they did have left would be safer in their homes. Banks failed. Manufacturing and agriculture slowed to a crawl. Millions of people lost their jobs. Bread lines formed. The world's other industrialized nations also saw their economies slide at an ever-increasing pace.

Alexei, struggling to ensure that Russia missed the worst of it, endured never-ending meetings with the Duma and his ministers, and every possibility of economic growth was put forth and debated. Throughout it all, the American capital that had been invested in the Russian economy dried up. Alexei, having foreseen that it would happen, began investing his own personal fortune in the economy. Other Russian industrialists followed suit, beginning with Felix Youssoupov. Alexei was relieved. *The Youssoupovs were always several times wealthier than my family,* he thought. *And they're a much smaller family. I'll bet Felix could invest more than I am and not even feel it.* All the same, he made sure that Felix was aware of his gratitude.

"This isn't just about you, Alyosha," Felix said one night as he joined Alexei for dinner at the Winter Palace. "It's about Russia too. My factories and mines employ tens of thousands of people. Everyone's lifestyle is at risk."

The next day, Alexei and Ileana set off across the Russian empire, checking in on factories to make sure they were still producing, touring mines to ensure that minerals and other commodities were still being extracted. They also stopped in the fertile areas of the Ukraine, whose black soil had always supplied the country with so much of its agricultural goods. There, Alexei saw that improved farming techniques he had implemented helped immeasurably.

"We're industrializing, but there's still so much to do," Alexei said as he and Ileana traveled back to St. Petersburg. He stared out the window, seeing the winter's barren trees and heaps of snow. *It's always winter in Russia,* he thought. *What have I done?* When he looked back at Ileana, his eyes were filled with tears.

"Alyosha, what's wrong?" Ileana asked, moving to the seat next to him.

"I'm *so* tired," Alexei said, burying his face in his hands.

Ileana put her arm around him. "These past couple of months have been very difficult," she agreed. "It's hard seeing so much suffering, but you're doing so much work, and you're doing it so well. The Russian people would be a lot worse off if it weren't for you."

"Really?" Alexei asked, finally looking at his wife.

"Yes, I really believe that," Ileana said, her gaze unwavering.

As the economic crisis deepened, Alexei buried himself in economic textbooks, trying to get a better sense of what was happening and how he could prevent it. *I may be learning a lot,* he thought, *but it's tedious too. I could use a break right about now.* As if on cue, he looked up to see Konstantin, now just past his fourth birthday, standing in the doorway of the study, smiling his wide, childish smile. Behind him, his governess hesitated in the hallway, giving him space. "Kostya," Alexei said. He went to the doorway and picked Konstantin up. "What are you doing here?"

"I'm just visiting," Konstantin said.

"Tired of your governess' company already?"

Konstantin laughed, a tinkling sound that filled the room. Then his eyes went to the small, child-sized desk that sat next to Alexei's. "Is that desk for me?" he asked, pointing a little finger at it.

"It can be if you want it," Alexei replied. Konstantin squirmed in his arms, and Alexei put his son down so that he could examine the desk more closely. "My father put that desk in his study for me when I was little," Alexei continued.

"This desk was yours?" Konstantin asked.

Alexei nodded. "I used to sit at it when I was your size."

Konstantin laughed again. "When were you ever my size?"

"When I was around your age," Alexei replied, still smiling.

"Naaawww," Konstantin replied. He looked back at the desk and ran his hand over the smooth, worn wood. "I can help you with your work?"

"Absolutely."

Konstantin paused, thinking. "I may do that," he said seriously as he walked back to the door, where his governess still waited. "But first I need to get my pens and paper."

Several days later, Alexei awoke as the sun rose. Morning light was just beginning to stream in through windows of his bedroom as he got dressed. Outside, the yellow summer sunshine filtered through the fog of the early dawn. Moments later, Alexei pulled on his right boot and felt his large toe hit something soft and soggy. "Eeeeuuuuugggh," he said, pulling off his boot as fast as he could. Behind him, Ileana sat up in bed, looking confused.

Alexei turned his boot upside down and shook it. A large, overripe strawberry came tumbling out and landed on the floor. "How did that get there?" Ileana asked.

Alexei bent down and picked up the strawberry, handling it carefully. "I'll bet it was Kostya," he said. "There were strawberries at breakfast yesterday."

"How do you know it was Kostya?"

"I did the same thing when I was his age. Only I didn't put it in my father's boot, I put it in the slipper of a lady-in-waiting."

Ileana shook her head. "I can't believe you did that," she said.

Alexei laughed. "Papa made me apologize immediately."

"Are you going to do the same to Kostya?"

Alexei contemplated the situation. "No," he said. "I have another idea."

At teatime that day, Alexei waited as the tea was served and the breadbasket was placed on the table. Then he picked up a small plate and put the strawberry on it. "This one is for you, Kostya," he said.

Konstantin took the plate, and when he saw the strawberry on it, he burst out laughing. Next to him, Dmitri and Rostislav watched intensely. "How come he gets a strawberry and we don't?" Dmitri asked.

"It's a mushy strawberry!" Konstantin said. "I put it in Papa's boot yesterday." All three boys looked at Alexei and laughed. Then Konstantin picked up the strawberry and threw it at Alexei.

Ileana was about to rebuke her oldest son when Alexei pulled off a piece of the biscuit in front of him and hurled it at Konstantin. A second later, bread was flying all directions as Dmitri and Rostislav joined the food fight. Ileana ducked to avoid being hit. For a full minute, food flew in every direction. Finally, Ileana hauled herself up onto her feet. "Stop!" she yelled.

Immediately, everything became quiet. The bread stopped flying through the air. Alexei, Konstantin, Dmitri and Rostislav stared at Ileana. Then they all burst into laughter. Ileana shook her head. Then she joined them.

Finally, Alexei stood to go back to his study. The servants moved forward to clean up the scene. "Help them clean up," Alexei ordered his sons.

In September, 1930, Alexei was about to put down his work for the evening when he received a phone call from Grand Duke Kirill. "As much as I hate to break this to you, Alyosha, I need to retire," Kirill said. "I love Moscow, and being Governor-General has been good for me, but I need some quiet time with my family."

"I understand," Alexei replied. "You've held that position for more than a decade." He looked out the palace window. A gray twilight had already descended on the Palace's park, enshrouding the trees and benches outside. Looking back at the portraits of his family that hung in his study, Alexei realized how dark it had become in the room as well, and he turned on the lamp on his desk.

"Still, I don't wish to inconvenience you," Kirill said. "Finding someone new takes a lot of work, and you certainly have enough to handle right now."

"I'll always have a lot of work. Do you have any thoughts as to who might succeed you?"

"Someone from your generation, definitely," Kirill replied. "I don't know if any of Igor's brothers want it, or maybe one of the Alexandrovichi princes? Your Aunt Xenia would certainly be pleased to have one of her sons in this position."

"Yes, I was thinking of Nikita in particular," Alexei said, picturing his tall, thin, dark-haired cousin who was usually smiling.

"The third son," Kirill said. "Interesting choice."

"I think he's the most refined of his brothers, and he seems to be in a more stable marriage than Andrei or Feodor."

"I think he'll do well here."

"Me too. I'll give him a call and see if I can arrange it."

That night, Michael joined Alexei, Ileana and their sons for dinner. Afterwards, when he and Michael withdrew to one of the drawing rooms, Alexei had the sense that Michael had something on his mind. As Michael seated himself in one of the mahogany-colored leather chairs, Alexei went to a cabinet and took out a bottle of vodka and two shot glasses. He handed one to his uncle.

"Thanks," Michael said as Alexei filled his glass.

Alexei filled his own glass and put the bottle on a small table before sitting across from Michael. "So, you too?" he asked.

Michael looked at him quizzically.

"Kirill called me today. He's retiring."

"Can't say I'm surprised," Michael replied. "But you're right, I'm looking to do the same."

Alexei sighed. "I've really appreciated your insight over the years, Misha. It's made a big difference."

"I don't think you've needed me as much recently as you did when you first became tsar. You've been a lot more independent these last few years."

"Still, trusted advisors are hard to come by."

"I'm motivated by the same forces that Kirill is," Michael said. "I'm fifty-four years old, and the men in this family don't have the longest life expectancy. I'd like to enjoy my life while I still can."

"Don't talk like that, Misha," Alexei said.

"It's true," Michael said with a shrug. "My father died at 49, Nicky at fifty-two."

"I know," Alexei said. "I don't blame you for wanting to enjoy your retirement, but I don't want you to disappear entirely."

"I won't," Michael promised.

In March 1932, while the world's economy had barely improved and the economic crisis remained dire, Ileana discovered that she was pregnant again. Alexei was ecstatic, but he sensed that Ileana did not share his joy. One night, he found her by the window outside their sons' nursery, staring out the window.

Outside, the storm that had been brewing all day had finally unleashed its fury, and the howling wind drove rain against the window with startling speed. Suddenly, a huge flash of lightning sprawled across the sky, lighting up the garden outside, which was still empty from the winter. A second later, a huge bang of thunder made the earth shake and the windows shudder.

Both Alexei and Ileana ducked, then looked towards the nursery, hoping that the noise had not woken their sons. But as the rain continued to splash against the windows, no sound emanated from the bedroom, and Alexei and Ileana relaxed. Soon, they were looking out the window again, and Alexei finally felt comfortable saying something. "Are you unhappy?" he asked.

"Not *unhappy*," Ileana said. "Just.... *worried*."

"About what?"

"The baby, I guess."

"Why?" Alexei asked, concerned. "Do you feel alright? Did the doctor-"

"It's not any of that," Ileana interrupted. "It's everything else- your hemophilia always made me worried that you'd be gone sooner rather than later. The economic crisis, which no one seems to know what to do about. Is this any type of world to bring a child into?"

"My hemophilia will always be an issue," Alexei agreed. "But I've spent my life managing it, and I haven't had an attack in a really long time. It's a reason to have another child- I need more heirs, not fewer." He shook his head. "Besides, we're fine, economically, for right now. My family's always been wealthy- you know that. And the country, as a whole, is doing alright for now. That seems to be the one positive thing about Russia being so far behind economically- we're still developing, and everything is moving forward."

Ileana heaved a breath and looked away, and Alexei could tell that she was not reassured.

"I really want this child," Alexei added. "I want this one as much as I wanted the others."

Ileana still did not look at him.

"What are you thinking?" Alexei asked finally.

"There are ways of ending a pregnancy," Ileana said. "Herbs I could take-"

"No!" Alexei yelled. "No!" Simultaneously, he and Ileana turned and looked at the nursery door. Not wanting to wake his sleeping sons, Alexei grabbed Ileana's arm and pulled her down the stairs and into another part of the Palace, where they would not wake their children even if they yelled.

"Alyosha, stop," Ileana yelped. "You're hurting me!"

Alexei dropped her arm immediately, and they stood in the long hallway of the Winter Palace, staring at each other. Finally, Alexei started talking again. "I love you, Ileana," he said, "and I will love all the children you bear for me. I agree that these are hard times- it's hard to even believe that there will be a future, but I will protect you and all of our children with every ounce of life I have!"

Ileana looked at him, and tears started rolling down her face. "I'm sorry," she said.

Alexei held out his arms, and Ileana ran to him. They wrapped their arms around each other and stood there for a few minutes. Finally, Alexei said, "promise me you won't do anything to harm the baby? I really want this child."

"I know," Ileana said. "Don't worry. This child will be as healthy as the others."

When the baby was born in October, 1932, she was Alexei and Ileana's first daughter. For the first time, the cannon salute stopped at 100 rather than continuing to 301, but none of that mattered to the child's happy parents. *I have three strong boys, any of whom can inherit my throne,* Alexei thought. *In contrast to my parents, I can enjoy this fourth child all the more because she is a daughter.* With that in mind, Alexei and Ileana decided to name her Anastasia.

Despite Alexei's familial joy, the world's economic woes only continued. A famine hit the United States, and Alexei was fearful that the whole world would collapse. After several days of checking his own country's food stores, Alexei made a phone call to Washington to see if President Franklin Delano Roosevelt would be willing to import Russian wheat and other items.

"Your Imperial Majesty, I've heard much about you from my predecessors," Roosevelt said. "I hope we have the chance to meet in person one day."

"You do me much honor, Mr. President," Alexei said. The conversation quickly shifted to business. "News of your harvest and food issues has reached Russia," Alexei said. "My country's latest harvest has produced a bumper crop, and I'm hoping this will assist you."

"That is most generous," Roosevelt replied. "But we are also trying to protect our own economy, and have encouraged our citizens to continue purchasing American products."

"With all due respect, Mr. President, your citizens are starving. Many don't have the money to buy necessities such as bread, and yet you continue with nearly fifty percent tariffs and essential items such as wheat. I don't understand your policies."

On the other end of the phone, Roosevelt sounded like he was smiling. "Our economy has been hurting," he said, as if Alexei needed reminding. "And these are the policies we've decided to pursue."

"I sure hope this economic crisis ends soon, Mr. President," Alexei said, *even if I don't think your policies will ease it at all.*

"Thank you," Roosevelt said.

When the phone call ended, Alexei put his head down on his desk, trying to rid himself of the frustration and despair that were threatening to overwhelm him. *I'm trying so hard to fix this,* he thought. *But I can't be of help if other countries won't accept the assistance.*

Alexei watched as his children grew fast. Already Konstantin was beginning his lessons, and Alexei made sure that he shared his schoolroom with boys his age. Marie's second son, Andrei Obolensky, and Igor's youngest son, Oleg, were first on Alexei's list. Two more noble boys, Vladimir Golitsyn and Alexander Dolgoruky, rounded out the list, and immediately, Konstantin began enjoying both his lessons and his new friends.

At the end of January, 1933, Alexei was listening to the news on the radio when it was announced that Adolph Hitler's Nazi party had gained the largest number of votes in the Reichstag in the German election a couple of months earlier, making Hitler chancellor.

Ileana came into Alexei's office a few minutes after the announcement to find Alexei white as a sheet. "Alyosha, what's wrong?" she cried.

"It's as I feared," he said, gesturing at the radio.

They both were silent as Ileana listened to the news. "You've been worried about this for awhile," she said.

Alexei nodded. "But no one else in the world has been willing to discuss the possibilities."

"It's time to try again."

"I'd start with the Americans again, if it weren't for how much they've been rebuking me over the last several years."

"People closer to home will listen to you more," Ileana said. "They're closer to the conflict."

"Alexander and Boris should be on our side, as are the Poles and the Finns."

"As are the Romanians," Ileana said with a grin.

"Oh, I would be wise not to underestimate the Romanians," Alexei said, smiling back. "But we're going to need some of the other big world powers."

"England's going to be the big draw here," Ileana said. "I can't imagine them aligning themselves with Hitler, especially with how popular Anastasia has become over there."

"Much as I hated to see my sisters married off for political reasons, I'm now glad they were. Maybe I should have married Marie to some American capitalist. Then maybe they'd listen."

"Talk about an unequal marriage," Ileana said. They both laughed.

As the meetings and talks about alliances progressed, Alexei, Boris and Alexander met towards the end of 1933, and then again in the middle of 1934. "Are the Brits definitely on our side?" Boris asked Alexei.

Alexei nodded. "I'm expecting to conclude a formal alliance with them by the end of the year."

"I've also been negotiating with the French," Alexander said. "I'm planning a state visit there in October to formalize our relationship."

"Paris?" Alexei asked. "I may go as well. If we're all at the negotiating table, maybe things will move faster than if it's piecemeal."

"You're welcome to try," Alexander said. "Though we're discussing Marseilles rather than Paris."

"Still worth it," Alexei said. The three men laughed and said their goodbyes.

"I'm glad we're going a few days early," Ileana said as they packed their trunks at the beginning of October. "I haven't been to Paris in years."

"You really like it there, don't you?" Alexei said. Ileana nodded.

The few days in Paris passed pleasantly enough, and soon Alexei and Ileana were in Marseilles on October 9, greeting Olga and Alexander. Alexei hugged his sister as they prepared for a procession through the streets of Marseilles. "It is always good to see you," he said.

The French president and other government officials joined them. When it came time to split into different cars for the procession, Alexei and Ileana went in the first car with Igor and Gorvenko. Behind them,

Alexander and French Foreign Minister Louis Barthou moved to the second car, leaving Olga to get in the car behind them. Olga frowned.

"Don't worry," Alexander told her. "I'll rejoin you once this is over."

Slowly, the cars, their tops down, proceeded through the streets. All around them, the crowd cheered, but there were a lot of people that were very close to the cars, and Alexei found himself feeling slightly claustrophobic. He looked at Gorvenko, and could see that Gorvenko was as nervous as he was. Taking a deep breath, Alexei reached for Ileana's hand in an attempt to calm himself.

A second later, gunfire sprayed through the air. Alexei ducked involuntarily, then grabbed Ileana and shoved her down. Behind him, Olga's screams tore through the air. Without hesitating, Alexei threw open the car door, slipped out of Gorvenko's grip, and leapt out onto the street.

But the gunfire had hit the second car behind him, not the third car. "Sandro!" Alexei yelled. Olga was still screaming as she scrambled out of the third car. Alexei raced to Alexander's car. Ileana was right behind him. Alexander's car had come to a stop, and Alexei pulled the back door open. Alexander stared back at him, his eyes unblinking. Next to him, Barthou was bleeding extensively.

"Sandro?" Alexei whispered. He put his hands to his brother-in-law's face and neck, and they came away covered in blood. Alexei tottered, and his knees shook.

By now, Olga had come running to her husband's car. "Sandro!" she screamed. Ileana, seeing the blood that covered Alexei's hands, pulled Olga away from the car and her dead husband.

Alexei stood, unmoving. His eyes were still fixed on Alexander. Alexander's eyes remained open, and a small smile was fixed on his face. "Sandro!" Alexei whispered again, certain that Alexander would move. Behind him, Olga continued to scream. Slowly, Alexei turned to face her. Already, policemen were pulling her away, shoving her towards the car behind them. A single drop of blood fell from Alexei's hand on to the pavement below him.

Suddenly, Alexei felt strong arms grabbing him and pulling him towards the car he had just exited. His body felt so leaden that he could not resist as Igor pulled Ileana back to their car, and Gorvenko pulled him away. Igor shoved Ileana into the back of the first car and raced around to the driver's side. Gorvenko shoved Alexei into the car and jumped in after them. "Drive!" Gorvenko shouted as he slammed the door behind him.

Igor obeyed, and the car shot forward. Alexei held Ileana under him, and Gorvenko had thrown himself over Alexei. Alexei could not see anything of the world outside the car, but he could hear the hoof beats of the Cossack guard that raced next to them. He could also hear the car's tires screeching against the pavement, could smell burning rubber. All the while, his heartbeat pounded in his head. *Sandro, Sandro.*

When the car finally came to a stop, Gorvenko slowly raised his head and looked around. Igor had already gotten out of the driver's seat and had come around to the back of the car. "It's quiet," he said.

Alexei slowly sat up and realized that they were back at the unassuming hotel where they had stayed the previous night. Cossack guards surrounded them, but no one else was nearby. Alexei got out of the car and pulled Ileana out after him. Tears streamed down Ileana's face, and Alexei still felt shockwaves coursing through his body. "Sandro," he whispered as Gorvenko and Igor pulled him and Ileana back into the hotel. Then he managed to say, more loudly, "Olga!"

"It looked like the guards got her out of there," Gorvenko said. "They killed the gunman too."

"Who would do such a thing?!" Alexei shrieked.

Inside the hotel, Alexei paced around, unable to stand still, until Ileana convinced him to at least wash Alexander's blood off his hands. Then he called Olga's hotel, hoping for some news. His nephew Peter answered the phone, and in a second, Alexei flashed back to the image he had of Peter in his bassinet when Olga and Alexander had come to St. Petersburg for Nicholas' funeral. *What's going to happen now?* Alexei wondered. *Is Peter now king?*

"Peter, it's Alexei," he managed to say. Tears started flowing down his face. On the other end, Peter started crying too. "I'm so sorry," Alexei said.

Then Alexei could hear the phone being taken away from Peter, and he frowned. A second later, Prince Paul, Alexander's first cousin, was on the line. "Alyosha, were you hurt at all?" Paul asked.

"No, I'm fine," Alexei said. "Paul, what's happening? Where's Olga?"

"She's back here at the hotel," Paul replied. "She wasn't hurt, but she was pretty hysterical. The doctors gave her something, and she's asleep."

"What's happening with… Sandro?" Alexei was still having trouble pronouncing his brother-in-law's name.

"I don't know yet," Paul said, sounding resigned. "It just happened."

"I know," Alexei said pointedly. "I was there."

"We're still trying to make arrangements," Paul said, trying to sound more conciliatory. "I'll let you know when everything has been decided."

"Yes, please call me," Alexei said. He hung up and went to find Ileana. She had changed out of her formal clothing, and Alexei did the same. Then he scrubbed his hands again. When he finished, he and Ileana wrapped their arms around each other. Then Gorvenko appeared at the doorway. Igor was behind him.

"Your Imperial Majesty, we should go back to St. Petersburg," Gorvenko said.

Alexei shook his head. "I'm *going* to Sandro's funeral, Ivan

Maximovich."

"I can't imagine that it's safe."

"It may not be," Alexei said. "But I'm going." He walked towards the doorway, hoping to slip past Gorvenko, but Gorvenko grabbed his arm. Alexei jerked away.

"I cannot let you go," Gorvenko said.

Losing his temper, Alexei whacked Gorvenko across the face. Gorvenko barely flinched at the blow, but his eyes betrayed his pain. Behind him, Igor and Ileana both cringed. "This is my brother-in-law!" Alexei cried. "Did you not hear my sister's screams?" He shook his head. "I really cared for Sandro, Ivan Maximovich. Not going to the funeral would be an act of cowardice."

The next day, the Yugoslav destroyer JRM *Dubrovnik* transported Alexander's body back to the port of Split, and from there, the body was moved to Belgrade. Alexei, Ileana, Igor and Gorvenko traveled to Belgrade by train. As they went, Alexei's hand, bruised from hitting Gorvenko, began to swell. He iced and bandaged it, concerned but distracted. Then he went to find Gorvenko. Bruises in the shape of Alexei's fingers had appeared on Gorvenko's face, and he stared straight ahead as Alexei approached him. "I am sorry, Ivan Maximovich," Alexei said. "My temper got the best of me."

Finally, Gorvenko looked at him. "I only have your safety in mind, Your Imperial Majesty."

"I know," Alexei replied, putting his hands on Gorvenko's shoulders. "Please forgive me."

In Belgrade, the Russian imperial family gathered for the funeral, and Igor looked relieved to be surrounded by his siblings and their families. Ioann kept his arm around Elena, who sobbed incessantly at her brother's violent murder. "This is unbelievable," Ioann said.

I can't disagree, Alexei thought as he grasped Ileana's hand. *What kind of world are we living in?* He eyed Vsevolod, who was standing behind his parents. Vsevolod's lips were quivering, and tears shone in his eyes. Alexei walked over to him and put a hand at his back. "I'm sorry," he said. "I know you and Sandro were close."

For a moment, Vsevolod stared past Alexei. Then his eyes focused on Alexei, and tears flowed down his face. "This is a disgrace, murdering a king," he said. "Are we going to war over it? I'm of age now and I'd be willing to fight."

Alexei took a deep breath, remembering the oath of loyalty that Vsevolod had taken when he had turned twenty earlier that year. "I'm hoping to avoid a war," he said.

"We have to do something, Alyosha," Vsevolod replied, looking Alexei in the eye. "We can't let this go unanswered."

Outside, a half a million Yugoslavians thronged the streets to see their king buried, but Alexei only had eyes for his sister, who looked as though she had spent the last couple of days weeping incessantly. Alexei kept his arm around Olga as all words failed him. By the time Alexander was buried in the Memorial Church of St. George, Alexei felt drained of his strength.

Alexei knew he had to return to St. Petersburg, but leaving Olga was one of the hardest things he had ever done. "Do you want to come to Russia?" he asked. "I'm sure you could use the change in scenery."

Olga's vacant gaze went through her brother, and her stare chilled Alexei. *She's looked this way ever since the funeral,* he thought. *It scares me.*

Slowly, Olga nodded her head. "I'll probably do that," she said. "We need to figure out how the government will be run- Peter's too young to reign on his own. If I'm Regent, I won't make it home, but if it's someone else..." Her voice trailed off.

"Let me know what happens," Alexei said. "You're always welcome in St. Petersburg."

"I'm worried about her," Ileana said as their train pulled out of the station.

"Me too," Alexei said. He looked over at Gorvenko. "Ivan Maximovich, could you do me a favor?"

"Absolutely," Gorvenko replied, standing at attention.

"I'd like to know everything you can figure out about Sandro's assassin."

Gorvenko nodded. "The French police killed him at the scene," he said. "But it shouldn't be too hard to get more information."

CHAPTER 5

A week after Alexei had returned to St. Petersburg, he got a call from Olga. "Is that offer for me to come home still open?" she asked.

"Absolutely," Alexei said, feeling the cold October breeze through the slightly open window of his study. "What's happening?"

"Paul is going to be regent. I'm not needed here, and I could use the time abroad."

"You're welcome here," Alexei said, concerned as much with the political situation in Belgrade as he was with the fact that Olga's voice was completely monotone.

"Paul is comfortable with me leaving the country," Olga continued. "At first, I thought it would be better if I stayed in Belgrade, but if Paul thinks it's alright..." Her voice trailed off.

Alexei stared across the room to the portraits of his father and Alexander II. "Do you need me to make travel arrangements for you?" he asked, holding the phone with one hand as his other hand picked at the corner of the papers in front of him.

"No, I can do it," Olga said. "I can be on the train as early as tomorrow."

When Olga arrived in St. Petersburg, Alexei arranged for Marie to meet her at the station. "I'm concerned about her," Marie confessed.

"Me too," Alexei said, deliberately not mentioning that Olga's screams in Marseilles had been haunting his dreams for the last several nights. "Be prepared, Masha. She's in bad shape."

"I would be too, if Nica had been murdered in front of me," Marie said. She stood up to go to the station. "We'll see you soon."

When Marie left, Alexei's shaking hands picked up Gorvenko's report on Alexander's assassin. Already, the news outlets had been reporting that the murderer had been a Bulgarian revolutionary, and the thought that Tatiana and Boris' countryman could have been involved was more than Alexei could bear. However, Gorvenko's report confirmed every rumor that Alexei had heard. By the time he was finished reading, his whole body felt drained.

In a second, however, he heard the sound of Olga and Marie returning to the palace, and he went to the window. Outside, a car with the imperial double-headed eagle had just stopped in front of the palace, and Olga and Marie were being helped out. Even from a distance, Alexei could see how haggard Olga looked. Her hair was unkempt and there were bags under her eyes.

Alexei hid Gorvenko's report and went downstairs to greet his sisters, forcing a smile as he did so. "Olga," he said. "I'm glad you made it. How are you?"

Olga shot him a look of exhaustion and despair. "I'm so miserable," she said.

"Olga," Marie whispered.

Olga looked down at the floor and took a deep breath. Then she looked back at Alexei and clasped his hands. "I'm glad you've let me come," she said.

"I hope you can rest while you're here," Alexei replied. "You've been through a lot."

"You look a little pale yourself," Olga said. "Is there anything I should know?"

"No," Alexei lied. "But it's been a rough time for all of us. I cared about Sandro."

"I know," Olga said. She looked around. "Where did the servants take my trunks?"

"I had a set of rooms cleaned up for you," Alexei said.

"Thanks," Olga said as she followed a pair of servants towards her new rooms.

Alexei nodded silently as he watched her go. Marie went after her older sister, but she turned around to face Alexei, walking backwards as she spoke. "I told Nica I'd be staying for supper if you'll have me."

"Good idea," Alexei replied.

At supper, however, Olga remained in her rooms, preferring to eat alone. "I was hoping she would join us," Ileana said. "I thought the company would do her good."

Alexei and Marie sighed simultaneously. "It's been tough for her," Marie said.

"But how long can she stay in her apartments and not go out?" Ileana asked.

"It might be awhile, unfortunately," Marie said.

I doubt her recovery will be hastened by that report on my desk, Alexei thought. He eyed his children, wondering how much they were listening and learning. Anastasia was eating away, seemingly oblivious, and Alexei almost smiled at the sight of his only daughter, who was so much like her namesake. Konstantin, Dmitri and Rostislav were listening, however, and Alexei could tell that Konstantin in particular understood what was happening.

"Would Aunt Olga care to see me?" Konstantin asked, making Alexei and Ileana smile. "Maybe she would feel better if I went to her apartments later."

"You're definitely welcome to try," Alexei said.

Several days later, as the late October sky was clouding over, Alexei noticed that the report on Alexander's murder was missing. Taking a deep breath, Alexei searched his study, just in case he had misplaced it. When a thorough search failed to reveal the missing document, Alexei felt a sweat breaking out all over his body. He had a hunch as to where that report had gone, and one hunch only. A minute later, he knocked on the door to Olga's apartments.

"Go away!" Olga said.

Alexei pushed the door open and found his sister lying on her bed, tears running down her face. The report sat on the table next to her bed.

"You knew," Olga said. "When were you planning on telling me that it was a Bulgarian who killed Sandro?"

Alexei looked at the floor. "I didn't have a plan," he murmured, feeling his face turn red.

In a second, Olga leapt up and raced towards Alexei, raising her hand.

Alexei ducked. "Don't hit me, Olga," he said, raising his hands over his head. "You know a bruise like that could kill me."

Olga let out a shriek of fury. She grabbed a small vase containing some roses and flung it across the room with force that stunned Alexei. The vase smashed against the wall, and the sound of broken glass filled the room as small shards flew everywhere. Water ran across the floor. "Damn Boris!" Olga screamed. "Did he plan this?"

"There's no way," Alexei said, feeling how dry his mouth was. "He and Tanya cared for Sandro as much as we did."

"That can't be true!" Olga yelled. "It's all politics, isn't it?"

Alexei shook his head, feeling how tight his neck muscles were, how tense his whole body was. "That's not true. Boris and Tanya are incredibly upset, even more so *because* the murderer was Bulgarian."

"How could you possibly know that?"

"I spoke to them yesterday. They left Sofia this morning to come here, to see if we could all work this out in person."

"What's to work out?" Olga asked. "Are they going to bring Sandro back from the grave?"

"Of course not," Alexei said. "But I think they're right- a conversation will go much further than spewing anger at each other from thousands of miles away."

"I can't bear to see them," Olga replied. She threw herself onto her bed and covered her face with a pillow. Alexei crept up to her bedside table and took Gorvenko's report. Then he quietly left the room.

Boris and Tatiana's arrival in St. Petersburg two days later made Alexei nervous. Outside, the wind howled, making Alexei think the weather was conveying his feelings. He looked at Tatiana and Boris intently as they sat across from him in his study. "Olga is not in good shape," he said, seeing no reason not to be honest. "She's been sleeping practically the whole time she's been here. She also stole my police report on the assassination, and we had a huge row over it."

Tatiana leaned forward. "Olga is my favorite sister," she said. "Growing up, I was closer to her than anyone else in the family. She can't possibly think I would condone anything like this. I'm hoping she'll let me reason with her."

Alexei looked doubtful. "I'm glad you're willing to talk to her," he said. "But I am afraid of the outcome."

Later that day, Alexei climbed the stairs to Olga's apartments with Tatiana and Boris behind him. As he knocked on Olga's door, his stomach felt like a crawling pit of snakes. There was no answer to his knock, and for a minute Alexei wondered whether Olga had gone out. "Olga?" he called. When there was no answer, Alexei put his hand on the doorknob. The door was unlocked, and Alexei pushed it open. The air in the room was stale. Nothing moved. Then Alexei saw Olga lying on her bed, her vacant gaze staring in his direction. "Tanya and Bo are here," Alexei said.

Slowly, Olga swung her legs over the side of the bed and stood up. Her eyes did not focus as Alexei, Tatiana and Boris came into the room. Alexei stood aside and looked back and forth between his oldest sisters. For a moment, silence reigned.

"Olga, I'm so sorry," Tatiana began.

Olga flew across the room and smacked her sister across the face. "How dare you?" she said, her voice dangerously low. She grabbed Tatiana's dress and began shaking her. "How could you do this to me? Sandro was my everything!"

Uncomfortably, Boris separated Olga from Tatiana. "I don't care about the killer's nationality- we had nothing to do with this," he said.

Olga swung her fist at Boris, who caught it and also grabbed her other arm to prevent any further violence. "You're lying!" Olga screamed. "This was one of your citizens! How could you not know?" She struggled and managed to free herself from Boris' grip.

"He was a revolutionary," Boris said, staying in front of Tatiana and putting a hand out behind him to make sure she stayed behind him. "They plot in secret. I would never condone the killing of another king, much less one who was my brother-in-law."

Olga spat in his face, and Alexei, disgusted, handed Boris a handkerchief as he pulled Olga back. "Olga, that's enough," Alexei said.

Olga let out another screech. "I wish I had weapons other than my hands!" she yelled. "Then I'd show you how I really feel!"

Tatiana had tears running down her face. "I swear, Olga- this is the last thing I would have wanted," she sobbed. "Don't you remember how eager we both were to grow up and get married, how we thought we would be old maids by the time the Great War ended?"

Boris finished wiping his face. "Will you please see reason?" he asked. "I could never have arranged Sandro's murder."

"The only reason I see is that Sandro is dead, and your countryman was behind it," Olga said. "My life might as well be over."

"That's not true!" Tatiana cried. "You have many years ahead of you!"

"And I want to spend the rest of them without ever seeing either of you again!" Olga shrieked. She shoved Boris and Tatiana out the door and shoved Alexei after them. "Make sure they find their way home," she ordered Alexei. Then she slammed the door in their faces.

Tatiana's tears flowed down her face again. Boris' eyes glistened, but he refused to cry openly. Alexei was not as stoic, and soon his tears were running down his face and dripping onto the floor. He was glad to see Ileana appear at the end of the hallway. He went towards her and she hugged him. Slowly, the dreary party went downstairs.

Alexei had nightmares for weeks after his sisters' fight. In some of them, Olga spent sleepless nights wandering, hunting for Alexander, wearing the long white dresses she had worn as a girl. In others, Alexei stood on the shores of the Black Sea with the paradise of the Crimea behind him. In front of him, far out to sea, Alexander waved to him, called to him. Suddenly, Olga would appear, again in her white dress, and try to get to her husband. She would even float on top of the water- to no avail. Alexander always disappeared, and Olga was always left crying.

One night, Alexei jerked awake after one such nightmare. His breath came in loud gasps, and he could feel his heart racing in his chest. Next to him, Ileana was breathing slow, deep, even breaths. Throwing back the covers, Alexei stood and went to the window. For a second, he thought he saw Olga, walking in the gardens in her long white dress, the heavy winter snow sparkling around her in the moonlight. Alexei looked over at his boots, which stood in the corner of the room. *Should I go out after her?* he wondered. But when he looked back outside, there was no Olga. Instead, a sentry paced, gun in his hand.

Alexei collapsed back into bed, willing himself to go back to sleep. Instead, he spent the next two hours watching the hands of the grandfather clock across the room, moving in their everlasting circular motion.

The next morning, Alexei was more than happy that he had no meetings scheduled and that his only work was the petitions and legislation on his desk. Ileana shared her husband's desire for stillness, so the two of them took breakfast alone as their children began their lessons for the day. Finally, Alexei checked his watch and folded his hand over his wife's. "I'll be in my study if you need me," he said.

The silence did not last long. Alexei had just become ensconced in legislation when a large bang shook the palace. In a second, Alexei knew that the explosion had come from his oldest son's schoolroom. "Kostya!" he shouted, and sprinted for the schoolroom. Igor was right behind him, fearing for Oleg's life.

They both burst into the classroom, which was a mess of smoke and debris. Alexei found Konstantin, grabbed him, and sprinted away. Igor was right behind them, carrying Oleg. Ileana, as if she had anticipated where her husband would take their son, met them upstairs. "What happened?" she asked forcefully. "Kostya, are you hurt? Oh my God, Oleg!"

It was then that Alexei saw that Oleg, like Konstantin, was covered in soot. But he also realized that both boys were laughing. "It wasn't a bomb, Papa," Konstantin said. "Volodya just messed up on his chemistry lesson."

Alexei, Ileana and Igor looked at each other, and Alexei felt like he was just starting to breathe again. "Is anybody hurt?" he asked. Konstantin and Oleg shook their heads. Alexei put his son down, and, taking his hand, led him back to his classroom. Ileana followed, and Igor, still holding Oleg, brought up the rear.

Inside the classroom, the boys' chemistry tutor was wiping his face with a handkerchief. Dmitri and Rostislav, who had been having their own lessons in a classroom just up the hall, appeared at the doorway of Konstantin's classroom, wearing identical expressions of bewilderment and fear. Marie's son Andrei, who was also covered in soot, was laughing. "Mama's going to hear about *this*, Uncle Alyosha," he said.

"Make sure she knows you weren't hurt," Alexei replied. He looked at Vladimir Golitsyn, whose error had caused the explosion. Both Vladimir and his last classmate, Alexander Dolgoruky, were quaking in fear. Alexei knelt down next to them and took Vladimir's face in his hands. Immediately, Vladimir started crying. "Are you hurt?" Alexei asked.

Vladimir shook his head. Alexei looked over at Alexander. "I'm fine," Alexander said.

"Then there's no reason to cry," Alexei told Vladimir.

"But this room is a mess," Vladimir said.

"It can be cleaned, and we have plenty of rooms for you to use in the meantime," Alexei said. "Everything will be fine, I promise."

It was three months later before Olga finally left her apartments, and even then, it was only to go to church. Alexei let the servants in to open the windows and clean up. He frowned as he looked around. *It's a mess in here,* he thought. The bedclothes were strewn on the floor, and Olga's clothes were spread out everywhere. Hardly any of her dresses hung in the closet. Instead, many were tossed on couches and chairs. Much of her jewelry had been piled up on one side of a bureau. The rest lay in boxes and in trunks. *That's a shame,* Alexei thought. *That jewelry is worth a fortune. Some of it is family heirlooms that Mama and Papa gave Olga when she married.* "Be careful with all this jewelry when you clean it and put it away," he ordered the servants.

They nodded, and Alexei turned to leave. He was almost out the door when his eye fell on the wastebasket in the corner of the room. It was full, and the crumpled papers on the top bore flowery handwriting in blue ink. Immediately, Alexei recognized Tatiana's handwriting. He returned to his study carrying the letter, smoothing its crumpled sheets as he walked.

"My dearest Olga," the missive began. "Leaving you a week ago was one of the hardest things I've ever done. I can only imagine how much you're hurting after the loss of your beloved Sandro. Your return to our homeland and childhood palace can only speed your healing.

"I want you to know that my heart is with you, and that it is both crying for your loss and praying for your recovery from this tragedy. Again I reiterate that a revolutionary's horrible deeds cannot be condoned or forgiven. Please believe that Boris and I knew nothing of that terrible man's plans or actions. If we had, he would have been dead long before he had the chance to act.

"I pray that one day you are able to let go of your pain, and to forgive. Fate and marriage have long since separated us physically, but every day, I miss your love, your telephone calls and your letters. It was always good to hear your voice, receive news of your children. You were good to me even in the months after Marie Louise's birth, when I could not return your kindness. Please know that my heart is still open to you.

"Yours always, Tanya."

As he put Tatiana's letter on his desk, Alexei felt an overwhelming sadness wash over him. *Tanya and Olga were so close growing up,* he thought. *And they've both been through so much. I hope this rift between them isn't permanent.*

Three weeks later, in the midst of a late February snowstorm, Alexei stood as Prince Paul of Yugoslavia was led into his study. King Boris of Bulgaria was led in right behind him. "Thanks for coming," Alexei said, gesturing for them to sit.

"Where's Tanya?" Paul asked Boris without looking at him. "Is she at least trying to work things out with Olga?"

Boris nodded. "Marie is taking them both to lunch and then back to her estate," she said.

Both Boris and Paul looked at Alexei as they all sat down. "I'm glad you're willing to host this meeting, Alyosha," Paul said. "Having it on neutral territory almost makes it palatable." His eyes shot daggers at Boris.

Boris glared back at him. "I had nothing to do with Sandro's murder!" he said. "To the contrary, we had a formal alliance between our countries!"

"Gentlemen," Alexei said calmly. "I am as upset as you are. I really cared for Sandro, and I'm worried that his murder might send us down the path to another Great War."

Paul and Boris looked away from each other, then down at the floor. The study remained silent, and Alexei felt discomfort and pain rolling off Boris and Paul like waves.

"I don't think any of us has forgotten than a murder just like this one led us all to the Great War," Paul admitted finally. "And Yugoslavia is a poor nation. Another war, even one just against Bulgaria, would bankrupt us."

"You shouldn't even be declaring war on us," Boris replied.

"Who then, the French?" Paul said. "I agree that their conduct was outrageous- providing hardly any police protection for a king!- but they would crush us in a week."

Boris and Alexei shared a look.

"What?" Paul asked.

"The assassin may have been a Bulgarian citizen, but he had Italian funding and weapons," Boris said.

"What?!" Paul yelped. "Are you sure about this?"

Both Alexei and Boris nodded. "But declaring war on Italy would mean Germany declaring war against you," Alexei said to Paul. "We would quickly be headed down the path to another Great War."

"Though Britain and France would probably hesitate to join us," Boris said gloomily. "They are even more reluctant to see another war than we are."

"Well, we can't just sit here and do nothing," Paul said. "Without our action, there could be more assassinations- any of us in this room could be next."

A thoughtful look came over Boris' face. "The assassin himself was killed at the scene," he said. "But he was working with a whole cadre of people, a couple of whom have been captured, and some of whom are still being hunted."

Paul arched his eyebrow. "If the Italians really did fund this, I'd love to go after Mussolini himself, but that would definitely start another war." He looked at Alexei and Boris. "Why don't we cooperate in arresting everyone in that conspiracy? Then we can decide on their punishment. I may even take a page out of your book at that one, Alyosha."

"How do you mean?" Alexei asked, genuinely confused.

Paul smiled. "Don't tell me you've forgotten having publicly hanged the communists who almost killed you outside of Moscow."

Alexei swallowed uncomfortably. He folded his hands on his desk and stared at them for a moment. "It's an episode I'd rather forget."

Paul smiled as he stood up. "That makes one of us, and I mean that as a compliment," he said. "I admire your methods, and your decisiveness."

Four months later, Alexei and Ileana were taking tea one morning when a servant opened the door nearest to their table. Alexei looked up, surprised and a little worried- he and Ileana were never disturbed at tea without prior instructions. Alexei was already standing up, his heart pounding, when Olga entered the room. Slowly, Alexei took a deep breath, willing his heart rate to slow down.

Olga waved a stack of newspapers, a triumphant look on her face. "The web of people behind Sandro's murder have been caught!" she said. "Their trial starts in Belgrade next week."

Alexei nodded. "I saw the headline this morning." *And I know more about it than that article does.*

"I called Paul this morning," Olga continued. "He thinks it's appropriate for me to go back to Belgrade."

She called him? Alexei thought. *That's more initiative than I've seen her take on anything since she arrived here.* "Are you willing to go?" he asked.

"I am now," Olga said. "It may be painful for me to be there, but maybe my pain will help get a conviction."

Two days later, Alexei, Ileana and their children said goodbye to Olga at the train station. Marie, Nicholas, and their children had come as well, and the whole group watched as Olga boarded the train. As the train pulled out of the station, Olga appeared at the window and waved goodbye.

Alexei waved back. "I think this is for the best," he said.

CHAPTER 6

As the 1930s wore on, the economy continued to improve. Still, progress was slow, and Alexei continued to make sure that bread lines, banks and factories were running. He also kept an eye on the German situation, making sure that Russia had a strong network of spies there. Then, in March, 1938, Ileana returned from a trip to Romania to find Alexei's study and the surrounding rooms awash in movement. Generals rushed around, and maps of Russia and Europe were being hung everywhere. In the middle of the hustle and bustle, Ileana looked for her husband and found him and Igor surrounded by ministers and Duma representatives, staring at the maps in front of them. Red pushpins stuck out of the maps in various places. "What's going on?" Ileana asked.

"You were travelling when the news hit," Alexei said. "Germany has annexed Austria."

For a moment, Ileana stood paralyzed. "Oh, my God," she stuttered. Then she looked around at the chaos that surrounded her, and realized how much of it was military. "Have you mobilized our army yet?" she asked, her mouth suddenly dry.

"Not yet," Alexei said, drawing out the words. He looked away from the maps and fixed his gaze on his wife. "But it's looking more likely. How is your mother doing?"

"Not well," Ileana said, feeling a lump rise in her throat. "And Carol has been restricting her access to the doctors.”

“He’s crazy,” Alexei said, and Ileana wished she could disagree. “Did he say anything about the political situation?”

“Nothing positive.”

“I was counting on having Romania as an ally,” Alexei said. “But if Carol won’t commit- or, even worse, if he commits to Germany, Russia will fight him.”

“I know that,” Ileana said, feeling like her heart was being ripped out of her chest. “But he really made it sound like he might join Hitler.”

Alexei shook his head and clenched his teeth. “Hitler’s armies are officially on the move,” he said. “He wants more territory than Germany received after the Great War, but I, for one, am not inclined to simply give it to him.”

Ileana nodded her agreement. “He’s going to have to fight for it,” she said. “Despite what my brother thinks, we’re not simply going to stand by and watch Hitler mow down all of Europe.”

On July 3, 1938, Alexei and Ileana took their annual vacation aboard the Standart. Alexei watched as his children played. Already, Konstantin had turned in a tall twelve-year-old, and his blond hair was as light as when he had been baby. Ileana joined Alexei. “You look happy watching the children, but you also look worried,” she said. “What’s bothering you?”

Alexei frowned as he stared out at the water that surrounded them. “For some time now, my sources in Germany have been reporting that the army is on the move again,” he said.

Ileana leaned against the boat’s railing for support, and felt the warmth that it had absorbed from the summer sun. “We can’t be the only country with an intelligence network there,” she said. “Other countries must see what we’re seeing. Why isn’t anyone trying to stop Hitler?”

“Because no one wants another Great War,” Alexei said. “It’s why no one declared war after Sandro’s murder.”

“And in the meantime, Hitler continues to grab more territory.” Ileana shook her head. “How long can this go on?”

Alexei took a deep breath and felt the warm air rush into his lungs. “I’ve been thinking of going to Germany to meet with Hitler. If that goes badly, we may go to war.”

Ileana pressed her hands to her face. “Why now?” she asked.

Alexei frowned. “What do you mean?”

“I just got a telegram from my mother, saying that her health has gotten even worse. It was followed, a few minutes later, from a telegram from Carol, saying that Mama’s health was improving and not to worry.”

Alexei felt the hot sun beating down, and still he shivered. "Who do you believe more?" *I'd have to vote for Marie.*

"Mama," Ileana said without hesitation.

"When we dock again, I'll send the children on to St. Petersburg with some of the guards," Alexei said. "We can go to Bucharest on our own."

During the voyage, Alexei ordered that his motorcar be brought to meet them where the Standart would dock. At noon of the last day of the voyage- July 18, 1938- Ileana received a phone call. When Alexei found her an hour later, she was still standing next to the telephone, tears running down her face. "Mama's dying," she said.

"I'm so sorry," Alexei replied. He hugged Ileana tightly to his chest. Then he gave the order for the Standart to go full steam ahead into the port, ending their vacation that afternoon rather than the next morning.

In a rush, Alexei and Ileana put their children back on the Imperial train to go to St. Petersburg. Then they jumped into Alexei's waiting car for the fifteen-hour drive to Bucharest. They arrived at the Romanian border very early the next morning. "Any word from the Palace?" Ileana asked frantically.

The guards recognized Ileana. "No, Domnitza, not yet," they replied, using the Romanian word for "Princess" as they checked their imperial visitors' papers.

She's Tsarina now, not a Princess, Alexei thought, but he held his tongue. "Maybe we'll get there in time," he said as they sped off. It was not until they reached the first large town across the border that they guessed otherwise. All the flags hung at half mast, and church bells tolled mournfully. "Ileana, I'm so sorry," Alexei said. Keeping one hand on the steering wheel, he put one hand on Ileana's shoulder as tears poured down her face.

Marie's body lay in state for three days at Cotroceni, giving Konstantin, Dmitri, Rostislav and Anastasia just enough time to join their parents for the full state funeral. The children brought some relief to Ileana, whose pain was palpable.

After the funeral liturgy, Marie's coffin, which was covered with red roses, was carried through streets of Bucharest to the train station. More than 250,000 people lined the route, waiting under mauve banners to say goodbye to their beloved queen. The trip, which normally took two hours, took six hours as the coffin slowly made its way through the streets.

Throughout the entirety of the trip, Alexei felt the hot sun beating down on him, and the wind blew a dry dust everywhere. Alexei constantly rubbed the dust from his irritated eyes, but Ileana's tears kept her eyes and face clean. All around them, hundreds of thousands of people knelt, holding lit candles and throwing flowers onto the open carriage that held Marie's coffin. An honor guard surrounded the casket on a flat car, and so many flowers were thrown that the guards looked like they were about to suffocate.

After the funeral, it was a quiet ride back to St. Petersburg. Alexei sat next to Ileana, and Konstantin sat on his mother's other side, holding her hand. Alexei looked at them, and then looked out the window. *Marie was very popular with the people, and Carol didn't dare do anything she would have opposed,* he thought. *But now that she's gone, he's free to join Hitler.*

Alexei spent the next several months in communication with Hitler's government. When it became clear that Hitler was relishing his country's newfound military might rather than backing down, Alexei arranged a face-to-face meeting. In the middle of January, 1939, as Dmitri, Rostislav and Anastasia made arrangements to go ice skating and take sleigh rides, Alexei, Ileana, Konstantin and Igor boarded the Imperial train to go to Berlin.

The four of them stood at the window as the train pulled into the German capital. Outside, they could see streets and buildings covered in with a fine layer of snow that was in direct contrast to the several feet of snow they had left in St. Petersburg. Alexei was surprised to see that the train's outdoor thermometer read zero degrees Celsius. "It's warm," he said.

He was just looking outside again when Sergei Kamensky handed him a telegram. Reading it, Alexei felt the blood drain from his face. He could see curiosity in Ileana's eyes, but he glanced at Konstantin. Ileana nodded and waited to hear the news.

The ride into the center of the city only increased Alexei's unease. Everywhere they looked, buildings were draped with the Nazi flag, and soon Alexei felt the bold red, black and white emblazoned into his eyeballs. He looked over at Ileana, who made a face at him over Konstantin's head. Alexei smiled through his gloom. *I am so lucky to have her,* he thought. *I was worried that I would be a burden to her, but she's proven to be my angel.*

In town, they checked into the one of the city's newest hotels, and their rooms and security took up most of the floor. Ileana made sure Konstantin was ensconced in his room before looking over at Alexei. "What was that telegram you got on the train?" she asked.

"The Nazis destroyed a synagogue in Nuremburg a few days ago."

"Why would they do such a thing?"

"I don't know," Alexei replied, his face twisting into a frown. "I never trusted Hitler or the Nazi party, but the more I hear about them, the less I like."

The next day, Alexei, Igor, Ileana and Konstantin were driven to the Reichstag. Inside the building's main hall, Alexei stood tall and polished in his uniform. Konstantin stood as sharply as he could in his child's version of a uniform, trying to look as grown up as possible. Alexei smiled at him. Next to them, Ileana stood in a long white lace dress. The pearl necklace that Alexei had given her for their engagement was at her neck.

Igor stood slightly behind them, tale and pale in his own uniform. "I'm honored that you've been serving me all these years, Igor," Alexei said.

"I wouldn't miss the excitement," Igor said with a smile. Then he became serious. "I want to prevent war as much as you do. If we fight, my brother, sons and nephews are all going off to battle."

"I know that," Alexei replied, just as seriously. "It's why I'm trying to avoid it."

A few minutes later, they all stood at attention as Adolph Hitler approached them. He was surrounded by some of his most famous generals and ministers. Alexei had been studying the Nazi party leadership and recognized Hermann Goering, Joseph Goebbels, Albert Speer, and Joachim von Ribbentrop. They marched in step, their shined boots moving at the same time and making a single sound as they hit the ground. They all wore the same uniform with the Nazi swastika on their left arms.

The group stopped as they neared their Russian guests, and Alexei found himself staring at Hitler in particular. Hitler's deep blue eyes glared from his face, and his habitual severe expression was unmitigated. Nevertheless, his first words were kind. "Welcome to Berlin," he said. "I hope your hotel accommodations are up to your standards?" He spoke in German, and Alexei was glad to have learned the language from Alexandra, despite how harsh he thought it sounded.

"Yes, the hotel is very nice," Alexei replied. "Thank you for hosting us." He introduced his family.

"Very pleased to meet you," Hitler replied, taking Ileana's hand.

"The pleasure is mine," Ileana replied, even if she felt the opposite.

"Konstantin, you are the oldest, correct?" Hitler asked, shaking the boy's hand.

"Yes, indeed," Konstantin replied, returning Hitler's handshake.

When Hitler got to Igor, he remembered that Igor was Alexei's cousin. *He did his research,* Alexei thought. Then Hitler affixed Gorvenko with a cold stare that Gorvenko returned without blinking. That made Alexei nervous. *It's not like Hitler doesn't have his own security,* he thought.

When the meeting started, Alexei and Igor were led into the building's official reception room. Gorvenko followed. Inside, huge Nazi flags hung on every wall. In the middle of the room, a long table with chairs awaited. The table was made of new mahogany, and the rich wood gleamed, even in the pale winter light that streamed through the windows. Pitchers of water and glasses sat at around the long table, one for every chair. When everyone was seated, Gorvenko stood in the corner of the room, watching everything that happened. Several Nazi officers stood around the room, also watchful.

Hitler's eyes fixed on Alexei. "Your Imperial Majesty, what are you hoping to get from this meeting?"

"I am hoping to forestall a war, Herr Fuhrer," Alexei replied. "The Great War only concluded twenty years ago, and its horrors are still etched in my mind."

"I served in that war," Hitler replied. "I, too, remember it well."

"Then perhaps we can work together to prevent another one."

Hitler smiled, but the expression only chilled Alexei further. "Perhaps we do, in fact, have some common goals," he said. "From what I understand, your family shares my views towards our Jewish population."

"My family has never supported the Yids, and many of my forefathers certainly hated them," Alexei admitted. "But in the years since the Great War, the Yids within my borders have proven themselves resourceful- many have invested in the economy, or run factories and mines. I may not agree with their religion or lifestyle, but persecuting them would be harmful for Russia."

Hitler's face hardened. "The Jews are the scourge of the earth," he said. "They are responsible for the world's problems."

Alexei frowned. "They are a tiny minority, and they're not politically organized. I doubt any of them is as dangerous as some of the military actions your government is planning."

"My military is only protecting my government and its people, Your Imperial Majesty."

"The security of your country and its people doesn't require the invasion of Czechoslovakia, Herr Fuhrer."

Hitler glared at Alexei, and his eyes seemed to reflect the reds, whites and blacks of the Nazi flags around him. "My country was quite hemmed in at the end of the Great War. I am only seeking *lebensraum* for my people."

"At the expense of other countries," Alexei said. "It is that path which will lead to another war."

Hitler's face twisted into a frown. "Maybe our political goals are not as aligned as I thought."

"No, unfortunately, Herr Fuhrer, it seems not," Alexei conceded, with sincere regret. *I truly was hoping to stop another war. Hitler seems intent on starting one.*

Everyone in the room rose, and Alexei realized the meeting was over. As he stood, he saw Hitler nod at one of the Nazi guards in the room. At the same instant, Goering, Goebbels, Speer, and von Robbentrap all exchanged a glance. *That can't be a coincidence,* Alexei thought. *What are they planning?* He shot a nervous glance at his police chief. Gorvenko caught his eye and nodded. He approached Alexei and covered his back as Alexei exited the room. Igor, too, moved towards Alexei as they got into the hallway outside the reception room.

Out in the hallway, Alexei took several long strides to put some distance between himself and his German hosts. Ileana and Konstantin, waiting in the hallway, saw that the meeting was over and started to come towards him. With a shake of his head and a quick gesture of his hand, Alexei told them to stay where they were. Konstantin did not understand the warning, but Ileana did, and she grabbed Konstantin's arm. Then Alexei turned back to face Hitler and his ministers.

As Alexei turned, the officer to whom Hitler had nodded at the end of the meeting moved forward with a quick gait. Alexei saw a flash of metal, then saw a pistol in the officer's hand. "No!" he yelled.

Immediately, Gorvenko stepped in front of Alexei. Alexei saw a flash of light burst out of the pistol. He ducked. A second later, two loud bangs reverberated through the hall almost simultaneously. Gorvenko collapsed and Alexei caught him. Then he saw that Igor had fired the second shot. The Nazi officer with the pistol collapsed, dead.

Behind Alexei, Konstantin and Ileana shrieked as a few of the family's Cossack guards surrounded them and rushed them out of the hall. The rest of the family's guards pulled their own guns and started firing. Igor helped Alexei haul Gorvenko's body into one of their waiting cars. The two of them jumped in as Ileana and Konstantin were practically thrown into the second car by the Cossacks. "Papa!" Alexei heard Konstantin wail as the cars raced away from the Reichstag in opposite directions.

"Where are they going?" Alexei yelled at Igor.

"We had an escape plan. This is it," Igor said, his face and eyes betraying his horror.

"I will see them again, won't I?" Alexei asked, his panic rising.

"I sure hope so," Igor said. He looked down at Gorvenko as their car continued to race through the streets.

Alexei also looked down at his police chief. Bloodstains covered both Gorvenko's uniform and Alexei's. It was only then that Alexei realized that Gorvenko was neither moving nor breathing. He looked up at Igor.

"He's dead," Igor confirmed.

Alexei looked back at Gorvenko. "I'm so sorry," he whispered. A few minutes later, the car finally came to a stop in an alley. "Where *are* we?" Alexei asked.

"At a smaller hotel across the street from the train station," Igor replied. "This is the back exit of the hotel. We'll go in this way, and another side exit should lead right to the Imperial train once we get it into the station."

"What about all of our belongings?"

"They're being loaded into carriages. They'll meet the train at another station along the way to St. Petersburg."

Several Cossacks arrived and lifted Gorvenko's body from the car. Tears fell down Alexei's face as he, too, alighted from the car. Inside, Ileana and Konstantin were already in the suite of rooms that had been rented as a security precaution. Alexei and Ileana flew at each other. "Alyosha, oh my God," Ileana said as Alexei wrapped his arms around her. Konstantin wrapped his arms around his parents, and both Alexei and Ileana left one arm around each other and put one arm around their son.

A few minutes later, the Imperial train pulled into the station and the three of them, followed by Igor and the Cossack guards, rushed to meet it. As they boarded, Alexei saw Gorvenko's body, wrapped in a sheet, being loaded onto the baggage car. As the train sped out of the station, he gave orders for a proper coffin to meet them at the same station that his trunks did.

The Imperial train moved, full steam ahead, through the whole afternoon and overnight. Almost immediately, it crossed the border into Austria, but Alexei did not feel safe until long after they had left Austria. Igor sat with Alexei overnight, neither of them sleeping. Alexei watched as Igor reloaded the ornate pistol he had carried to the meeting with the Nazis. "That's quite a weapon," he said. "Where'd you get it?"

"From the Armory in Moscow when I was visiting Nikita a few months ago. It's from an updated line of the one I gave you before your meeting with Lenin."

Alexei thought of the gun he had held all that time ago. "You're still looking out for me after all these years," he said.

"And I will continue to do so until I can't take another breath," Igor said.

When the train finally came to a stop, it was in a small town halfway through Czechoslovakia that Alexei could not name. "The train has been moving too fast for our belongings to catch up with us from Berlin," Igor reported.

"That's fine," Alexei said. "My family is more important to me than our trunks. What about the coffin for Ivan Maximovich, though? That, I think, is important."

"I cabled ahead to ask," Igor said. "It's ready. We'll also be taking on food supplies, but it shouldn't take long."

When the train had been waiting in the station for a few minutes, its blinds drawn, Alexei peeked out the window long enough to see Gorvenko's coffin being borne back to the train by the Cossacks and other officers who served as part of Alexei's security detail. Without telling anyone, Alexei slipped out of the train and stood at attention, saluting, until the coffin was loaded back onto the train. He did not care that it was snowing again, or that the winter's bitter wind made his eyes tear.

Then the train began moving again. For the rest of the ride, Alexei sat at the window, his eyes a steely blue. Ileana sat across from him. "Alyosha, what are you thinking?" she asked.

When Alexei turned to look at his wife, his look chilled her. "Diplomacy is done," he said. "This means war."

Part III

CHAPTER 1

February 3, 1939.

Alexei stood in front of the Winter Palace, dressed in his warmest overcoat. He had a square fur hat on his head and yet he could still feel the cold digging into his face. *Even my eyeballs are cold*, he thought. Every breath he exhaled became white fog as it exited his mouth. The night before, a storm had blown through St. Petersburg, leaving an extra 10 inches of wet snow in its wake. Now, in the brief daylight, everything was bathed in a pure whiteness. Even so, Alexei felt nothing but dread as regiment after regiment of the Russian army marched before him in parade, their black polished boots hitting the ground in sync. *These men's lives are my responsibility*, he thought.

Just yesterday morning, Alexei, with the full support of the Duma, had declared war on Germany. The general order of mobilization had gone out in the afternoon. *I've spent the last several months watching Britain and France appease Hitler- enough is enough*, Alexei thought. *As if trying to kill me weren't bad enough, Hitler invaded Czechoslovakia and Belgium and is about to invade Poland. There has to be some response.*

In front of him, the parade of tall soldiers in full uniform suddenly came to a halt and presented arms. Alexei, with Konstantin, Dmitri and Rostislav behind him, began marching up and down the line, reviewing the troops. His young sons examined the soldiers in front of them with awe, reminding Alexei of his own experience during the Great War. Feeling an enormous weight on his shoulders, Alexei made eye contact with each and every soldier that he passed.

Once the review was over, Alexei took a microphone from his new police chief, Feodor Mikhailovich Ivanov. "Gentlemen," he began, and his voice soared. "I am proud of you and of each of the Russian soldiers who will be marching out to defend our country. But I did not make the decision to declare war lightly. It was only because of the threat to Russia, and to each of us personally, that Nazi Germany and Adolph Hitler represent. We mean to live our lives as free Russians, worshiping God in the Orthodox tradition. They mean to dominate us and incorporate us into a German empire where God does not exist.

"We also will not let an attempt on the Tsar's life go unanswered. Let us show the Germans what real strength looks like. Let us show them what real love of our country looks like. Let us show them what it looks like to have something to fight for- freedom that emanates from ancient traditions and an ancient homeland! Let us wipe the scourge of Nazi Germany off the face of the Earth!"

When Alexei finished speaking, a roar went up from the troops in front of him. Then, on a single command, the troops faced right and marched out. Alexei knew that his mobilization order meant that a similar scene was taking place all across his empire, from St. Petersburg to Siberia.

When Alexei and his sons returned inside, Ileana, Anastasia, Marie, Nicholas Obolensky, Igor and Sophie were waiting for them. "All of Europe is at war again," Igor said. "Our allies have joined us as expected."

"Indeed," Alexei said. "Yugoslavia, Bulgaria, Britain and France all declared war against Germany within an hour of our declaration. The Scandinavian countries all expect to join the war on our side within the next forty-eight hours."

"I'm still hoping that the Americans will join in, now that war has actually started and they can't keep pressing for peace," Igor said.

"That would be a welcome event," Alexei agreed.

Outside, a loud cheer went up. Konstantin, Dmitri, Rostislav and Anastasia ran to the window to watch as more regiments marched by.

"It won't be an easy fight, though," Igor said. "Germany, Austria, Japan, Italy and Hungary have all declared war against us."

"I know," Alexei said. "I fear for our world if we keep fighting like this every generation."

Tears ran down Sophie's face. "My father's assassination started the first Great War," she said. She looked at Alexei. "Your near-assassination started this one."

Ileana moved to Sophie's side to console her.

"It isn't just about Hitler nearly killing me," Alexei said. "It's bigger than that. Hitler will take over all of Europe if we don't stop him."

"And yet it is my son that's going off to war, not yours," Sophie said. "Peter thinks his regiment will deploy as early as next week."

"Your sons and nephews were foremost on my mind when I signed the declaration of war," Alexei said, as he thought of all of Igor's siblings, each of whom had sons who would be fighting. "These are my relatives too. Each of their lives is precious."

A week later, Vsevolod deployed with his regiment. Ioann and Elena wept as they hugged their oldest son. Then they watched as Vsevolod hugged his five younger siblings and the large extended family.

Alexei and Igor exchanged a look as Vsevolod marched out without even a glance back. *We're the only two people in the family, besides Sevka himself, that know that he won't be with his regiment after they leave St. Petersburg,* Alexei thought. *Sevka has spent years training as a spy, but Ioann and Elena don't know that.* He took a deep breath. *Our army really needs the intelligence, but I fear for Sevka's life.*

The next week, Peter's regiment was called up. Igor hugged him, and Nicholas, Oleg and Sophie did the same. As Alexei embraced Peter, he saw that Igor's teeth were clenched, but Peter looked as excited as Alexei had ever seen him. "Please come home safely," Igor beseeched his son. "I want you home alive when this is over."

"Don't worry, Papa," Peter said with a grin. "I'll be home before you know it."

Wherever Russian soldiers marched with their allies, Nazi armies were there to meet them, and huge battles roared. Casualties flooded Russian hospitals, and Ileana worked day and night, overseeing supplies, recruiting doctors, and assisting in operations as needed. She and many of the imperial family's women took nursing classes and became certified nurses.

One night, Marie smiled at Ileana after they had spent the day cleaning and bandaging wounds. "Anastasia and I were too young to become nurses during the last war," she said. "But Mama, Olga and Tatiana trained for it and were at the hospitals every day. Nastia and I were so jealous."

Ileana smiled back. "I'm more worried about our family at the front than I am about myself," she said.

"At least two of our boys are together," Marie said, reminding Ileana that Konstantin and Andrei still had their lessons together. "I'd rather that than they march off with their regiments. I'm worried enough about Sasha," she added of her oldest son, who was at the front.

Two days later, Alexei was meeting with his ministers when the news came that Poland had surrendered to the German forces that had completely overrun their country. "Damn," Alexei cursed.

"I'm not surprised, unfortunately," said Mikhail Timofeievich Bazanov, the Minister of War. "The Poles fought for every inch of their country, but the Nazi army is a well-oiled machine. It wasn't much of a contest."

Alexei frowned as he examined photographs of the damage in Poland. Whole city blocks had been leveled, and bodies could be seen in the streets, many of them twisted into strange positions. "Are these civilian casualties?" he asked, feeling nauseous.

"Yes, Your Imperial Majesty," Bazanov said. "The Luftwaffe is deadly, and the Germans are taking full advantage of it."

"So they kill thousands of people without ever sending in their army," Alexei said. "At most, their pilots get shot down, and even then, it's a bigger loss for the countries they're bombing." He shook his head. "It's a different type of warfare than the last Great War."

"Have you spoken to Stanislaw Czartoryski?" asked Anatoly Andreievich Demetrikov, Alexei's Foreign Minister. "One of his sons is fighting in the war. I can't imagine what he's going through."

Three hours later, Alexei, holding the phone, waited as one of Czartoryski's aides ran to get him. Igor sat behind Alexei, listening in on the conversation. "Hello, Alexei," Czartoryski said a minute later, sounding as if he had aged several decades in the last few weeks.

"Is the news as bad as I've heard?" Alexei asked.

"No, it's worse," Czartoryski replied. "My army has been completely destroyed. The Nazis are already here in Warsaw."

"Is there no way for you to keep fighting?"

"No, none at all. I have no forces left to fight with."

"I'm really sorry," Alexei said.

"Me too," Czartoryski replied. "The Poles have spent so long fighting for their independence, and once more we've been reduced to rubble."

"What of your son?"

"The Germans have him," Czartoryski said, his voice breaking.

"What?!"

"They captured him in the fighting, and I hear he's being taken to a POW camp somewhere- no one could tell me where, exactly."

"Oh my God."

"Alexei, could you do me a favor?"

"Absolutely."

"Could you beat the Germans? Could you wipe them off the face of the Earth?"

"We're working on it." When Alexei hung up, his hands were shaking and his heart felt like it was rattling in his chest. He looked at Igor.

"There's no way his son will survive," Igor said, confirming what Alexei was thinking. "The Germans will kill him, if they haven't already."

"There's a part of me that hopes the Germans will keep him alive as some sort of leverage."

"Leverage for what?" Igor asked. "The Nazis have spent the last several weeks crushing Europe. They don't need anything to negotiate with."

The day after the Polish rout, and with the Nazis marching across the Ukraine and much of western Europe, Alexei called an urgent meeting with his top generals. Soon, he was sitting around a table with Prince Konstantin and the rest of the generals on his staff: Zhukov, Timoshenko, Tukhachevsky, Antonov, Chuikov, Rokossovsky, and Kulik.

Igor grinned as he hugged his brother. "It's always good to see you," he said.

Konstantin nodded. "It's a relief that I'm still safe," he said.

When the meeting began, Tukhachevsky spoke first, detailing his plans for a counter-attack. "I'd start by having these tank divisions here," he began, pointing at the map in front of him.

Kulik interrupted him. "Tanks are overrated," he said. "Our horse-drawn guns are what will determine our win over the Nazis."

The room fell silent as everyone looked at Kulik. He looked back at them, daring them to challenge him.

"You can't be serious," Alexei said finally.

"Of course I am," Kulik said. "Our cavalry performed admirably in the last war. Your Imperial Majesty, your Cossacks are still pretty fearsome. Perhaps you should consider sending them into battle."

"We are talking about an all-out war against German planes and tanks," Alexei said, struggling to control his disbelief.

Kulik looked at Timoshenko and Zhukov. "You both started your careers in the cavalry," he said. "I'm surprised you wouldn't support the greater of use of horse-drawn guns."

Timoshenko and Zhukov looked at each other and shifted uncomfortably in their seats. "The Panzer blitzkrieg has devastated Poland and the Ukraine, and the Nazis will probably march on Moscow and St. Petersburg," Zhukov said finally. "I can't believe you would even contemplate switching back to horse-drawn weapons."

"Grigory Ivanovich, are you truly serious in this argument?" Alexei asked Kulik.

"Yes, Your Imperial Majesty, I am."

"We cannot fight this war that way."

"I will lead my regiments the way I see fit."

Alexei shook his head. "No, you won't," he said. "I want your resignation. We need to beat the Nazis, not have them overrun all of Russia."

"Are you firing me?" Kulik asked.

"Yes, I am," Alexei replied. His face remained calm, but his heart was racing in his chest as he tried to control the desperate fear that was rising up within him. *I declared war with this general on my staff?*

"You'll regret that decision," Kulik said.

"You are incapable of fighting a modern war," Alexei snarled back, his voice rising.

Kulik stood up and glared at Alexei. "So are you," he yelled. "Russia would only have a chance at winning if your father were still on the throne."

"Get out!" Alexei shouted in reply. "You're not going to make me regret my decision by insulting me!"

Finally, Kulik grabbed his belongings and stormed out of the room, slamming the door behind him. Stunned silence filled the room, and Alexei could see the discomfort on the faces of the generals around him.

His heart still racing, Alexei took his seat again and took a deep breath. "I thought highly of Kulik because of his service under my father," he said finally. "My father always spoke highly of him."

Veiled expressions descended on the faces of the generals in front of him, and Alexei could tell they did not agree with him.

Alexei sighed. "Mikhail Nikolayevich," he said to Tukhachevsky. "You were discussing your plan of attack. Let's continue that discussion- *including* the use of the tanks."

The first week in July, Alexei took Konstantin to Rovno to visit hospitals and wounded soldiers. Many tales of the troops' heroism had reached Alexei's ears, and such tales vied for the space in his heart that was not filled with fear at Russia being overwhelmed by the Nazis. "There are three soldiers in particular that I want to award the Order of St. George for their gallantry," he told Konstantin. "Their names are Evgeny Yefimovich Vetrov, Iosif Ivanovich Dorokhin, and Leonid Yurievich Klepin."

Konstantin nodded and opened one of the three smooth boxes

bearing the decorations. The black and orange ribbon and white enamel star stood out against the black felt at the bottom of the box.

In Rovno, as Alexei and Konstantin were driven from the train station, they could see evidence of the war all around: huge piles of rubble and burned out buildings surrounded them. Smoke rose in several places. Very few people were out, and the streets felt empty. Alexei could see heat shimmering off the rubble as sweat dripped down his back.

At the hospital, Alexei and Konstantin greeted Grand Duchess Marie Pavlovna, who was stationed there as a nurse. Soon, they were discussing how close the fighting was and the safety precautions that the staff was taking. "The Germans have been bombing here regularly," Marie said.

"It certainly looked that way outside," Alexei confirmed as Konstantin looked nervously out the window.

"Do you want to visit our patients now?" Marie asked.

"Yes," Alexei said. Ostensibly, Marie led the tour, but Alexei was definitely the focus. In many rooms, the soldiers recognized him and Konstantin, and cries of "the Tsar!" and "the Heir!" were common. Konstantin looked back at the soldiers, his eyes shining with interest, and he listened intently to their stories of escaping German fire. As the soldiers whose rooms they visited had increasingly worse wounds, however, Konstantin's expression changed from interest to horror.

In the last room, the three soldiers for whom Alexei had the Cross of St. George waited. One was missing a leg, another an arm, and the third had his head wrapped completely in bandages. The smell of gangrene was unmistakable. "What happened to you?" Konstantin stuttered, directing the question at all three men.

"I'm an airman," replied Evgeny Yefimovich Vetrov, who was missing a leg. "I bombed the hell out of the Germans until the Luftwaffe came after me. I had to bail out of my plane not far from here."

"My cousin is a pilot," Konstantin said of Prince Konstantin's son Sergei. "He's gone on several missions already."

"I am a lieutenant in charge of about a hundred men," said Iosif Ivanovich Dorokhin, who was missing an arm. "We were losing our battle, but I pulled my wounded men to safety. It wasn't until afterwards that I realized I'd been shot too."

Leonid Yurievich Klepin, whose head was completely bandaged, could not speak, so Marie spoke for him. "He sets mines in enemy territory," she said. "Three days ago, one blew up and he was too close."

Alexei watched his son's pallor take on a green hue. *Can't say I blame him,* he thought as he pinned the Order or St. George on each of the soldiers. He had barely finished when Konstantin rushed from the room. Marie slipped out after him and Alexei let them go. Only when the medal ceremony was over did Alexei excuse himself to find his son.

Out in the hallway, Konstantin was cleaning himself up after having thrown up in a nearby basin. Marie had been comforting him but went back into her patients' room when Alexei appeared. "Sorry," Konstantin said.

"It's alright," Alexei said, putting his arm around Konstantin's shoulders. "This isn't easy." All of a sudden, a loud siren wailed. Alexei and Konstantin jumped. "Air raid," Alexei said. "We have to get into the bunker!"

"The soldiers!" Konstantin exclaimed. "We can't leave them!"

They rushed back into the room in front of them. Dorokhin was already out of bed and moving. "I can get down there on my own," he said. "Help them!"

Immediately, Konstantin rushed towards Vetrov, who was out of bed and on his crutches. Konstantin stood on Vetrov's left side, and Vetrov put his arm around Konstantin's shoulders and started hobbling. They made it out into the hallway as the air raid siren continued to wail. Behind them, Alexei was helping Marie carry Klepin. All around them, nurses were helping other wounded patients toward the bunker.

Next to Konstantin, Vetrov continued to hobble. "We're not moving fast enough!" Konstantin said. "Come on!" Vetrov leaned on him, and Konstantin managed to carry him towards the bunker. Alexei and Marie, still carrying Klepin, moved faster to keep up. Konstantin was relieved to see the entrance to the bunker just up ahead.

"Move, Kostya, move!" Alexei ordered, and Konstantin rushed forward. Alexei and Marie were right behind him, followed by a host of other nurses and patients. Konstantin reached the bunker entrance and dashed down the stairs.

Alexei heard the unmistakable growl of the Luftwaffe. He looked out the window and saw German planes at the horizon. Below them, smoke rose where their bombs had been dropped. "Hurry!" he cried.

In the darkness of the bunker, Konstantin struggled to see with only the barest of candles around him. Making his way over to an empty chair, he stopped and eased Vetrov into it. Vetrov closed his eyes and sighed as he clung to Konstantin's jacket. "Thank you," he whispered.

Konstantin felt a hand clasp his shoulder. He looked up, expecting to see Alexei. Instead, it was Dorokhin, who was holding Konstantin's shoulder with his one remaining hand. "Nice work," he said.

"Thank you," Konstantin said. All around them, the bunker shuddered. Konstantin ducked.

"Those are the bombs," Dorokhin said.

Konstantin looked around in fear. "Papa?" he called.

"Over here," Alexei replied, and Konstantin found him with Marie, still tending to Klepin. For the first time, Konstantin saw bandages sticking out of Klepin's shirt and pants, and realized that his whole body, not just head, had been burned.

As other nurses and a doctor surrounded Klepin, Alexei backed off to let them work. Konstantin looked back up the stairs and saw nothing but darkness. "Don't worry, everyone's down here and the bunker's been sealed," Alexei said. Then he wrapped his arms around Konstantin. "Nice work. We'll be safe down here until after the raid is over."

Back at the Winter Palace a week later, Alexei stood outside Konstantin's classroom. He was about to talk to his son's tutors about Konstantin's academic progress when he heard Konstantin discussing the air raid with Oleg, Andrei, Vladimir and Alexander. "It was scary," Konstantin was saying. "It made me glad I'm not in the trenches with a machine gun."

"I don't know," Oleg said. "I wish I were old enough to go off and fight."

"Petya is already at the front, and Nicky will be going soon too," Andrei reminded him. "I'm surprised your parents haven't locked you in a closet to stop you from enlisting."

They almost did, Alexei thought.

"It seems like half of our family is off fighting," Oleg said. "Vsevolod, Sasha and Sergei are also at the front."

"My older brother is fighting too," Vladimir said, "but I'm just as happy to be here in the capital. I want to enroll in the University when we're done with our studies here. I'd hate to be killed at the front before I can do that."

"What would you study?" Alexander asked him.

"Chemistry," Vladimir said without hesitation. "Our best lessons have been chemistry lessons."

"They're only fun when you blow stuff up," Konstantin said, remembering Vladimir's experiments gone wrong. The group laughed, the first real mirth Alexei had heard in awhile.

The discussion with the tutors can wait, Alexei thought. *Let them have their fun.*

CHAPTER 2

Summer turned to fall, and still Russia and her allies struggled against the Axis war machine. "This was never going to be an easy fight, Your Imperial Majesty," War Minister Bazanov said as he and the rest of Alexei's ministers gathered at the Winter Palace for one of their regular strategy meetings.

"I know," Alexei replied. "I'm not as naïve as we were at the beginning of the first Great War, to think that Russia would win easily."

"At least we have a lot more on our side that we didn't have in the last war," Bazanov said. "That includes our network of spies and the intelligence they provide."

"Including Vsevolod," Alexei said with a smile, catching sight of the trees in the park, which were singing with shades of red, orange and yellow. "Though his parents don't know he's a spy. They think he's at the front with his regiment." He shook his head, his smile gone. "I'm just waiting for *that* bomb to drop."

"We've been most impressed with the intelligence that His Serene Highness has provided," Bazanov said. "Unfortunately, this time it includes something you're not going to like."

"What is that?"

"Romania has decided to join the war- against us."

"*What?!*" Alexei shrieked. "Carol decided to fight against his own sisters?"

"I'm sorry, Your Imperial Majesty…." Bazanov began, but Alexei was already rushing to the phone.

"Are you going to call Carol directly?" Foreign Minister Demetrikov asked. His discomfort was reflected in the expressions of everyone around him.

"There must be some mistake," Alexei said. "I always thought Carol was crazy, but I didn't think he was *this* crazy."

"Hello, Alyosha," Carol said a minute later, sounding self-satisfied. "By now I'm sure you've heard the news."

"I can't believe you've declared war against us!" Alexei replied. "Why in hell would you join the Nazis?"

"Because they're going to win," Carol answered. "I don't want Romania wiped off the face of the Earth."

"Is there anything I can do to make you change your mind?"

"No, there isn't. I've already committed my army."

Alexei hung up the phone and sunk into his chair. "I can't believe it," he said. His ministers watched him as the silence grew. Then Alexei sat up straight, his jaw set. "We need to beat the Nazis," he said. "What's the best way to launch an offensive?"

Later that evening, Alexei had to break the news to Ileana, a conversation he dreaded. As she always did, however, Ileana sensed that something was wrong, so Alexei saw no reason say anything but the truth.

"How could he do such a thing?" Ileana shouted. "I'm here, Mignon is married to the Danish king, Elizabeth to a Greek prince, and Carol enters the war against all of us?"

Alexei's chest constricted. "I don't understand his decision at all," he said.

Ileana collapsed into a chair and wept. Alexei put his arms around her. Ileana took a deep, shuddering breath. "When my mother died, I thought it would give Carol freer reign to join the Nazis," she said. "Mama would have opposed it, and the Romanian people would have followed her lead."

Alexei knelt next to his wife. "Ileana, I know you're hurting, but I also want to defeat Germany. I deeply believe that the Nazis are evil."

"So do I," Ileana said. "I'm just scared of what their defeat will mean for Romania."

As October became November, Alexei sat at his desk, leafing through a stack of official correspondence from all parts of the war. Notes from his generals always made it to the top of his pile, but today, his mail contained an envelope whose handwriting he did not recognize. The lack of an official postmark also told him that the letter had not gone through the usual channels to reach him. Frowning, Alexei opened the envelope, if only to discern its contents. "Dear Alyosha," the letter began. "By now my official intelligence on the camps in Poland must have reached your desk, but there is more I need to say."

Realizing that the letter was from Vsevolod, who was still undercover, Alexei took a deep breath and continued reading. "My intelligence had to be edited to make for an official version whose clarity made the message easy to disseminate," Vsevolod's letter continued. "However, the full truth weighs upon my conscience, so I have taken it upon myself set down my full impressions of those camps, even if writing this letter compromises my cover.

"Make no mistake, Alyosha, those camps are death camps, and the Nazis will exterminate all who are in them, mostly Jews. Each person there is being led to their death, and the Nazis mean to kill all of them in the most horrible way possible. Many of the people in these camps are innocent civilians who are being carted in, not only from Poland, but also from Germany itself, which has long been promulgating laws against its undesirables.

"The camp I went to see is called Treblinka, and the Germans pronounce the name with relish. Its shower facilities act with gas rather than water, and Nazi guards pack in as many people as they can. The smell of death hangs in the air all around this place- the smell of flesh burning, the smell of thousands of dead bodies being removed from the showers. I will never forget that smell, nor the sound of so many dead people being moved and piled up, for the rest of my life.

"The worst part of it, Alexei, is that these are all innocent civilians who have never raised a finger, much less a weapon, against the Nazi regime. I know our family's anti-Semitism is practically ingrained at this point, but my religious father made sure my siblings and I saw past our princely rank to the humanity of the people around us. It is in this spirit that I beg you to help these innocents.

"Besides, if the Nazis succeed in this gruesome extermination, who might be next? Might we be next, Alexei? Might the Nazis turn on our family because of the royal blood that runs in our veins? If all these innocent people die, and we Romanovs do nothing to help them, their blood will be on our hands more so than the Nazis that we kill.

"We are at war with Hitler and his army, but these innocent people need saving. I implore you to take action in some way to derail the Nazi's evil agenda. Yours truly, Vsevolod."

By the time Alexei finished reading, his hands were shaking, and his insides felt like they were quaking along with them. *I haven't forgotten how Hitler started our meeting trying to turn me against the Yids,* he thought. *I have to do something about those camps, even if I'm having trouble understanding them. How could the Nazis, who are in the middle of a war across all of Europe, divert their resources to a project like that?*

Alexei put Vsevolod's letter back on his desk and took a deep breath. *What to do about this?* he wondered. *Our armies are fighting as hard as they can, and yet we just started this war. It won't be over for a good while, and by then it will be too late for the people in those camps- and for many more like them. The Germans are killing machines, there's no doubt about it.*

As a plan began to form in his mind, Alexei called a meeting with his Interior Minister, Viktor Danilovich Smirnov, and Demetrikov, his Foreign Minister. When they arrived, Alexei explained the situation and the intelligence he had been receiving. "I want to save as many people as we can," he said.

"What do you propose?" Smirnov asked.

"I want to get as many Jews as we can out of Germany and the countries the Germans occupy. Get our ambassadors in those countries involved. See if we can get Russian visas for as many of them as we can."

"I don't know how many of them would be willing to come here," Demetrikov admitted. "And the German Jews are still our enemies."

"Then forge visas or passports for other countries."

Smirnov looked uncomfortable. "Do you know how illegal that is?"

Alexei's eyes bored into him. "It's less illegal than putting these people in death camps and killing them."

Smirnov swallowed and looked away. "There are shortages of war materials and sometimes even food, Your Imperial Majesty, and you want to pursue a project like this?"

"Yes, I do," Alexei said. "The Germans are monsters. We Russians are not. If you don't want to do this, tell me, and I'll find someone else who is willing." His pointed glare remained unabated.

"I'll see what I can do," Smirnov said finally. "I'll get in touch with our ambassadors and other contacts as soon as I get back to my office."

"Make sure you keep this as quiet as possible," Alexei said.

"We will," both ministers said in unison.

Several weeks later, when Konstantin and Oleg's lessons were done for the day, Alexei and Igor waited for them in the hallway outside their classroom. "Come on," Alexei said. "We're going for a drive."

A few minutes later, the four of them were being driven across the city, past the sparkling waters of the Neva, past the gleaming bronze statue of Peter the Great, to a residential block of flats that had been vacant until recently. "Where are we going?" Konstantin asked.

"We're meeting some of the people that Hitler has been trying to get rid of," Alexei said.

"Other than our soldiers?" Oleg said.

Alexei nodded. "There are a lot of people within Germany and the countries that Hitler has conquered that he considers undesirable."

"So he's trying to kill them?" Konstantin asked. Alexei nodded. "And you've arranged for them to come to Russia instead?"

"As many as possible," Alexei said as their car stopped and they all got out.

By the time they made their way inside the building, it was obvious that their arrival had been announced. People crowded in the hallways outside the flats, hoping to catch a glimpse of Alexei. Smiling, Alexei went through the group, introducing himself and shaking hands. Konstantin and Oleg were on his heels, taking in everything that was said. Igor hung back only slightly.

"What's your name?" Alexei asked an older man with a shock of gray hair as he shook his hand.

"I am Benjamin Rosenthal," the man replied.

"What is your profession?"

"I am a physicist. Some of your scientists have invited me to join them in creating a new, very explosive bomb."

"Good for you," Alexei said. "I hope you finish the project soon." He turned to a woman nearby. "Welcome to Russia," he said. "What is your name?"

"I am Frieda Gold. I am a writer and a musician."

For several hours, Alexei, Igor, Konstantin and Oleg listened to the life stories of the people in front of them. When they finally got back into their car, the sun was already approaching the horizon, sending long waves of light across the deep blue sky.

"Why would Hitler want to kill those people, Papa?" Konstantin asked.

"Because they're Jewish, Kostya," Alexei said, turning to look at his son.

"But those people are the smartest, most educated citizens he's got," Konstantin said. "That physicist who's building a bomb- he could have been building it for Germany! Instead he's building it for us, and we'll probably drop it on Germany."

Now both Alexei and Igor were nodding. "Hitler has always hated the Jews," Igor said.

"So you're trying to bring them here?" Konstantin asked. "Have many have come?"

"Not as many as I'd hoped," Alexei admitted. "Many are too scared to leave Germany and its conquered territories. Many others whom we've tried to help escape have been killed en route. It's dangerous."

Konstantin shook his head. "We need to wipe Hitler off the face of the Earth. I wish I were old enough to enlist."

By early 1941, warnings were trickling in to Alexei's office, both from Vsevolod and from other spies across the front, that the Germans were planning on marching to Moscow, under the code name Operation Barbarossa. *Can't say I'm surprised,* Alexei thought. *St. Petersburg will probably be next.*

By February 1941, as the Germans marched towards Russia's ancient capital, Alexei was forced to deploy further regiments, and Nicholas was deployed as a sniper. "My second son deployed," Igor said. "I was hoping the war would be over before that happened."

"So was I," Alexei said. "But we would have been foolish to think we could end this war in a year and a half. Besides, Nicky's skills are needed at the front."

"Yeah, I work with the big guns," Nicholas said with a grin. "The Imperial family's first sniper."

"Just be careful," Alexei warned him. *I am really nervous about this. I can't believe the Nazis have gotten as far as they have. Our armies are fighting really hard. How much longer can we do this?*

Three months later, as the snow was beginning to melt across the Russian empire, Alexei scanned the telegrams and reports in front of him, which dealt with casualty reports on both the Russian and German sides. *Until now, the numbers were pretty even- we're really slugging the Germans, but we're getting slugged ourselves,* Alexei thought. *These numbers are slightly better- we're starting to have fewer casualties than the Germans. Maybe the tide is turning.*

Then Alexei picked up a telegram that he thought listed the wounded. Instead, it was from Peter's commanding officer. Alexei suddenly felt chilled. He looked out the door to where Igor was discussing the latest offensive with some of the generals. When went to the door, Igor and the generals all looked at him. "Igor, do you have a minute?" he asked.

Igor looked at the telegram in Alexei's hand and turned pale.

Alexei grabbed his elbow and steered him towards a bench that sat against the wall in the hallway. Behind them, the generals watched nervously. When they were both sitting, Alexei said quietly, "Petya has been wounded."

"Oh, no," Igor moaned. "Is it bad?"

"Too soon to tell. He's being transported to a hospital here in St. Petersburg. He's expected to get here the day after tomorrow."

"He might not make it that long!"

"You can't think like that, Igor. It may just be a superficial wound."

Igor shook his head. "I know my Petya," he said. "He'd still be fighting if it were a superficial wound." He stood up and grabbed the telegram from Alexei's hand. "I have to get Sophie." He dashed out of the Palace.

Two days later, Igor, Sophie and Oleg were sitting at Peter's bedside when Alexei and Konstantin visited the hospital. Sophie was pale and Igor sat hunched over. Next to them, Peter lay in bed, groaning, his midsection wrapped in bandages. Alexei grimaced. Konstantin went over to Oleg and put a hand at his back, and Alexei was reminded of the years the two boys had spent together in the schoolroom. *This must be as hard on Kostya as it is on Oleg,* he thought. *Petya was like an older brother to him, too.*

Igor stood when he saw Alexei and they went out into the hall to talk. "It's bad, Alyosha," Igor said.

Alexei pressed his hand against Igor's forearm. "I'm so sorry," he said. "Is there anything I can do?"

Igor shrugged. "Do you think Nicky could make it back from the front to see him?"

Igor's listless tone depressed Alexei. "I'll send a telegram to his commanding officer," he said. "I'm sure he'll make it back in time."

Then Igor's brothers piled into the hospital. Gavril wrapped his arms around Igor, who finally lost his composure and wept. Ioann and George looked at Alexei. "How bad is it?" George asked.

Alexei bit his lip and looked towards the doorway of Peter's room. Ioann sighed and went in to see his nephew. His brothers followed him. Alexei swallowed and thought of their sons, all fighting at the front. *Most of them should be able to make it back to the capital,* he thought. *The only one I'm worried about is Vsevolod. There's no way I can pull him from the front. It's too dangerous, and his intelligence is too valuable. I'll send a telegram to the rest of the family, though.*

For five days, Peter lay in his hospital bed, moaning. His fever ebbed and flowed. It was not until the sun was setting on the fifth day, sending both shadows and golden light through the windows, that Nicholas finally hauled himself to his brother's bedside, holding his huge sniper rifle. His boots were wet from the remnants of the melted snow outside. Nicholas frowned as he took stock of the scene- Peter's bandaged midsection and gray pallor, his parents' grim expressions.

But then Peter opened his eyes and smiled at Nicholas. Laying down his weapon, Nicholas went to his brother's bedside. Igor and Sophie moved to let him through. "How are you feeling, Petya?" he asked.

"Never better," Peter whispered.

"Liar," Nicholas said, but he was smiling.

"It's good to see you," Peter said. "Though I'm sorry you had to take a break from killing the Germans."

"I've picked off more than a hundred of them so far," Nicholas said. "I'm sure they're glad to see me go."

When Peter drifted off to sleep, Alexei and Nicholas convened in the hallway, and Ioann, seeing a chance to talk to Alexei, followed them. "I was hoping Vsevolod would make it back too," he said.

"I contacted his commander," Alexei lied. "He can't make it back right now without risking being killed. It's too dangerous."

Ioann took a deep breath, and his eyes glistened with tears. "Petya may not make it," he said. "I think Sevka deserves to be here. My brother and all of my nephews are on their way back."

"I know," Alexei said. "But Sevka is in a particularly dangerous part of the fighting right now. I don't want to risk his life any more than I have to." Ioann looked unhappy, but he disappeared back into Peter's room. When he was gone, Alexei looked at Nicholas. "Have you really killed more than a hundred Nazi officers?" he asked, certain that Nicholas' statement was nothing more than bravado.

But Nicholas nodded seriously. "I'm up to 112 confirmed kills so far," he said. "Several generals, a bunch of colonels, many other high-raking officers." He took a deep breath. "And if Petya doesn't make it, all the more reason to kill a few more."

Alexei clenched his teeth. "Let's hope Petya makes it," he said. "Tell me more about the fighting at the front."

Nicholas sighed. "It's tough," he said. "The Germans have their sights set on Moscow, and my regiment has already had to pull back from Voronezh. The fighting is intense."

Suddenly, there was a wail from inside Peter's room. Nicholas, recognizing his father's voice, dashed into the room. Alexei was on his heels. The doctor that had been attending to Peter shook his head, and Alexei felt his heart sink. "I'm so sorry," the doctor said. Nicholas dropped to his knees next to his brother's dead body.

"Oh, no!" Igor wailed. Alexei put his arms around him as he wept.

As Alexei and Konstantin made their back to the Winter Palace a couple of hours later, Alexei kept his teeth clenched as he stared straight ahead. *If I do anything else, I'm going to cry as hard as Igor was,* Alexei thought. *The last thing Kostya needs is to see me that way.* He risked a sidelong glance at Konstantin and saw a tear sliding down his son's face. *I'm not the only one who's hurting,* he realized. He put his arm around Konstantin. "I'm sorry," he said as his own tears started flowing.

"Poor Oleg," Konstantin sobbed. "He was so proud when his brothers deployed."

"I know," Alexei said. *It's even worse for Igor. He wanted each of those sons so much.*

At the Winter Palace, Ileana took one look at her husband and son's red eyes and faces and guessed what happened. "I'm so sorry," she whispered, hugging them both.

That night, after their children had gone to bed, Alexei and Ileana sat up, talking about Peter. Alexei had stopped crying, but only because his tear ducts had stopped producing. His eyes now felt so dry that he was sure they would stick to his skull, and his nose was red where his handkerchiefs had chafed it. A pile of wet handkerchiefs sat on the table in front of him.

"I feel so guilty, Ileana," Alexei said.

"Why?" Ileana asked. "You didn't shoot Peter."

"I know," Alexei said. "But I declared war on Germany, and I gave the mobilization order."

Ileana held her husband's hand. "You can't blame yourself for this," she said.

Alexei shook his head. "You didn't see Igor's pain," he said. "Or Nicky's, or the rest of the family's."

"I don't need to see it to understand it," Ileana said. "Igor has practically lived here at the Palace since he became your ADC. Oleg has been like another son to us."

"I know," Alexei said. He disentangled his hand from Ileana's and put both of his hands on the table in front of him, making sure to avoid the damp handkerchiefs. Then he pushed himself into a standing position. "I'm going to check on the children," he said. "I doubt Kostya will be able to sleep much tonight."

"I'll come with you," Ileana said.

Two days later, the state funeral procession wound through the streets of St. Petersburg. All of Alexei's ministers and their families attended, as did most of the members of the Duma. As the priests chanted, Igor wept copiously, alternatively leaning on Sophie, Nicholas and Oleg for support. Alexei, too, tried to comfort his cousin, but the guilt of having sent Peter into battle nearly choked him.

Alexei eyed Konstantin, who was surrounded by his schoolroom buddies Andrei, Vladimir and Alexander. Only Oleg was missing from the tight-knit group, and only because he stood next to his parents and Nicholas, the latter of whom was still in his uniform. At one point during the services, however, Oleg, his face covered in tears, turned around. His eyes sought Konstantin, Andrei, Vladimir and Alexander. Four tear-stained faces looked back at him, and Alexei could almost feel their pained energy being shot back and forth.

After the funeral, the Imperial family went back to Pavlovsk, and Alexei could tell that Igor was glad for the familiar surroundings. Even so, when it came time for Nicholas to gather his belongings and head back to the front, Igor shot Alexei a beseeching look that Alexei could barely handle. "I don't suppose Nicky could remain in the capital?" Igor asked Alexei, a hand at his son's back.

"While my regiment remains in the field, defending Moscow?" Nicholas asked. "You know I couldn't live with that. Besides, we snipers are playing a huge role in the city's defense." He shook his head. "My regiment needs me. My *country* needs me. I'm going."

Alexei was glad for Nicholas' words as he struggled to respond. When Igor's eyes filled with tears again, Alexei's did also.

"Come on, Papa," Nicholas said, wrapping Igor in a bear hug. "I'll be home again before you know it. The war will be over, and bands will playing."

Igor looked at Alexei as he released his son. "Can we make sure that happens?"

"Don't worry, Igor," Alexei reassured him. "Ending this war on our terms is my top priority."

CHAPTER 3

As the war stretched through July and August, an intense heat wave burned through Russia, and Alexei struggled to remember a time when he had seen as many sunny days and such high temperatures. On the other side, the Nazis finally started showing the effects of the long war and the long front and supply lines. *The Germans have been losing as many men to exposure and starvation as to the fighting,* Alexei thought. *Their supply lines are stretched thin. Maybe this is the time to start a new offensive.*

By September, 1941, the Germans had retreated slightly, and Moscow seemed marginally safer. After a long day of meeting with his ministers and generals, Alexei stared at the maps in front of him. *The Germans are advancing on St. Petersburg,* he thought. *They must have given up on Moscow for now and turned their attention here.* He shook his head. *I'll bet anything my family and its palaces will be their targets, just as much as our armies.*

With that in mind, Alexei invited his uncles, aunts and cousins to dinner. "Can Oleg come?" Igor asked. "He and Kostya have lessons together anyway. He could just stay at the Palace."

But Alexei shook his head. "I don't want the children to be a part of this discussion," he said. "Convey that to your brothers as well."

Igor frowned. "Even our younger children are nearly adults now."

Alexei glared at him. "This isn't a social visit."

Three nights later, Alexei sat at the head of a long table in one of the halls traditionally used for formal state banquets. Ileana sat next to him.

Throughout the first courses of the meal, the volume of the chatter rose as the family caught up, told stories, cracked jokes. Alexei grinned as he watched his aunts, Olga and Xenia, trade jokes and stories as their husbands and children looked on. Next to Xenia, Felix and Irina Youssoupov alternately listened and shared some private conversation. Five of Xenia's six sons were scattered around the table with their wives next to them. *Only Nikita is missing,* Alexei thought, *and only because he's in Moscow.* Farther down, Ioann and his youngest brother, George, sat next to Prince Vladimir Kirillovich, the Grand Duke Kirill's only son. Igor sat next to Alexei, his hand often clasping Sophie's when neither of them was eating. Igor's brother Konstantin sat on Igor's other side, his arm around Pilar.

This would be so much nicer if it weren't for the war, and the reason that I've called everyone together, Alexei thought.

During a pause in the food service, after the borscht and pickled fish had been cleared, Alexei called the table to order. "Thank you for coming," he said. "I know you're all busy with the war effort, and I want to thank you all for everything you've done. Having the imperial family visibly involved has made a large difference, both in morale, and in our fighting strength."

He took a deep breath. "I've asked you all here on something of a more personal note. The Germans have already invaded Russia's frontiers, and they've set their eyes upon both of our capitals- first Moscow, and now St. Petersburg. I fear that as members of the Imperial family, we will become the Germans' targets- not only our persons but our palaces as well."

"You think the Germans would bomb our palaces?" Ioann asked. "They're our homes!"

"That's precisely the point," Alexei said. "Besides, our palaces are huge buildings that make for easy targets for the Luftwaffe."

Konstantin looked at Ioann and nodded. "Sergei said the same thing, even when he had just started flying. He could pick out all of the palaces from the air."

"What about all our belongings?" Vladimir asked. "Our palaces are filled with priceless art, jewels- everything- that's taken our family hundreds of years to accumulate."

"That's why I'm having this discussion," Alexei said. "As the Germans have attacked the cities where our largest factories are, we've started moving the factories east, to the Urals and Siberia, so that production will be as uninterrupted as possible. I propose we do the same with as much as we can from our palaces."

"Is that even possible?" Xenia asked. "Alyosha, you know how much stuff our family has."

Alexei nodded. "That's why I think we should start now. Our armies have been holding the Germans at bay as best we can, but the Germans have destroyed as much of Europe as they can. I'd like to prevent that from happening to our palaces, while we can still spare the trains and manpower to pack and move everything."

"What about evacuations of civilians?" Pilar asked.

"I've started making plans for that as well. We've also begun building the city's food stocks and securing supply lines, just in case the Germans make it as far as our gates." Alexei saw the unhappy expressions around the table, and felt his chest constrict with his own unhappiness. Silence hung in the air.

"I thought we were prepared for this war, Alyosha," Igor said finally. "Didn't we spend the last fifteen years or more investing in the country's railroads and production of everything from heavy machinery to guns, tanks, and airplanes? What was the point of any of it if our enemies are going to overrun the capital and come after us in particular?"

"I didn't say that any of that would definitely happen, Igor," Alexei replied. "All I said was that we can't underestimate our foes. And I think we've been fighting as good a war as we can because we've spent the last twenty years preparing for it."

Igor stared down at his plate, and Alexei was sure he was thinking of Peter and Nicholas.

"This war has been hard on all of us, Igor," Ioann said, and Alexei was relieved for his input. "I've barely heard a word from Vsevolod since he deployed to the front, and now it looks like my two other boys will be conscripted as well." He shook his head. "I finally understood how our father felt, watching five of his sons march off to fight in the Great War."

Gavril nodded as he looked from Igor back to Alexei. "Any way we can help the war effort is worth it to me. I'll start by taking an inventory of the items in our palaces. That way, at least we'll know what to start packing."

Ileana also looked at Alexei. "I'm happy to be in charge of everything at our palaces," she said.

"That makes a lot of sense," Alexei agreed.

Later that night, after the discussion was over and the extended family was leaving, Konstantin crept into the room. "Let me help, Papa," he said, and Alexei was certain he had been hiding outside, listening to the conversation. "Everybody else is off fighting or serving Russia some other way. Why can't I do something?"

"Because you are only fifteen, and you haven't had any military training," Alexei said. "Nobody in their right mind is going to send you into battle."

"Then send me to one of my regiments. I can train at Krasnoe Selo until I'm old enough."

Alexei smiled at his son. "Our men aren't conscripted until they're eighteen," he said. "The war will over by the time you're old enough."

"I can volunteer when I'm sixteen," Konstantin said.

"Not if we don't let you," Ileana said.

Konstantin made a face at her.

As Alexei walked through the Winter Palace a few weeks later, he could already see the effects of Ileana's moving efforts. The priceless paintings and scrolls that had covered the walls were gone. Sculptures that had sat in the middle of the rooms were gone too. So were carpets and gilded furniture. When he reached his study, he saw that the portraits of his parents, grandparents and other ancestors had been removed, packed, and shipped east. The antique books and bookcases were also gone, crated and placed into trains that had just left the capital.

This place feels like a tomb, Alexei thought as his feet struck the parquet floor and echoed around the empty room. *The rest of the Palaces must be the same way by now- the Alexander Palace, Peterhof, Alexandria... Did I do the right thing here?*

Alexei collapsed into the chair behind his desk, feeling a wave of despair wash over him. Before he could help it, he had placed his head on his desk. *I was the one who declared this war*, he remembered. *What have I done?*

In November, as the German army continued to close in on St. Petersburg, Alexei moved his family to Tsarskoe Selo. "Why do we have to move?" Dmitri asked. "I like the Winter Palace."

"I do too," Alexei replied. "But it's right in the center of the city. I don't want to take the chance that we'll get bombed." As he spoke, the lights in the train flickered, and the train began to slow down.

"Why did the lights flicker?" Rostislav asked. Next to him, Anastasia began crying.

Ileana stood up and tried to comfort her daughter. Then she looked out the window. "Are there cars that can take us the rest of the way?" she asked.

Alexei nodded as the train came to a complete stop.

"Must be the German bombs," Konstantin said. "They've been bombing rail lines, so it's been harder to get supplies to the front and food to the capital."

When the family arrived at Tsarskoe Selo, additional cars began arriving with their belongings. The electricity in the Palace was also out, so Alexei made sure the Palace's traditional white and blue stove was lit as

Ileana lit candles.

"Are we going to be warm enough?" Anastasia fretted.

"Absolutely," Alexei said confidently. "This stove has always warmed the palace. It will work just fine now."

That night, shortages of food in the city meant that the family's supper was limited to soup and the main course. At the table, Anastasia pushed the soup around in her bowl but did not really eat it. "Not hungry?" Alexei asked his daughter.

"The soup tastes funny," Anastasia complained.

"The cook hasn't been able to get all the ingredients because of the war," Alexei explained. "But I think it tastes fine."

"Well, I don't," Anastasia bellowed, and both Alexei and Ileana were shocked at how loudly their little daughter could yell. Konstantin, Dmitri and Rostislav watched their sister cautiously, even as they ate their soup without complaining. In a second, Anastasia threw her spoon across the room. Ileana ducked to avoid being hit, and the spoon hit the wall with a loud clang. Konstantin, Dmitri and Rostislav stopped eating and looked at Anastasia incredulously.

Alexei and Ileana put their napkins on the table simultaneously. Alexei got up to retrieve the wayward spoon as Ileana knelt next to Anastasia. "Nastia, you can't behave this way just because you don't like the soup as much as usual," Ileana said quietly as Alexei put the spoon next to Anastasia's bowl.

"Why not?" Anastasia yelled. "Don't I deserve decent food?"

"This is decent food," Alexei said. "In fact, it's better than decent. It's quite good, and it's more food than most people in this city are eating right now."

"I don't care about anyone else in the city," Anastasia said petulantly. "I don't understand this war, or why we're fighting it."

"Well, perhaps you should have gone with Papa and Mama to visit Hitler and watched as he tried to kill Papa," Konstantin said. "Or maybe you should have gone to the front with Papa and seen the soldiers with missing limbs, or watched the Luftwaffe bomb us." He shook his head.

"You were at Petya's funeral and you still don't get it?" Dmitri asked his sister. "There's no hope for you."

At the mention of Peter's funeral, both Alexei and Ileana sighed, and Anastasia finally sat up in her chair. "I remember Petya's funeral, and Igor and Sophie crying," she said. "This soup is not as bad as that was."

Ileana stood up and went back to her chair. "It's hard on everyone, Nastia," she said. "But it could be a lot worse."

"I'm sorry, Mama," Anastasia said, and, picking up her spoon, she finished her soup.

A few days after the family's move to the Alexander Palace, Alexei stood at the window of his study. Outside, the sun was setting, sending streaks of pink and purple across the sky. The trees of the palace's park cast long gray shadows over snow. *This is peaceful,* Alexei thought. He had barely completed the thought when he heard the familiar whine of planes overhead.

A second later, explosions rattled the windows. Alexei threw himself to the floor. He could hear windows breaking in other parts of the palace and loud explosions all around him. "Ileana!" he yelled, jumping up and dashing out of his study. He barely got past the door when the whole Earth shuddered around him. Alexei nearly lost his balance, and grabbed the door to steady himself.

Ivanov suddenly appeared in front of him. "The Luftwaffe is right overhead!" he said. "You must to get safety!"

"I must find my children!" Alexei yelled back. He raced upstairs to his children's nursery. "Kostya!" he yelled. "Mitya! Slava! Nastia!"

Ileana was also racing towards the nursery. Konstantin came racing from the library, and Dmitri, Rostislav and Anastasia raced out of their bedrooms. "What's happening?" Anastasia shrieked.

"We're being bombed!" Alexei said. "Into the cellars! Now!"

The whole family raced into the basement, followed by all of their servants and footmen. The Earth continued to shudder around them. Alexei cringed as he heard several crashes in other wings of the Palace. *I'm so glad we evacuated most of our belongings,* he thought. He put his arms around Dmitri and Rostislav as Ileana put her arm around Anastasia and held Konstantin's hand. Alexei tried not to show his fear, and he could tell from the way Ileana bit her lip that she was scared. Dmitri, Rostislav and Anastasia all looked terrified, but Konstantin was simply frowning. *What is Kostya thinking?* Alexei wondered. *Is he hiding his fear? Or is he simply brave- or stupid- enough not to be scared?*

After the bombs had subsided, it was quiet for a long while before Alexei felt comfortable allowing everyone to go upstairs. The Palace was eerily silent. Alexei gasped as he saw the huge bomb crater in the main hall. The columns around it teetered, and Alexei feared they would collapse. He pushed his family outside, but the park was in no better shape. Many of the tall trees that Alexei had been looking at from his study now lay sideways on the ground. Holes of varying sizes littered the park where the bombs had missed the Palace. Smoke rose in columns, filtering the sunlight into a gray sheen.

Alexei turned back to the Palace. Smoke and fire rose from it too, and for the first time, Alexei could hear the fire brigade coming. "We must get you out of here," Ivanov said.

Alexei nodded. "Have my family and servants driven back to the Winter Palace," he said.

"You must go as well, Your Imperial Majesty," Ivanov said.

"I need to see what condition this Palace is in," Alexei replied as the Fire Brigade arrived and began dousing the smoldering Palace with water.

"I don't like that at all," Ivanov replied. "The Germans could come back at any moment."

"Get my family to safety," Alexei ordered. He watched as Ileana and his children were hustled into the family's motorcars and whisked away. Then he began to circle around the Palace with Ivanov at his side. The entire right wing of the Palace had taken a direct hit, and had nearly been obliterated. The center of the Palace, which had housed its rotunda and reception rooms, was also severely damaged. Alexei stared at the destroyed palace in which he had grown up, and tears fell from his eyes.

At the Winter Palace more than an hour later, Alexei lifted the telephone in his study to call Igor. *He needs to know to come here rather than Tsarskoe,* he thought. But his call to Pavlovsk did not go through, and Alexei frowned. Then he tried the Marble Palace.

"Hello?"

"Ioann, it's Alyosha," Alexei said, feeling relief surge through him.

"Alyosha, thank God you're alright," Ioann said. "We just got word that Pavlovsk was bombed! Its only luck that my family and I were visiting Gavril when it happened!"

"What!?" Alexei shrieked. "The Alexander Palace too! The Germans must be targeting us!"

"Is anybody hurt?" Ioann asked.

"We barely escaped! I was in my study working when I heard the planes overhead. Luckily we made it to the basement in time."

"God, Alyosha. What was the damage?"

"It's bad," Alexei replied, feeling his stomach sinking. "I can't live there anymore."

Ioann sighed. "My siblings and I heard about Pavlovsk from our servants that were over there. Thank God Igor was at his mansion on the Neva when it was hit, and Pilar and the kids were at Strelna. We're all going over there tomorrow to see how bad it is." He sniffed, and Alexei could tell he was crying.

"Be careful," Alexei said. "I don't want the Germans coming back for another round."

"We will be," Ioann said. He shook his head. "That was my childhood Palace, Alyosha."

"I know that," Alexei said forcefully. "I grew up in the Alexander Palace. The Germans have destroyed everything."

"They've been targeting our monasteries and churches too," Ioann said. He shook his head, and his voice remained thick with pain. "It makes me want to go out to the battlefield again and kill more Germans."

December 8, 1941.

Alexei tossed and turned in bed, unable to sleep. Finally, he sat up and felt around for his pocket watch. Its hands were not visible in the early morning darkness, and Alexei had to run his hands over his bedside table again to find his flashlight. Once illuminated, the watch read five o'clock. *There's no way I can get back to sleep*, Alexei thought.

Slowly, Alexei pulled on his uniform. A few minutes later, he was sitting in one of the palace's drawing rooms, heating up the samovar to make tea. As steam started rising from the spout, Alexei could hear the water bubbling, and he was glad. He poured himself a mug of tea, and felt its warmth between his hands.

Suddenly, the telephone rang. Alexei jumped, nearly spilling the hot tea in his lap. Cursing, he went to the phone, fearing the worst. "Your Imperial Majesty, this Mikhail Timofeievich," Alexei's War Minister said on the other end. "I hope I didn't wake you."

"I haven't slept well since the beginning of the war," Alexei reassured him. "Still, it's unlike you to call before six in the morning. Is something wrong?"

"Your Imperial Majesty, the United States was attacked yesterday."

"What?!" Alexei shrieked. "Where?"

"The Japanese navy attacked the American naval base in Pearl Harbor, Hawaii. The first news is that the American fleet was destroyed, and thousands of Americans were killed."

"Oh my God," Alexei said, holding onto the cabinet in front of him until he could find a chair. His knees knocked together as he sat. "I can't imagine that the Americans would let this go unchallenged."

"To the contrary, a declaration of war is expected as early as today."

"Let's hope so," Alexei said. "Listen, Mikhail Timofeievich, I think we should go to the Tauride Palace to meet with the Duma about this."

"Absolutely," Bazanov replied. "The whole course of the war is about to change."

When he hung up the phone, Alexei waited a full three seconds and called Igor. By nine o'clock that morning, news of the attack on Pearl Harbor had spread across the country. "I can't believe this is happening," Igor said.

The atmosphere in the Tauride Palace was tense as Alexei and Igor arrived. Outside, the sun was just rising on another cold Russian day. Inside, torches and candles had been lit to supplement the flickering electrical light. All day, the debate raged as news about the bombing trickled in. "This can only be to our advantage," Alexei argued. "I think we should coordinate our forces with the Americans so as to take out both Germany and Japan as quickly as possible."

"We need to see what the Americans do first," Bazanov replied. He eyed the radio he had been turning on and off throughout the day. "There hasn't been any news from Washington."

"There will be," Alexei said.

At eight-thirty that night, Bazanov finally heard what was listening for. "This is it!" he shouted. "President Roosevelt is addressing the American Congress!"

Silence descended in the chamber. The large radio in the front of the hall was turned on, and a radio engineer carefully tuned it to the proper channel. Alexei, standing stiffly with his arms crossed across his chest, leaned forward, feeling his ears strain to catch every word. Microphones were placed next to the radio's speakers, and in a second, Roosevelt's voice could be heard throughout the chamber.

"Mr. Vice President, and Mr. Speaker, and Members of the Senate and House of Representatives," Roosevelt began. "Yesterday, December 7, 1941- a date which will live in infamy- the United States of America was suddenly and deliberately attacked by naval and air forces of the Empire of Japan."

For seven tense minutes, Roosevelt spoke of the attack's surprise, and of the destruction that it caused. In the Tauride Palace, three hundred delegates of the Duma were present, and no one moved an inch. The air that surrounded them was both unmoving and thick. Nothing but the sounds of Roosevelt's speech could be heard.

"Always will our whole Nation remember the character of the onslaught against us," Roosevelt said. "No matter how long it may take us to overcome this premeditated invasion, the American people in their righteous might will win through to absolute victory."

He's going to declare war, Alexei thought, feeling sweat trickle down his face and back.

"I ask that the Congress declare that since the unprovoked and dastardly attack by Japan on Sunday, December 7, 1941, a state of war has existed between the United States and the Japanese Empire," Roosevelt said.

In the Tauride Palace, whoops filled the air. Delegates threw pens and books towards the ceiling and hugged each other. Alexei remained standing tensely. Only his eyes moved- to Igor's face. Igor smiled, and Alexei relaxed just a little. "Finally," Igor said. "With the Americans on our side, this war might finally end."

CHAPTER 4

Two weeks after the Americans' entrance into the war, Alexei, Igor, and Bazanov sat tensely in Alexei's study in the Winter Palace as Alexei called the Governor-General's Palace in Moscow. *The Germans renewed their assault on Moscow, contrary to all my expectations,* Alexei thought. *They were retreating in the fall but have resumed their assault in the winter. I hope the city's communication system hasn't been bombed out of existence.* As the phone rang and rang, Alexei felt his chest constrict. He sent Igor a stricken look, an expression that was mirrored on Igor's face.

"The Germans have been attacking Moscow for some time now," Bazanov said. "Maybe having your cousin as Governor-General wasn't the best idea."

Alexei glared at him. "Nikita has led Moscow for more than a decade," he said. "Our generals say he's shown great courage during the war."

The phone stopped ringing. Both Alexei and Igor leaned forward, and Alexei felt like pulling the phone out of the wall when someone finally answered. "Hello?" Nikita said on the other end. He was out of breath and his voice sounded like a croak.

Alexei and Igor fell back into their chairs. "Nikita, it's Alexei. Is everything alright?"

"Yes, I was down in the basement. We just got through an air raid drill.”

“You’re still getting attacked by air?” Alexei asked.

“Actually, it hasn’t happened for a couple of days- the Germans are retreating.”

“I can’t tell you what a relief that is.”

“For me too. It’s been hell.”

“Tell me about it.”

“A lot of civilians fled, and I don’t know if they’re coming back. Our forces here have been fighting tremendously. The Germans never made it into the city proper, but they captured Novgorod. I could hear the fighting, even see it from the tower of St. Basil’s.”

Alexei swallowed. “Losses?”

“A lot on both sides,” Nikita admitted. “The fighting isn’t over and we’re still counting, but the Germans have lost close to two million men. We’ve probably lost a little over a million. We downed more than two hundred of their planes, though, and we’ve neutralized over 4000 of their tanks.”

“That’s incredible work,” Bazanov said.

“It’s not over yet,” Nikita reminded him.

“What about Nicky’s unit?” Igor asked.

“Nicky’s still alive, and his whole regiment has been amazing. The snipers have neutralized so many German officers that it’s hindered Nazi operations.”

Igor looked so relieved that Alexei wanted to hug him.

“I think the Germans’ operations are shifting,” Alexei said. “Since September, we’ve been fighting them very heavily in Tsaritsyn, and they’ve also been closing in on St. Petersburg. I’m thinking of moving Nicky’s regiment, at least, to Tsaritsyn. The few snipers that are there already have made a huge difference, and General Zhukov has asked that more be stationed there.”

“Just don’t leave Moscow unprotected,” Nikita pleaded. “I’d hate to see our gains reversed.”

“Don’t worry, I won’t.”

“So, Tsaritsyn,” Nikita said. “I heard that at one point, many years ago when the Communists still thought they would win the revolution, Stalin had his eyes on renaming that city after himself.”

“He lost his chance,” Alexei joked.

“Maybe you should rename it in his honor,” Nikita teased. “Stalingrad has a certain ring to it.”

“Only to you,” Alexei replied, but he was smiling. “Besides, that’s shaping up to be one of the biggest battles we’ve fought so far. If we win, it should honor the tsars, not the Communists.”

“Make sure we win, Alyosha,” Nikita said. Suddenly, Alexei, Igor and

Bazanov could hear gunfire in the background. "I have to go," Nikita said, and the line went dead.

Alexei, Igor and Bazanov looked at each other uncomfortably in the sudden silence. Outside, the long winter night was approaching, and the light in the room had turned a dull gray as the sun set. "Come," Alexei said as he stood up. "The Germans may be retreating from Moscow, but they're still approaching St. Petersburg."

"It's a real threat," Bazanov said as they went from the study to the large meeting room with their maps and intelligence. "The Germans have already overrun Denmark and are eying Finland. If the Finns weren't our allies, we'd be in trouble."

Alexei nodded. "Giving the Finns their freedom was a difficult choice, but I'm certainly happy about it now."

Within a few days of Alexei's conversation with Nikita, Nicholas' regiment, as well as several reserve divisions, were on their way to Tsaritsyn. "I'm glad to hear that," General Zhukov said over the phone when Alexei informed him of the move. "The battle here is intense beyond words."

"You've been saying that for months now, Georgy Konstantinovich."

Zhukov sighed. "The Germans have been throwing incredible resources into this battle," he said.

"So have we," Alexei said. "These new regiments, as well as the snipers, are a testament to that."

"I know that, and I'm grateful for it," Zhukov said. "And I'm looking forward to working with Nicky again."

Igor smiled.

"Don't worry, Your Imperial Majesty," Zhukov added. "If we win this battle, and I think we will, it will be the beginning of driving the Germans out of our homeland."

For three more months, the battle at Tsaritsyn continued to rage in an epic battle of urban warfare. By the end of March, 1942, Alexei began having trouble reviewing the casualty reports. *We've lost millions of men there,* he thought. *Is the battle worth it? Is any of this war worth it?*

Photos of the fighting had also reached his desk, but Alexei, after seeing image after image of crumpled, burned out buildings and rotting German corpses, had stopped looking. *I can't deal with it anymore,* he realized.

Alexei looked at his watch, glad he had a meeting with his ministers, even if that, too, would be about the war. He walked into one of the nearby reception rooms of the Winter Palace, once more feeling how empty it was now that the paintings and almost everything else had been sent east. Only the table, chairs, and telephone remained.

Alexei's ministers rose when he and Igor entered the room. "Please be seated," Alexei said. The words were barely out of his mouth when the telephone rang. It was a secure line, so Alexei knew that it could only be one of his generals calling from the battlefield. He grabbed the phone. "Hello?"

"Your Imperial Majesty, this is General Zhukov, calling from Tsaritsyn." Zhukov's voice came smoothly over the line.

"I hope you have good news for a change," Alexei said.

"Yes, indeed," Zhukov replied. "The Germans have surrendered. We are victorious."

Alexei threw up his hands and cheered. His ministers joined him, and Igor's eyes glowed as he howled with joy. "Our armies have fought bravely for the city," Alexei said to Zhukov when the room got quiet again. "I'm glad the Germans finally acknowledged our superiority." He could almost hear Zhukov smiling on the other end. "Tell me the details," he ordered. "Was it General Paulus himself who surrendered?"

"No, it was one of his colonels," Zhukov said. "General Paulus was killed yesterday- by Nicky."

"What?" Alexei yelped.

"Indeed. The Germans surrendered shortly after his death. I guarantee that this will go down as Nicky's top kill." He paused. "Is Prince Igor in the room with you?"

"Yes, he is," Alexei said, and handed the phone to Igor. Then he smiled, watching Igor's face as he got the news.

Igor's jaw dropped. "My Nicky got General Paulus?" he asked. The ministers looked at him as if nailed to the floor. The expressions on their faces were both stunned and admiring.

"Thank you, General Zhukov," Alexei said when he took the phone back from Igor. "I can't tell you how relieved I feel."

That night, Alexei's voice rang out over the airwaves, out over the public speakers in the streets of St. Petersburg, into private homes across the country, and out over the small radios being played by soldiers at the front. "Tonight, the Russian people announce their victory in the Battle of Tsaritsyn," he said. "With the encirclement of 90,000 elite German troops and the death of General Freidrich Paulus, the German army has surrendered to superior Russian forces. The end of this battle, which was defined by intense urban warfare and hand-to-hand combat, is a significant victory for the Russian Imperial Army.

"The tide of this war has now turned. The Wehrmacht, once the dominant military force in Europe, is now in retreat. Rest assured that Russian might and ingenuity will not rest- nor will its armies, air force, or navy- until the forces of Nazi Germany are completely destroyed."

As Alexei finished speaking, artillery salutes across the country celebrated the victory. 324 guns across St. Petersburg fired 24 salvoes, and the colors lit up the sky and all of the buildings. Alexei smiled as he listened to the noise. He draped his arm around Ileana as the walls of the Winter Palace seemed to shake with the force of the guns.

"Hopefully we'll be doing another salute soon when Moscow and St. Petersburg are fully liberated," Ileana said.

"When that happens, the war will be nearly over," Alexei said.

It was the next night, after supper was over, with Igor and Sophie sitting with him and Ileana, watching Konstantin and Oleg play chess, that Alexei really began to process the events of the previous day. Nearby, Rostislav and Dmitri played dominoes, and Anastasia sat drawing in her sketchpad, her pencil scratching against the paper. *The Allied armies have started to defeat the Germans all across Europe*, Alexei thought. *Even so, Tsaritsyn was a huge win. We may not be fighting this war much longer, but even a short conclusion could mean another couple of years of fighting. Unless….*

Alexei took a deep breath and eyed the chessboard on which his oldest son was playing. As he watched, Oleg took one of Konstantin's rooks with his queen and announced, "check."

The Germans surrendered pretty quickly after Nicky killed General Paulus, Alexei thought. *Maybe we can end this war more rapidly if we kill of more of the Germans' leadership.*

"What are you thinking, Alyosha?" Igor asked. "I know that look. It means you're planning something."

"I'm thinking of how to defeat the Germans," Alexei said honestly.

"Are you thinking of sending Nicky after the rest of their generals?" Igor asked. His expression was one of amusement and sadness. "Much as I would like my son to have that kind of glory, I also want him back alive."

"The Germans already killed one of my sons," Sophie added. "And one was more than enough."

Igor reached out and took his wife's hand as Alexei spoke. "Petya is never far from our minds," he said. "And I will do anything to spare Nicky's life."

It may not be Nicky who goes after the highest-ranked Nazis, Alexei thought. *But whoever goes will cause his parents worry.*

Two days later, Alexei sat in one of the Palace's drawing rooms with Ileana and their children. It was several hours after the rationed electricity had been cut off. Ileana was reading by candlelight, and Dmitri, Rostislav and Anastasia were playing a card game. Konstantin sat by the window, a book open on his lap. Instead of reading it, however, he was staring out the window as if he were watching for the Luftwaffe.

Kostya knows what's coming, Alexei thought. He cleared his throat. Ileana looked up from her book, and Konstantin slowly turned his head away from the window. Dmitri, Rostislav and Anastasia continued their game. "Mitya, Nastia, Slava, listen up," Alexei said, and his youngest children finally dragged their attention away from their game. Alexei forced himself to remain calm, even as what he was about to say tore at his insides. "The Germans have been getting closer to St. Petersburg, and our intelligence says they're intent on surrounding the city."

"What does that mean?" Ileana asked, closing her book and putting it on the table next to her.

"We started evacuating civilians this morning," Alexei said. "It's going to be a slow process, because most of our materials are dedicated to the war effort, but we got three trainloads out today. I'd like our family to be next."

"We're abandoning the capital?" Konstantin said angrily, tossing his book onto the table and standing up.

"Where would we go?" Ileana asked.

"I'll be sending you east, past the Urals."

Ileana eyed her husband. "You're not coming with us?"

"No, I'll be staying here to oversee the fighting. I'd like Konstantin to stay here too."

"No!" Ileana said immediately.

"Yes," Konstantin said, just as quickly. "I am not a baby! I will stay here and defend the city!"

"You aren't even sixteen," Ileana reminded her son.

"I'll be sixteen in June," Konstantin shot back. "What difference does six months make?"

"You may not live to see your birthday," Ileana said. "That's the difference it makes." She looked at Alexei. "I can't believe you're thinking of letting him stay. When my family evacuated Bucharest during the first Great War, the whole family went, not two thirds of it."

"I'm aware of that," Alexei said. "But many of my cousins will be staying here too- Igor, Ioann, Gavril and George are staying, but they're sending their wives and children east. Their mother and sisters are going too."

"Oleg is evacuating?" Konstantin asked.

"Yes," Alexei said. "Igor already had one son killed at the front, and a second one is still fighting. Neither of us is willing to risk Oleg. If that changes your mind, Kostya, you're welcome to go with the rest of the family."

Konstantin looked back and forth between Alexei and Ileana. Then he swallowed and looked back out the window.

Dmitri stood up. "I think you should stay here, Kostya," he said. "If I were old enough, I would stay here."

"If I were old enough, I would enlist!" Rostislav said, jumping to his feet.

"Me too!" Anastasia chorused, jumping up and swinging her arms. "If I were old enough, I would have enlisted *yesterday*!"

Alexei and Ileana looked at their daughter and laughed. Then they looked at Konstantin.

"They're right," Konstantin said. "I should stay here."

The next night, at midnight, Alexei and Konstantin helped move packed trunks into waiting cars. Alexei was dressed in several layers and still he felt the chill of the early spring night. It was pitch black, and yet they moved with minimal light. Nothing that could attract the attention of the Luftwaffe was in sight. The hard soil crunched underneath Alexei's boots as he walked, and the weight of the suitcases he carried felt light in comparison to the weight in his chest and stomach.

When he looked behind him, Konstantin was on his heels. Further back, Ileana was exiting the palace with Dmitri, Rostislav, Anastasia, two ladies in waiting, and three aides-de-camp. All of them were carrying trunks, which were loaded into the car.

Alexei hugged Ileana, and his eyes filled with tears. "Our most trusted guards will meet you at the train station and ride with you all the way east," he said. Ileana hugged her husband tightly in return. "Please get there safely," Alexei begged in a whisper.

"We will," Ileana said fiercely.

Alexei let her go, and hugged Dmitri, Rostislav and Anastasia as Ileana hugged Konstantin. Far in the distance, Alexei heard gunfire and felt his chest constrict. "You must go," he said. "The train will be waiting for you at the station."

Alexei and Konstantin watched as the cars pulled away from the Palace and through the gates. At the last minute, Ileana turned and put her hand on the car's back window. Alexei and Konstantin waved back simultaneously. *I love you,* Alexei thought as his tears seem to freeze against his face in the cruel darkness.

As Alexei made plans for his extended family to evacuate, he received a troubling phone call from Vsevelod's commanding officer. When the call was over, all Alexei could do was stand at his desk, immobile and staring straight ahead.

Igor came into his study. "Sophie and Oleg are ready to leave," he said. "So are my mother and sisters, and all of my brothers' wives and daughters." Then he saw how white Alexei was. "What happened?"

Only Alexei's eyes moved as he looked at Igor.

"It's not Nicky, is it?" Igor shrieked, throwing himself at Alexei. "Did a German sniper finally get him?"

"No, no, no," Alexei said quickly. "It's not Nicky, it's Sevka. The Fritzes captured him. His commanders are certain that his cover is blown."

"Shit," Igor yelped. "You *have* to tell Ioann!"

"What am I going to say? We're the only ones in the family who know Sevka's a spy!"

As if on cue, Ioann appeared in the doorway of Alexei's office. Gavril and George were behind him. "I heard Sevka's regiment is coming back to St. Petersburg to help defend the city," Ioann asked, looking more hopeful than Alexei had seen him in awhile. Then he noticed Alexei and Igor's expressions, and his eyes narrowed. He entered the study, and Gavril and George followed.

Ioann fixed his eyes on Alexei. "Has something happened to Vsevolod?"

Alexei swallowed, trying, and failing, to get his tongue to work.

In two strides, Ioann closed the space in between them. He grabbed Alexei's shoulders and shook him. "Talk to me, Alyosha! Has something happened to Sevka?"

Uneasily, Igor raised his hand to stop his brother. "Ioannchick, his hemophilia-" he began.

Ioann pushed Igor's hand away without even looking at him. His steely gaze remained on Alexei.

Alexei finally spoke. "There's something you should know, Ioann," he began.

"Is he alive?" Ioann yelled.

"Yes," Alexei said. *For now.* "But he never deployed with his regiment."

"What?!" Ioann shrieked. Behind him, Gavril and George looked confused and uneasy. "Where has he been all this time?" Ioann asked, his voice lower, venomous.

"He's been all over Europe, conducting intelligence missions-"

"Are you telling me he's a *spy*? How long has this been going on?"

"Since the beginning of the war. His intelligence has been invaluable. It's a major reason our armies have been so successful."

Ioann looked at Igor. "You knew this, didn't you?"

Igor nodded silently.

"How long have you known?"

"Since the war began."

"And you never told me?" Ioann stepped forward and smacked Igor across the face.

"Ow!" Igor recoiled, and Gavril grabbed Ioann back.

Ioann looked at Alexei to find Alexei eyeing him uncomfortably. "There's more, isn't there?"

Alexei nodded. "I'm sorry, Ioann," he said, "but I just got news that the Fritzes captured Sevka this morning."

Ioann, Gavril and George gasped, and Ioann's eyes shot daggers at Alexei. "They know who he is, don't they?" he yelled. Alexei nodded mutely. "They're going to kill him immediately, just because he's my son! How could you do this? You put him directly in harm's way!" He dove at Alexei, his fist raised.

Igor immediately leapt in front of Alexei. "Don't hit him, Ioann," he said. "Killing a tsar in wartime won't help anyone, least of all Sevka."

"Stand aside, Igor," Ioann said, his voice a menacing snarl.

"No," Igor said firmly.

Without further warning, Ioann's fist connected with Igor's face. A loud crunch crackled through the tension-filled air. Bright red blood poured down Igor's face. George and Gavril grabbed Ioann and dragged him across the room. Then George rushed to Igor and pressed his handkerchief to his brother's face. Alexei handed George the pile of extra handkerchiefs he kept in his desk as Igor's tears mingled with his blood. Then Alexei looked nervously back at Ioann, who was still glaring at him.

Ioann jerked away from Gavril, grabbed a glass inkwell from the table next him, and hurled it at Alexei. Alexei threw himself onto the floor to avoid being hit. The inkwell smashed into the wall behind him and shattered. Small shards of glass and little drops of ink flew everywhere. The majority of the ink adhered to the wall, and turned into a black blotch. Small rivulets quickly ran down the wall. "What are you doing to find Vsevolod?" Ioann bellowed.

Suddenly, Sergei Kemensky rushed into the room. "Vsevelod's commanding officer is on the phone again," he said. "Vsevolod escaped the Fritzes! He's safe behind Russian lines!"

"Can I talk to him?!" Ioann yelled, pulling away from Gavril again and racing towards the door.

Alexei felt his relief flowing through his body faster than his blood. "Is Sevka on the line?" he asked as he followed Sergei and Ioann out of the room. Gavril was right behind them, but George put a hand on Igor's shoulder to make sure he stayed put until his nose stopped bleeding.

"It's just his commander right now," Sergei said, "but maybe they can patch Vsevolod through."

Alexei raced for the phone, Ioann on his heels. "Yuri Mikhailovich," Alexei said when he picked up the phone. "Are you sure Sevka is safe?"

"Yes, he is," General Volodin replied. "I just spoke to him."

Alexei gave Ioann a nod, and Ioann threw up his fists and whooped. Gavril put an arm around him. "What happened?" Alexei asked Volodin.

"Our air force bombed the train carrying Sevka. He escaped when the train derailed, and our army was right nearby."

Alexei looked at Ioann, who was leaning forward, trying to hear the other end of the conversation. "Are you still on the line with Sevka?" Alexei asked. "His father his here and hoping to talk to him."

"I think I can do that," Volodin replied.

A minute later, Vsevolod's voice was audible, and Ioann grabbed the phone from Alexei. "Sevka, are you alright?" he asked, tears brimming in his eyes.

"I am now," Vsevolod said. "I just got away from the Germans, and I'm with the Russian army."

Ioann's tears flowed down his face. "Your regiment is returning to St. Petersburg to defend the city," he said. "I don't suppose you could join them?"

"I haven't been with my regiment since the beginning of the war, Papa."

"So I heard," Ioann replied, glaring at Alexei. "But I still want you home."

"I'll be home when the war ends," Vsevolod replied. "Speaking of which, Yuri said Alyosha had another mission for me, one that he thought could end the war. Could you put him on?"

Ioann continued glaring at Alexei, but he handed the phone back to him. "I do have something in mind," Alexei told Vsevolod. "But I have to firm up the plans before I give you any orders."

When he hung up, Alexei realized that Igor and George had finally joined them. Igor's nose had stopped bleeding, but bruises were beginning to show on his face. Ioann put his arm around Igor's shoulders. "I'm sorry," he said.

Alexei looked back and forth between them for a minute before speaking. "I had Ileana and the kids evacuated already," he said. "How fast can your wives and children be ready to leave?"

"Everyone is packed and ready to go," Ioann said. "We're only still in the capital because we were hoping to see Sevka."

"I'm sorry," Alexei replied. "But we need to get our family out of the city quickly as possible. The Germans can't be more than a day or two outside our gates. I heard gunfire as I loaded Ileana and the kids into cars, and that was in the middle of the night."

Less than an hour later, Alexei and Konstantin were at the train station with as Igor, Ioann, Gavril, and George said goodbye to their families. "Hurry," Alexei said. "Hurry." But finally, the train inched its way out of the station before picking up speed. Alexei looked at his cousins and saw a hard look set on each of their similar faces.

"We fought the Germans in the first Great War," Ioann said as he watched the train carrying his family disappear. "Let's fight them again now."

"That's goddamn right," Igor replied, and cocked his rifle.

In two cars, the men traveled back to the Winter Palace. They were all living in the servants' basement apartments for safety, and yet Alexei was comforted by the presence of his cousins, grizzled warriors from the last war that had raged across the world.

CHAPTER 5

Twilight slowly lit the sky over the Russian capitol as March became April. As the sun made its entrance into the day, Alexei sat decoding a telegram as it came into the Palace. "Arrived safely," it read. "Children and I unharmed. Ileana."

Alexei whooped with relief and rushed to tell Konstantin the good news. He had barely said two words to his son when the familiar wail of an air raid siren tore through the air. Alexei grabbed Konstantin's arm and they raced into the basement of the Palace. As they ran, Alexei looked out the window and saw German planes in the distance. "Shit!" he yelped.

Suddenly, both he and Konstantin saw several flashes of light. Three German planes exploded in the air and a fourth, hit in the wing, took an immediate nosedive and disappeared. "Wow!" Konstantin exclaimed. "Those were our anti-aircraft missiles!"

"Alyosha, Kostya, get into the basement now!" Igor shouted.

Suddenly remembering the wailing siren around them, Alexei and Konstantin continued their sprint into the basement with Igor just ahead of them. Ioann, Gavril, and George were already downstairs. In the dark basement, it was impossible to tell what kind of battle was being waged outside, and Alexei was disappointed. For the first time in his life, he felt jealous of the men serving at the front. *I am Tsar of the all the Russias,* he thought, *and I'm hiding in a basement as my citizens protect me.*

They spent the night in the basement, sleeping fitfully on camp beds. In the morning, the battle in the city seemed over and the all quiet was given. Half an hour later, General Zhukov arrived at the palace to give

Alexei an update. "Last night's attack was just the Luftwaffe, and we downed more than twenty of their planes," he said. "But the battle is not over."

"How close are the German infantry and tanks?" Alexei asked.

"About 150 versts," Zhukov replied. "We're expecting an attack as early as tomorrow."

Alexei nodded and dismissed him so that he could get back to the fighting.

As the weeks went by, the Russian army beat the Germans back, only to be beaten themselves the next day. The same several versts were gained and lost by both armies more than once. One night, Alexei swallowed hard as he pushed a door open and stepped out onto the roof of the Winter Palace. He walked to the edge of the roof and looked out over the city. It was the middle of May, and the heat of the summer was still several weeks off. In the distance, Alexei could see fires from the Luftwaffe's bombs and the reports of firing soldiers, and he imagined that he could feel more heat than was actually in the air. The electricity was being rationed, and the night's darkness seemed unnatural as Alexei strained to see through it. Curfew was also in place, and Alexei could hear little but the occasional gunfire.

Alexei pictured the millions of Russian soldiers in the field, both those in the capital and those stretched out across all of Europe and Asia, fighting for their lives and for their homeland. Tears welled up in his eyes and fell down his cheeks. *They are all people's sons, brothers, husbands, nephews and cousins,* he thought. *And they are all fighting at my command. I'm so sorry.* He struggled to take a breath.

Just as he felt air was reaching his lungs, Alexei heard a sniffling sound nearby. Frowning, he looked around, and for the first time, he saw a tall figure nearby. Moving closer, Alexei saw that it was Ioann, but he could only ascertain that by the light of the flame that leapt from Ioann's cigarette lighter. As Alexei watched, Ioann tried to light his cigarette twice, but his shaking hands prevented it.

"Let me do that, Ioannchick," Alexei said, walking over to his cousin and holding out his hand.

Ioann jumped. "You startled me," he said.

Now that he was closer, Alexei could see tears running down Ioann's face. "Is everything alright?" he asked worriedly.

Instead of responding, Ioann handed Alexei his lighter and held out his cigarette. Once Alexei was holding the lighter, he could see the Imperial double-headed eagle engraved on it.

Ioann remained silent until after his cigarette was lit and he had taken a long drag from it. "I miss my family," he said finally. "Did you know that Elena and I haven't been apart since I was fighting the Germans in the last war?"

"No, I didn't," Alexei said.

Ioann wiped his tears away with his hand and took another drag from his cigarette. "Back then, I was fighting at the front and she was taking care of three little babies by herself- Vsevolod, Ekaterina and Elizaveta. Now she's taking care of our three daughters as our three sons are off fighting, though Sevka is God knows where."

"I know where he is," Alexei said. "He's safe now."

"For how long?" Ioann asked, fixing his tear-filled eyes on Alexei. "I know he's training for whatever mission you still have in store for him."

"He's one of the best men we have, Ioann," Alexei said. "Not putting him on that mission would be a mistake."

Ioann's gaze bore into his cousin. "He's so good at what he does that he's kept me and Elena in the dark these past four years. I have no idea what he's been through or what kind of danger he's been in." He flicked ash away from his cigarette. "This is my *son*, Alyosha, my first born child."

"I know that," Alexei said, his tears welling up in his eyes again. "I'm planning on getting him home when this mission ends, believe me."

"If he survives."

"Sevka's a fighter, Ioannchick. He's been through a lot, but he's survived, and fought to survive, in situations where lesser men around him didn't."

Ioann looked at Alexei, and his eyes narrowed. Alexei could tell he wanted to know more, but just then, they heard the door to the roof being pushed open. They turned to see Gavril folding his tall frame through the doorway.

"Alyosha, Ioannchick, are you out of your minds?" Gavril demanded. "You know the palaces are targets for the Luftwaffe. What the hell are you doing lighting cigarettes on the roof?"

"Just getting some air," Ioann mumbled as he put out his cigarette and walked towards his brother. Alexei followed.

"Get inside," Gavril ordered.

As the battle for St. Petersburg raged on, the German armies inched ever closer to the gates of the city, even as they sustained terrible losses doing it. As the fighting encircled the city, food and other supplies were often cut off. Alexei felt the lack of water the most as the July heat engulfed the city, and thirst engulfed Alexei's throat. Finally, he called his cousins and son together and described the situation. Igor and his brothers looked at each other. "I'm joining the fighting," Ioann said. "I'm not sitting here pretty while my sons fight the enemy and the rest of my family is fleeing for its safety."

"Hear, hear," Gavril replied, raising the huge sniper rifle he had spent the last six months learning how to use. "I'm going to make use of this thing. Nicky may be the family's first sniper, but he's still at the front. I'll be defending the capitol."

Igor and George looked at their older brothers and set their teeth. "We're coming with you," Igor said. "The Germans already got my Petya. They're not getting the rest of the family too."

They all stood and headed for the doors of the palace. Alexei stood too. "Gavril?" he said. Gavril looked back at him. "Shoot straight," Alexei ordered.

Gavril snapped into a salute. "Yes, Your Imperial Majesty," he said. Then he followed his brothers out of the Palace.

Alexei took a deep breath, struggling to control the fear and worry he felt. Every muscle in his body was tense, and he stood up stiffly. In the sudden quiet of his wood-paneled study, Alexei looked at Konstantin. "Come," he said. "Let's go out. I need to see what shape the city is in."

Outside, the sun was approaching the horizon, sending the shimmering white light of the summer night across the city as Ivanov drove Alexei and Konstantin down Nevsky Prospect. Theirs was the only car on the road, and the city's silence seemed to hang in the air like smoke. All around them, the normally white cobblestones had been turned black with soot. Only a couple of bombs had gotten through the Russians' defenses, and yet whole buildings had been reduced to a smoky rubble. A few people began to emerge from their homes, but it was mostly to look for food.

"Oh, man," Konstantin sighed.

Alexei put his arm around his son.

"There's got to be something we can do, Papa," Konstantin said. "I want to wipe the Germans off the face of the Earth." He had barely finished speaking when he saw a familiar face. "Volodya!" he yelped, and opened the car door to get out. Ivanov brought the car to a stop, and Konstantin rushed out.

"Kostya, wait!" Alexei said. "It's too dangerous!" But Konstantin did not listen, and Alexei jumped out of the car as well.

"Volodya!" Konstantin yelled, and ran towards his schoolroom buddy.

"Kostya!" Vladimir replied, and they threw their arms around each other in the middle of the street.

"What are you still doing here?" Konstantin asked. "I thought most of the city's civilians had evacuated."

"No, plenty of us are still here. Some of my professors at the

University decided to stay, so I've been attending classes where I can. I can't believe *you're* still here."

"Most of my family left, but my father and I and some of our cousins decided to stay," Konstantin replied. Alexei appeared behind him.

Vladimir immediately bowed. "Your Imperial Majesty-" he began.

Suddenly, the air raid siren ripped through the air. Alexei cursed. "We'll never make it back to the Palace!" he said.

Ivanov raced from the car towards Alexei. "This building has a bunker in it!" he yelled, pointing the office building in front of them.

Alexei grabbed Konstantin's arm and pushed Vladimir in front of him. Together, the four of them raced inside.

"This way!" Ivanov said, and they ran down a set of stairs, joined by the building's workers, who were also racing into the bunker for their own safety.

"How do you know about this place?" Alexei asked Ivanov.

"My officers and I have been keeping tabs on all of the bunkers built in the city since the start of the war, in case you ever had to leave the Palace."

Inside, the bunker was dark and the air smelled dank. When the people around them realized that Alexei and Konstantin were seeking shelter among them, they were appalled. "Why are you even outside the Palace, Your Imperial Majesty?" one asked.

"Many of my cousins are fighting the Fritzes," Alexei replied. "We are not afraid."

"Many of us would have preferred you evacuate the city," another man said.

"My wife and younger children evacuated," Alexei said. "We stayed so that I could supervise the fighting."

As the bombs fell around them, the Earth seemed to shudder. Alexei, seeing the fear on the faces of the people around him, sought to reassure them. "Our anti-aircraft missiles are getting the best of most of the Lufftwaffe's planes," he said. "Besides, the Luftwaffe is an advance guard. If the Germans are still sending their planes in, it means their army isn't advancing."

After he finished speaking, Alexei grabbed a chair and went to the darkest corner of the bunker. Konstantin, Vladimir, and Ivanov followed him. Alexei sat with his back to the wall. Konstantin and Vladimir sat facing him, and Ivanov hovered behind them, keeping an eye on everything. In the darkness of the bunker, Alexei could not see past his police chief.

Konstantin draped his arm around the top of Vladimir's chair and beamed at his father. "I know that look, Papa," he said. "You have a plan, don't you?"

"I do," Alexei admitted. "One that I've been thinking of for awhile."

He looked at Vladimir. "You said you were taking classes at the University?"

Vladimir nodded. "Yes, Your Imperial Majesty. I'm studying chemistry."

"So you're still blowing things up?" Alexei said.

"Yes, sir, I am!" Vladimir said, grinning at the memory of his mishaps in the Winter Palace.

"Do you know how to build a bomb?"

"That's all we've been learning."

"What about a bomb small enough to fit inside an inconspicuous briefcase, yet powerful enough to rip through a room and kill as many people as possible?"

"I can do that."

"What are you thinking, Papa?" Konstantin asked.

Alexei glanced around the bunker, and took in the damp darkness. With Ivanov keeping watch, most of the workers had migrated to the other side of the bunker. Alexei looked back at Konstantin. "Our armies may be starting to get the best of the Nazis, but I don't think the Germans will surrender until their leaders are gone."

"Like when Nicky killed Paulus at Tsaritsyn," Konstantin said.

Alexei nodded.

"You're thinking of trying to kill Hitler," Vladimir said.

Alexei nodded again.

"How?" Konstantin asked.

"Same way he did to me in '39- with a face to face meeting."

Konstantin shook his head. "If Hitler knew you were coming, he'd send orders to kill you before you got anywhere near Germany."

Alexei smiled. "I'd have to send someone that he wouldn't be afraid of."

Konstantin and Vladimir looked at each other. "You're thinking of sending us?" Konstantin asked.

"I am," Alexei said, still smiling. "I can't imagine that Hitler would turn down a diplomatic meeting with a sixteen-year-old boy and his Aide De Camp, especially if you're acting on my behalf because I just had a really bad hemophiliac attack."

Vladimir looked horrified. Then he realized the attack would be faked. Konstantin poked his friend in the side, and they both laughed.

Alexei looked behind them and realized that people were leaving the bomb shelter. "It looks like the air raid is over," he said. "Let's go."

Out in the street, Alexei and Konstantin stared at the spot where their car had been. What had been a car was now a mangled bed of steel. "Oh, my God," Alexei said. He looked around. The Luftwaffe's bombs had missed the side of the street where they had been hiding, but the opposite side of the street was completely demolished. What had been buildings only an hour before was now a burning pile of rubble, and Alexei could feel the heat from the fires.

"Your Imperial Majesty, we must get you to safety," Ivanov said.

At that moment, the Fire Brigade, followed by two police vehicles, arrived at the scene. Ivanov commandeered one of the police vehicles from his subordinate and held the door open for Alexei, Konstantin and Vladimir. A second later, he was at the wheel, and they were driving back to the Winter Palace at an incredible speed.

Alexei watched the Fire Brigade spray down the burning buildings as they left. Then he looked at Konstantin and smiled. "The last time I was driven back to the Palace by the police, it was because I was out joyriding with your mother."

Konstantin and Vladimir burst into laughter. "Really?" Konstantin asked.

Alexei nodded. "Ileana always liked fast cars."

The next day, Alexei convened a meeting of his top generals and made sure that Konstantin and Vladimir were there. After receiving reports on the success of Operation Bagration in the Ukraine, Alexei said, "it sounds like our armies might make their way onto German soil soon."

The generals nodded in agreement, and it was General Timoshenko who spoke first. "Even so, I don't think Germans will surrender until they can no longer muster an army," he said. "Russian soldiers will have to take Berlin before the Germans surrender."

"I have come to that conclusion myself," Alexei admitted, as the rest of his generals nodded. He looked at General Zhukov. "And yet, your victory at Tsaritsyn has given me an idea for a quicker course of action."

"How so?" Zhukov asked.

"The Germans surrendered pretty quickly after General Paulus was killed. Would the whole German army surrender if Hitler were killed?"

Silence hung in the room as Zhukov contemplated the question. "I certainly think it's possible," he said. "A lot of the intelligence we've gathered says that many German soldiers and generals realize that they're being beaten. It sounds like Hitler is the one keeping them in the war because he can't bring himself to surrender."

"And yet, if the Russian Army appears in Berlin, it will be a huge fight," General Antonov said. "The Germans aren't going to let their capital city go to the enemy any more quietly than we were willing to let the Germans take Moscow or St. Petersburg."

"It will also be a different type of fight than what our army has seen so far," Zhukov warned. "Berlin is an urban environment that's guarded to the hilt."

"Would your experience at Tsaritsyn give you a way forward?" Alexei asked.

"Certainly," Zhukov said. "But I think the battle for Berlin will be even more intense."

"Which is why I'm thinking of getting rid of Hitler first," Alexei said.

An amused smile graced Zhukov's face. "How do you plan on doing that?" he asked. "Our army can be as secret as possible in approaching the city, but we won't get anywhere near Hitler without a massive fight."

"I propose to send in someone whom Hitler won't think is Army- someone that looks like a peace offering but has a bomb behind him."

Timoshenko's eyes had already flickered past Alexei to where Konstantin and Vladimir sat. "You're thinking of sending the Heir, aren't you?" he said.

"Yes, I am," Alexei replied.

Igor leapt to his feet, shaking his head vehemently. "No!" he yelled. "He'll get killed!"

"I won't be sending him there alone," Alexei said. He looked at Zhukov. "General Zhukov, what kind of firepower can you muster against the city of Berlin?"

"No!" Igor said again. He grabbed Alexei's arm. "Petya's already been killed, and still half of our family is fighting at the front. How many more of our sons' lives are you going to put at risk?"

"How many more Russian soldiers' lives do we need to put at risk?" Alexei shot back, pulling away from his cousin. "I'm trying to *end* the war, remember?"

"By sending in an inexperienced sixteen-year-old!"

"He's willing to go on this mission."

"Of course he is. He's a kid who has no idea what the danger is."

"I know the danger, Igor," Konstantin said. "I've accompanied Papa to the front and seen the soldiers' wounds. I've also been training in the reserves of my regiment for six months now- that's more training than some of our soldiers going to the front have."

"And I'll be sending our best regiments to protect him," Alexei said. "That includes Vsevolod's regiment of spies, who have been in Berlin for weeks now, gathering intelligence."

"Great, both of them will be killed at once," Igor said sarcastically. He shook his head. "Kostya will be a target the minute he steps onto German soil."

"I'm well aware of the danger," Alexei said. He looked back at the generals in the room. "General Zhukov, what kind of attack on Berlin can you prepare for?"

"I can prepare for an intense battle that will force the Germans to surrender," he said confidently. "But I still would not be comfortable sending the Heir on the kind of mission you're contemplating."

"What do you think are its chances of success?"

Zhukov took a deep breath before answering. "My intelligence sources have long confirmed that Hitler remembers meeting the Heir, and has spoke of wishing to see him again under the right circumstances. He may well be taken in with a plan like this."

Alexei walked to the window and stared out to the shimmering heat of the park in front of it. The room became completely silent around him. Alexei took a deep breath and made up his mind. Then he turned around and looked back at Zhukov. "Prepare for a full campaign against Berlin," he said. "Let our spies know that Kostya is coming, and the nature of his mission. I want them to protect him, and I want a full assault on the city once he's out of there. This must be the last campaign of the war."

As preparations for Konstantin and Vladimir's mission moved forward, Alexei said, "I'll issue the medical bulletins, putting out a warning about my health. When they're out, we'll give Hitler a call." Then he called his generals to warn them of the impending news and its falsity. "I want each of our men to continue fighting as hard as possible," he said. "The war is not over. When it is over, it will be because we won. And be careful with the news of my illness. It won't be effective if the Germans learn it's false."

"The battle for St. Petersburg is a draw so far," Timoshenko shouted into the phone from outside the city, trying to make himself heard above the crackle.

"What can I do to help?" Alexei asked. "Should I divert more units?"

"Yes," Timoshenko said.

By early afternoon, the medical bulletins had gone out, first across St. Petersburg, and then across the rest of Russia. Alexei waited a few hours, and then, with Konstantin and Vladimir in the room, he turned on the radio to a BBC broadcast. "It is with great sadness that I report that German bombings over St. Petersburg have injured the Russian emperor, whose health now lies in the balance…"

Alexei looked at Konstantin and Vladimir and grinned. "Let's give it a little time to sink in before I call Hitler," he said.

Overnight, Vladimir snuck onto the grounds of the University to mix the ingredients of the bomb he would carry. Then he returned to the

Winter Palace. Early the next morning, with Konstantin and Vladimir back in his study, Alexei picked up the telephone with a secure line and dialed out. "Herr Fuhrer," he said into the phone a minute later, making his voice sound as weak as possible. "This is Alexei Nikolaievich of Russia."

"Ah, Your Imperial Majesty, I was wondering when I might hear from you," Hitler said, and even over the phone, Alexei shuddered at the man's sliminess. "How is your health? Are you calling to talk peace?"

"I would be willing to discuss it, but I am incapacitated at the moment."

"So I heard. It's too bad you evacuated your ambassador from Berlin. Perhaps he would have been of use to you."

"I propose to send a different ambassador to negotiate with you," Alexei said. His heart beat faster, and he could feel sweat starting to trickle down his back.

"It better be someone with real power," Hitler replied. "I wouldn't trust anyone less."

"I propose sending my oldest son and heir to my throne. You met him when we were in Berlin."

"Yes, of course," Hitler said. "I see now that this is a mission of real importance to you."

"His safety means everything to me," Alexei agreed. *That's the only honest thing I've said so far,* he thought.

"Don't worry, Your Imperial Majesty, I will put an order out across my empire that he is to travel unharmed."

"Thank you, Herr Fuhrer." Alexei replaced the receiver, noticing that it was covered with the sweat from his hand. The he looked at Konstantin and Vladimir.

"A protection order from Hitler himself," Konstantin said, rubbing his hands together.

Alexei would have smiled at his son's sarcasm, but for the implications of the offer. "In line with Vsevolod's intelligence, it means that Hitler has his own plans for you," he said seriously.

"Even so, we'll have to play along," Vladimir said. "If we want to kill him, we're going to have to get near him."

Police Chief Ivanov stood with Konstantin and Alexei as Vladimir joined them, trunks in hand, including the all-important briefcase. "You'll be protected by my best men," Ivanov told Alexei. "But I'm still unhappy about leaving you here."

"My son is more important than I am," Alexei replied. "This is a dangerous mission and I want you to protect him." He looked at Vladimir.

"Your father called a few minutes ago. Call him back. He needs to know you won't be home for awhile."

Vladimir immediately went to the phone, and Alexei and Konstantin listened to his end of the conversation. "Hello, Papa, it's me, Volodya," he began. "Don't worry, I'm unharmed…. No, I'm still at the Winter Palace with Kostya and His Imperial Majesty…. We're all unharmed…. But Papa, listen, His Imperial Majesty has decided that he'd prefer to see me and Kostya evacuate the city. Most of the Imperial Family has evacuated, so we're going too… No, Papa, it's fine, I'm sure I'll be safe. Papa, I really need to leave- the train is coming for us in a few minutes…. I'm sorry, Papa. Yes, I hear the gunfire too. I promise I'll be careful… Goodbye, Papa. Say goodbye to Mama for me too."

Vladimir hung up and looked at Konstantin. His teeth were clenched, and his lips were shaking. "Let's do this," he said.

Konstantin nodded, and Alexei hugged them both. "Please be careful," Alexei said. "I want to see you home alive."

At the train station, Alexei watched as the Imperial train pulled away. A feeling of dread washed over him. "I hope this isn't a mistake," he said to Boris Andreievich Vostov, Ivanov's top deputy.

"It may be our best chance," Vostov replied. "Hitler never trusted your ambassador, but he seemed genuinely interested in seeing His Imperial Highness again."

"He may only be eager to see Kostya because he's planning on capturing and torturing him," Alexei said. "Vsevolod has been in Berlin for weeks now, and he said it was all the Germans could talk about. It scared him, and he's seen a lot these past few years."

Vostov looked at Alexei as the Imperial train disappeared out of their line of sight. "You can always end the mission, you know," he said. "It's still within your control. If you're nervous about it, have the Imperial train turn around. Tell Hitler you've changed your mind."

Alexei swallowed hard and stared in the direction that the train had gone. He felt the sun on his skin. "I don't know what to do," he said. "It's such a gamble, but we've already put so much preparation into it."

They were both silent as Alexei contemplated the situation. All around him, Alexei felt the unnatural silence of the station as he remembered the hustle and bustle of the Imperial family's travels in past years. *Our lives were very happy before this war,* he thought. *Hitler has changed all that.* He felt tears rise up in his eyes as he thought of Peter's funeral, and of all the horrors that he knew Vsevolod and Nicholas had endured at the hands of the Nazis. Then he clenched his teeth as he thought of how Hitler had nearly killed him the last time they had met. *I want to return the favor, and I kept Kostya here in the city for that very reason.*

Vostov saw Alexei's eyes harden and realized that he had made his decision. Both men were silent as Vostov drove Alexei back to the Winter Palace. The Germans had stopped bombing the city, but had taken to shelling it instead, and Alexei clutched the side of the door as Vostov swerved around the incoming shells. Up ahead, a number of women and children waited in line for bread, and Alexei sighed. "The rationing still hasn't let up," he said. "I've been hungry for weeks now, and so has the rest of the city."

"The Germans have cut most of our supply lines, Your Imperial Majesty," Vostov agreed.

"They're trying to blockade the city," Alexei said. "But the battle has been a draw so far. My generals and I have a huge offensive that we're starting tonight. I just hope it works."

As he continued watching the bread line, incoming shells from the nearby German artillery continued to fall on the streets. Suddenly, the shells rained down on the civilians waiting for food. The people scattered immediately, women grabbing their children as they dove for cover. As Alexei watched in horror out of the back window of the car, one shell hit an elderly man, who immediately collapsed onto the street, his head severed from his body.

Alexei let out a shriek. "Stop!" he yelled.

Vostov shook his head. "Can't do that, Your Imperial Majesty," he said. "I have to get you to the safety of the Palace."

Once they were in the Palace's garage, Alexei tumbled out of the car, heaving. In a second, he was vomiting as tears rolled down his face. Vostov gave him a minute to collect himself, but when Alexei remained doubled over, Vostov pulled him to his feet. "I'm sorry you had to see that, Your Imperial Majesty," he said. "But this is war. Even with the incident you just witnessed, the streets of St. Petersburg are still a better sight than the trenches were during the first Great War."

Alexei stared into the space in front of him, not seeing anything. "This war is all my fault," he said. "None of this would have happened if I hadn't declared war on Germany."

"The Nazis are evil and they tried to kill you," Vostov said without hesitation. "If I weren't employed in Your Imperial Majesty's personal protection, I would have gone to the front in this war too."

Finally, Alexei looked at him. "You're right," he said. He turned from the cars in front of them and stepped over the pile of his own vomit to go back into the Palace. "The Nazis would have invaded all of Europe if we hadn't declared war. Now I just hope Kostya succeeds in killing Hitler, and ending this war for good."

Inside, the Palace was silent, and Alexei began to take stock of just how alone he really was. At that moment, Alexei's secure telephone rang, and his heart rate shot up. *That can't be Kostya already?* he thought, and dove at the phone. "Hello?"

"Oh my God, Alyosha, are you alright?" Ileana said on the other end. "Those medical bulletins- they said you'd gotten hit by a German bomb!"

"I know, I know," Alexei said, trying to calm her down. "It's false propaganda. We're trying to get Hitler to let his guard down."

"Oh my God!" Ileana wept. "You have no idea what effect that had on me!"

"I'm sorry," Alexei said genuinely, feeling a lump close his throat and tears sting his eyes. "But we needed the bulletins to be as realistic as possible." Ileana sniffled on the other end of the line, and Alexei hastened to distract her. "How are the kids? How was your trip east?"

"The kids are fine, but we had a hell of time getting here. Many of the rails have been blown apart. There were often cars to meet us, but sometimes it was horse-drawn carts, and German planes flew over more than once. We had to drive like maniacs through a lot of virgin forest to avoid the bombs."

Alexei took a deep breath, and tried to steady his shaking hands. "Was anybody hurt?"

"No, but we had a few close calls."

"What about the rest of the family- Elena, Sophie, Pilar, their kids?"

"They had a harder time of it than we did," Ileana said. "They got out later, when the Germans were closer to the capital. They lost a lot of their belongings- their train derailed when the Germans bombed the track just in front of them. We had to treat them for injuries when they got here. Oleg broke his arm, and almost everyone else had cuts and bruises."

Alexei's tears fell from his eyes. "I'm so sorry for all of this," he said. "I should have evacuated everyone sooner."

"Oleg has been incredible, though- even with his broken arm, he carried two of the younger kids out of the train wreckage and to safety. The whole family is really courageous."

"Oleg takes after his father," Alexei replied. "Igor and all of his brothers went out to their regiments to help defend the city."

"Amazing," Ileana agreed. "Oleg will be pleased to know that. Where is Kostya?"

"At the University with Volodya," Alexei lied, feeling his guilt rise like bile. "They and the chemistry professors are trying to find better bomb formulations."

"So Volodya is still blowing things up after all these years," Ileana said. She laughed, and Alexei pretended to. "I was hoping to talk to Kostya, though."

"I'll tell him you called," Alexei replied.

After he hung up, Alexei's tears continued to flow. Wiping at them first with his handkerchief and then with his hands, and Alexei went back down to the Palace's basement, into the two-bedroom servants' suite that he had been sharing with Igor before Igor and his brothers had departed for the fighting. For a moment, he hesitated in the doorway of Igor's bedroom, hoping to catch the scent of his cousin's cologne. Instead, he spotted a letter sitting on a small table in the corner.

Picking it up, Alexei saw that it was many pages long but had been scribbled hastily- the handwriting was uneven and often sloped downward on one side. Flipping to the last page, Alexei saw Nicholas' signature written sloppily across the bottom, and a date from just a few weeks prior. *He must have written to Igor from the battlefield at Tsaritsyn*, Alexei realized.

"Dear Mama and Papa," the letter began. "I hope this letter finds you and Oleg safe at Pavlovsk. How I miss the evenings we all used to spend there as a family, sitting by the warm stove as Petya cracked jokes and played games with me and Oleg. I would give anything to see Petya returned to this Earth.

"Here at Tsaritsyn, the fighting is beyond description. Many of the snipers that arrive here don't live more than a day or two, so I wonder how it is that I've managed to stay alive these last few months. Is it possible that God took Petya but is ensuring my safety?

"It is almost inconceivable to think of God in this place. We lost 70,000 men in one day alone last week, but at least the Germans have been losing even more. Blood runs through the Earth here like water down the Neva, and the stench of death is everywhere. I have lost count of the number of limbs that I have seen blown through the air by German bombs and bullets. Even the men that survive their initial injuries aren't always the better for it- many simply watch as gangrene eats their whole body. My clothes smell of death, and my fingernails smell of the infection.

"Each night, I am certain that I will never see another sunrise, and yet each day, my bullets reach the heads of German officers. My clean shots make the Germans fall without any damage that I can see. My dirtier shots spray their brains across whomever is standing nearby. My work is only made bearable by the thought that any of those officers could have ordered the attack that killed our Petya, and that any of them would happily order an attack on the rest of the family and the rest of Russia.

"My shift has just ended, and I must go to sleep, so that I can continue my work in the morning. The rest of the soldiers here are brave beyond belief, and I must join them in their bravery- that it is the only thing that gives me hope that we may end this battle, and the war.

"Your truly, Nicholas."

Alexei put down the letter and doubled over as his tears poured down his face. His stomach felt as though a truck had just driven through it. Slowly, Alexei grabbed a nearby chair to steady himself. Then he managed to rock back onto his knees. The chair's smooth wooden handles felt cool to the touch, and Alexei had to work up the strength to pull himself into a standing position. When he could walk again, Alexei went to the phone and called General Timoshenko. "Where are the regiments that were on their way from the East?" he asked.

"They're just arriving," Timoshenko replied.

"Good," Alexei said. "Launch the counterattack with full force as soon as possible- as soon as the additional regiments have fully arrived and the counterattack can be done with full force."

"Thank you, Your Imperial Majesty, we will."

CHAPTER 6

The Imperial train moved through the desolate Russian countryside, avoiding the towns that had been bombed and the railroad tracks that had been blown up. Vladimir Golitzyn stared out the window, his teeth clenched, his tears threatening to overflow.

Konstantin put his arm around his friend. "Now is the time to cry if you need to," he said. "You must be in control of yourself when we meet with Hitler."

Vladimir glared at him. "I may have just said goodbye to my father for the last time," he said. "And I did it by lying to him."

Konstantin stared back at Vladimir, and his blue eyes seemed to go black with anger. "Don't you think I feel your pain?" he said. "The last time I met with Hitler, he tried to kill my father in front of me. I know you were at Petya's funeral, but that was *my* cousin- you would have to know Igor and his brothers to know just how much pain they were in, and their other sons are still fighting at the front!"

"I know that!" Vladimir shot back. "I've been feeling pretty unimportant, stuck in the capital while everyone else goes off to fight."

"I know the feeling," Konstantin said. "My father acutely feels the loss of every Russian. He's kept me on a tight leash too. This has been my first chance to do anything meaningful, and I intend to make it count!"

Finally, Vladimir reached out and took Konstantin's hand. "Your family has been very visible since the war began," he said. "The fact that Petya, Nicky, Vsevolod and the rest of them all went off to fight made a huge impression on the country, as did Petya's death. You may have evacuated your women and children, but it only shows your humanity, especially as Igor, Gavril, Ioann, and George have taken up arms outside St. Petersburg."

Konstantin swallowed and looked away. "I just hope they all survive it," he said. "That's a very large part of my family we're talking about."

"I know," Vladimir said, squeezing Konstantin's hand. "That's why I'm doing this."

Konstantin nodded as he looked back at his friend. "Show me the bomb you made, and explain how it works," he commanded. "I need to know everything, just in case."

"Sure," Vladimir said, and they walked over to his small briefcase. He opened it and pointed to a smaller, square-shaped object inside. "I can remove it from the briefcase," he said. "I'm hoping to walk in there with the briefcase, remove the bomb while we're meeting with Hitler, and then walk out with the briefcase, to raise as few suspicions as possible."

Konstantin stared at the small square. "That's really tiny," he said. "Are you sure it's powerful enough? Is it completely set up?"

Vladimir nodded. "All I have to do is flip the detonation switch, and then we'll have four minutes to get out of there before it blows. And yes, I mixed together enough materials that we'll be killed too if we're not far enough away."

That night, Konstantin and Vladimir pushed their camp beds together and slept next to each other, taking comfort from each other's presence. By the time they finished their breakfast rations the next morning, the train was pulling into Berlin, and a car draped with the Nazi flag waited for them. A Nazi officer stood next to the car door and saluted them as they exited the train. His whole arm flared out in a Nazi salute, but Konstantin and Vladimir returned a simple military salute as Ivanov sized up the situation. Then they all got into the car and were driven to the Reichstag.

Konstantin and Vladimir kept neutral expressions on their faces as they looked at the city around them. *The Allied armies may have turned the tide against Germany, but we haven't reached the capitol yet,* Konstantin thought. *All of these buildings are intact, and the people here are well fed and going about their business.* Still, he could not help but notice the number of German regiments in the city, or the number of tanks in the streets. *Before we left St. Petersburg, I heard that General Zhukov was amassing our forces outside the city. I hope this works.*

Up ahead, Konstantin saw the Reichstag, where huge Nazi flags hung, the largest they had seen yet. The car stopped in front of the building, and Konstantin and Vladimir got out. For a moment, Konstantin took a deep breath of fresh air, inhaling the smell of the nearby flowers and trees.

The driver exited the car and stood at attention. "I will be waiting here when you finish," he said.

"Thank you," Konstantin said.

On the steps of the Reichstag, there were so many Nazi officers waiting to escort him and Vladimir inside that Konstantin nearly felt claustrophobic. *They're not taking any chances with us*, he thought. He waited for Vladimir to reach his side, and they both entered the building together. Behind them, Ivanov kept an eye on their surroundings and a hand on his pistol, especially as they got inside and more German soldiers searched both Konstantin and Vladimir. *Damn,* Konstantin thought as the soldiers immediately found the pistol he was carrying. *I should have left the gun in the car. Then maybe I'd have a chance at getting it later.*

The Nazis removed the pistols both Konstantin and Vladimir were carrying, and Konstantin finally found himself becoming scared. *We're going in there unarmed, except for Feodor,* he thought. *And except for the bomb.* Then the guards searched Vladimir's briefcase, and when they opened it, Konstantin was sure the game was over. But the soldiers saw Vladimir's pens and papers and nothing more, and when they closed the briefcase, Konstantin started breathing again.

When the search was over, Konstantin, Vladimir and Ivanov were led into a light, airy conference room. Hitler, Hermann Goring and Joseph Goebbels all waited for them. The three men rose in unison as Konstantin and Vladimir were led in. *The old guard,* Konstantin thought, remembering the last time they had met.

"Your Imperial Highness, you have really grown up since the last time I saw you," Hitler said with his slimy half-smile.

"Indeed," Konstantin agreed. "Thank you for meeting with us."

"Our pleasure."

"This is my Aide-de-Camp, Vladimir Golitzyn."

"Pleasure to make your acquaintance," Hitler said, and gestured at the chairs around the table. "How is the Emperor?" he asked as they all sat.

"He's still quite ill, unfortunately," Konstantin replied smoothly.

As Konstantin spoke, Vladimir placed his briefcase on the floor and extracted some papers and a pen from it. Then he loosened the bomb from the briefcase and slid it to the floor. Within a second, he was straightening up, holding the papers and pen, which he put on the table in front of him. Once he was sitting up, he used his feet to push the bomb towards the other side of the table.

"This is the worst hemophiliac attack Papa has had in awhile," Konstantin said. "And they take some time to heal."

"That is unfortunate."

"Yes, it is."

"But I'm glad you've come in his place," Hitler said, leaning forward. "I know your father was hoping to make peace."

"Yes, that's true. Our armies may be gaining the upper hand, Herr Fuhrer, but we don't wish to see your citizens murdered any more than necessary."

Hitler smiled. "We disagree with your military assessment. Our armies remain strong, and our soldiers will fight to the death."

"So will ours," Konstantin said candidly. "Russian soldiers have always been brave, especially when fighting for our homeland."

"The same is true for my soldiers. I see no reason to stop fighting."

"We seem to be at a stalemate, Herr Fuhrer. Do you not wish to consider peace at this time?"

"Unfortunately not," Hitler said. "I will let my armies do the talking."

"Very well," Konstantin replied. "Thank you for meeting with us."

As Konstantin stood, Vladimir pushed the bomb's detonation button with his foot. Then he grabbed his briefcase and put his papers and pen back in it as he and Konstantin walked towards the door. Behind them, Hitler, Goring and Goebbels stayed seated. Hitler's half-smile remained on his face.

Once outside the conference room, Konstantin, Vladimir and Ivanov took the longest, fastest strides they could without appearing to be in a hurry. *There's no way I'm taking the time to get my gun back*, Konstantin thought as he counted down the minutes until the bomb detonated. In a minute and a half, he, Vladimir and Ivanov exited the Reichstag into the bright summer day. Konstantin was expecting the same serene urban scene he had left when he had entered the Reichstag. Instead, he walked right into a gunfight.

Immediately, Konstantin, Vladimir and Ivanov hit the ground. Konstantin heard a bullet fly right above his head, and he rolled down the steps of the Reichstag to avoid it. All around him, the bodies of dead Nazis littered the steps. Konstantin took it as an opportunity to seize one of their pistols, as well as extra bullets that had tumbled out onto the steps.

When he looked up, the car in which he had been driven was open and waiting, but it was also full of bullet holes. The Nazi officer who had driven him from the train station lay next to the car, also riddled with bullets. Next to the dead Nazi, another Nazi officer was firing at other officers across the street, and he was an incredible shot- each of his bullets downed a target. All around him, other Nazi soldiers sprayed bullets across the street. Ivanov pulled his pistol out of its harness, but he could not tell where to start shooting.

"We have to get to the train," Vladimir cried, and Konstantin saw that he too had grabbed a gun and extra bullets from a dead Nazi.

"Kostya, get into the car!" the officer next to it yelled.

As he and Vladimir ran to the car, Konstantin suddenly recognized the officer. "Vsevolod!" he yelped as he and Vladimir dove into the back seat.

Konstantin and Vladimir were hardly in the car when Vsevolod jumped into the front seat and jammed his foot on the accelerator. "Stay down!" he yelled. Konstantin and Vladimir obliged as Konstantin pulled the back door shut behind him. The car raced forward as Vsevolod continued shooting out the front window. Behind them, the Nazi officers continued firing. Bullets sprayed the back of the car.

"Feodor!" Konstantin yelled, watching his police chief firing at the Germans behind them as they sped away from the Reichstag.

"We can't help him!" Vsevolod yelled back. The car jumped, and Vsevolod cursed. "One of our tires has been blown out!"

No sooner had he said that than the whole car began to rattle and sway, even as it continued moving forward. Then another round of bullets sprayed the car, and Konstantin, even as he kept his head down, could see German soldiers- whole regiments of them- lining the street and firing at them. Their fire was being answered by that of Russian troops. *Zhukov's forces must be invading,* Konstantin thought.

Vsevolod shook his head as the car careened out of control. "This car isn't going to last much longer," he said. "We'll have to get out. As soon as we do that, fire at the Germans."

"Sevka, the station is still nearly a verst away," Konstantin said as he made sure his gun was fully loaded.

"I know," Vsevolod replied. "We'll have to find another way to get there, even if it means stealing another car."

Their car swerved and crashed into a lorry. Konstantin, Vladimir and Vsevolod threw open the doors and rolled out onto the street. Immediately, they were fired upon, and Konstantin did his best to return fire and avoid being hit. Amid the shooting, a sudden explosion ripped through the air. Konstantin dared a glance behind him and saw that the Reichstag was burning. *Yes!* he almost shrieked. *That was our bomb! Hitler must be dead!*

But there was no time to celebrate. The explosion at the Reichstag was answered by a round of explosions several times the size. They seemed to be coming from farther off, but still Konstantin threw himself to the ground, sure his body was going to be blown apart. Bullets flew all around him, and artillery shrieked overhead. Discarded weapons lay all around- broken guns, cracked rifles, even swords and bayonets. Konstantin felt all the air get sucked out of him as he watched the artillery level a tall building nearby, killing all of the German soldiers inside. "That's our artillery," Vsevolod yelled at Konstantin, throwing him an extra handgun that had tumbled onto the street. "Use this!"

Konstantin caught it mid-air and fired twice. Two German soldiers in front him fell. Out of the corner of his eye, Konstantin saw Vladimir shoot at more German soldiers as they ran. Up ahead, Russian tanks suddenly appeared a block over, mowing down everything in their path. Still, more German soldiers rushed at Konstantin, Vsevolod, Vladimir and the Russian soldiers that surrounded them.

One German general in particular dashed at Vsevolod, his eyes gleaming. Vsevolod saw him coming, and froze. In a second, Konstantin could tell the two men recognized each other- and that the German was gaining on Vsevolod. Vsevolod raised his gun and fired- to no avail. He was out of bullets. Vsevolod ducked and rolled away, and the German's bullets flew over his head. Konstantin fired at the general, but his shots hit other German soldiers that were covering for him.

The general raced after Vsevolod again. Vsevolod grabbed an abandoned bayonet, leapt to his feet, and swung at the general's neck. The general's head flew up from his body but didn't completely separate from it. His body collapsed onto the street, and Vsevolod grabbed his rifle.

From a block over, German tanks began to answer the Russian ones, and as Konstantin continued firing at the enemy soldiers around him, he saw one Russian tank get hit and roll over. Two Russian soldiers ejected and sprinted down the street, carrying AK-47s. They had just arrived to help Konstantin, Vsevolod and Vladimir when their tank, now upside down, burst into flames.

"We have to get to the train station!" Vsevolod yelled at Konstantin.

"There are lorries a block over!" yelled one of the soldiers with the AK-47s. "You go! We'll cover for you!"

Konstantin, Vsevolod and Vladimir sprinted away, covered by the fire of their comrades, who followed them as they fired. Several meters over, Vsevolod broke open the doors of the first lorry they came upon. Konstantin and Vladimir climbed in the back with one of the tank operators, and Vsevolod and the other operator climbed in the cab. Vsevolod jacked the ignition and slammed on the accelerator. The lorry jumped forward and sped away from the fighting.

In the back, the tank operator looked at Konstantin and Vladimir. "Stay down," he said, keeping his AK-47 cocked. Konstantin and Vladimir ducked into crouching positions but kept their weapons at the ready. The tank operator smiled as the lorry continued to race forward. "I'm Misha," he said. "My comrade in front is Anatoly."

"Kostya," Konstantin replied with a nod.

"Volodya," Vladimir said.

"Kostya, did you tell the train to wait for you?" Konstantin heard Vsevolod yell from the front of the truck.

"Yes!" he yelled back.

A minute later, the truck came to a screeching halt. Misha pushed the back door open and scanned around them. It was so quiet all of a sudden that Konstantin was sure he had gone deaf. "We're at the station," he heard Vsevolod say, and he and Vladimir leapt out of the lorry and followed Vsevolod and the two other soldiers to the train at a run.

All of a sudden, the Imperial train, which was sitting on the tracks in front of them, started moving. "The Germans must have gotten to the train!" Konstantin shouted. Vsevolod moved the fastest, and in one flying leap, he jumped onto the train, grabbing its back handle as he landed. Konstantin and Vladimir were right behind him. Vsevolod held the rail with one hand and caught his leaping cousin with his other arm. Konstantin grabbed Vladimir's arm as Vladimir jumped. Vladimir's momentum shoved Konstantin into the back door of the car, which gave way. Konstantin fell into the car, and Vladimir fell on top of him. Behind them, Misha and Anatoly were also making flying leaps for the train as it picked up speed.

Vsevolod stepped over Konstantin and Vladimir to get into the car, reloading his pistol as he did. "We have to find those Germans," he said.

Konstantin and Vladimir leapt to their feet, keeping their pistols handy. Vsevolod dashed ahead of them, and Konstantin and Vladimir quickly followed as the train moved even faster. The three of them raced towards the front of the train, with Misha and Anatoly right behind them. Each car was empty as they moved through it. Finally, Vsevolod sped into the first car and sprayed it with bullets. The four German officers in it collapsed immediately, and Vsevolod made his way to the engine car, where the engineer was driving the train.

Konstantin followed him, his pistol cocked. Inside the engine car, Vsevolod pressed his gun to the back of the engineer's head. "We just killed four of your comrades," Vsevolod said. "Are there any more besides you?"

"No!" the engineer yelled.

"Where do you think you're taking us?"

"My orders were for Munich!"

"Turn the train around!" Vsevolod shouted, pressing his pistol harder against the man's head. "Take us to St. Petersburg, and you *might* live to tell about it!"

The train changed course and headed north. It was only then that Konstantin felt his shoulder twinge. Vsevolod, seeing him cringe, asked, "what's the matter?"

"My shoulder hurts," Konstantin replied. He began removing his uniform's overcoat, then winced. "Ow!"

Vladimir moved to help him, and it was only when the coat was half off that Konstantin saw the hole in the coat- and the blood soaking it. "Shit!" Vladimir yelped. "Kostya, you've been hit!"

"Anatoly, guard the engineer," Vsevolod ordered. "Make sure we stay on course for St. Petersburg. Kostya, follow me." Vsevolod grabbed his cousin's good arm and guided him into the car that Alexei had always used as his study. He guided Konstantin to the couch and helped him lay down.

Vladimir saw the Imperial family's first aid kit in the corner and grabbed it. He opened it and pulled out bandages and iodine as Konstantin groaned in pain. Misha stood guard at the doorway of the car. He watched Konstantin uneasily and kept his AK-47 raised.

Vsevolod pulled bandages and ointment from a hidden compartment in his coat. "Your adrenaline is wearing off," he said. "That's why it's starting to hurt now."

"I didn't even notice getting shot," Konstantin moaned.

"There was a lot going on," Vsevolod said. He pulled a small bottle from another hidden compartment in his coat, removed its top and took a pill from it. "Take this," he ordered.

"What is that?' Konstantin said.

"It's for the pain," Vsevolod said. He went to a small table next to one of the compartment's armchairs and fiddled with it until the top popped open. Then he reached inside and removed a small container.

Konstantin watched his cousin with amazement. "Whaaat?"

"I helped Alyosha outfit the train once he declared war," Vsevolod said. "This is a container of water. We wanted to be sure we had a source of water that no one knew about, so that we could be sure it wasn't contaminated."

Konstantin took the pill and swallowed it. Then Vladimir helped him remove his uniform so that Vsevolod could examine his wound. Vsevolod cleaned the wound even as Konstantin cringed. "There's no bullet," Vsevolod said. "It must have been a through and through."

As Vsevolod bandaged Konstantin up, Vladimir looked out the train window. "I'm surprised the Luftwaffe hasn't been bombing the hell out of us," he said.

"I think our air force bombed the hell out of them," Vsevolod said. "Right after the Reichstag exploded, there was another round of explosions."

Konstantin nodded. "I certainly heard that."

"The Luftwaffe kept their planes stored in the direction those explosions were coming from," Vsevolod said. "Given how quiet they've been since then, I'm betting they lost most of their planes." Then he noticed that Konstantin was watching him with a certain amount of wonder, a look that was replicated on Vladimir and Misha's faces. "What?" he asked.

"All of it," Konstantin replied. "You rigged the Imperial train for wartime, you know how to bandage wounds, you have stores of stuff hidden in your jacket."

"You never know what you might run into at the front," Vsevolod replied.

"Ain't *that* the truth," Misha said from the doorway, cocking his rifle again. Vsevolod eyed him, his concern obvious, and Misha realized his statement had been taken the wrong way. "Please relax," he said. "I am here to *protect* you, not harm you."

"I certainly hope so," Vsevolod replied.

Konstantin started to stand up. "I'm going to find my sleeping car," he said. "I need to lie down." He swayed a bit. "Whoa." Vsevolod caught his good arm, and Vladimir put a hand on his back. "Wow," Konstantin said when he was steadier. "I feel that pain stuff."

Vsevolod looked amused. "It's pretty intense," he said. "Come on, I'll help you get to bed."

Vladimir followed them, tears gathering in his eyes. When they were in Konstantin's sleeping compartment, Vsevolod helped Konstantin onto his cot and covered him with a blanket. "Thank you," Konstantin mumbled as he drifted off.

When Konstantin awoke several hours later, Vladimir was sitting on a chair next to him, and Vsevolod was sticking his head into the car. "I'm fine," Konstantin told them. Then he tried to sit up, and his muscles refused to obey. "Ooohhh, maybe not."

"It's going to hurt for awhile, Kostya," Vsevolod said, coming into the car. "You should try to eat something, but you'll probably be sleeping for most of the way home."

"How far from home are we?" Konstantin asked.

"It'll take us a couple of days," Vsevolod said.

"I was hoping we'd travel through the night."

"We will. The German engineer will have to sleep at some point, but Misha, Anatoly and I can drive the train while he does."

Konstantin tried to sit up again, and this time he succeeded. "How much of that pain medication do you have?" he asked.

"Enough to get us home," Vsevolod said.

In the dining car a little while later, Misha and Anatoly joined Konstantin and Vladimir for dinner as Vsevolod guarded the engineer. They were only eating soldiers' rations, but Konstantin did not care. As they ate, he could see the soldiers eyeing the plush train. *I doubt they're accustomed to this type of traveling,* he thought. "So what are your full names?" he asked. "We got out of Berlin so fast I didn't get to ask."

"Anatoly Alexandrovich Voronov. I'm from Ekaterinburg."

"I'm Mikhail Timofeyevich Kalashnikov. I'm from Kurya originally, but I was stationed in Moscow for awhile, and have served all over during the war.”

“Kalashnikov?” Konstantin asked. “The weapons designer?”

Misha nodded, Konstantin could tell he was impressed at being recognized. “These AK-47s are my design.”

“I’ve heard about you- you served with my cousin Nicky, didn’t you?”

“Oh, Nicky,” Misha said with a smile. “He’s an incredible shot. Did you know he tested some of my first gun designs?”

Konstantin smiled back. “He couldn’t stop talking about it. You both served under General Zhukov.”

“Yes. Zhukov was also the general leading our troops into Berlin.”

“I know. I was at the meeting where Papa put him in charge.”

Misha eyed him. Then he looked away and heaved a breath. After a minute, he stood up and went to the window of the car. Outside the train, the scenery sped by.

“What is it?” Konstantin asked.

Misha sighed again before responding, and Anatoly was having trouble looking at Konstantin too. “All of this is incredible to us,” Misha said finally. “We’re just regular soldiers, and yet we’re serving alongside the Tsar’s family, even his heir.”

“Russian blood flows in our veins, the same as yours,” Konstantin said. “We’re as willing to die for our country as you are. Nicky’s brother was killed in action.”

“Yes, I remember that well,” Misha said. “Nicky was heartbroken.” He clenched his teeth and looked out the window again.

Konstantin sensed that he had more to say, and waited for him to speak.

Finally, Misha turned from the window and looked directly at Konstantin. “I was just a baby when your father became tsar,” he said. “But the generals I’ve served under- Zhukov, Rokossovksy, the lot of them- all remember your grandfather’s reign and the unrest during the first Great War. The Communist threat was real then, and many generals I’ve served under think they would have joined the Communists if they had come to power.”

Konstantin frowned, contemplating Misha’s words.

“But now I’ve spent much of this war serving alongside the imperial family,” Misha continued. “Nicky, and now Vsevolod and you.” Misha continued to stare Konstantin directly in the eye. “You’re barely old enough to volunteer, and yet here you are on one of the war’s most dangerous missions.” He looked away and shook his head. “You Grand Dukes and Princes are some of the bravest men I’ve ever met. It would have been a shame to depose the dynasty.”

Konstantin smiled. “Thank you,” he said.

On the third night they were traveling, Konstantin joined Vsevolod in the engineering compartment as the engineer slept, guarded by Anatoly. For a moment, Konstantin looked out the front window with interest. "You should really be resting," Vsevolod said. "I don't want you to be a total mess when we get home."

"I won't be," Konstantin promised.

"I mean it," Vsevolod said. "I didn't make it through these last four years just to have your father kill me because I didn't protect you."

"He won't," Konstantin said, smiling. "Besides, I spent the whole afternoon sleeping. I just got up a little while ago."

Vsevolod stared straight ahead in such a way that said he did not believe his cousin.

"Sevka, who was that German general that you practically beheaded while we were fighting in Berlin?" Konstantin asked. "It looked like you knew each other, and that he was coming after you."

Vsevolod grimaced. "I'm sorry you saw that," he said.

"Who was he?" Konstantin repeated.

Vsevolod stared ahead silently as he continued driving the train forward. "I met him when I was stationed in Poland at the beginning of the war," he said finally. "It was my first assignment, and I was undercover as a Polish officer." He took a deep breath. "That general was only a colonel back then, but he was a sadistic son of a bitch."

"So why didn't you kill him then?"

"Because they didn't know who I was, and I didn't want to blow my cover. Then he left Poland for another part of the fighting."

Konstantin shook his head. "I'm sorry for everything you must have gone through."

Vsevolod looked back at him. "You have nothing to apologize for," he said. He looked at Konstantin up and down and smiled. "You have grown up so much since I left for the front."

"It's been a few years, Sevka."

"I know. These past few years have been *crazy*. I feel like I've lived a few lifetimes since the war began."

"I'd like to hear about it," Konstantin said. "I spent most of the war in St. Petersburg. Mostly Papa's been protecting me."

"That's appropriate," Vsevolod replied. "He is Tsar, and you are his Heir. Besides, you're not giving yourself enough credit."

"What do you mean?"

"This was a *dangerous* mission, Kostya, going to Berlin to kill Hitler, with only another sixteen-year-old and your police chief to cover for you. That certainly takes balls."

"We had all of Zhukov's army behind us."

"Zhukov is an incredible general," Vsevolod agreed. "And getting his forces into Berlin as we were leaving was amazing work. But he still wasn't in the Reichstag with you. Hitler could have killed you himself."

"I didn't think I'd get out of there alive," Konstantin admitted.

"You almost didn't. It took our whole army to get you out of there, but you and Volodya showed courage too. You got yourselves out of there as much as we soldiers did."

Finally, Konstantin smiled, and Vsevolod put his arm around him.

The Imperial train pulled into St. Petersburg just as the sun was rising. Immediately, Konstantin, Vsevolod and Vladimir could see the police presence around the station. Vsevolod drew his gun as the train came to a full stop. "Anatoly, guard the engineer as we leave the train," he said. "Kostya, come out in front with me. Be prepared to shoot if you have to."

Outside, however, two policemen exited their car with their hands raised. "They guard the Palace!" Konstantin said.

"Do you trust them?" Vsevolod asked.

"Yes," Konstantin answered.

"Fine," Vsevolod said, but he kept his gun raised. He gestured for Anatoly to take the engineer off the train. More Russian police moved forward, and Vsevolod gestured at the engineer. "This man was part of the plot to get the Imperial train out of Berlin," he said.

Two policemen put the engineer into their car and drove off. Konstantin, Vsevolod and Vladimir piled into the first waiting police car they had seen. Misha and Anatoly got into the second car. "Take us back to the Winter Palace," Konstantin ordered. "Make sure the two soldiers in the other car come to the Palace too."

Both police cars started moving.

"Oh my God," Vsevolod said a few minutes later, crossing himself as they passed St. Isaac's Cathedral. "I never thought I'd see this city again."

*　　*　　*

Inside the Winter Palace, Alexei sat at the desk in his study, examining a copy of the Germans' formal surrender. At the same time, he tried to quash the feeling of worry rising in his stomach. *Volodya's bomb did its task, that much I know,* he thought. *But I've had no news of him or Kostya.*

Then Alexei heard the sound of motorcars just outside the Palace. He got up and went to the window. Outside, two police cars pulled up in front of the Palace, and Alexei feared the worst. Then he saw five people getting out, and three of them were familiar. "Kostya!" Alexei shouted. "Volodya! *Vsevolod!*" His heart bursting with joy, Alexei ran to the front of the palace and dashed out the doors.

"Papa!" Konstantin shrieked. "I'm safe!"

But Alexei noticed that his son was moving unsteadily. "What happened?!" he yelped as he grabbed his son's good arm.

"I got shot," Konstantin said.

Alexei fixed his gaze on the policeman next to them. "Call the doctor," he ordered. "Tell him it's an emergency." He let Konstantin go long enough to wrap Vsevolod in a bear hug. "I'm so glad to see you," he said. "And your father will be even happier." Alexei gave Vladimir a hug as well. "Your bomb worked," he said. "Hitler is dead, and the Germans have surrendered."

Konstantin, Vsevolod and Vladimir screamed with joy and jumped up and down. Misha and Anatoly joined their howls. It was not until after they were quiet that Konstantin thought to introduce Misha and Anatoly to Alexei. "They helped us get out of Berlin," he said.

Both soldiers bowed deeply to Alexei and kissed his hand.

"Come inside," Alexei said. "You'll have lunch with us. I also need to make sure Kostya is alright." He looked at the policemen that were still next to them. "Where is the doctor?"

"On his way, Your Imperial Majesty."

"What about the fighting here in St. Petersburg?" Konstantin asked as they walked towards the Palace doors.

"Reinforcements arrived just after you left, and I launched a counteroffensive," Alexei answered, supporting Konstantin as they walked. "After two days of heavy fighting, the Germans started to retreat. Then the news of your work came in, and that was the end of it."

Behind them, Vsevolod had backed up a few paces, and was staring at the Palace. Alexei looked at him, and then back at the Palace. He could see Ioann, Igor, Gavril and George at the window. Vsevolod threw open his arms and grinned. "Papa!" he cried.

"Vsevolod!" Ioann bellowed, loud enough to rattle the window in front of him. He disappeared at a dead sprint. His brothers disappeared after him.

Vsevolod burst into laughter and dashed towards the doors of the Palace. In a second, Ioann was throwing open the doors and sprinting towards his son. "Papa!" Vsevolod yelled again. They both dove forward and threw their arms around each other.

"I never thought I'd see you again," Ioann said. Tears were coming down his face. His brothers ran out of the palace and threw their arms around them.

Alexei laughed as he, Konstantin and Vladimir continued moving towards the Palace. "We wouldn't have gotten out of Berlin without Vsevolod," Konstantin said. "The Germans were waiting for us. It was a trap."

"I was afraid of that," Alexei said. "Vsevolod was a part of a whole network of Russian spies in Berlin. I made sure they were on high alert from the minute you left here."

"They all deserve a medal," Konstantin said.

"Or several," Vladimir said. "Those are some of the bravest men I've ever seen."

When Ioann, Gavril, Igor, and George piled off Vsevolod, Alexei waved his arm at them. "Let's go inside," he said.

As they walked, Ioann's arm remained tightly around his son's shoulders, but Igor caught up to Alexei and Konstantin. His grin lit up his face. "Nicky is alive and safe and on his way home," he said.

"Hooray!" Konstantin whooped.

They had just made their way into the Palace's first drawing room when Dr. Golov's car pulled up to the Palace. "Over here," Alexei called as the doctor raced inside.

Golov helped Konstantin off with his coat. Konstantin winced.

"What *happened?*" Igor asked as he came into the drawing room.

"The Germans were waiting for us," Konstantin said as Golov helped him remove his shirt and started examining him. "I got hit."

Igor let out a string of curses as he watched Golov unwrap Konstantin's bandage. His brothers gathered around him and eyed Konstantin's wound. Next to Konstantin, Alexei watched the doctor work, tears gathering in his eyes. Behind them, Misha and Anatoly retreated into a corner of the room. Vladimir remained next to Konstantin. Tears gathered in his eyes too.

Konstantin winced again as the doctor examined him. "Who bandaged you up?" Dr. Golov asked.

"Sevka."

"He did a good job."

"It still hurts."

"Yes, and it will until it heals," Golov replied as he treated and bandaged the wound.

Only when he was finished did Alexei, Igor, Ioann, Gavril, George and Vladimir sit in chairs around Konstantin. Alexei, noticing that Misha and Anatoly were still hiding in the corner, waved them forward and ordered them to sit as well. Then he introduced them to his cousins.

Anatoly and Misha bowed deeply as they were introduced. When the introductions were finished, Misha eyed Igor. "Is Your Highness Nicholas' father?" he asked.

Igor nodded and smiled. "He definitely said plenty about you."

"It was my honor to serve with him. I was very sorry to hear about your older son."

Igor sighed. "That never gets any easier."

Then Vsevolod came into the room, and Alexei realized that he had been changing out of his Nazi uniform and into a Russian one. He smiled.

That night, Alexei delivered his victory address to the country. Standing in the Tauride Palace, in front of a room packed with the Duma delegates and their families, as well as the members of his own family that were in the capital, Alexei began to speak.

"For four years, our nation has been locked in a desperate struggle against an aggressive, fascist state. Their well-trained armies attacked us with the intention of occupying the Motherland and wiping our people off the face of the Earth. Today, it warms my heart to announce that victory is ours. The troops of the First Belorussian Front, supported by the troops of the First Ukrainian Front, both led by the best Russian generals of our generation, have captured the German capital of Berlin. All of Germany lies in ruins. Its army is in ruins. Its evil leader has been killed by a bomb of Russian making, brought all the way to Berlin under a plan of Russian ingenuity.

"German generals have already signed their country's terms of surrender, watched over by the Russian generals who captured them. It is truly a great day for our country, but we could not have done it alone. Tonight, I pay tribute to each of our Allies, the brave nations of the United States of America, Great Britain, France, Yugoslavia, Bulgaria, Poland, Denmark, Finland, and Sweden. Your brave armies and your insightful leaders have led the free world to a decisive victory over hatred and imperialism. Your strong civilians came together in support of the war effort, increasing production of war materials throughout every year of the fighting. Without your soldiers' efforts, without your constant influx of war supplies, we would not be declaring victory now. Tonight, we stand together in freedom and brotherhood. Tonight, I call on God to bless each and every one of you. Thank you and good night."

Alexei's address was broadcast by radio to the whole country. In St. Petersburg, people gathered outside the Tauride Palace and in public spaces all across the city, listening as their Tsar paid tribute to their suffering, and to the country's victory. When the speech ended, the huge crowds burst into cheers. Families hugged families, and strangers kissed strangers.

Inside the Tauride Palace, Alexei was mobbed by the crowd around him. Duma delegates and their families surrounded him and congratulated him. When his own family finally made their way over, Konstantin and Igor wrapped Alexei in a big bear hug. When they had separated, Alexei looked at them and the rest of his cousins. "Shall we head back to the Winter Palace?"

"I'm just sorry Sevka couldn't be here to see this," Ioann said as they left. "But he was sleeping so soundly I couldn't bear to wake him."

"I think that was the right choice," Alexei said. "He's been through a lot these past four years."

"Still, he was so instrumental in bringing the country to victory that he should take part in the celebrations."

"He will," Alexei said with a grin. "This is the beginning of the celebrations, not the end."

Ioann smiled, but worry lines still creased his forehead. "I hope he's alright," he said. "He's been so completely asleep since we ate lunch that I felt for a pulse a couple of times. If he's still in that state when we get back to the Palace, I might have to call a doctor."

Igor put an arm around his brother. "Let him sleep," he said as they walked to their cars. "This is probably the safest he's felt since he deployed."

The next night, even as the sky remained light from the summer twilight, Alexei ordered a salute to the Russian armed forces. He, Konstantin, Igor, Ioann, Vsevolod, Gavril, and George piled on to the roof of the Winter Palace to see the artillery rent the sky. Shells flew into the air and exploded, sending fireworks in every direction. Alexei looked below him and saw crowds of people gathered in the street. Between bursts of artillery, he could hear the people singing the national anthem.

Alexei put his arm around Konstantin and turned to see Ioann standing with one arm around Vsevolod and the other around Igor. Alexei's face split into a grin. "It's over," he said. "This war is finally over."

Over the next several days, civilians poured back into the city, and trains carrying returning Russian soldiers poured in as well. Overnight, Russian flags and banners had sprouted all across the city, and the civilian population had taken to the streets, wearing colorful clothing and waving banners and icons of Alexei, Ileana and Konstantin. Alexei and Konstantin met each train of returning soldiers as they arrived at the station. A huge crowd, mostly families of the returning soldiers, surrounded them.

"Hurrah!" the crowd yelled as a train carrying Russian soldiers emptied out. "Hurrah!"

The sound was deafening. Alexei could not keep the smile from his face. In front of him, the soldiers, seeing their Tsar and his Heir at the station to meet them, snapped into a salute. "Nice job, soldiers!" Alexei boomed.

"Thank you, Your Imperial Majesty!" the regiments shouted before marching smartly down the street.

The next day, Alexei received word that the Imperial family was on its way back to the capital, en masse. He, Konstantin, Igor, Ioann, Vsevolod, Gavril, and George went to the station to wait together, craning to see each train as it pulled into the station. Alexei could feel every fiber in his body waiting to jump forward. *Ileana!* he thought. *I-le-an-a!*

Several trains of returning soldiers pulled into the station, and Alexei, with his family behind him, greeted each of them with a salute and words of thanks. Huge crowds had surrounded the train station again, augmented by the soldiers that had returned the day before.

There was a pause in the trains pulling into the station, and as the pause grew longer, Alexei could feel his impatience growing. Finally, another train came into view and inched forward. As it pulled into the station, Alexei could see Ileana in the first car. Her face lit up with a grin, and her eyes beamed happiness. "Ileana!" Alexei yelled.

Ileana waved back furiously. Next to her, Anastasia, Dmitri and Rostislav were waving and yelling. As soon as the train stopped, Ileana dashed out and into Alexei's arms. Dmitri, Rostislav and Anastasia threw themselves at Konstantin and whooped for joy.

Then Nicholas stepped out from the train behind them, still in uniform and surrounded by the soldiers of his regiment. They all saluted Alexei. Alexei let go of Ileana and saluted back before opening his arms. Nicholas wrapped him in a bear hug. Then he dove towards Igor. "Papa!" he shouted. "I'm home!"

Igor wrapped his son up in his arms as Sophie and Oleg, his arm still in a cast, joined him on the platform, and the rest of the Imperial family poured out of the train. The huge crowd around them began singing "God Save the Tsar."

As the familiar words swelled around them, Alexei and Ileana walked to the edge of the platform and waved to the crowd. "Hurrah!" the soldiers yelled. "Hurrah!"

When the national anthem was finished, the entire crowd joined the soldiers: "Hurrah!" they shouted. "Hurrah!"

TRIUMPH OF A TSAR: CHARACTER LIST

Alexei II: Tsar of Russia
Princess Ileana of Romania, later Tsarina Ileana: Alexei's wife
    Tsarevich Konstantin Alexeievich: Alexei and Ileana's oldest son
    Grand Duke Dmitri Alexeievich: Alexei and Ileana's second son
    Grand Duke Rostislav Alexeieveich: Alexei and Ileana's third son
    Grand Duchess Anastasia Alexeievna: Alexei and Ileana's daughter

Tsar Nicholas II: Alexei's father
Tsarina Alexandra Feordorovna: Alexei's mother
King Ferdinand of Romania: Ileana's father
Queen Marie of Romania: Ileana's mother
Prince Carol of Romania (later King Carol II): Ileana's oldest brother

Dowager Empress Marie Feodorovna: Alexei's grandmother
Grand Duke Michael Alexandrovich: Alexei's uncle, Nicholas II's brother
Grand Duchess Olga Alexandrovna: Alexei's aunt, Nicholas II's sister
Grand Duchess Xenia: Alexei's aunt, Nicholas II's sister

Grand Duchess Olga Nicholaievna: Alexei's sister
Prince Alexander of Serbia (later King of Yugoslavia): Olga's husband
    Prince Peter of Yugoslavia: Olga and Alexander's oldest son
    Prince Paul of Yugoslavia: Alexander's cousin
Grand Duchess Tatiana Nicholaievna: Alexei's sister
King Boris of Bulgaria: Tatiana's husband
    Princess Marie Louise: Tatiana and Boris' daughter
Grand Duchess Marie Nicholaievna: Alexei's sister
Prince Nicholas Obolensky: Marie's husband
Grand Duchess Anastasia Nicholaievna: Alexei's sister
Prince Henry of England: Anastasia's husband

Prince Igor Konstantinovich: Alexei's cousin and Aide-De-Camp; son of
    the Grand Duke Konstantin Konstantinovich
Princess Sophie of Hohenburg: Igor's wife
    Their children:

Prince Peter Igorievich
Prince Nicholas Igorievich
Prince Oleg Igorievich
Prince Ioann Konstantinovich: Igor's oldest brother
Princess Elena of Serbia: Ioann's wife
>Their children:
>Prince Vsevolod Ioannovich
>Princess Ekaterina Ioannovna
>Princess Elizaveta Ioannovna
>Princess Kira Ioannovna
>Prince Vyacheslav Ioannovich
>Prince Gleb Ioannovich
Prince Gavril Konstantinovich, Igor's older brother
Princess Maud, nee Lady Maud Emma Louisa, daughter of the Duke of Devonshire (England): Gavril's wife
Princess Tatiana Konstantinova- Igor's sister
Prince Konstantin Konstantinovich: Igor's brother
Princess Pilar of Bavaria: Konstantin's wife
>Their children:
>Prince Sergei Konstantinovich
>Prince Boris Konstantinovich
>Princess Olga Konstantinova
>Princess Marie Konstantinova
Prince George Konstantinovich: Igor's younger brother
Princess Vera Konstantinova: Igor's sister
Grand Duchess Elizaveta Mavrakievna: Igor's mother

Grand Duke Pavel Alexandrovich: Alexei's great uncle, Nicholas II's uncle
Grand Duke Dmitri Pavlovich: Pavel's son
Grand Duchess Elizabeth Feodorovna: Alexei's aunt, Alexandra's sister
Grand Duke Kirill Vladimirovich: Alexei's cousin. Governor-General of Moscow through 1930.
Prince Nikita Alexandrovich: Alexei's cousin. Governor General of Moscow beginning in 1930.
Grand Duke Nicholas Nikolaievich: Alexei's cousin

Prince Felix Youssoupov: Prince of Russia
Princess Irina Alexandrovna: Alexei's cousin, Felix's wife, daughter of Grand Duchess Xenia

ABOUT THE AUTHOR

"Triumph of a Tsar" is Tamar's second novel. She has a history of writing about the Romanovs. Her first book, the nonfiction biography entitled "The Russian Riddle," was the first biography of Grand Duke Sergei Alexandrovich. In addition, one of her short stories about the Grand Duke Konstantin Konstantinovich and his sons, "Rumors of War," was published in *The Copperfield Review* in May, 2017.

Tamar's first novel, "The Last Battle," was published in 2017.